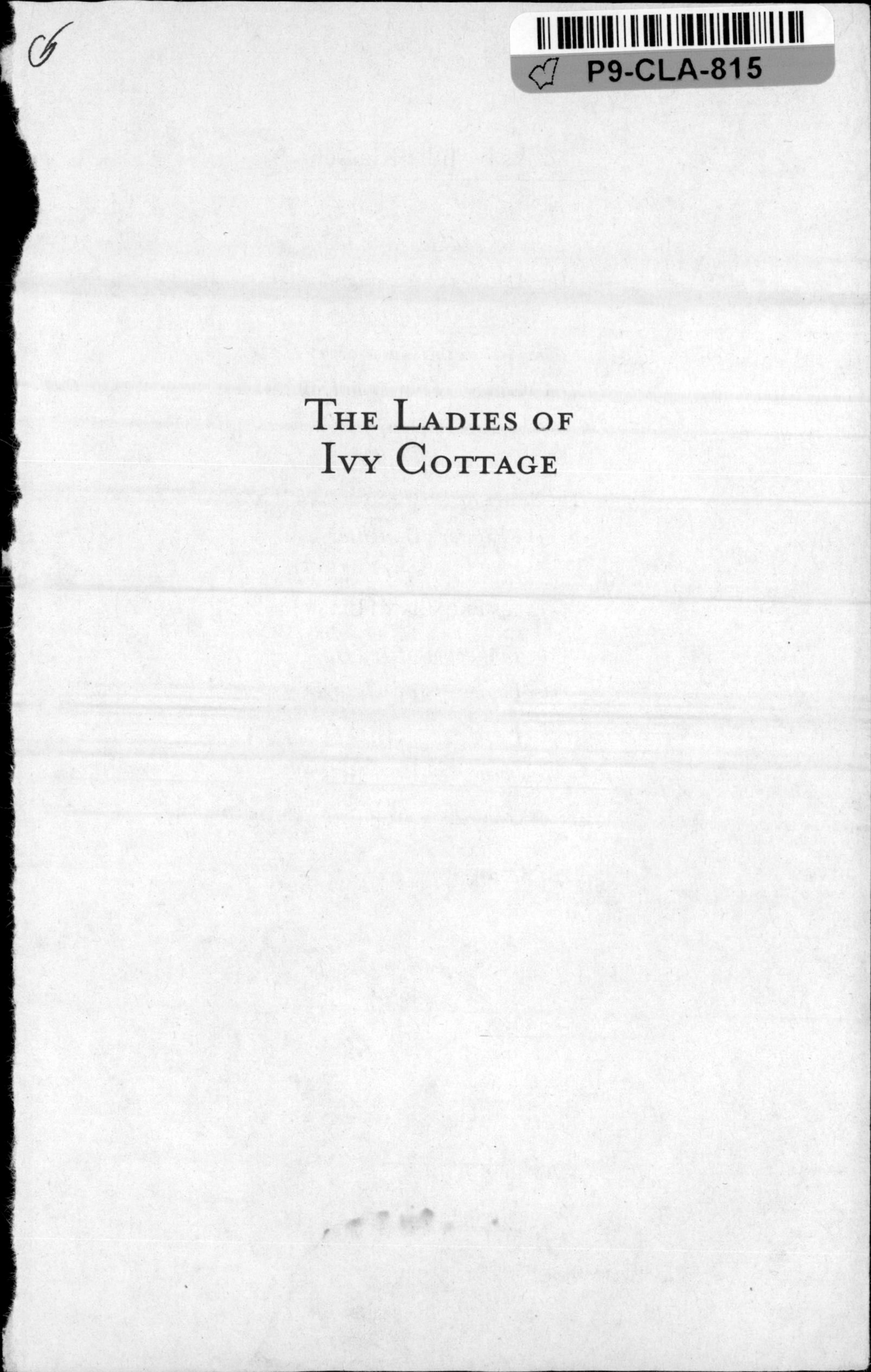

The Ladies of Ivy Cottage

Books by Julie Klassen

Lady of Milkweed Manor

The Apothecary's Daughter

The Silent Governess

The Girl in the Gatehouse

The Maid of Fairbourne Hall

The Tutor's Daughter

The Dancing Master

The Secret of Pembrooke Park

The Painter's Daughter

TALES FROM IVY HILL

The Innkeeper of Ivy Hill

The Ladies of Ivy Cottage

Tales from Ivy Hill · Book Two

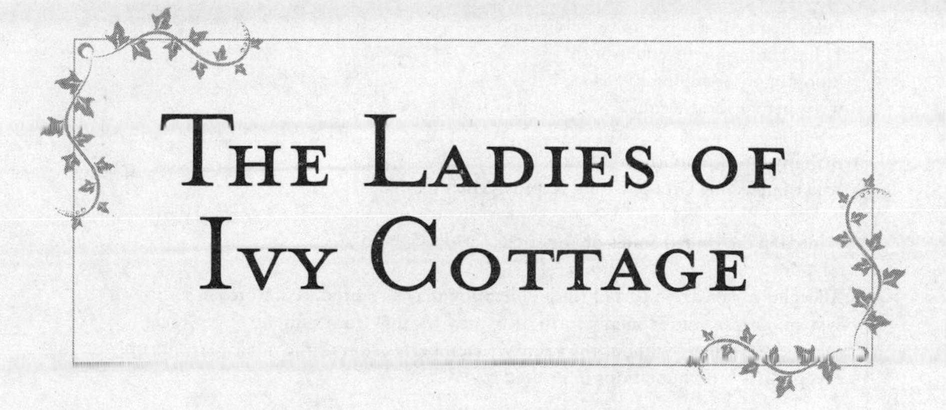

The Ladies of Ivy Cottage

Julie Klassen

Bethany House
a division of Baker Publishing Group
Minneapolis, Minnesota

Published by Bethany House Publishers
11400 Hampshire Avenue South
Bloomington, Minnesota 55438
www.bethanyhouse.com

Bethany House Publishers is a division of
Baker Publishing Group, Grand Rapids, Michigan

Printed in the United States of America

Library of Congress Cataloging-in-Publication Data
Names: Klassen, Julie, author.
Title: The ladies of Ivy Cottage / Julie Klassen.
Description: Minneapolis, Minnesota : Bethany House, a division of Baker Publishing Group, [2017] | Series: Tales from Ivy Hill ; 2
Identifiers: LCCN 2017030031| ISBN 9780764218163 (hardcover : acid-free paper) | ISBN 9780764218156 (softcover)
Subjects: | GSAFD: Christian fiction. | Love stories.
Classification: LCC PS3611.L37 L3 2017 | DDC 813/.6—dc23
LC record available at https://lccn.loc.gov/2017030031

Unless noted, Scripture quotations are from the King James Version of the Bible.

This is a work of fiction. Names, characters, incidents, and dialogues are products of the author's imagination and are not to be construed as real. Any resemblance to actual events or persons, living or dead, is entirely coincidental.

Cover design by Jennifer Parker
Cover women photograph by Mike Habermann Photography, LLC
Cover village photograph by Victoria Davies/Trevillion Images
Map illustration by Ben Cruddace Cartography & Illustration

Author is represented by Books and Such Literary Agency.

17 18 19 20 21 22 23 7 6 5 4 3 2 1

With love to my brothers' beautiful daughters,
my much-loved nieces:
Kathryn, Alexandra,
Julia, and Lia

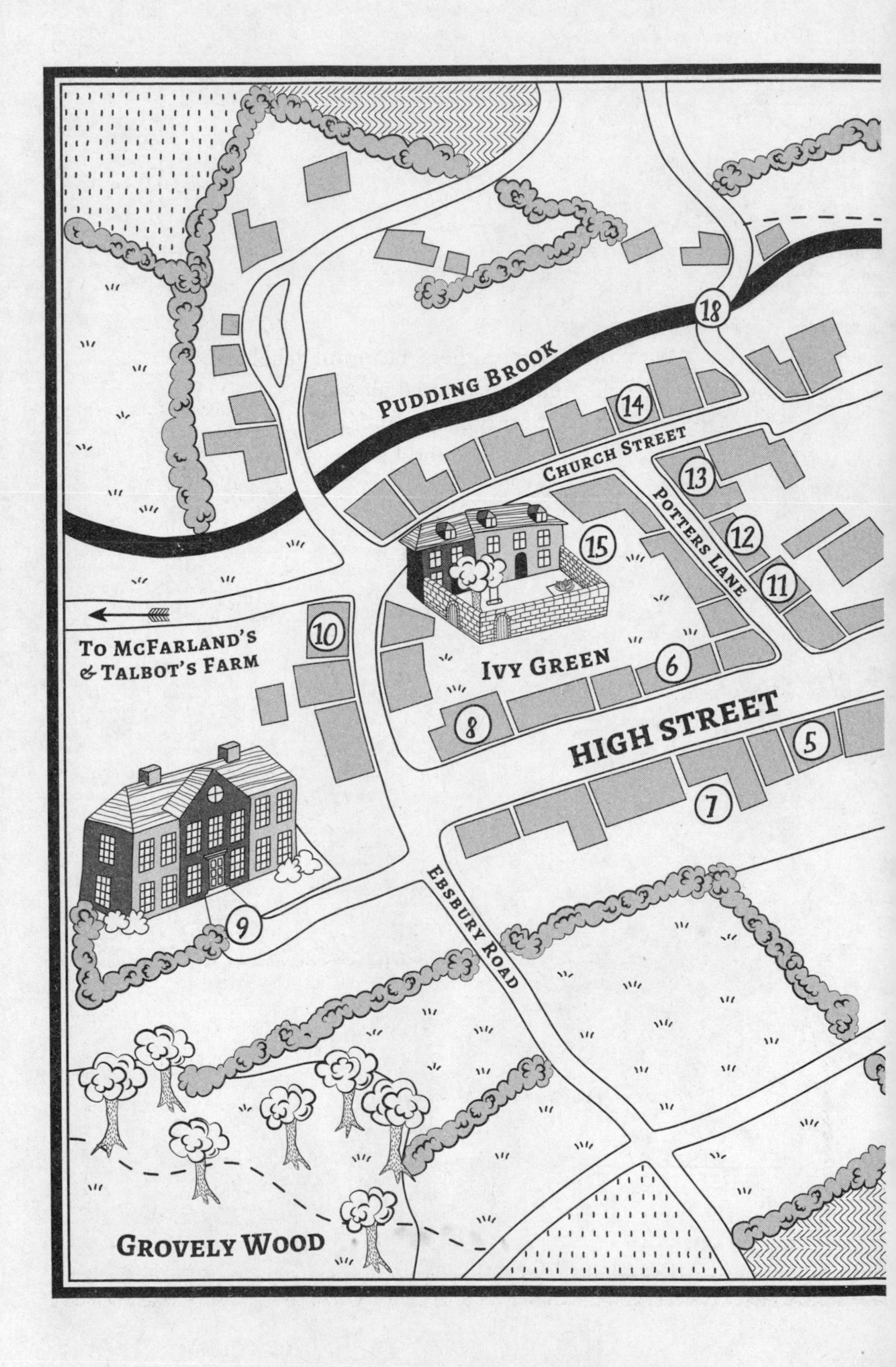
PUDDING BROOK
18
14
CHURCH STREET
13
POTTERS LANE
12
11
15
10
TO MCFARLAND'S
& TALBOT'S FARM
IVY GREEN
6
8
HIGH STREET
5
7
9
EBSBURY ROAD
GROVELY WOOD

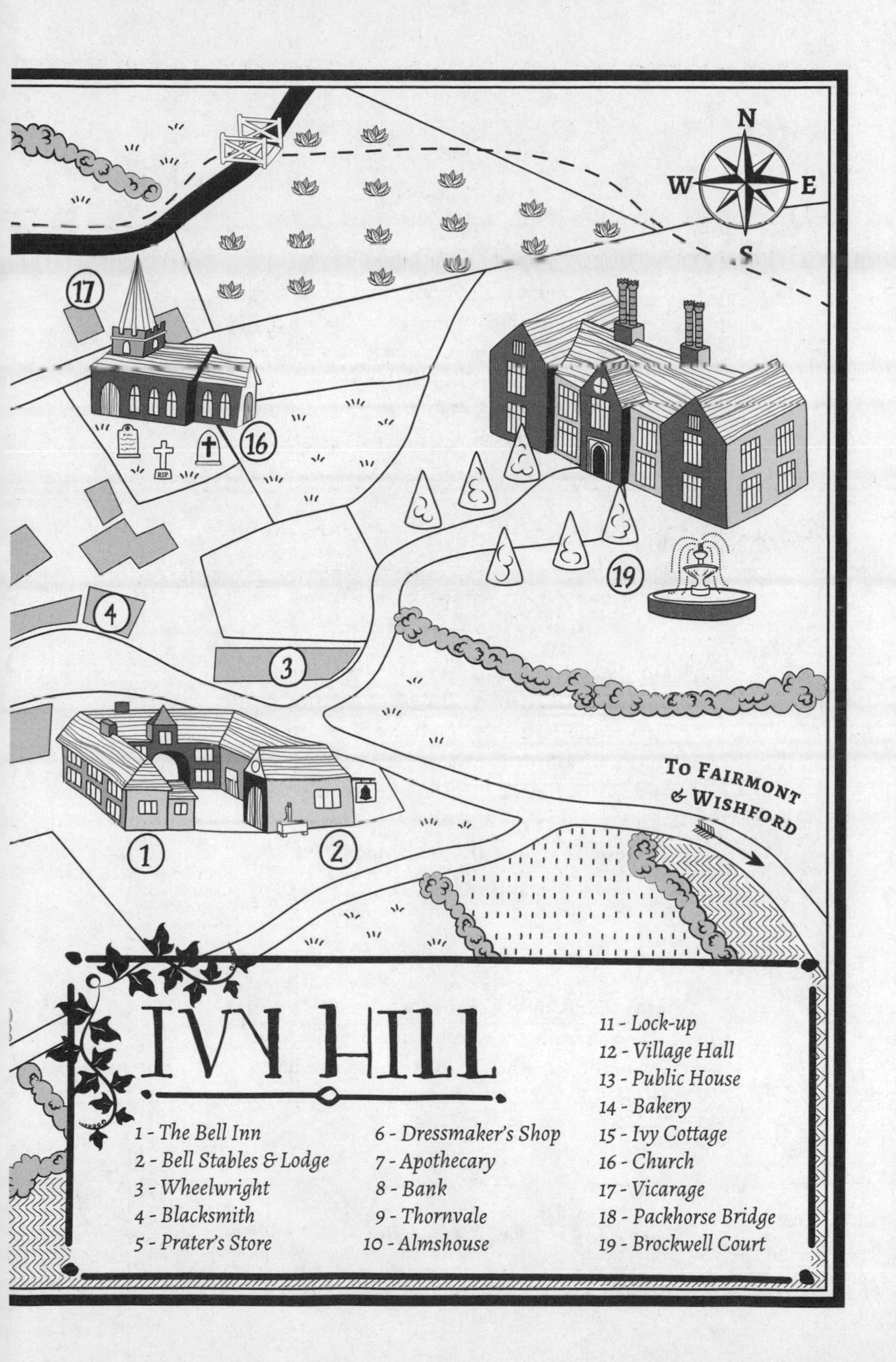
N
W
E
S
17
16
19
4
3
1
2
RIP
To Fairmont
& Wishford
Ivy Hill
1 - The Bell Inn
2 - Bell Stables & Lodge
3 - Wheelwright
4 - Blacksmith
5 - Prater's Store
6 - Dressmaker's Shop
7 - Apothecary
8 - Bank
9 - Thornvale
10 - Almshouse
11 - Lock-up
12 - Village Hall
13 - Public House
14 - Bakery
15 - Ivy Cottage
16 - Church
17 - Vicarage
18 - Packhorse Bridge
19 - Brockwell Court

Circulating Libraries:

Where charming volumes may be had
Of good, indifferent, and bad.
And some small towns on Britain's shore
Can boast of bookshops half a score . . .
Which afford a more than common measure
Of pleasant, intellectual treasure.

—*Poetical Sketches of Scarborough*, 1813

Messrs. Wright and Son's Royal Colonade Library . . .

This establishment contains eight thousand volumes of History, Biography, Novels, French and Italian, and all the best Modern Publications. The Reading Room is frequented both by Ladies and Gentlemen, and is daily supplied with a profusion of London morning and evening papers . . .

—*Brighton As It Is*, 1834

Jesus did many other things as well. If every one of them were written down, I suppose that even the whole world would not have room for the books that would be written.

—John 21:25 NIV

CHAPTER ONE

September 1820
Ivy Hill, Wiltshire, England

Rachel Ashford wanted to throw up her hands. Her private education by governess had not prepared her for this. Standing in the Ivy Cottage schoolroom, she paused in her prepared speech to survey the pupils. Fanny whispered to Mabel, Phoebe played with the end of her plaited hair, young Alice stared out the window, and Sukey read a novel. Only the eldest pupil, Anna, paid attention. And she was the most well-mannered among them and therefore least in need of the lesson. Whenever Mercy taught, the girls sat in perfect posture and seemed to hang on her every word.

Rachel was tempted to raise her voice but took a deep breath and continued evenly. "Always wear gloves on the street, at church, and other formal occasions, except when eating. Always accept gentlemanly offers of assistance graciously. Never speak in a loud, coarse voice, and—"

Fanny grunted. "That's the only voice I've got!"

A few of her classmates giggled.

"Girls, please try to remember that boisterous laughter is not acceptable in polite company. A lady always speaks and moves with elegance and propriety."

"Well, I am not in polite company," Fanny retorted. "I'm with you lot."

Rachel bit the inside of her cheek and persisted, "Vulgarity is unacceptable in any form and must continually be guarded against."

"Then don't venture into the kitchen when Mrs. Timmons is overcharged by the butcher. You'll hear vulgarities to make you blush, Miss Ashford."

Rachel sighed. She was getting nowhere. She picked up *The Mirror of the Graces* from the desk. "If you will not heed me, then listen to this esteemed author." She read from the title page. "'A book of useful advice on female dress, politeness, and manners.'"

"Oh bother," Fanny huffed.

Rachel ignored the groan, turned to a marked passage, and read. "'The present familiarity between the sexes is both shocking to delicacy and to the interest of women. Woman is now treated by men with a freedom that levels her with the commonest and most vulgar objects of their amusement. . . .'"

The door creaked open, and Rachel turned toward it, expecting to see Mercy.

Instead, Matilda Grove stood there, eyes alight. Behind her stood Mr. Nicholas Ashford, looking ill at ease.

Rachel blinked in surprise. "Miss Matilda. The girls and I were just . . . trying . . . to have a lesson on deportment."

"So I gathered. That is why I asked Mr. Ashford to come up with me. What better way to instruct on proper behavior between the sexes than with a demonstration. So much more engaging than dry text."

"Hear, hear," Fanny agreed.

Nicholas Ashford cleared his throat. "I was given to understand that you wanted assistance, Miss Ashford. Otherwise I would never have presumed to interrupt."

"I . . . It is kind of you to offer, but I don't think—"

"'Always accept gentlemanly offers of assistance graciously,'" Mabel parroted Rachel's own words back to her.

Apparently, she'd been listening after all.

Rachel's neck heated. "Very well. That is, if you are sure you don't mind, Mr. Ashford?"

"Not at all."

Miss Matilda opened the door wider and gestured for him to precede her. The lanky young man entered with his long-legged stride.

The girls whispered and buzzed in anticipation while Rachel tried in vain to shush them.

He bowed, a lock of light brown hair falling over his boyish, handsome face. "Good day, Miss Ashford. Ladies."

Rachel felt more self-conscious than ever with him there to witness her ineptness.

"Why do you not act out the proper and improper behavior the book describes?" Matilda suggested. "First, I shall introduce you. For you know, girls, you are not to give your name to just any blade who happens along. One must wait to be introduced by a trusted friend or relation."

"Why?" Phoebe asked.

"To protect yourself from unsavory connections. Or from being corrupted by low company. Let's see now. I have always loved a little playacting, though as a thespian I am nothing to your dear departed father, Miss Rachel." Matilda raised a finger. "I know—I shall pretend to be some great personage, like . . . Lady Catherine de Bourgh from *Pride and Prejudice*. Wonderful novel. Have you read it?"

Rachel shook her head.

"Oh, you should. So diverting and instructive."

"I'm afraid I don't care much for books."

Matilda's mouth stretched into a long O. She sent a significant look toward the students.

"That is," Rachel hurried to amend, "I am sure books are quite worthwhile. For learning especially. I read many in my own years in the schoolroom. And my father loved books."

Matilda nodded. "Very true. At all events. For now, we shall dispense with rank and introduce you as social equals." She began in a royal accent, "Miss Ashford, may I present my friend Mr. Ashford. Mr. Ashford, Miss Rachel Ashford."

Sukey murmured, "That's a lot of Ashfords."

"How do you do, sir." Rachel curtsied.

Nicholas bowed. "Miss Ashford. A pleasure to meet you."

"Excellent," Matilda said. "Now let us progress to how to deal with impertinent males." She picked up Rachel's book, skimmed, then read aloud, "'We no longer see the respectful bow, the look of polite attention, when a gentleman approaches a lady. He runs up to her, he seizes her by the hand, shakes it roughly, asks a few questions, and to show he has no interest in her answers, flies off again before she can make a reply.'" She looked up at Nicholas. "Can you demonstrate this—how *not* to approach a lady."

His mouth parted. "I would never—"

"I think it will be all right this once, Mr. Ashford. It is for the sake of the girls' education, after all." Matilda said it innocently, but Rachel saw the mischievous glint in her eye.

"Ah. Very well. In that case."

Nicholas retreated a few paces, then advanced on Rachel in two long strides, grabbing her hand and shaking it vigorously. "I say, Miss Ashford. What a beautiful day it is. You are in good health, I trust? Well, we must take a turn soon. Good-bye for now." He turned and strode out the door.

The girls giggled and applauded. Nicholas stepped back into the room, blushing furiously. He sent Rachel an uncertain look, and she smiled encouragement in return.

Matilda shook her head in mock disapproval. "Such shocking familiarity! Icy politeness is a well-bred woman's best weapon in putting vulgar mushrooms in their place."

"Mushrooms?" Mabel echoed. "Mr. Ashford, she called you a mushroom!"

"I've been called worse."

"Now, let us repeat the scenario. But this time, Miss Rachel, if you will demonstrate the proper response?"

Again Nicholas Ashford stepped forward and took her hand

in both of his. She glanced up at him from beneath her lashes. He was tall—and looking down at her with warm admiration. His fair gaze traced her eyes, her nose, her cheeks. . . .

When she made no move to rebuke Mr. Ashford, Miss Matty prompted from the book, "'When any man, who is not privileged by the right of friendship or of kindred, attempts to take her hand, let her withdraw it immediately with an air so declarative of displeasure, that he shall not presume to repeat the offense.'"

Matilda stopped reading and Rachel felt her expectant look, but she could not bring herself to jerk her hand from his. Not when he had offered to marry her. Not in front of an audience. It seemed so heartless.

"Is it ever all right to let a man hold your hand?" seventeen-year-old Anna Kingsley whispered hopefully.

Matilda turned from the uncooperative couple to answer. "Well, yes. But remember, Anna, a touch, a pressure of hands, are the only external signs a woman can give of entertaining a particular regard for someone. She must reserve them only for a man she holds in high esteem."

With another glance at the frozen pair, Matilda closed the book and cleared her throat. "Well, girls. What say we end a bit early and go outside for recess. You don't mind if we cut our lesson short, Miss Rachel? No, she does not. All right, girls. Out we go."

Rachel pulled her gaze from Mr. Ashford's in time to see the amusement glittering in Matilda's eyes as she shepherded the pupils past her demonstration partner, who still held fast to her hand.

When the door shut behind the girls, Rachel gave a lame little chuckle and gently tugged her hand from his. "The lesson is over, apparently."

He clasped his own hands together. "Do you think it helped?"

Helped . . . what? she wondered, but replied casually, "Heavens, who knows? More than my poor attempts to teach them at any rate." She stepped to the desk and tossed her notes into the rubbish bin. "I have no talent for teaching. I must find another way to contribute here. Or find another livelihood."

He followed her to the desk. "You need not be anxious about supporting yourself, Miss Ashford. You have not forgotten my offer, I trust?"

"No. I have not. Thank you." Rachel swallowed and changed the subject. "Shall we . . . um, walk together, Mr. Ashford? You did mention it was a beautiful day."

"Oh. Of course. If you'd like."

Did she want to be seen strolling side by side with Nicholas Ashford? She did not want to encourage the inevitable tittle-tattle, but nor was she ready to remain alone with him—and his offer—in private.

She retrieved her bonnet, then led the way downstairs. There, he opened the front door for her and ushered her through it.

Which way? Not toward the busybody's bakery or Brockwell Court, she decided. She gestured in the opposite direction. "Shall we walk this way?"

He nodded, and at the corner they turned down Ebsbury Road and passed the almshouse.

She took a deep breath to steel herself. They would soon reach Thornvale. Beautiful, beloved Thornvale. When they reached its gate, she looked at the fine, red-brick house with its dark green door. Oh, the happy years she had spent there with her parents and sister before their troubles started. It was also where her brief courtship with Timothy Brockwell had begun, and then ended all too soon. When her father died, the house went to Nicholas Ashford—his heir and distant cousin. He and his mother lived there now.

If Rachel married him, she could leave life as an impoverished gentlewoman and return to her former home. Should she? She could not keep him waiting forever.

His voice penetrated her reverie. "Shall we turn here?"

"Hm? Oh, yes."

Diverting onto the wide High Street, they passed the bank, now closed. A few houses. Fothergill's Apothecary, its window displaying colorful bottles of patent medicines. The butcher's with his gruesome slabs of hanging meat and dead fowl, and the greengrocers with crates of produce.

Nicholas gestured toward Prater's Universal Stores and Post Office. "Do you mind if we stop here? I have something to post." He pulled a letter from his pocket.

Rachel acquiesced but said she would wait for him outside. She avoided smug Mrs. Prater whenever she could. The sour shopkeeper's wife had once treated her with fawning respect, but that was before her father's financial ruin

While she waited, Rachel glanced toward The Bell next door, wondering if she had time to stop in and greet Jane before Nicholas returned. But at that moment, two people on horseback rode out through the coaching inn archway—Jane Bell and Sir Timothy Brockwell. Rachel's stomach twisted at the sight.

They did not notice her, talking companionably as they directed their mounts down the Wishford Road. Both were well dressed Jane in a striking riding habit of peacock blue. Together, they were the picture of a perfectly paired couple.

Rachel found herself transported back to her youth. She, Jane, Timothy, and Mercy were all from the area's leading families. The other three were close in age, but Rachel was a few years behind them. Judged too young to tag along, Rachel had frequently been left behind when the others went off together on some adventure. Especially Jane and Timothy, who had always been far more active and athletic than she or bookish Mercy Grove.

Standing there on the High Street, Rachel felt twelve years old all over again. That plump awkward adolescent, watching the enviable adults ride away together.

The shop door opened behind her, and Rachel turned toward it.

Nicholas followed the direction of her gaze and nodded toward the riders. "Who is that with Sir Timothy?"

"My friend Jane Bell."

As if sensing their scrutiny, Sir Timothy glanced over his shoulder at them but did not smile or wave.

Nicholas studied her face. "He has never married?"

She shook her head.

"I wonder why."

So do I, Rachel thought, but she made do with a shrug.

"Has he ever courted anyone?"

"Not in years, as far as I know."

"But you two are . . . friends?"

"Family friends, yes. But that doesn't mean he would confide something of such a personal nature to me."

Nicholas turned to watch Sir Timothy again as he and Jane disappeared down the hill. "I gather he is considered quite the eligible bachelor. A desirable catch."

"Yes, he would be," she answered truthfully. "For the right woman."

Rachel had once thought that she might be that woman. But that was eight years ago. She took a deep breath. It was long past time to forgive, forget, and move forward.

She gestured across the street toward Potters Lane. "Shall we continue on together?"

For a moment Nicholas held her gaze, his eye contact uncomfortably direct. "Yes, I very much hope we shall."

Jane Bell inhaled a deep breath of fragrant autumn air—apples and blackberries, hay and oats drying in the sunshine. The green leaves of chestnut trees and underbrush were beginning to mellow and yellow, which made the colors of the remaining flowers and ripening fruit seem more vibrant. Riding past, she noticed a goldfinch feeding on burst pods of thistle seed, and in the distance, workers harvested a field of oats.

She and Timothy talked sparingly as they cantered along Wishford Road. Dressed in the new riding habit she'd given in and purchased, Jane felt prettier than she had in a long while. Sir Timothy was well turned out as always in a cutaway coat, leather breeches, and Hessian boots.

When they slowed their mounts to a walk, he looked over at her. "Is that a new habit?"

"Yes, it is."

"I like it. You looked like a bedraggled sparrow in that old brown one."

She mock gasped. "Thank you very little, sir! You are most ungallant."

Inwardly she was pleased that he felt free to tease her. It made her feel closer to him—to the Timothy of old, her childhood friend.

He smiled. "I am glad we can ride together now and then. I missed it."

"Me too. Who did you ride with all those years we . . . didn't?"

"On my own mostly. Occasionally with the farm manager to look over the fields, or sometimes with Richard, though he comes home less and less."

Jane had not seen his brother in years. "But no friends?"

He shook his head. "If you think about it, there is a dearth of men my age around Ivy Hill."

"I never really considered it. I had Mercy and Rachel, but you had few friends close by."

"I didn't need more friends." He sent her a sidelong glance. "I had you."

Their gazes met and held, and Jane felt a poignant ache beneath her breastbone.

He lightened the moment with a wry grin. "Oh, don't feel sorry for me. Horace Bingley wasn't too far away, but I saw more than enough of him at school."

"Feel sorry for the lord of the manor?" Jane teased. "Hardly." Although she did, a little. His life, his family, his responsibilities were not always easy.

He looked down, then asked, "Did you and Mr. Bell ride together? I never saw you, if you did."

She looked at him in surprise. He almost never asked about John.

"No. My father sold Hermione while I was away on our wedding trip, and John was always too busy with the inn."

"Then I am glad you have Athena now. She suits you."

Jane stroked the mare's sleek neck. "Yes. I am grateful to have her."

She thought of Gabriel Locke, who had given her Athena. His ruggedly handsome face shimmered in her memory, along with the feel of his strong, callused hands holding hers.

Timothy's gaze swept over her again. "It is good to see you out of mourning, Jane. Are you . . . over the worst of your grief?"

She considered that. "I am, yes." *At least where John is concerned.*

"Will you ever marry again, do you think?"

Jane coughed at the question.

"Dust," she mouthed, but knew he wasn't fooled. She swallowed and said, "I don't know. Maybe. In time."

He winced. "Tell me truthfully, Jane. Did you marry Mr. Bell because you wanted to or because I disappointed you?"

Jane drew in a sharp breath and stopped her horse. Timothy had never broached the subject so directly before.

He reined in close by. "Had I not hesitated. Had I not—"

"Fallen in love with someone else?" she supplied.

Again he winced, but he neither confirmed nor denied it.

He didn't need to. At Rachel Ashford's coming-out ball, Timothy had looked at her with a powerful admiration beyond anything Jane had ever noticed directed at herself. He'd begun treating Rachel with formal deference, almost like a stranger—an intriguing, beautiful stranger. It had stung at the time. Jane knew Timothy had felt himself honor bound to *her*, so he had hesitated to act on that attraction. But Jane had not wanted him to marry her for duty's sake. For simple loyalty or the expectations of others. What woman would? Perhaps if John Bell had not pursued her with such singular determination, she might not have noticed the warm devotion missing from Timothy's eyes.

"I cannot deny that turn of events influenced my willingness to be courted by John." Jane looked at him. "Timothy, why did you never marry? I had wed someone else. You were free to marry as you liked."

"Free? Ha. You know why I did not marry."

She saw the anguish in his eyes, and her heart went out to him.

He referred to more than his obligation to her, she guessed. His family had high expectations.

She said gently, "You know how much you mean to me, Timothy, don't you? And how grateful I am that our friendship is on better footing again?"

"I value our friendship as well, Jane. That is why I need to ask. You are not waiting for . . . anything more from me, are you? I know how presumptuous that sounds, but God help me, I don't want to disappoint you again."

Jane took a deep breath. "You did disappoint me—I can't deny it. But that was a long time ago. You have every right to marry someone else." She reached over and squeezed his hand. "Truly. I want you to be happy."

"Thank you. I am glad we agree. I wanted to be certain before I . . . do anything else."

They rode on. Jane hoped Timothy had not waited too long to act now that Nicholas Ashford was on the scene. Or was he thinking of someone besides Rachel?

With that in mind, she added, "However, I hope you will marry for love, not family duty."

He frowned. "I don't know that I can separate the two. It has been ingrained into me since I was a child: Marry the right person for the family's sake, and love and happiness will come in time."

"Like our own parents did?"

"Yes. Mine barely knew each other."

"Were they happy, do you think?"

"Daily evidence to the contrary, Mother claims they were. She was devastated when he died."

Jane nodded. "I am sure she was. And you were too, no doubt. I'm sorry I was not there for you. Again, I am glad our friendship is on better terms now."

"Me too." He smiled at her, but it was a sad smile. A smile of farewell.

Would she have been happier if she had pretended not to notice his feelings for Rachel, rebuffed John Bell, and married Timothy anyway?

Jane shook off such futile second-guessing. Timothy was master of Brockwell Court and must have an heir to leave it to, which was beyond Jane's abilities.

They stopped to let the horses drink from a clear stream. Jane inhaled deeply, then exhaled the final lingering remnants of what might have been. With a determined smile, she said, "Now, let's not spoil our ride with any more gloomy talk. I have to return to The Bell shortly to greet the one o'clock stage."

He nodded. "I agree. Shall we . . . race back?"

Her smile became genuine. "With pleasure."

As they galloped home, once again that question went through her mind: Would she have been happier if she had married Timothy? If she had forgone marriage to an innkeeper, the death of that innkeeper, and taking his place at The Bell?

No . . . she realized, oddly startled at the revelation, and at the peace that flowed over her as she pondered it. She would not give up where she was today, and who she was today, to go back in time and marry Sir Timothy Brockwell.

CHAPTER TWO

The next morning, Rachel sat down to breakfast with the Miss Groves and asked Mercy how her campaign was going. Her friend's goal was to open a charity school to educate many, if not all, of the parish's girls and boys—regardless of ability to pay. As it was, Ivy Cottage could house only about eight pupils.

"Not well," Mercy explained as she buttered her toast. "Lord Winspear has not yet replied to my request for a meeting. And yesterday I learned Lady Brockwell is against educating the poor. Sir Timothy said he *might* support the project in future but for now has other obligations to attend to. Apparently the almshouse needs a new roof and the church has a long list of pending repairs. And Mr. Bingley says that if the Brockwells and Winspears agree to put money toward the cause, he will as well, but not before." She ended on a sigh.

"I'm sorry."

"Don't worry, Rachel." Matilda patted her niece's hand. "Mercy will not give up. She will succeed in the end."

"From your lips to God's ear, Aunt Matty."

Later, as they finished their meal, the Groves' manservant brought in the post and handed Rachel a letter. She thanked him, and Mr. Basu left the room as silently as he'd come.

Recognizing her sister's handwriting, Rachel excused herself to read the letter in private.

Dear Rachel,

Greetings, little sister. I hope this letter finds you happy in your new home. Do you remember how we admired charming Ivy Cottage as girls? I admit I imagined living there myself when I was young and secretly admired George Grove. Thankfully I did not break my heart over him. I might have done, until I learned he planned to pursue a career in India. Yes, I think I can date my recovery to that precise moment.

I do hope the Miss Groves are treating you well. Have they banished you to the attic, or pressed you into service like Cendrillon, the poor orphaned stepsister? Are you sharing a bed with four wriggling schoolgirls with odiferous feet and worse breath? I hope not. Or perhaps girls do not produce as many foul odors and sounds as boys do. I am sure we never did, as ladylike as Mamma raised us to be. Speaking of foul, do you ever see the she-dragon who now lives in our old house?

Rachel shook her head, a wry twist to her mouth as she read the rest of her sister's letter. Then she moved to the desk in the sitting room to write her reply.

Dear Ellen,

Thank you for your letter. Rest assured, I am content here in Ivy Cottage. Of course the Miss Groves are as kind as could be. More kind than I deserve.

And no, they have not put me in the attic. I have my own bedchamber here. It isn't grand, but it is comfortable. I believe it was the boyhood room of George Grove, before he left the country.

It was thoughtful of you to send a coin under the seal and offer to send more, but that is not necessary. I have a little money left and have been able to make small contributions to my upkeep, which eases my mind about accepting what would otherwise be charity.

On a happier note, you will be glad to learn that Jane Bell and I have reconciled. I missed her friendship even more than I realized and am grateful to have her back in my life. Although she is busy with the inn, we find time to talk every week—either she stops by Ivy Cottage or I walk to The Bell and have coffee with her there.

You asked about the new residents of dear Thornvale. I see Mrs. Ashford only in passing. She remains aloof, but her son is very amiable, and his warmth makes up for her coolness. People here hold Mr. Ashford in high regard already. Some tease about his awkward ways, but it is not unkindly meant. Mrs. Ashford, however, shows no interest in befriending anyone except the Brockwells and the Bingleys.

That is the news from Ivy Hill for now. I hope you continue in good health, especially as your confinement nears. Give my love to Walter and William.

Fondly,
Rachel

Rachel folded and sealed the letter. Writing it had reminded her that she had not yet contributed to her room and board for the month. She went upstairs to remedy that oversight.

In her room, she retrieved her reticule from the side table. She shook the contents onto her palm, but only a few ha'pennies and a button tumbled forth. The button had fallen off her blue spencer at church, but she had not remembered to sew it back on.

Pennies would not be enough, so she opened her trunk at the foot of the bed. From it she retrieved her knitted coin purse. She had a little money from a small annuity she'd inherited from her mother. But the dividend would not last long. Rachel extracted a coin, then looked again at the loose button. She *should* sew it back on then and there. Do something productive. After all, needlework was one thing she was good at.

Instead, she dug deeper in the trunk. She moved aside the winter clothes stored there along with the one dress of her mother's she had kept. Near the bottom, she peeled back a layer of tissue, and there it was—the pink gown she had worn to her coming-out ball eight years ago. Seeing it, thoughts of buttons and spencers fled.

She spread the fine, rosy-pink gown across the bed and admired it anew. She supposed it was foolish, but she could not bear to part with it.

She remembered how she'd felt wearing it. When Rachel had looked in the mirror that night, she had, for the first time in her life, liked what she saw. The graceless adolescent was gone. The gown flattered her figure and complemented her coloring. In it, she felt feminine, grown up, and attractive. And based on Timothy Brockwell's reaction, he had thought so as well. She could still see him standing wide-eyed at the bottom of the stairs as she descended and hear him stammer, "You look . . . astounding—that is, beautiful. Astoundingly beautiful."

Rachel's chest tightened at the memory. That night had been almost perfect, and yet—

Someone knocked and Rachel jumped. Hand to her chest, she called, "Yes?"

Anna Kingsley popped her head in. "Pardon me, Miss Ashford. Alice and Phoebe are not in here, are they? We are playing hide-and-seek, and I can't seem to find them."

"No. Have you checked the linen closet? They hid there the last time."

"Good idea." Anna's attention was captured by the pink gown. "Ohhh . . . what a pretty dress," she breathed.

Rachel glanced over her shoulder. "Thank you. I have always liked it."

Anna backed from the room. "I'll go look in the closet now. Thank you for the clue."

Alone again, Rachel repacked her trunk. Her gaze fell on her mother's Bible on the nearby side table, but she did not open it.

Instead Rachel went to find Mercy and stoically confessed her situation. "My meager funds will not last long, I'm afraid. The only things I have of value—a few remembrances of my mother, and my father's books—I cannot sell. Nor have I any talent for teaching, as you no doubt realize by now, though of course I am willing to help however I can. I can sew, but I've already caught up on all the mending. I must find another way to contribute."

She expected Mercy to deny her poor assessment of her teaching abilities, or insist Rachel not worry about contributing.

Instead Mercy nodded thoughtfully. "You are right. There must be something more you can do. I know I would not like to feel as if I were not being useful. God has given us all gifts to use in serving others, Rachel. We shall have to try harder to find yours."

"How do we do that?"

"Pray for wisdom and direction, of course."

"Um-hm . . ." Rachel murmured noncommittally. She felt uncomfortable asking God—asking anyone—for help.

Mercy added, "Beyond that, the counsel of friends is a good way to start."

"Are you sure I should be here?" Rachel whispered to Mercy, nervous at the prospect of attending that evening's meeting of the Ladies Tea and Knitting Society.

"Of course," Mercy assured her. "Any woman is welcome to visit."

They had arrived at the village hall early, and Rachel helped arrange chairs while Mercy heated water for tea on the room's corner stove.

Soon others began to enter, chatting to one another as they came. Several sent curious looks her way.

Rachel was acquainted with the dressmaker, Mrs. Shabner; Mrs. Klein, the piano tuner; and Mrs. Burlingame, who had helped move her belongings from Thornvale to Ivy Cottage two months before. She recognized the lace women, the Miss Cooks; the laundress, Mrs. Snyder; and a few others as well. Did they know who she was and look down on her for her father's failings, as many did?

A woman with reddish-brown hair and fair eyes introduced herself as Mrs. O'Brien, the chandler. Rachel smiled and gave her name in return, silently wondering, *Miss Ashford, the . . . what?*

Jane Bell entered, and Rachel's heart lifted at the sight of her.

"Rachel! Welcome." Jane embraced her. "I am glad to see you here."

"Are you? Good." Rachel exhaled a relieved breath. "I feel so out of place. But then, I feel that way everywhere since leaving Thornvale."

"I understand. I felt out of place at my first meeting as well. Here, sit by me."

Rachel did so, and Mercy sat on her other side. Bookended by two old friends, Rachel felt better already.

A stocky woman with a ruddy complexion drew up short at seeing Rachel. "Good heavens. Another one?"

Jane said, "Mrs. Barton, this is Miss Ashford, who is visiting us for the first time tonight."

"I know who she is. Who's next—the royal princesses?"

Judith Cook sighed wistfully. "Ohh, the princesses. Wouldn't that be grand?"

Mrs. Barton rolled her eyes, then turned to Mercy. "I heard Miss Ashford was helping out at your school. But does she fancy herself a woman of business now too?"

Rachel spoke up. "I don't know what I am, truth be told. All I know is I need to find a way to support myself."

Mercy amended, "Miss Ashford helps us at Ivy Cottage in several ways. But she longs to secure her own livelihood, now that her family home has gone to her father's heir. I thought we might help her think of something suited to her abilities."

"Did your father leave you and your sister nothing?" Charlotte Cook asked. "That young man got it all?"

Rachel's face burned. "My sister received a few things passed down from our mother. And I inherited my father's collection of books."

One young woman whistled, impressed. "Well, that's something."

"Is it?" Rachel wasn't convinced.

Mrs. Snyder nodded. "Books are dear, indeed. Worth a fair sum, I imagine."

Rachel shook her head. "Not when his will stipulates that I cannot sell them but must keep the collection intact."

Judith Cook gave another wistful sigh. "A whole library of books for your own use . . . I should never get any lace made were they mine."

Mrs. Klein added, "I've taken to visiting the circulating library in Salisbury when I travel there. But that's a long way to go to return a book."

Rachel shrugged. "You are welcome to read any of my father's you like. I'm afraid I am not all that fond of books myself. They will receive precious little attention from me."

"How many books have you?" Mrs. Burlingame asked.

"I don't know. Hundreds. My father's heir has allowed me to leave them in Thornvale for the time being, since they would not fit in my bedchamber at Ivy Cottage."

"Mrs. Klein has given me an idea," the chandler said. "How about starting a circulating library here in Ivy Hill? Is there anything in your father's will to prohibit that?"

Rachel stared at Mrs. O'Brien, stunned. *What a notion!* She tried to recall the lawyer's wording. "No, not that I remember."

"Well then, there you are. That's settled." Mrs. Barton leaned back against her chair with heavy satisfaction. "Now I would like to talk about my cows."

"But . . . !" Rachel sputtered. "Nothing is settled. Far from it. While I appreciate the suggestion, it is entirely impractical. I could not presume to open a circulating library in Thornvale, which is not my home any longer."

"Why not? I've seen the way that young man looks at you," Mrs. Burlingame said. "He'd do anything you ask, I'd wager."

"But I daresay his haughty mamma would not," Mrs. Klein said. "Won't hire me to tune that old pianoforte either."

Rachel could not disagree. "Even if Mr. Ashford would allow it, it would not be appropriate to take advantage of his generosity."

"You could use our library at Ivy Cottage," Mercy said. "Most of the books we use regularly are kept in the schoolroom. I think we have more ornaments than books on our library shelves. I would have to talk to Aunt Matty first, but we rarely use our formal drawing room and might give over at least part of that as well, if more space were required."

"Oh, Mercy, I couldn't. It's too much."

"Not at all. What a boon it would be to have all those books under our roof. What a benefit to our school. Assuming you would let the girls borrow them."

"Of course I would. You may do, as it is. I didn't realize you would be interested."

"Oh, yes. I have long admired—dare I admit, coveted—your father's library."

Rachel raised her hands in agitation. "I don't even know how a circulating library operates."

Mrs. Klein spoke up. "The one in Salisbury charges an annual subscription rate, and then I pay an additional two pence for every volume I borrow."

Mercy nodded. "I recall a similar arrangement at the circulating library near my parents' home in London."

"I'll help you cart the books over," Mrs. Burlingame offered.

Jane nodded her approval. "And I could promote the library at The Bell. I'm sure frequent guests would appreciate being able to borrow popular, diverting books to help pass the long hours while traveling."

"I don't know that my father's books could be called either popular or diverting. Most are academic in nature, I believe. Histories, biographies, works of philosophy . . ."

"Then perhaps you might accept donations of popular books and novels from others," Mercy suggested. "We have many."

"We have several as well," Charlotte Cook added.

Rachel held up her palm. "I don't want charity."

Jane squinted in thought. "Then to those who donate books, you could . . . reduce their subscription fee, or give them a credit toward borrowing other books. Either of those would be a fair exchange."

"Though hopefully some will pay for subscriptions outright," Mrs. Klein said. "She can't make a living if we all just trade books."

Mrs. O'Brien nodded. "I'm sure many will be willing to pay for a subscription. I know I would."

Mrs. Barton said, "Me too—if the price isn't too dear."

Rachel shook her head. "Heavens, I'd have no idea what to charge. But let's not get ahead of ourselves. You have given me a great deal to think about, and talk over with the Miss Groves. Thank you. Now, I've taken enough of your time. What's next? Mrs. Barton's cows, was it?"

"That's right," the dairywoman said. "I've got too much milk on my hands. My bossies are producing exceedingly well at present. And I've already got more cheese than I can sell this month."

"I've been thinking, Mrs. Barton," Jane said. "Could you make cheese in the shape of a bell, by any chance? Perhaps I could sell them at the inn?"

"Like the Stilton cheeses other inns sell?"

"Exactly."

Mrs. Barton considered, lips pursed. "Bell-shaped, hm? Interesting idea."

The meeting proceeded, and Rachel was relieved when the focus shifted off of her. She sat quietly, but her mind remained busy dissecting the circulating library idea. Could she make a success of such an enterprise? Or would she end up a mortifying failure? The latter seemed far more likely.

CHAPTER
THREE

They convened the library planning meeting the following afternoon. Rachel and Mercy went in early to tidy the Ivy Cottage drawing room. Matilda joined them a few minutes later with a tray of tea things and paper for note taking. Jane would be arriving soon. She had asked if she might bring Mr. Drake, who was currently renovating Fairmont House—Jane's former childhood home—into a hotel. The man was knowledgeable about business matters and had probably seen many successful circulating libraries in the course of his travels.

Rachel had agreed but was nervous about a man she barely knew joining them. She had met Mr. Drake at a party held in Jane's honor recently at The Bell. He had been friendly, but she had found his polished good looks and worldly experience intimidating.

While they waited for their guests, Rachel asked Mercy, "Would you not need to ask your parents' permission? Ivy Cottage is still theirs, is it not?"

Mercy nodded. "Legally, yes. Though when George left and I came of age, they relinquished the house to Aunt Matty and me and moved to London."

Matilda explained, "By the time my father wrote his will, it was clear I would remain unmarried, so he put the house in my brother's name and the furnishings in mine, with the understanding that I would live here, supported by Earnest, for my lifetime."

"Will he object to my operating a circulating library here?"

Matilda replied, "You leave Earnest to me."

"And Mrs. Grove?"

"Oh, she won't like it." Matilda made a face. "She wasn't keen on Mercy keeping a school here either. But since she inherited her family's house in London, and prefers city living, she isn't here often enough to complain. Not overly much, at any rate."

"Be that as it may," Rachel said, "that doesn't mean I ought to take over their drawing room as well as their library." She gestured through the archway to the adjoining room.

"The girls receive their visitors here in the drawing room," Mercy said. "But perhaps we might keep part of this room furnished with comfortable chairs for reading or talking?"

Matilda added, "Visitors come primarily on Sunday afternoons, so it wouldn't be much of a conflict. Or perhaps the library might not open on Sundays?"

"Yes, that would probably be best," Rachel agreed.

Jane and Mr. Drake arrived, and their conversation paused as greetings were exchanged. Jane wore her new lavender dress, which brightened her complexion and hazel eyes. Mr. Drake, handsome in gentleman's attire of claw-hammer tailcoat and trousers, politely greeted the ladies.

The two newcomers were informed of what had been discussed so far. Then together they all walked through the existing library before returning to the drawing room to reclaim their chairs and teacups.

Mercy surveyed the drawing room. "To begin with, we'll need more shelves in this room."

Jane followed her gaze. "I agree. Mr. Kingsley might help. He seems a capable builder."

Mr. Drake nodded. "The Kingsleys' work at the Fairmont has been excellent. In fact, Joseph Kingsley is working on a project for me right now."

"Then he is probably too busy to build shelves." Rachel bit her lip, then added sheepishly, "Nor have I much money to pay him."

Mr. Drake looked at Jane, his green eyes brightening. "What about using the shelves we removed from the Fairmont library? We stored them in one of the outbuildings. Might they not, with some alteration, suit this room?"

Jane looked around once more. "I think they might."

Rachel's face heated. "I haven't the funds to purchase them."

He waved away her concern. "You are welcome to them. Not doing anyone any good sitting where they are. Some assembly would be required to reinstall them, but I am sure Mr. Kingsley would be equal to the task. Let me talk to him, see what he thinks."

"Very well. Thank you, Mr. Drake."

Mr. Drake sipped his tea and relaxed back against the cushions. "This room is most comfortable. I can easily imagine sitting here browsing for hours. Many libraries offer reading rooms, you know, and stock the latest periodicals for the purpose."

"No, I did not know," Rachel said, beginning to feel overwhelmed again.

"Remember, I will be happy to promote the library to our guests," Jane said. "And perhaps we should go to Salisbury and visit the circulating library there. See what else we might need in terms of furnishing and organization."

Mr. Drake nodded. "Excellent notion."

Rachel pressed her hands to her cheeks. "This is all happening so quickly."

Jane turned again to Mr. Drake. "What about a license? Will she need one to start a business here?"

"I am not sure," he replied. "But Sir Timothy Brockwell would know."

Jane looked at her. "Will you ask him, Rachel, or would you like me to?"

"I . . . suppose I will do it, since it is to be my library. What strange words to utter! But does it really make sense to open one here?"

Mr. Drake nodded. "I think your scheme an excellent one, Miss Ashford. Granted, circulating libraries are most popular in spa towns and the coast. But located on the Royal Mail coaching route, as we are, we receive our share of travelers too. And like Mrs. Bell, I too will be happy to recommend a subscription to my regular guests." He winked at Jane. "When I have any."

"Thank you. Again, thank you all." Rachel managed a smile, though inwardly she quailed.

Good heavens. What have I got myself into!

After the meeting, Jane walked with Mr. Drake back to The Bell, where he had left his horse.

"Thank you for coming today."

"My pleasure, Jane. You know I am always happy to help. And I like your friends—intelligent, well-spoken, resourceful . . ."

"I agree."

"And pretty, which a woman should be, if at all possible." He gave her a roguish grin. "Though no one holds a candle to you, of course."

"Now, that's going it a bit brown."

"Not in my view. At all events, I was impressed with your ideas today. You do remember what I said at your license hearing? That I consider you one of the keenest women of my acquaintance?"

"I remember."

His eyes glimmered. "I also said I looked forward to a long relationship with you." He took her arm and laced it through his as they walked.

She sent him a sidelong glance. "What you said was a 'mutually profitable' relationship. Not exactly romantic."

"We were in front of the magistrates, after all. But we are not now." He drew her closer to his side.

She tried to tug her hand free, but he held fast, stopping to face her.

"Jane . . ."

"Yes, James?"

"Have dinner with me tonight at the Fairmont."

She hesitated, recalling his veiled offer when she'd toured Fairmont House. She had doubted his sincerity, but either way, she had not been ready to consider it. Jane shook her head. "I will be gone to Salisbury the better part of tomorrow, so I had better not be absent tonight as well."

Disappointment shone on his handsome face.

She added, "But you are welcome to join me in The Bell coffee room."

"And eat Mrs. Rooke's cooking instead of my chef's?" He exhaled a long-suffering sigh. "A sacrifice I'd make only for you, Jane Bell."

She dug a playful shoulder into his, and he escorted her the rest of the way home.

A short while later, Jane and James sat together at her favorite table—two high-backed benches near the front windows, where she or Patrick could see the street and any coaches coming up the hill. The cheerful coffee room was where the staff, coachmen, and locals generally ate, while most passengers preferred the formal dining parlour.

Seeing Jane alone with Mr. Drake, a few of The Bell regulars sent them interested glances, and Patrick came over to greet them.

"Evening, Jane. Mr. Drake."

"Mr. Bell, how are things here?"

"Busy. More traffic lately, thankfully."

James nodded. "Probably due to hunting season and the harvest."

"Ah. I wager you're right. Well, whatever brings business to little Ivy Hill, we'll take it. Right, Jane?"

"Definitely."

"Now I'll leave you two to enjoy your dinner."

Patrick walked away as Alwena brought them the evening's special of roast beef and potatoes.

Jane picked up her knife and fork. "Do you know, you never fully explained why you came here to 'little Ivy Hill' in the first place."

"Besides to tease you, do you mean?" Appealing grooves dimpled his cheeks. "Actually, I thought I had explained. When I saw plans for the turnpike, I sensed an opportunity and came looking."

"And *I* sense there was more to it than that."

"Clever girl." He cut a piece of meat.

Jane ate a bite of roast and was quiet as she chewed, and chewed, and finally swallowed. "Have you found everything you hoped for here?"

"Not yet. But what I have found has captured my interest."

She raised a skeptical brow. "At least for now, do you mean? I cannot imagine Ivy Hill holding your attention for long."

He nodded. "For now."

She shook her head. "You are a mystery, James Drake. Can nothing be plain and straightforward with you?"

He lifted a forkful of stringy meat. "Like dry roast and plain potatoes, do you mean? Personally, I prefer a bit of complexity to savor."

"You certainly know how to dish it out."

"I hope that means you find my company interesting, Jane. For I enjoy yours a great deal. In fact, there is almost no one I would rather see across the table from me."

"Almost no one? At least you are tempering your flattery now. I might almost believe you."

A slow smile tilted his mouth, but it did not quite reach his eyes.

The next morning, Jane rose a little earlier than usual to dress and prepare for their trip into Salisbury. Mercy wanted to join them, but Lord Winspear had finally agreed to a meeting to hear her case for the charity school. She needed his support, so Jane and Rachel would go alone.

Jane selected an old but becoming carriage dress of russet red for the trip, and a hat with a matching ribbon.

"It is such a pleasure to help you dress now that you are out of mourning, Mrs. Bell," Cadi said as she curled Jane's brown hair. "I hope that isn't impertinent to say."

"When has that ever stopped you?" Jane teased the girl, who was friend as well as maid.

Entering the inn a short while later, Jane spoke briefly with Colin, Alwena, and Mrs. Rooke. She found herself missing Thora. She and Talbot were still away on their wedding trip. But hopefully all would continue to go well during her absence. Then Jane stopped at the desk to remind Patrick of her plans for the day.

Patrick leaned back in his chair. "No problem, Jane. You go and enjoy yourself. You have been working hard for weeks. I'll take care of things here."

"Thank you." Jane realized she believed him. She'd become increasingly comfortable leaving the inn in Patrick's hands. He still liked to spend too much time in the taproom, hobnobbing with guests, but overall he was proving himself a capable manager.

"Can I bring you back anything?" Jane asked.

He looked around. "A new registry if you happen to pass the stationers. With the increase in traffic lately, this one's nearly full. An excellent problem to have."

Rachel stepped through the front door wearing a long mauve redingote trimmed in black, her blond hair crowned by a matching bonnet.

Seeing her, Patrick let out a low whistle. "Or *I* could go to Salisbury with Miss Ashford, and you could stay here." He gave Jane an impish grin.

Jane rolled her eyes. "You would find her immune to your charms, Patrick, as she has a promising new suitor."

"The young man who inherited Thornvale, while I own nothing? Don't remind me." Petulance flashed across his face, then disappeared. He stepped to the side door, opening it with gallant address. "Miss Ashford. Jane. Right this way. Your carriage arrives in two minutes. Safe journey, ladies. I shall be here, ever vigilant, when you return."

Jane shook her head in tolerant amusement and followed Rachel out into the courtyard to await the mail coach. Two minutes later, the Quicksilver arrived right on schedule.

Seeing Jane, the Royal Mail guard waved. As the coach slowed, he hopped down. Approaching the ladies, he bowed smartly, and Jane introduced her friend.

Rachel blushed, whether disconcerted to have a guard formally introduced to her, or to have a dashing man smile at her so warmly, Jane could not be sure. Jack Gander did cut a fine figure in his red coat, his dark hair and eyes in striking contrast to his fair skin.

He shifted his smile to Jane. "How are you, Mrs. Bell? Everything shipshape here at my favorite coaching inn?"

"I am well, Jack. And so is The Bell, thankfully. And you? How is the new coachman getting on?"

"Oh, he is all right. He's no Charlie Frazer, but who is?"

They referred to his former partner—the coachman who had recently vied with Walter Talbot for Thora's affections. He had taken a new post far from Ivy Hill.

"He is quite a character—that is for certain," Jane agreed. "We miss him."

"As do I. But the new man is a decent fellow. So, where are you ladies bound for today?"

"Only to Salisbury."

"Off for a bit of shopping? A fine day for it. Allow me." He opened the door and handed in Rachel, then Jane, before returning to his duties.

"Goodness, he is handsome," Rachel breathed.

Jane blinked innocently. "Is he?"

"Almost as handsome as your husband was."

Jane looked at her in surprise. "Did you think John handsome?"

"Of course. Don't you remember when we first met him in Bath? Come to think of it, didn't we meet him at the circulating library in Milsom Street?"

"It was a bookshop, but no matter."

"Ah. Well, in any case, I could not believe you wanted to look at books, of all things." Rachel grinned. "Had you seen a handsome man through the shop window?"

"I had not!"

"Is it all right that I tease you, Jane? Or do you prefer not to talk about him? I would never want to hurt you."

"It's all right. It feels strange but oddly good to talk about John. I so rarely hear his name anymore. Especially now with Thora gone."

Rachel shook her head. "I am still surprised neither Ellen nor I recognized Mr. Bell, since we lived in the same village. But he was so well dressed and looked every inch the learned gentleman, especially reading a book, as he was."

Jane nodded, thinking back. She remembered how John had looked at her—as though she were the most beautiful woman in the world—and felt a nostalgic ache at the thought. "I learned later he was staying in Bath with Thora's sister. He studied for a time under a tutor there. He always rather saw himself as a gentleman."

Rachel nodded. "I admit, I have often wondered what might have happened if we realized from the beginning he was the innkeeper's son. I'm afraid Ellen and I would have dismissed him instantly. Instead she encouraged you to dance with him in the lower assembly rooms that night. If you had known who he was from the first, would you have allowed yourself to fall for him? Or . . . might things have turned out differently?"

Was she asking if Jane would have married Sir Timothy instead? Jane took a deep breath and exhaled. "They might have, yes." She leaned forward. "But things worked out as they were meant to, Rachel. Timothy and I are friends, but that is all."

"Even now that John is gone?"

Jane nodded. "Even now."

"Well, that is more than he and I are. We barely speak, even when we see each other in church or on the street."

"Perhaps that will change."

"After eight years, why should it?"

Jane hesitated, not wanting to speak out of turn. "And what about Mr. Ashford? Are you . . . 'allowing yourself to fall for him'?

I have only met him in passing, but I confess I like the young man." She grinned. "After all, he has good taste in women."

Rachel ducked her head, her cheeks reddening in embarrassment or pleasure or both.

And again Jane feared Timothy had waited too long, now that Nicholas Ashford was pursuing his pretty cousin.

Rachel remained quiet after that, looking out the coach window at the passing Wiltshire countryside. Soon they were rattling along Salisbury's streets and through the archway into the Red Lion's courtyard. The handsome Royal Mail guard appeared again to let down the step and help them alight.

He tipped his hat. "Enjoy your day, ladies."

"Thank you, Jack," Jane said. "See you soon."

From there, Rachel and Jane walked down the narrow cobbled lane to the wider High Street, with its colorful shops and medieval gate. They turned at Catherine Street and walked until they found Fellows's Circulating Library.

Inside, they introduced themselves to the proprietor. Mr. Fellows said he would be happy to show Miss Ashford around his establishment and advise her on setting up her own. He apparently judged Ivy Hill too small and too distant for Rachel's library to pose any serious competition.

The short man led them into a back room filled with floor-to-ceiling bookcases and gestured toward them with evident pride. "Our collection boasts over fifteen hundred volumes, which subscribers may borrow for an annual fee." He next led them to a separate seating area. "Our reading room here is frequented both by ladies and gentlemen, and is daily supplied with the latest London morning and evening newspapers, as well as journals and magazines."

He described his methods of labeling and cataloging books, as well as record keeping, accounting, and advertising.

"Goodness," Rachel breathed, again feeling overwhelmed by it all.

Jane added, "Very impressive, Mr. Fellows."

They thanked the man for his time and advice, and left the establishment.

As they walked away, Jane squeezed her hand. "Don't be anxious, Rachel. You needn't try to compete with Mr. Fellows. Start small. And you know Mercy, Matilda, and I will help you."

"Thank you, Jane." It was difficult to admit it, but she would need all the help she could get.

They stopped at the stationers for the promised registry and to order cards for Rachel. Then Jane said, "Shall we see the cathedral while we're here? It is what brings most tourists after all."

"Why not?" Rachel smiled, but her heart was not in it.

As they approached the cathedral, Rachel gazed up at England's tallest spire, struck by its majesty, her thoughts naturally drawn to God. A prayer leapt to the tip of her tongue—a plea for help in this scary new venture—but she suppressed it. How small and inconsequential her problems must seem from so far above.

CHAPTER FOUR

The next afternoon, Rachel changed into her best blue walking dress, then stood before the mirror to rebrush and pin her blond hair. She'd had to learn to dress her own hair since releasing her lady's maid, Jemima, to take a place at Brockwell Court. Rachel wasn't very good at it but was slowly improving. The ladies of Ivy Cottage helped one another morning and night with fastenings and lacings. Their boarding pupils did the same for one another. The Miss Groves did employ one maid, along with their cook and manservant. Agnes Woodbead cleaned the house and laid fires in the female bedchambers, while Mr. Basu tended the gardens, hauled coal and wood, and helped Mrs. Timmons with the heavy work of the kitchen. At all events, everyone was too busy to help with something as frivolous as arranging hair.

Rachel sighed at her reflection and stuck in one last pin for good measure, hoping the coil of hair at the back of her head would remain in place. She wanted to look calm and collected for the meeting to come.

Leaving Ivy Cottage a short while later, she crossed the village green and followed the High Street past the shops and coaching inn. Seeing The Bell reminded her of Jane's offer to talk to Sir Timothy on her behalf. Now Rachel regretted saying she would do so herself. Nerves tingled in her stomach, and she felt prickles of perspiration that had nothing to do with the exertion of the walk.

The brick chimney stacks of Brockwell Court appeared above the tree tops. She walked toward them, turning up the long curving drive until the house—the largest in the parish—came into view.

Brockwell Court was an Elizabethan manor three and, in places, four stories tall. Artfully shaped topiaries lined the drive, and a nearby ornamental fountain lofted water in a graceful arc.

When Rachel was young, she had often visited Brockwell Court with her parents and sister—parties, Christmas gatherings, the occasional concert—but it had been years since she'd been there, or received an invitation to call. She had not been invited to call today, either, and wondered how she would be received.

A young footman she had never seen answered her knock. He said he was not sure where Sir Timothy was at the moment but that he would try to find him. Rachel nodded and stepped inside, knowing the Brockwells' exacting butler, Carville, would never have admitted he was unaware of any of the family's whereabouts, and he would no doubt have formally instructed her to wait while he went to see if Sir Timothy was "at home to callers."

As Rachel stood in the hall rehearsing what to say, Lady Brockwell came down the stairs—tall, black-haired, and regal in afternoon dress of deep green. With her dark coloring, hooded eyes, and long nose, she looked like an Italian *donna*.

Seeing her, anxiety pulsed in Rachel's veins.

Lady Brockwell glanced up and paused at the bottom of the stairs. Some emotion crossed her face, but it was not pleasure.

"Miss Ashford. I am surprised to see you. Were we expecting you?"

"No, I—"

"I suppose Justina invited you? That child is forever inviting people to call."

"No, she did not. I was hoping to speak with Sir Timothy."

The woman's eyes flashed a warning. "My son is very busy, Miss

Ashford. In fact, I believe he is meeting with our farm manager as we speak."

"You needn't worry, your ladyship; this is not a social call. I was hoping to talk with him about a . . . matter of village business. But I can return another time."

Justina appeared in the drawing room door. "Mamma, the tea is growing cold. Oh, Rachel! I did not see you there." The young woman with golden brown hair, dark eyes, and delicate features crossed the hall to her, all smiles. "What a wonderful surprise. I do hope you are staying for tea."

"Thank you, Justina. But I have only come to speak to your brother on a matter of business."

Justina's brows lifted. "Business?"

Rachel hesitated to describe the proposed venture with Lady Brockwell standing there.

Noticing her discomfort, Justina said, "Then I shall fetch him. He is in the billiards room, but I am sure he'll come directly once he knows you're here."

Meeting with his farm manager, indeed, Rachel thought. "I do not want to interrupt. I shall speak to him another time. Does he keep regular office hours, or . . . ?"

Justina shrugged. "Mornings, usually. But he won't mind. Not for you."

Lady Brockwell said, "Justina, if he is finished with his day's duties, we ought to let your brother rest."

"Mamma, Miss Ashford is an old friend. He would be unhappy if we sent her away."

The same young footman crossed the hall again, apparently still looking for his master, and Justina called, "Andrew, Sir Timothy is in the billiards room. Please let him know Miss Ashford is here and would like to speak with him on a village matter."

"Very good, miss."

Justina turned back to her. "It is so good to see you, Rachel. I haven't spoken to you since your farewell dinner party at Thornvale." The girl's face fell. "Forgive me. I suppose that is an unhappy topic."

"Not at all," Rachel assured her. "It was a lovely evening." *Until Nicholas and his mother arrived.*

Justina looked at Lady Brockwell. "It was a pity you missed it, Mamma. You stayed home with a cold, remember?"

"A trifling cold. I rarely take ill." She turned to Rachel, as if reading her thoughts. "By the way, I have since met Mrs. Ashford and her son at church. She seems a decent sort of woman."

Rachel replied neutrally, "I am glad you think so."

Justina teased, "And rumor has it that the amiable Mr. Ashford has made clear his interest in a certain distant cousin. . . . " The girl smiled, eyes alight.

"How rumors do spread." Rachel shifted uneasily, the insinuation all too obvious. "Mr. Ashford and I are not . . . That is, there is no . . . " She'd been about to say there was no understanding between them, but that was not quite true. She said instead, "I don't know who told you that, but nothing is settled between us."

Justina shrugged. "I have seen you with him myself, talking at church, or walking home together afterward. And don't forget, your Jemima is my lady's maid now."

Ah, that explained a great deal. Had the maid eavesdropped during Mr. Ashford's proposal? Rachel wondered. Probably.

Lady Brockwell said, "It was your suggestion, Justina tells me, that I engage your lady's maid for her."

Rachel nodded. "Yes, I am grateful. And Jemima is an excellent maid." *And an excellent gossip.*

"I was sure Mamma would insist I didn't need a lady's maid. Instead she agreed rather quickly."

Rachel smiled politely at Lady Brockwell. "It was kind of you to give her a place."

"It was time Justina had a maid of her own. She is a marriageable young woman now."

"Mamma, not that again," Justina groaned. "As with Rachel, nothing is settled. Ah. Here comes Timothy."

Rachel turned to watch his approach. She felt Lady Brockwell's gaze on her profile but pretended not to notice, clasping her hands over her nervous stomach and pasting on a serene expression.

"Good day, Miss Ashford." Sir Timothy crossed the hall in long strides. "A pleasure to see you. Nothing is wrong, I hope."

"No. Nothing . . . specific."

"The footman mentioned some village matter you wished to discuss?"

Rachel darted a look at his mother, who showed no intention of excusing herself.

She swallowed. "Yes. But I can return another time if now is not convenient. I did not realize you kept morning office hours."

He waved away her concerns. "In general, when I can. But it is no trouble to speak with you now." He pointed to his right. "My office is just there, if you would prefer to talk privately?"

"Yes, thank you. I shan't keep you long."

"Excuse us, Mamma."

"But your tea, Timothy."

"Go on without me. I shall join you later."

"Very well." Lady Brockwell smiled coolly and strode away, Justina trailing behind.

Sir Timothy gestured for Rachel to precede him. In the office, he hesitated only a moment before closing the door. "You must forgive my mother. She has always been protective of my time."

Rachel thought, *Yes, I remember*.

She did not recall ever being in this office before. It had been Sir Justin's domain, where he performed magisterial duties, as his son did now.

Being in close proximity to Sir Timothy, she noticed his dark side-whiskers were threaded with silver, though he was only thirty. His father, she recalled, had greyed early as well. Yet Timothy was still as handsome as ever, with strong regular features, pronounced cheekbones, and cleft chin. He was tall and shared his mother's dark hair and regal bearing. Rachel had always looked up to him, literally and figuratively.

He removed a book from one of the chairs facing his desk. "Please, be seated."

She did so, and he took his own chair, interlacing his fingers on the desk. "Now, what can I do for you?"

"I hope you might answer a question for me. You see, my father left me his collection of books, though his will stipulates that I am not to sell them."

Sir Timothy nodded along, but his tense expression told her he was wary about what she was leading up to.

"Surely he left you some means of support as well?"

"He was not able to. I have a little money from my mother, which allows me to contribute toward expenses at Ivy Cottage. The Miss Groves don't require it, but I insist."

He frowned. "Miss Ashford, as I told you before, if you need anything, I—"

"Please just hear me out," she interrupted. "I am not here to ask for financial help." She took a deep breath and pressed on, "Some of the village ladies suggested I might open a sort of circulating library with Papa's books as a way of earning a living. Mercy has offered me the Ivy Cottage library for the purpose. I am here to ask about any required licenses or ordinances."

He slowly shook his head. "First Mercy, then Jane, and now you. How the world has changed." He held up his palm. "I mean no censure. I am only surprised. And honestly unsure what to think. Three gentlewomen in business . . ."

"We are only trying to do the best we can with the resources we have."

He nodded, eyebrows lowered in thought. "No doubt your father's collection would be useful for Miss Grove's pupils. But . . . what about Mr. Ashford?"

She lifted her chin. "What about him?"

"Forgive me. I heard there might be an understanding between you. And then I saw the two of you out together the other day."

"We were only walking."

"So . . . there is not an understanding between you?"

Was that hope in his eyes? No—probably only her imagination.

He continued, "That is, I assume there is not. If there were, you would have no need and, I would guess, no desire to pursue such a venture."

"He has asked me to marry him."

He sat back, expression somber. "Has he indeed? But is he not a few years younger?"

Rachel nodded. "But he sees that as no impediment, and I suppose neither do I."

Why was she telling him this? Was she hoping he would regret letting her go? Feel jealous? Feel . . . something? "He asked before I departed Thornvale. He did not like being the cause of my having to leave my home. He said he felt responsible for me."

"That was noble of him."

"I thought so."

"But you did not accept him?"

"Not . . . initially."

"Oh?" His eyebrows rose. "Are you saying you wish to see if this library will be a success before you decide whether or not to accept him?"

"No. How callous you make me sound! Is it wrong to want to become better acquainted with the man I might one day marry? To be certain I could care for him, and he for me? Who knows how long that might take. A few months? A year? In the meantime, I cannot live off the Miss Groves' generosity. I must earn my own way. The circulating library is the only idea I have at present. I have to try something." She paused for breath, feeling flushed and winded.

"It is not immoral or even unusual to marry for security, Miss Ashford."

Why would he say that? Was he encouraging her to marry Mr. Ashford?

She said, "If security was all I wanted, I suppose I would have accepted him in the first place. But that has never been all I wanted. Not now, and not when—" She broke off and squared her shoulders. "In any case, none of that is why I am here. Apparently you helped Jane obtain the necessary license for The Bell. She suggested I ask you if I would require a license to operate a library."

"Did she? Then I gather you and Jane are on better terms now?"

"We are."

"I am glad. I have always regretted how things ended between you. Between . . . us."

Rachel licked dry lips. Did he mean between him and Jane, or him and *her*? Before she could ask, he cleared his throat and went on.

"At all events, as an innkeeper, Jane was required to obtain a victualler's license. That particular license does not apply in this case. But let me consult with the magistrates and village council about any other ordinances or concerns."

"Thank you." She rose. "I would like to know any requirements before I begin."

He nodded. "I will let you know what I find out." He crossed the room and opened the door for her. "And will you let me know what you decide?"

She mulled his words. "What I decide about the library or . . . Mr. Ashford?"

"Yes." He met her gaze but did not expand on his oblique reply.

As Rachel walked back to Ivy Cottage, she reviewed their conversation in her mind. Sir Timothy had been perfectly polite but terribly formal. How different than he had once treated her—for a short time. At the thought, she allowed herself to recall his first visit to Thornvale about a week after her coming-out ball. . . .

Rachel and her father were sitting in Thornvale's drawing room together, Rachel bent over her embroidery hoop, while Sir William scowled at a letter.

"Bad news, Papa?"

He glanced up. "That seems to be all I receive these days. But no matter." He refolded the letter and stuck it in his pocket, then picked up a leather volume from the side table. "Why dwell on unhappy tidings when there is a good book at hand, eh?"

"If you say so."

Rachel returned to her embroidery, but when she looked up a few minutes later, she was disconcerted to see him staring blankly over the top of the book without having turned a single page.

"Papa? Are you all right?"

"Hm? Oh, yes. Of course. And you shall be as well."

"What do you mean?"

Jemima appeared in the doorway and announced in an excited whisper, "Miss, Mr. Brockwell is here to see you. He has flowers in his hand! Are you at home?"

"Of course." Rachel's heart soared. She reminded herself that it was traditional for a gentleman who'd escorted a lady into supper to pay a call the next day, and a week had passed. She hoped he had not come out of obligation alone.

Sir William set aside his book, and Rachel rose as Timothy entered.

He bowed. "Miss Ashford. Sir William. I hope I don't intrude. I have come to congratulate your daughter on her great success last week."

Rachel curtsied. "Thank you."

"Good of you to call, Brockwell," Sir William said. "You are always welcome, as you know." He looked at Rachel. "And were you pleased with your coming-out ball, my dear?"

"I was, Papa. It was almost perfect."

Her father raised one brow. "Almost?"

"If only dear Mamma had been with us."

"Ah, yes. Though she was, in a way, for you are more and more like her."

"Thank you, Papa." She turned back to their guest.

"These are for you." Timothy Brockwell stepped forward and handed her a small bouquet of peach-colored roses, which looked delicate and out of place in his masculine hand.

"They're lovely." She drew the nosegay to her face. "Oh! And smell heavenly. Just like my mother's."

"I asked Mrs. Bushby to order these especially. I know they are your favorite."

Pleasure tingled through her. "Thank you. Will you be seated?"

He did so, his dark eyes tracing her face, her cheeks, her mouth. Then he abruptly turned to Sir William. "And how are you, sir?"

"Better now you're here, Brockwell. But . . ." Sir William rose. "Propriety be hanged, you two have known each other all your lives, and I trust you implicitly. Besides, there's a glass of claret awaiting me in my study. If you will excuse me."

"Of course, sir. I can't stay long myself. I am traveling with my father to the quarter sessions in a fortnight, and there is much to do to prepare."

"Ah, yes. No doubt a great deal of news exchanged there among the men of the county."

"So I understand."

"Well, don't believe everything you hear."

Feeling uneasy, Rachel watched her father leave the room. But when she looked back at Timothy and found his admiring gaze resting on her face, her concerns fled.

"I enjoyed your ball as well." A small smile curved his lips. "And apparently that night was not a dream after all, for you are just as enchanting by daylight."

Her cheeks warmed and her pulse pounded. "Thank you."

He sobered. "But . . . forgive me. I don't mean to get ahead of myself. I realize you may have expected a call sooner, but I wanted to be considerate of the feelings of . . . others. I trust you understand?"

"I do."

"May I call again?"

"Of course. I would be happy if you did."

"Perhaps you could come to Brockwell Court. I know Justina would love to see you." He looked up in thought. "We might . . . pick strawberries together or stroll through the gardens."

She sent him a wry glance. "You are not really the strolling and strawberry-picking sort of man, Mr. Brockwell. I think you would prefer archery or riding."

"That I can't deny, but I want you to enjoy yourself as well."

"I have never ridden."

"I know. And that is all right. You need not—"

"But I would like to learn," she interjected. "Might you teach me?"

He studied her face. "Would you truly like to?"

"I would, yes. Though I confess the prospect is a little frightening."

He leaned forward, voice warm and reassuring. "I shall remain close and keep you safe."

Her stomach tightened. "That would help indeed."

"Worth every moment, if you might learn to love horses as I do."

And as Jane did as well, she knew. But this was not about Jane. This was about herself and Timothy. At the ball, Rachel had assumed he could have no serious romantic interest in her—not when everyone assumed he would marry Jane—but that was not what she read in his expression now. Seeing it, dreams of romance blossomed.

He took his leave soon after, and Rachel glanced down at the nosegay once more, noticing a small card tucked beneath the ribbon.

To the lovely Miss Ashford. Congratulations, and all the best for the future.—TB

A future that was proving to be nothing like she had dreamed.

CHAPTER
FIVE

Mercy Grove entered the silent schoolroom, pausing a moment to close her eyes and inhale the peaceful, familiar smells of chalk dust and old books. Opening her eyes, she noticed a crumpled piece of paper on the floor. She picked it up and carried it toward the rubbish basket. The lines on the paper piqued her curiosity and she peeled open the wad to see what was scrawled there.

One of the girls had drawn this? She felt a stab of hurt. For the image was clearly a caricature of her, and not a flattering one. The center-parted curtain of flat, dark hair. The long oval face and even longer neck. The exaggerated needle nose like an exclamation symbol over a small thin mouth. Fanny's work, she guessed. Mischievous Fanny Scales enjoyed making people laugh, often at the expense of someone else. But Mercy had never been the target of one of her cutting jokes before, at least as far as she knew.

Mercy regarded the image again. Perhaps Fanny had been practicing her drawing skills and this was simply what she saw when she looked at her teacher, and no joke or insult was meant. The rendering was rather accurate, she could not deny.

Mercy knew she was plain—had always known it. Her mother had never said so aloud, but Mercy heard it in every admonition to not stand up quite so tall, to do something with her hair, or in asking the dressmaker to pad the top of her long stays and tighten the bottom. "You were such a beautiful baby, Mercy," her mother had told her more than once, ending on a sigh, which left little room for misinterpretation. If Mercy had ever been beautiful, she had grown out of it. She had certainly grown. The current dress style was both a blessing and a curse. The high, indistinct waistlines, lower necklines, and shapeless skirts revealed her long neck and thin bosom, yet concealed her trim waist—the best feature of her triangular figure, in her view. But at least the full skirts hid her disproportionately generous backside.

Fanny walked in and stopped abruptly at the sight of Mercy standing there, wrinkled drawing in hand. Her mouth parted, and she looked from the caricature to her teacher with wary eyes.

"You display talent, Miss Scales," Mercy said kindly. "The nose is especially clever. Did you know our note of exclamation comes from the Latin exclamation of joy? We really ought to find a drawing master to help hone your skills."

The girl swallowed. "I was only having a bit of fun. I meant no disrespect, Miss Grove."

Mercy gave the girl a gentle smile. "None taken." She dropped the note into the rubbish and walked to her desk.

Fanny remained. "Miss Grove? Why did you never marry?"

Mercy turned in surprise. "Do you mean, beyond my looks, which you so accurately captured?"

Fanny had the decency to blush and looked down at the floor. "I am sorry about that."

"I had no intention of begging an apology, Fanny. It is no secret that I am plain."

"Not *so* plain." The girl shrugged one shoulder, still not meeting Mercy's eyes. "Some plain girls marry, don't they?"

Ah . . . Mercy thought. Fanny was somewhat plain herself, or at least, not as attractive by worldly standards as, say, pretty Anna Kingsley or sweet little Alice. And her often sour disposition did nothing to help her looks. But Fanny was still so young. Was she already concerned about her looks and marriage prospects? Very possibly. After all, Mercy had been made aware of her own deficiencies at a young age.

Mercy realized that for most girls, marriage was their primary goal in life. Unless one happened to be a rare independent heiress, the importance of marrying a good provider was undeniable. Mercy, however, did not believe a woman needed to marry to be whole, valued by God, and to live a fulfilling life. After all, look at her aunt Matilda. But Mercy was in the minority with this view, she knew.

"Yes, Fanny. Plenty of plain girls marry. And plenty of plain men."

"But . . . not you?"

Mercy shook her head. "Not me." She gently lifted the girl's chin. "Remember, Fanny, there is more to life than beauty, which doesn't last anyway. There is character and virtue. Gentleness and sweetness of temper."

"I haven't got those either."

"You are young, Fanny. With God's help, you will . . . in time."

"Will you ever marry, do you think?"

"Heavens, I don't know. At my age, it seems unlikely. Now, let us prepare for class."

Fanny took her seat, and Mercy opened her lesson book.

Though Mercy had cherished hope of marriage and children when she was younger, she'd never had a promising suitor. Her parents had made several matchmaking attempts over the years but had eventually given it up. Now she was at peace, for the most part, about her single state. But in her secret heart, she hid a sadness over her childless state. She was very fond of her pupils, and of Alice, in particular. But it wasn't the same as having a child of her own, as being someone's mamma.

God was good, she did not doubt. But that did not always mean He gave you everything you wanted.

What would her life be like someday when Aunt Matty passed? Would she grow old alone?

A favorite verse whispered itself in her heart, reminding Mercy not to worry . . . *but in every thing by prayer and supplication with thanksgiving let your requests be made known unto God. And the peace of God, which passeth all understanding, shall keep your hearts and minds through Christ Jesus.*

"Thank you." Mercy whispered a little prayer and turned her thoughts to the next class.

The following day, Rachel wrote another letter to her sister, revealing her plans to open a circulating library with their father's books. She hoped Ellen would not be too scandalized. After she'd finished, she walked to The Bell, longing to tell Jane about her visit to Brockwell Court.

When she entered the inn, Jane looked up from the desk. "Rachel! How good to see you again." Jane came from around the desk to embrace her, then gestured toward the coffee room. "Do you have time for coffee or tea? Or we could go over to the keeper's lodge, if you'd rather talk in private."

Rachel hesitated. "No, this is fine. Coffee sounds heavenly."

They sat amidst the pleasant clamor of laughter and conversation from coachmen, guards, and locals. A maid brought them coffee and a pitcher of cream.

Rachel sipped the dark, delicious brew, then began. "I went to Brockwell Court yesterday. I have not been so nervous in years. I went to speak to Sir Timothy about the library, as you suggested, but his mother met me in the hall and was not pleased to see me. She clearly meant to discourage a social call, though I assured her it was not."

Jane frowned. "I am sorry to hear it. Perhaps she was just surprised to see you? Your families have always been friends. And Justina looks up to you as the sister she never had, your being closer in age than the rest of us."

Rachel clarified, "Our families *used* to be friends and Justina *used* to look up to me, but that was a long time ago, before the scandal."

Jane sadly shook her head. "If I had known you dreaded going there, I would have inquired about the license on your behalf."

"No, Jane. It is time I learned to do for myself. As you have here."

Jane bit her lip. "If it makes you feel any better, Lady Brockwell is not especially warm toward me either. She hasn't invited me to call since I married an innkeeper."

Rachel glanced up and noticed James Drake enter the coffee room.

"Hello, Jane. Ah, forgive me, you have company." He bowed. "Miss Ashford, a pleasure to see you again. How go plans for your new venture?"

"Well, thank you. We visited the circulating library in Salisbury, and the excursion was most helpful. I will begin packing up the books this week."

"Excellent. I am afraid I have not seen Mr. Kingsley in the last few days, so I've not yet had a chance to ask him about the shelves. That's why I stopped by—that and to see his progress here."

Jane explained to Rachel, "We are expanding our dining parlour on Mr. Drake's advice." She smiled up at the man. "Thank you for sparing Mr. Kingsley for a few days."

"My pleasure."

"He has agreed to oversee repairs on the stable as well," Jane added. "But those will have to wait awhile longer."

"Yes, he and his men still have much to do at the Fairmont. Well, I'll just go take a look, if you don't mind. You two ladies go ahead with your coffee."

Rachel rose. "I was just going, Mr. Drake. Don't leave on my account."

Jane laid a hand on hers. "Can you stay a few more minutes? I would like to introduce Mr. Kingsley to you, in case he might be able to help with the library."

James Drake nodded. "Good idea. By the way, Jane, there are several crates of your family's books stored in the Fairmont attic. Perhaps you might go through them, keep any you like, and give the rest to Miss Ashford to expand her collection?"

Rachel quickly interjected, "That is very considerate, Mr. Drake. However, I don't want—"

"Considerate, bah." He winked. "I shall expect a discounted rate on my subscription."

Rachel sputtered a protest, but Mr. Drake had already turned and strode from the room. The women exchanged bemused looks, then followed him past the booking desk to the public dining room, where the walls of one private parlour were being taken down to expand the main room.

A man, his brown wool coat stretching across wide shoulders, picked up several lengths of lumber and directed a younger man to haul away the heap of rubble created so far. He looked up as the three of them entered and straightened to his full, impressive height. He was in his mid-thirties, Rachel guessed, with a broad, pleasant face, sandy hair, and brown eyes.

Mr. Drake stopped in front of the man with a grin. "Mr. Kingsley, how goes it?"

"On schedule, Mr. Drake. I should be able to return to the Fairmont in two days. My brothers continue their work there, I trust?"

"Yes. Laying new paving stones on the veranda when I left." Mr. Drake crossed his arms. "Remember those bookcases you took down?"

"Of course."

"How much work would it be to reinstall them in another location?"

"Depends on the location. Why?"

"Miss Ashford here is planning to open a circulating library and could use more shelves."

Mr. Kingsley pursed his lips as he considered. "Could be done, but I'm afraid I'm rather busy at present. At Thornvale, is it?"

Rachel spoke up, "No, in Ivy Cottage. I am living there with the Miss Groves now."

"Ivy Cottage?" he repeated. "The girls school?"

"That's right."

"Then I'll come over and take a look. Depends on the height

difference of the room compared to the original, the mouldings, and so on. Once I see the place, I can better judge how difficult it would be."

"Thank you, Mr. Kingsley, but I wouldn't want to take you away from your work, especially as I am not at all certain I shall be able to afford your services."

He shrugged. "I'll come by after work one evening this week, if that will suit."

"Yes. If you are sure. Thank you."

Jane and Rachel bid Mr. Drake and Mr. Kingsley farewell and turned to go, chatting as they returned to the entry hall. Rounding the desk, they were nearly bowled over by a man a few years younger than Rachel—Jane's porter and clerk.

"Pardon me, ladies." His fair face blushed. "I should know better than to try to tally a guest's bill whilst walking."

Jane said, "Miss Ashford, you have met Colin McFarland, I believe?"

"Yes, in passing."

"Miss Ashford, you live in Ivy Cottage now, is that right?" Mr. McFarland asked.

"That's right."

"Do you know . . . do the Miss Groves teach only girls there?"

"Yes, only girls. Why?"

"Only curious."

Jane asked, "Thinking of your sisters, are you?"

"Yes, that's it. Well, if you'll excuse me." He hurried back to the desk.

Jane quietly confided, "He struggles a bit with some of his duties, but he works hard."

Patrick Bell stepped out of the office, a ruled page in his hand. "Colin! You undercharged Mr. Sanders again. . . . Oh. Hello, ladies." He bowed and continued to the desk.

Jane walked Rachel out. As the two women stepped outside, Rachel teased, "My goodness, Jane. No wonder you enjoy working here. You are surrounded by handsome men every day. Far different from living in a girls school, I assure you!" She looked at Jane hopefully. "Have any of them captured your interest?"

Jane met her gaze, humor in her eyes and a shimmer of . . . wistfulness. She shook her head. "And that's as well, as it would be unprofessional to moon around like a lovesick calf for someone I work with."

Did that mean she wouldn't rule out someone *not* working at The Bell, like James Drake? Or was she thinking of someone else?

Rachel and the Miss Groves were sewing together in the Ivy Cottage sitting room when Mr. Basu opened the door and Sir Timothy Brockwell entered, well dressed as usual, hair carefully groomed.

He bowed. "Good afternoon, ladies."

When he straightened, his gaze rested on hers. Rachel's foolish heart lurched in her breast.

"Sir Timothy." Matilda beamed up at him. "What a pleasant surprise. Do be seated."

"Thank you. I wanted to let Miss Ashford know that Lord Winspear and the village council have approved the circulating library."

"That is excellent news." Matilda turned to her expectantly, and Sir Timothy did as well.

Rachel swallowed. "I . . . yes, thank you."

He said, "While I am here, I also want to invite you and your pupils to our orchard to pick apples. The trees have produced exceptionally well this year."

"That is very generous of you, Sir Timothy," Mercy said. "The girls would no doubt enjoy such an outing."

Matilda grinned. "And we shall all enjoy the apples."

"Perhaps sometime next week?" he suggested.

Mercy and Matilda nodded in agreement, and then looked at Rachel.

She hesitated. She didn't like the idea of going to Brockwell Court to collect fruit, as though a poor cottager gleaning fields. It reminded her of the baskets of produce and game that began to appear on Thornvale's kitchen steps after her father's fall from grace. Cook had been grateful for the anonymous gifts, but Rachel had been reluctant to accept them.

She replied, "Em, yes. I can help supervise the girls."

Sir Timothy smiled. "Excellent. I shall look forward to seeing you there." They agreed to a time, and then he bowed again and took his leave.

Matilda's gaze followed him from the room. "That was very well done of Sir Timothy." She shifted toward Rachel, eyes sparkling. "I presume we have you to thank for the invitation. Sir Timothy has never invited us to pick apples before."

Rachel shook her head. "No, you heard him. They have an unusually good crop this year."

"Um-hm," Matilda murmured, though she did not look convinced, and her eyes continued to sparkle.

After church on Sunday, Rachel walked out of St. Anne's with Nicholas Ashford. She clasped her hands tightly, knowing she could not put off this conversation any longer. Not only had Lord Winspear and the council approved the library, but the Miss Groves had already begun relocating their personal belongings to the family sitting room and attic to free up space.

She took a deep breath and began, "I would like to remove my father's books from Thornvale, when it is convenient."

He turned to stare at her. "What? All of them?"

"Yes. I hope you don't mind. I suppose empty shelves will look strange, and I'm sorry. Have you books of your own? If not, perhaps I could leave a few."

"Where will you put them all? I said I was perfectly happy to keep them for you. I hope you didn't feel as if you were . . . I don't know, taking unfair advantage, or in my debt and unwilling to be."

"No, that is not it," Rachel assured him. She went on to explain her plan to open a circulating library in Ivy Cottage.

As she spoke, his long face lengthened even more. "I don't

understand. Or perhaps I don't want to understand what this seems to mean."

"It means I feel I need to try to earn my own livelihood."

He dipped his head. "It would be my pleasure, my privilege, to provide for you."

"I know, and I have no doubt you could do so admirably. But . . . I need more time."

He frowned and seemed about to argue, but instead he said, "Of course. Remove them whenever you like. I will help you pack them up myself."

"Thank you for understanding."

"In fact, we shall make a party of it. I know Mrs. Fife and her maids will be happy to lend a hand, and I'll ask Cook to provide refreshments while we work. How does that sound?"

She smiled at him. "Excellent. You are very kind."

CHAPTER SIX

Under a bright autumn sun, the ladies of Ivy Cottage walked to Brockwell Court, broad bonnets in place, and baskets in gloved hands. Rachel still felt ill at ease about the outing, but seeing the girls' excitement, her hesitation faded away beneath the cheerful chatter and sunshine.

Soon they were strolling along the bridleway behind the manor, Matilda praising its formal gardens, and the girls ohhing and ah-hing over the large topiary house. Seeing the house-shaped yew with doors cut into either end, a stab of nostalgia hit Rachel. She and Justina had often played inside when they were young.

Sir Timothy came down the rear steps of the manor and strode toward them. Dressed in informal trousers, striped waistcoat, and tan country coat, he looked more relaxed than Rachel usually saw him. The breeze tousled his wavy dark hair, and he smiled from one person to the next, his gaze lingering on her. Rachel's heart squeezed and she smiled back.

"Welcome to Brockwell Court, ladies. Please follow me." He led them down the orchard path where they gathered around the apple trees. "I see you brought your own baskets, but there are also bushel baskets here if you need them. Feel free to gather as many apples as you wish."

Mabel's eyes rounded. "As many as we wish?"

"Well, as many as you can carry." Timothy winked.

Fanny asked, "May we eat one now?"

"You may indeed. All I ask is that you don't waste them and that you save room for a picnic we'll share in an hour or so."

At that, the girls looked at one another with gleaming grins.

Timothy gestured toward the trees. "Go on now."

For a moment the girls hesitated, looking at Mercy. She nodded encouragement and waved a shooing hand. The girls buzzed with excitement and dashed into the trees in twos and threes.

Little Alice ran to the nearest tree and stretched up on her tiptoes, trying in vain to reach a large apple dangling from a high branch. Before Mercy or Rachel could react, Sir Timothy asked her, "May I give you a boost?"

Eyes on her prize, Alice nodded, and he lifted her up to reach the beguiling fruit. Then he set her back down and whistled appreciatively. "Good eye. That is the most perfect apple I have seen this year."

Alice gave him a shy, dimpled smile and carefully placed the prize in her basket.

A ladder stood propped against one of the taller apple trees, and Rachel decided to use it to reach the upper branches. She slid her small basket over her arm and began climbing the rungs, which to her dismay were worn smooth and seemed precariously loose.

"Take care, Miss Ashford," Sir Timothy warned.

"I shall." But at that instant her foot slipped and she flailed for balance.

Strong hands flew out to help, grazing her backside before grasping her waist.

"Em . . . pardon me. Only trying to stop your fall."

Rachel burned all over at the accidental touch. "Th-thank you. Not the best shoes for climbing ladders, apparently."

He kept his hands on her waist as she descended the final rungs.

Turning around, she darted a look at him, then away again. Was he red in the face as well, or was that a hint of sunburn?

He looked instead at the ladder. "Perhaps I ought to take this to the barn before one of the girls tries to climb it. Don't want anyone getting hurt."

He stowed the ladder, then rejoined them, picking apples from a tree beside Rachel's. Working at a steady pace, he filled a bushel far more quickly than she did.

Beyond Sir Timothy, Rachel noticed Fanny pick up a rotten apple from the ground. She looked at Mabel with a mischievous smirk and reeled back her arm. Realizing what Fanny intended, Rachel opened her mouth to call a warning, but too late. The apple flew. In a flash, Sir Timothy's hand shot out and caught the apple with a smack before it reached its mark.

Fanny turned to him, eyes wide.

"An impressive arm," he said. He tossed the bruised apple onto the compost heap, then shook burst fruit from his glove. "But no aiming at living creatures, please."

"No, sir. Sorry, sir."

Sukey ran over to Timothy, swinging her full basket. "May we feed an apple to the horses, sir?" She motioned past the orchard, where several horses grazed in the fenced paddock.

He looked from the girls to the animals. "I don't see why not, if you give each only one."

The girls hurried to the gate with their offerings. Timothy accompanied them, showing the girls how to hold their palms flat to avoid the horses' teeth.

Rachel watched them from a distance, and Matilda came and stood beside her. "He is surprisingly good with them," she observed.

Rachel nodded. "He is an experienced older brother after all."

As if in response to Rachel's reference to her, Justina came out to join them, wearing a striking icy blue dress. The girls gathered around the pretty young woman as though she were a princess.

Timothy walked over and stood beside Rachel, his gaze resting on his sister with almost paternal pride. Rachel looked up at him and noticed a smudge of apple pulp on his cheek. Splatter from his recent catch, she guessed.

"You have a little, em . . ." She pointed to her own cheek.

He frowned and swiped ineffectually at his face.

Seeing the girls' attention still fixed on Justina, Rachel reached up and picked the offending speck from his skin.

He stilled, eyes holding hers.

She stepped back with a closed-lip smile, showing him the piece of fruit—her excuse to touch him—before flicking it away.

Soon afterward, footmen came outside and spread blankets on the ground beneath the shade of several lime trees. Then they brought out trays bearing ham and chicken, fresh fruit, biscuits, and glasses of lemonade. At their host's invitation, they all sat down to enjoy the cold repast from the Brockwell Court kitchens.

Sir Timothy disappeared for a few minutes and returned with a book in hand. "I have just discovered this poet and would like to read one short poem to you, if you will oblige me."

He sat back down and crossed his legs, reminding Rachel of the lanky youth he'd once been.

Opening the book, he said, "I can think of no better place to read it than out of doors on a beautiful autumn day."

Rachel expected Fanny to groan or complain, but instead the girl watched Sir Timothy with a soft expression, clearly smitten with the handsome man who was treating them so kindly. Rachel could not blame her.

"This poem is called 'To Autumn,' by John Keats." He cleared his throat and began reading in his rich baritone voice.

As Rachel listened, the words wrapped themselves around her, sensuous and laden with meaning. She looked around the orchard and gardens, everywhere seeing images evoked by the poem.

> "Season of mists and mellow fruitfulness,
> Close bosom-friend of the maturing sun;
> Conspiring with him how to load and bless
> With fruit the vines that round the thatch-eves run;
> To bend with apples the moss'd cottage-trees,
> And fill all fruit with ripeness to the core;

To swell the gourd, and plump the hazel shells
With a sweet kernel; to set budding more,
And still more, later flowers for the bees,
Until they think warm days will never cease,
For summer has o'er-brimm'd their clammy cells—"

"What are clammy cells?" Phoebe blurted, breaking the sweet spell.

Sir Timothy paused, unruffled by the interruption. "Honeycombs overflowing with honey. The bees think summer will never end. But we know better, don't we. Winter must come in its time."

He read on, and Rachel saw with new eyes the beauty of autumn, which, like spring, "hast thy music too."

As Timothy read the final lines about birds preparing to fly away for the winter, Rachel could almost feel the cold wind on her neck.

He slowly closed the book, and a thoughtful silence followed. Timothy asked the girls what they thought the poem meant, and they discussed their favorite seasons. Rachel listened, her heart warming toward the man, and toward poetry in general.

After the picnic had been cleared away, Phoebe asked Justina, "May we play hide-and-seek, Miss Brockwell? There are so many places to hide, with the trees and gardens and outbuildings. . . ."

"Of course you may."

"For a little while, but then we should really go," Mercy amended. "And stay out of the house, girls, and out of the stables. We don't want to frighten the horses."

Phoebe implored, "You will play too, won't you, Miss Brockwell?"

Justina looked at Rachel. "I shall if Miss Ashford will join us. Come, Rachel. For old time's sake?"

"Very well."

Little Alice had fallen asleep, her head in her teacher's lap, so Mercy remained where she was. And Matilda declared she was too full to move.

Sir Timothy offered his hand to Rachel to help her up. Feeling self-conscious, she placed her hand in his. He easily pulled her to her feet, holding her hand a little longer than absolutely necessary for the task.

Justina turned to her brother. "Timothy, will you be the first seeker?"

The girls looked at him in anticipation.

"Please, sir, will you?" Sukey entreated.

"I will, but I warn you that I know every hiding spot on the estate." He grinned, dark eyes alight with challenge. "So hide thee well."

Timothy began counting, and the girls scattered to hide. Of old habit, Justina took Rachel's hand and pulled her toward the topiary house. Rachel ducked her head and followed her inside.

"This will probably be the first place he looks," Rachel whispered.

"You're right." Justina peered about, then slipped out the other door.

Rachel thought of following her, but before she could, Timothy's voice called out, "Ready or not, here I come!"

Rachel backed into the arms of bushy yew, hoping the branches and darkness would conceal her.

A moment later, Sir Timothy folded his tall form through the low door and gingerly straightened within the small shadowy space.

Rachel held her breath.

At first he didn't move, his vision perhaps not yet adjusted to the dim light. Then the whites of his eyes turned in her direction. He took a step toward her, closing the distance between them.

Barely breathing, Rachel blinked up at him, trying to make out his features. Then she drew in a shallow, shaky breath. Being alone with him in the dark, out of view of the others, sparked in her a secret thrill.

He reached out as though blind and touched her shoulder. "Miss Ashford," he whispered.

"Yes?" she whispered back, traitorous fingers longing to touch him again.

For a moment, his hand lingered, then he stepped back. He bent and slipped out the low door without announcing he'd found her, without saying anything at all.

Rachel stood there, heart beating hard, feeling foolish and uncertain. A moment later, she heard him call, "There you are, Justina. I see you."

Rachel felt illogically deflated. He had found her. Again, he had found her . . . and had walked away.

In the Ivy Cottage sitting room a few days later, Mercy held little Alice on her lap while the girl quietly wept.

"Shh. There, there, my dear. You're all right."

Mr. Basu appeared in the open threshold and gestured a tall man inside. Mercy recognized him as one of the Kingsley brothers, the local builders.

He wore trousers and work boots. A white collar and neckerchief showed beneath his brown coat and waistcoat, and he carried a well-worn tweed hat in his hands.

Mr. Basu departed without introducing the man.

Mercy filled the gap. "Hello. Mr. Kingsley, I believe?"

"That's right. Joseph Kingsley." He fiddled with the hat brim. "And you're Miss Grove."

"Yes. I would rise to greet you properly, but I've got my hands full at present, and Alice is too big to carry." She smiled at the man, hoping to put him at ease. "Anna Kingsley is your niece, I believe?"

"That's right. My older brother's girl."

"She is one of our best pupils. It is a pleasure to have her here. She helps the other girls and would make a fine teacher herself one day, if she likes."

"Not surprising. Her father is the only bright one among us."

She gave him an indulgent grin. "I am sure that is not true. Well, you've come about the bookcases, I imagine?"

He nodded, looking at the sniffling child and back again. "I have come at a bad time."

"That's all right. Alice here has taken a tumble and scraped her knee. One of the girls laughed at her, which, I believe, hurt even worse. She'll be all right by and by. Won't you, Alice."

The girl rubbed her runny nose and shook her head in adamant denial.

Undeterred, Mercy went on, "Miss Ashford mentioned you would be stopping by sometime this week. She is outside with the older girls at present, but if you'll give me just a few moments, I will fetch her."

"Don't trouble yourself, or Miss Ashford. I'll just look at the rooms in question, if that's all right. Take a few measurements."

"Of course. The drawing room is across the corridor and the library adjacent to it." She gave him another little grin. "It's the one with books."

"Ah." He nodded, mouth quirked. "Clever. No wonder you're a teacher."

She chuckled. "Let us hope more than that qualifies me."

He held her gaze but did not laugh in reply. Instead he cleared his throat. "Well, I'll be as quick as I can, and let myself out."

"Thank you, Mr. Kingsley. Take your time."

Delivery of the Fairmont bookcases was scheduled for two days later. Knowing several workmen were coming to Ivy Cottage that morning to unload, Mercy dressed quickly and urged the girls to hurry down to breakfast. Passing her in the hall, Aunt Matty swiped the muslin cap from Mercy's head. After the girls had eaten, Mercy made sure they were safely ensconced in the schoolroom out of the workmen's way.

Mr. Kingsley and one of his nephews arrived first. Mercy welcomed them and offered coffee, but both declined. Shortly after, men from the Fairmont rattled up Church Street with shelves and lumber loaded on carts, Mr. Drake riding a horse alongside. Rachel came downstairs in time to greet them.

Mr. Kingsley directed the men where to stack the materials, and he and his assistant helped them unload.

Rachel smiled up at the hotel owner. "Thank you, Mr. Drake. This is very kind of you."

"My pleasure, Miss Ashford." He looked at Mr. Kingsley. "I suppose this means you won't be able to work at the Fairmont for a while?"

"No. I'll be there tomorrow. I'll install these on my own time, in the evenings, if the ladies don't mind."

"Of course we don't mind, Mr. Kingsley," Mercy assured him and Rachel both. "As long as it's before the girls' bedtime, and mine." She smiled. "I don't believe hammering at all hours would be conducive to an early morning of learning."

"No, indeed," the builder agreed.

Rachel added, "And you have yet to give me a cost estimate."

He shrugged. "I mean to donate my time, so don't worry about it."

"Donate your time? Mr. Kingsley, I cannot accept that. I must pay you for your services."

"I don't mind. It should only take a few weeks."

"But . . . why would you do that? As much as I appreciate your generosity, this is not a charity."

He hesitated. "I know it isn't. My niece is a pupil here. And as her uncle, I'd like to contribute to her education in this small way. Is there any harm in that?"

Mercy shook her head, impressed by his offer.

"Gratis, eh?" Mr. Drake grinned at the man, but Mercy saw questions sparking in his eyes. "I must be paying you too well."

Mr. Kingsley looked down, humor quirking his lips. "I'll not be the one to admit that. Not and bring down my brothers' wrath upon my head."

Mercy's gaze lingered on his tall frame and broad shoulders. Here was a man to look up to, in more ways than one. She wondered if he was married. She'd thought she'd heard all the Kingsley brothers were, though with several working in the village, as well as elsewhere across the county, she might be mistaken. Mercy had never paid much attention . . . before now.

CHAPTER SEVEN

Jane Bell left the innkeeper's lodge, several flowers in her gloved hands. She did not go to the churchyard as often as she once did—only now and again, when loneliness swamped her. Reaching St. Anne's, she pushed open the swinging gate and walked past listing, moss-covered headstones until she came to her husband's grave. John had been gone some sixteen months now. She had accepted his passing and the events that led to his untimely death, but other losses brought her there today.

Jane lowered herself to sit on the back of her legs and laid the small bouquet onto the grave—a single red chrysanthemum for John and five white ones for the children she had lost. She knew John had been laid to rest in that spot but knew not where her children were buried. So this was the best she could do—the closest she could come.

She thought of each one and calculated how old he or she would have been by now, had God spared them. Crouched there, her womb cramped and her heart ached. Oh, how she had wanted and prayed for and loved each little life. . . .

A creak of the gate hinge startled her, and she looked up. A frail, elderly woman in faded black entered the churchyard, a few forlorn Michaelmas daisies trembling in her hands. She looked mildly familiar, but it took Jane a moment to hit upon the woman's name—Mrs. Thomas, the glazier's wife. Jane could not recall the last time she had seen her.

Suddenly self-conscious, Jane rose and watched the woman from the corner of her eye.

Mrs. Thomas wandered through the headstones and crosses, her eyes darting this way and that, her mouth a loose gap of dismay. Had she lost a loved one? Jane had not heard of any recent burials.

Jane remained where she was, not certain she could gaze upon fresh grief at the moment and keep her own composure.

Then the small woman swayed unsteadily, looking weary and uncertain, and compassion overcame Jane's reserve. She walked tentatively toward her. "May I help you? Are you . . . looking for someone?"

"I tried, but I can't find her." Mrs. Thomas's eyes were large and pleading. "He said she's passed on, but how can that be, my sweet wee girl?"

"What is her name? Perhaps I might help you find her?"

"You can't find her. She's gone." The old woman shook her head. "She was bad took. But no, we could not help her. Too late. Too late!" The flowers shuddered in her thin, knobby hands.

The elderly sexton—flat cap atop stringy grey hair—emerged from a work shed nearby, carrying a spade. Mr. Ainsworth maintained the grounds and dug the graves and, as Jane had recently learned, made pets of the church mice.

He propped the spade against the shed and ambled toward the grief-stricken woman. "Come, missus. Here be the place for your posies." He gestured with soiled work gloves along the west churchyard wall, to a rock the size of a quartern loaf of bread.

The slight woman followed him, and Jane held her arm to steady her as she knelt and laid the flowers on the spot, weeping as she did so. "My poor wee girl . . ."

Behind them, the vestry door opened and the Reverend Mr. Paley came striding out, brows low in concern as he glanced from Jane to the sexton to the old woman.

"There now, Mrs. Thomas. Slipped out again without your

husband, did you? You know he'll worry." The vicar nodded to her. "Hello, Jane." Then to the sexton. "You may return to your work, Mr. Ainsworth. I'll take the matter in hand."

Jane spoke up. "She was looking for someone's grave."

"My sweet girl," Mrs. Thomas whimpered.

Mr. Paley laid a comforting hand on her shoulder. "Now, Mrs. Thomas, you're confused."

"Has she lost a daughter or granddaughter?" Jane whispered, wondering if this would be her in thirty years. Heaven help them both.

The vicar shook his head. "She hasn't any family buried here. Except perhaps some distant ancestors. She lost a grown daughter years ago, but she lived and died elsewhere. As I said, she is confused—increasingly so, poor creature."

He bent and gently took the frail woman's arm to help her up. "Come now. Let's get you home."

Movement drew Mr. Paley's attention over the churchyard gate. "There's your husband now, Mrs. Thomas. Shall we go and meet him?"

Jane glanced over and saw the glazier striding purposely up Church Street, expression somber.

The parson escorted Mrs. Thomas to the gate, carefully matching his stride to hers and helping her over the uneven ground.

Jane watched the uneasy reunion, questions and pity coursing through her.

Beside her, the sexton retrieved his spade and leaned on its handle. "Parson don't know everything."

She glanced at him. "Oh? *Has* Mrs. Thomas a loved one buried here?"

He shrugged thin shoulders. "She does if she thinks she does."

Jane was not sure how to respond to that. Everyone said the sexton was an odd man, and Jane could not refute that. But beneath his scruffy appearance lurked a streak of kindness, she believed, at least for small, overlooked creatures.

Jane stopped by Ivy Cottage on her way home. Mercy greeted

her warmly and showed her the progress on the library—mostly a lot of stacked shelving and furniture pushed to one wall.

"Mr. Kingsley warned us it would look worse before it looks better, and apparently he was not exaggerating." Mercy grinned. "By the way, Rachel is not here, if you were hoping to see her. She has gone to Thornvale to pack up her father's books."

"That's all right. I had a question for you, actually. Are you well acquainted with Mrs. Thomas?"

Mercy looked up in surprise. "Mrs. Thomas? A little. Aunt Matty knows her better. Why do you ask?"

"I saw her in the churchyard just now, looking for someone's grave. She seemed rather upset and confused, though Mr. Paley told me she has no close relatives buried there."

Mercy slowly shook her head. "Aunt Matty says Mrs. Thomas has been declining for some time—in body and mind. She is increasingly housebound, poor dear. I am surprised her husband let her venture out alone."

"I take it she left without his knowledge. He hurried over to escort her home."

"I see."

Jane added, "Mr. Paley did say the Thomases lost a grown daughter years ago, but that she is apparently buried elsewhere."

"Yes, their daughter and son-in-law both died a long time ago. They lived in Portsmouth, I believe. The couple had one child, but she . . . lived elsewhere as well."

"How sad. I wonder if Mrs. Thomas was looking for her daughter. She muttered something about trying to find her 'wee girl.'"

Mercy nodded, expression distracted. "It's possible. Or perhaps she was looking for someone else."

"Like who?"

Mercy opened her mouth but seemed to think the better of what she'd been about to say. Instead she sighed. "Poor old dear must be confused indeed."

It wasn't like Mercy to be secretive. Jane had a feeling there was more to the story than what she'd said.

Mercy changed the subject. "And what took you to the church-yard this morning, if you don't mind my asking? Some special anniversary or . . . ?"

"No, nothing like that."

Mercy tilted her head to one side. "Are you all right, Jane?"

"Hm? Oh yes. Just a little melancholy."

Mercy regarded her thoughtfully. "Come and sit down and tell me what's going on."

Jane hesitated. She had never told Mercy about the children she had lost, but decided it was time, past time, to confide in her dear old friend.

As arranged, Rachel went to Thornvale to begin packing her late father's books. Nicholas had assured her they had plenty of crates and boxes on hand, left from their recent move to Thornvale. All she needed to bring was herself, and perhaps some idea of where she wanted to start and how she wanted to organize the collection.

A young footman she did not recognize answered her knock and opened the door for her. In the middle of the hall stood a new round table topped with a large arrangement of silk flowers, but otherwise, things looked much as she remembered them.

The footman said, "Mr. Ashford is in the library, if you would like to follow me."

"I know the way, thank you. Just . . . give me a moment."

"Very good, miss." He bowed and left her.

As Rachel stood there, memories of the day she had left Thornvale washed over her. She could still recall her churning emotions, and how she had stiffened her spine in resolve and carried her valise into the library, determined to show Mr. Ashford she planned to leave immediately, hoping to avoid a reprimand after the uncomfortable dinner party the night before.

She remembered stepping silently into the room, and seeing Mr. Ashford standing before one of the windows, hands folded behind his back, spinning his thumbs in impatience—or so she'd thought, never guessing how nervous he was, or the astounding offer he planned to make her.

Now as Rachel entered, he turned with an eager smile on his boyish face. "There you are. Right on time."

She smiled in return. "Thank you again for offering to help." She looked at the stacked boxes and large crates with their waiting, yawning mouths. "You are certainly prepared."

Her former housekeeper, Mrs. Fife, came in, directing a second footman to set one more wooden box in the corner. "This is the last of them, Mr. Ashford. I hope these are enough."

"We can always make more trips, as needed." Nicholas smiled at the woman. "Thank you, Mrs. Fife."

Rachel turned to her as well. "Hello, Mrs. Fife. How are you keeping?"

"Miss Ashford. A pleasure to see you again. I am well, though we miss you, of course."

"And I you." Mrs. Fife had treated her with maternal warmth after her mother's passing, and Rachel was surprised to realize how much she had missed the woman.

The housekeeper patted her arm. At the gesture, Rachel felt a poignant little ache in her breast.

"Thankfully, we are all fond of our new master." Mrs. Fife did not, Rachel noticed, mention their new mistress.

At that, both women turned to look at Nicholas.

He gestured toward the waiting bookcases. "Shall we begin?"

Mrs. Fife and the footman worked together on one side of the room, while she and Nicholas started in on the other. Together, they packed up the heavy books, shelf by shelf.

An hour or so later, one of the maids brought in a tray of tea things and cake. The housekeeper and other servants excused themselves to take their refreshments belowstairs.

"You are welcome to join us here," Nicholas offered.

"Thank you, sir. But we'll be more comfortable in the servants' hall. And you two might like a chance to talk alone." Her eyes glinted with speculation as she looked from him to Rachel, and at that moment, Rachel was reminded of Matilda Grove.

After she left, Nicholas slanted Rachel a grin. "Wise woman."

The two sat down to take tea together, talking over her plans for the circulating library. Nicholas admitting he sometimes missed his days in an office, managing a business. Rachel decided it was as pleasant to talk with the amiable young man as it was to work side by side with him. If she married him, would their days be like this? How could they be anything but happy there in beautiful Thornvale?

After their respite, they resumed their packing. Nicholas stepped out to find a second step stool to reach the higher shelves, promising to return shortly. A few moments later, Rachel heard footsteps and turned, expecting to see him, the words "That was quick" on her lips.

Instead, Mrs. Ashford entered, looking officious in a tall hat and military-styled redingote with a row of frogging clasps.

Rachel took a steadying breath and greeted her politely.

Mrs. Ashford said, "I thought I would look in and see the dismantling of Thornvale's library."

Guilt and indignation punched the air from Rachel's lungs. "I trust you remember, Mrs. Ashford, that my father left his books to me."

"Yes. In fact I recently verified the terms of his will. Though I doubt this was what he had in mind." She gestured toward the crates. "Do you think he would approve of this? Of his daughter doing what you propose?"

Rachel lifted her chin, hoping the woman would not see it tremble. "I think he would be glad to know I have taken an interest in books at last."

"Perhaps. But I'm sure he never imagined you would use your inheritance to enter *trade*."

Mortification seared Rachel's cheeks.

She was spared having to reply by Nicholas Ashford returning, carrying a step stool. He looked from Rachel to his parent and frowned. Had he overheard her last words? "Come to help, Mother?" he asked, a note of irony in his voice.

"No. I am on my way out, along with Thornvale's library, I see."

"Sir William's library. It was never ours. And now it belongs to Miss Ashford."

The woman laughed, but it was not a pleasant sound. "I am sure he never meant for her to turn it into a business for profit."

"Mother, don't forget that business profits supported us before I inherited Thornvale, and they support us now."

"I don't forget."

"I think you'd like to."

"Well, I have seen what I came for. Good day, Miss Ashford."

Rachel nodded. "Mrs. Ashford."

At the door, she turned back. "Don't toil too late, Nicholas. Remember we have been invited to dine with the Bingleys this evening."

"I remember."

The woman swept from the room, and Nicholas stood there, apology written across his young, appealing face.

"I am sorry. Was she even worse before I returned?"

"Let's just say I am glad you came back when you did."

"That is something, I suppose." Nicholas grinned, but then the expression faded. "My mother likes to pretend that we are some genteel family—ladies and gentlemen who have never had to work in their lives. But that is inaccurate and unfair. Just as she was unfair in her assessment of your new venture."

"Do you think so?"

"Yes."

"Why does she dislike me so?"

"I don't think it's so much that she dislikes you, as that she had her heart set on my marrying a . . . different sort of woman."

"What sort? An heiress, I suppose? Or at least someone with an impressive dowry? Which I don't have, by the way."

He shrugged. "Personally, I think it would be disheartening to be pursued for one's wealth alone."

Rachel chuckled. "Well, heaven knows, I have never suffered from that." She sobered. "Does your mother think I am pursuing you for your money . . . or Thornvale?"

"Are you pursuing me? I had not realized." He stepped closer, eyes shining.

Rachel flushed. "I only meant . . ."

"I am teasing you. But as far as my mother . . . she is a conundrum. She was offended to learn you did not accept me straightaway. But had you, she would no doubt have accused you of that very thing."

"It seems I cannot win where she is concerned."

"It isn't her approval I hope for, Miss Ashford. I cannot deny I am disappointed you have not yet accepted me, but I admire your courage, and your determination to make a go of your library."

Earnest gratitude filled her. "Thank you." She laid an impulsive hand on his sleeve.

He took her hand in his and kissed it. She was afraid he would not let go, or beg for an answer. Instead he released her with a smile. "Now, no shirking. Let's get back to work."

CHAPTER EIGHT

Mr. Kingsley returned late that day to begin installing the bookcases. Rachel met him in the library, answered his questions, and then left him to work, telling him to be sure to let her know if there was anything he needed. Then she went and joined Mercy and Matilda for dinner.

Mercy said, "It is very kind of Joseph Kingsley to offer to work in the evenings like this."

"Are you sure you don't mind?" Rachel winced as something heavy dropped in the next room, and a mild epithet reached them.

Matilda bit her lip, then offered kindly, "At least we don't have the whole contingent of Kingsley brothers working here. We'd hear worse than that, I don't doubt." She looked toward the library. "I thought one of his nephews assisted him?"

"Needed at home in the evenings, apparently," Rachel said. "By the way, Mr. Kingsley assures me he will install the shelves in a manner that will not harm the walls should the venture fail and we need to remove them again. Well, he didn't specify the reason, but that's probably what he meant."

"I'm sure he didn't mean that," Mercy reassured her. "But yes, it's good of him to think ahead and preserve the integrity of the room for . . . the distant future."

"I still don't feel right about not paying him," Rachel said, "whether his niece attends here or not."

"It is generous of him to help." Matilda's eyes brightened with speculation. "And I suppose being a widower, his evenings are free."

Mercy looked at her aunt in surprise. "A widower? I did not know that."

"Nor did I. But I have my ways." Matilda winked.

Mrs. Timmons brought in their dinner. "It's not my fault the Yorkshire pudding fell flat with all that banging going on."

"That's all right, Mrs. Timmons. I'm sure it will taste just as good."

Mr. Kingsley himself appeared in the doorway. Sawdust sprinkled his hair and plaster dust whitened one trouser leg. He looked at Mercy, then shifted his gaze to Rachel and cleared his throat. "Sorry about the noise, ladies. I'm going to have to plane down some pieces because the floor slants a bit, as is often the case in old houses. But I shall return tomorrow, if that suits."

"Perfectly," Matilda answered for them all.

He nodded and awkwardly turned to go. "Well, good night, then." He ducked slightly to avoid hitting his head on the low doorway.

"Good night," they all said together.

Rachel noticed Mercy's gaze trail him from the room.

The next morning, someone knocked on the lodge door, and when Jane opened it she was surprised to see James Drake. He was well dressed, as usual, his green cutaway coat bringing out the color of his eyes. Behind him stood a horse and wagon, loaded with several wooden boxes. Two workmen waited nearby.

"Good morning, Jane."

"Hello, James. What brings you here?" She glanced at the wagon and raised one eyebrow. "Have you become a traveling peddler since I saw you last?"

He grinned. "If it were more profitable, I might." He nodded toward the wagon. "I hope you don't mind, but I culled some books from the old Fairmont library, stored in the attic. A selection I thought might appeal to patrons of Miss Ashford's circulating library."

"That is kind of you." Jane wondered if Mr. Drake had shifted his attentions to Rachel. He was being awfully generous.

As if reading her mind, he said, "I know she is your friend, Jane, and for that reason alone, I am happy to oblige. However, I wanted to give you the opportunity to go through them first. Keep any or all you like. I wouldn't want to give away anything with sentimental value."

"Thank you. That was very thoughtful of you."

His dimples appeared. "My, my. Today I am kind *and* thoughtful. You flatter me, dear Jane. Take care, or your sweet words shall go to my head."

Jane gave him a skeptical smile. "I doubt it. How many books have you brought?"

"Two crates' worth. I didn't count."

"Goodness. Do you plan to demand a share of Miss Ashford's profits?"

"Ah, now you wound me. Thank you for checking my pride."

The sparkle in his eyes assured Jane her words had not injured him. She doubted she could. Words and situations seemed to bounce off him like a frozen pond that she, or anyone else, rarely penetrated.

He gestured toward the crates. "May I bring them inside?"

"Oh. Of course." She felt a little flustered at the prospect of Mr. Drake entering her private domicile but decided not to object.

"I didn't think you'd want them cluttering up the inn," he said and signaled to the men, who hefted the crates out of the wagon and carried them over. Mr. Drake accepted the first one at the door and placed it inside, then stepped back out to receive the second.

Jane went in, pulled the lid from the first crate, and began sorting through the books.

A moment later, James Drake returned with the second crate, set it on the table, and opened its lid as well.

"Oh, my goodness. I forgot about these." Jane lifted out three matching books. "My father bought me this set. They were some of my favorites."

Jane felt the long forgotten memory pass over her. The warm comfort of sitting in her father's lap as he read to her in his low melodic voice . . .

She felt unexpected tears prick her eyes. "I loved these books as a child."

James gazed at her warmly. "Then save them for your own children."

She looked down, feigning interest in another book.

Her discomfort must have shown on her face, for he added, "I know you are a widow, Jane. But you are still young and might marry again."

She might marry again one day, Jane privately allowed, but have children who lived long enough to be read to? When she had not been able to bring one to term in seven years of marriage to John?

"I hold out no such hope or plan." With a quick smile, she added lightly, "What about you? Want a whole quiver full, do you?"

"I have . . . other priorities. Besides, I don't think I am cut out to be a father. My own was not the best example."

"I am sorry to hear it. Are the two of you not close?"

He shook his head. "I avoid being in range of his cutting criticism whenever I can."

"But you are a successful man. Surely he is proud of you."

"Ah, Jane." He tapped her nose and gave her that charming smile that did not reach his eyes. "Not everyone thinks as highly of me as you do. It is one of your most endearing qualities."

"Have you some serious character flaw I have yet to see?"

"Of course I have. Probably more than one. We all have our flaws. And our secrets."

Mercy sat at the secretaire desk in the sitting room, where she wrote letters and dealt with correspondence and finances related to her school. Today, she wrote to Lord Winspear, the parish's senior magistrate, who lived near Wishford. As he'd requested after their short meeting about the proposed charity school, she provided more detailed plans and projected expenses—teacher's salary, wood and coal, candles, books, paper, and other supplies. Mercy suspected he'd asked for the information to keep her too busy to trouble him for a time, but she hoped she could sway him yet.

Next, she wrote a letter to successful newcomer Mr. Drake, explaining her wish to start a school to educate more of the parish's girls and boys, especially those unable to afford education otherwise. She invited his questions and financial support as well.

Mr. Basu appeared and gestured a visitor into the room. Mercy looked up, surprised to see Colin McFarland standing there, hat in hand.

"Good day, Mr. McFarland."

"Miss Grove. And it's Colin, if you don't mind."

"Very well, Colin. How is your mother keeping?"

"Better, thank you."

"Has she enough work?"

"She has a fair amount of sewing these days, thanks to the women of the village, though she could always use more. But that's not why I've come."

Mercy gestured to a chair. "Please, have a seat."

He sat, frowned at his hat, opened his mouth, and closed it again.

She prompted gently, "Is everything all right at the inn?"

He winced and finally began, "Miss Grove, I know you put in a good word for me with Mrs. Bell and helped me get the job there. And I am grateful, don't mistake me."

"What is the matter, Colin?"

"May I tell you something in confidence?"

Mercy hesitated. "Yes, unless saying nothing would harm Jane

Bell. She is my friend, and I would do nothing to hurt her." Mercy's conscience nipped at her. She was already keeping one secret from Jane, though at least that one did not affect her personally.

"Of course not," Colin replied. "I hope it will help her."

"Help her? Is something the matter with Jane?"

"Only that her clerk is incompetent."

"Don't say that. Surely that is not true."

"I can do some of the job well. The portering. Dealing with patrons and coachmen. But it's the office work I stumble over."

"Colin, we discussed the types of duties you would be required to perform before you even applied. You told me you could do the work."

"I may have . . . stretched a bit, ma'am." He hurried to add, "I didn't lie. I can read, and I write a fair hand. I doubt a teacher like you would think so, but I get by."

"Then what is wrong, Colin?"

"I am. Far too often." He twisted his hat brim. "It's the ledgers and bills and fares. I can't get my head around all those figures. I've made mistakes in customer's tallies and fare prices, and in subtracting payments from accounts. I try to make myself scarce, or busy, when there's arithmetic to be done. I've taken to asking others to sum the inn tally forms for me as I hurry off on some errand or other. Yesterday a coachman offered five passengers a fifteen percent fare reduction due to a repair delay, and I didn't know how to figure it. No one else was around to ask. I stood there, mortified, staring at the numbers and wishing the floor would open up and swallow me. I could hear two of the ladies whispering behind their hands, and one young buck smirked, so superior. I couldn't concentrate! Finally, Bobbin—that's the barman—came out of the taproom and helped me. He's figured out my secret, and it won't be much longer until everyone else does and I'll be out on my ear."

Colin slowly shook his head. "That settled it for me. I have to learn. I know this is a girls school, but I was hoping you might teach me. I could pay you something. Not much, I'm afraid—my mother depends on my wages—but a little. Or maybe I could do some work for you here—whatever needs doing—in return for lessons. I have an hour respite during the afternoon lull, and two hours on Sundays."

Mercy exhaled, glad his problem was something fixable. She intertwined her long fingers and considered what was best to be done. "You were once an apprentice in the building trade, were you not?"

He nodded. "A stonemason's apprentice. But I did not finish my term after my father . . . after his health problems."

Mercy knew his father's problems stemmed from drink but did not say so. "Have you any carpentry experience?"

"Some, yes. I'm forever patching up my parents' house or repairing a broken chair or banister or something. Why?"

"We are having bookcases installed in the drawing room and several added to our existing library. Miss Ashford plans to open a circulating library here."

"I heard something about that. Who is doing the work?"

"Mr. Kingsley."

"Neil Kingsley?" Wariness shone in Colin's eyes.

"Joseph," she clarified. "Why?"

"My father asked Neil Kingsley for a job once, but he turned him down flat." Colin raised his hands. "Not that I blame him. This was a few years ago, when Pa was . . . ill . . . every day. He's got better. Somewhat."

"I am glad to hear it."

"But if Joseph Kingsley doesn't mind my help, I will do my best to be useful."

She nodded. "I will talk to him about it." Mercy paused, thinking. "How would you feel about someone else teaching you? It isn't that I would mind doing so, but I am spending more time than usual away from Ivy Cottage at present, trying to raise support for a charity school."

"By someone else teaching me, do you mean your aunt?"

"No, Aunt Matty is not all that quick with numbers herself. Miss

Ashford might, but she is busy organizing her library. However, one of our pupils, our eldest, is excellent in all her studies, including arithmetic. She already tutors the younger girls and shows natural teaching ability. But she is younger than you are. Would that make you uncomfortable?"

He shifted in his chair and his neck reddened. "Well, it's not something I'd trumpet about—that's for certain. Could we . . . keep it between ourselves?"

"Anna is a very sensible girl and not given to gossip. I trust her, and you can too."

His fair brows rose. "Anna . . . ?"

"Kingsley. Oh. I did not think. Neil Kingsley's daughter. Will that be a problem?"

Colin sighed. "I'll get over it. We McFarlands are accustomed to being humbled by Kingsleys."

Mercy acknowledged his self-abasing humor with a gentle smile.

The next day, Jane and Colin reorganized the tables in the newly expanded dining parlour. Afterward she stopped in the coffee room to see if Alwena needed any help. Rain began to fall and the wind picked up—a sudden storm blown in over the Salisbury Plain. Out in the courtyard, Tall Ted and Tuffy hurried to finish changing a team in the downpour, wincing and wiping rain from their eyes and then dashing into the stables as soon as they finished. Mr. Sanders came in the front entrance, the door banging open in the wind. He strained to close it, then went to dry himself by the coffee-room hearth.

Plop. Plop. In the entry hall, a leak sprouted from the ceiling and began puddling the floor. Jane groaned. It was always something. Mr. Broadbent had repaired the gutters, but they were still waiting for the slater to replace the broken tiles in that section of the roof.

With a sigh, Jane went to find buckets in the scullery.

Returning a few minutes later, Jane positioned the buckets to catch the leaks, then glanced up. Through the open taproom door, she saw Mr. Drake greet the barman and take a seat, shaking rain from his hat. The taproom was quiet, except for Mrs. Burlingame and Mrs. Klein at a corner inglenook, sitting over cider and a long talk.

Jane noticed a wilted flower on the hall table, and as she paused to pull it from the vase and tidy the arrangement, she overheard Bobbin say, "Haven't seen you for a spell, Mr. Drake. How goes it at the Fairmont?"

"A few problems and delays. The usual growing pains."

Bobbin set a pint before him. "Pains, ey? That reminds me. You asked me about a Miss Payne a while back. Did you ever find her?"

Mr. Drake shook his head. "No. I thought I remembered that she had stayed here in Ivy Hill with relatives as a girl. I was merely curious what became of her."

Mrs. Burlingame, the carter, spoke up. "I believe the Thomases have relatives by that name who used to visit now and again."

Mr. Drake turned to her. "Oh? And where do those relatives live?"

She narrowed her eyes in memory. "I can't recall the particulars at the moment." She looked to her companion. "Can you, Kristine?"

"No, I never met anyone named Payne around here. They must not have a piano."

"I will ask Mrs. Snyder for you. She knows everybody's laundry—clean and otherwise."

"Thank you. As I said, I was only curious." Mr. Drake's brow furrowed. "Mr. Thomas is the glazier, right? He's done some work for me at the Fairmont. But I had no idea he had any family at all."

Mrs. Burlingame nodded. "That's him, all right. A tight-lipped fellow."

Picking up his glass, James appeared to shrug off the topic, but there was an awkward vulnerability in his expression Jane had rarely seen. Or perhaps she was reading too much into his discomfort.

His eyes lit up when he saw her. "Jane! Just the person I hoped to see. Come and cheer me up."

He pulled out a chair for her, and she accepted a small glass of cider.

He said, "By the way, I received a letter from your friend Miss Grove, asking me to support a charity school here in Ivy Hill."

Jane nodded. "Mercy has always been a proponent of education. Even when we were little she loved playing school. Although trying to teach our dolls to read and write was not terribly fruitful."

He smirked. "Those dolls were probably more attentive than I was as a lad. How I detested sitting for long hours on end. I would have done better had we been allowed to decline Latin verbs while riding or fishing."

"No doubt. I can well imagine you an energetic and mischievous boy, James Drake."

He smiled at her, his gaze tracing her features.

She shifted. "At all events, Mercy is a gifted teacher. I have already made a donation, though I wish it could have been more. We have to build up our cash reserves, for who knows how long it shall be until that crafty new *hôtelier* begins stealing our customers."

"I shall try," he said. "But you are up to the challenge, Jane. I don't doubt it for a moment."

His words reminded her of what Gabriel Locke had said to her before he left. *"You'll be all right, Jane Bell. I know it. I have every confidence in you."*

Why was she thinking of him now? Gabriel had left, with no plans to return, while James Drake was here, and would be for the foreseeable future. She determined to give James her full attention.

He watched her face with interest. "What are you thinking of, Jane? Of me, I hope? When you look at me like that, I am tempted to think it means something."

"It means I am striving to be a good listener. A good . . . friend."

"Is it such a struggle?"

"You know it is not."

He nodded. "Then, I shall meet with your friend Miss Grove and give her campaign every consideration."

"Thank you. She will appreciate that, and so will I."

He dipped his head in acknowledgment, then waved away Bobbin's offer of another pint.

From the front window, Jane saw a sleek two-wheeled curricle pass, pulled by a pair of matched bays, its leather hood raised against the rain. She recognized Timothy's profile. Beside him sat a young woman in carriage dress and plumed hat, the feather drooping from the damp.

James asked, "Who is that with Sir Timothy?"

"His sister, Justina."

"Ah. I thought perhaps it was some young lady he was courting."

"No."

James studied her with interest. "Would you mind if it were? I hope it isn't an impertinent question, but I had heard the two of you were once a couple."

"That was a long time ago."

James leaned nearer, face alight with humor and admiration. "You had your chance to marry a baronet and instead married a business owner. That shows excellent taste on your part. I must say, it gives me hope."

Jane shook her head. "James, James, James. I don't know how well you mastered Latin verbs, but you have certainly mastered the art of flirtation."

"Thank you." His eyes gleamed. "It is one of my proudest accomplishments."

Jane enjoyed another half an hour of diverting conversation with the handsome, charming man. Was diversion all it was? Or could there be more between them?

CHAPTER NINE

That evening, as Mercy walked down the Ivy Cottage corridor, she heard Mr. Kingsley and Anna in the library.

"Hey-ho, Annie-girl. How is my niece today?"

"I am well, Uncle Joseph."

"More than well, I'd say. You're clever and kind, Anna Kingsley. And don't forget it."

Mercy reached the doorway in time to see Anna grin up at him. "I shan't."

"Hang on. . . . What's this?" He reached behind her ear and pulled something forth. "How did you come to have a wood screw in your ear? Hard to learn with a screw loose, little girl."

"Uncle Joseph!" Anna gave a good-natured groan. It was clearly not the first time he'd performed the little trick.

Their fond teasing warmed Mercy's heart.

"I am not a little girl any longer." Anna straightened to her full five feet.

"As I see." He gave her a wistful smile. "But don't be in too much of a hurry, Annie-girl. I won't know what to say to a fine lady." He glanced over and noticed Mercy standing there. "Never do . . ."

Mercy crossed the threshold. "Hello, Anna. Good evening, Mr. Kingsley."

He swiped the cap from his head. "Miss Grove."

"Sorry to interrupt. I only wanted to ask if having Colin McFarland's help would be beneficial now and again. He has offered his services."

"I'd be glad of his help, if he can spare the time."

"Excellent. Thank you." She smiled at him. "Well, I will leave you to work in peace."

Anna walked out with her, and together they went upstairs to check on the younger girls.

Mercy asked, "Where does your uncle live, Anna? I don't know that I've ever heard."

"In the rooms above the family workshop." She pursed her lips in thought. "I believe he used to have a house when I was little, though. Uncle Matthew slept above the workshop, too, before he married. We have our own house, and Uncle Frank has my grandparents' old place."

"I see."

Mercy wondered why Mr. Kingsley no longer had a house, and what had happened to his wife, but she decided it would be rude to ask.

A few days later, Rachel surveyed the progress in the library. Mr. Kingsley and Colin had finished most of their construction work in the main room and had moved on to the adjoining drawing room, where she had arranged groupings of comfortable furniture as a reading room of sorts. More bookcases would be added there as well, and perhaps eventually a partitioned stand to hold periodicals. She would have to ask Mr. Kingsley if he would be willing to build one when he had time.

Becky Morris arrived with a hand-painted sign and laid it on the desk for Rachel's inspection. The sign read *The Ashford Circulating Library* in fine lettering. The amiable young woman also handed Rachel a trade card printed with *Mr. Morris, Painter* and the amount owing scribbled at the bottom.

"It's perfect," Rachel declared. "Did you paint this yourself or did Mr. Morris?"

"There is no Mr. Morris—not anymore."

"Oh, sorry. I saw Mr. Morris on your card and thought he might be your husband."

"No. No husband. I haven't found *him* yet. Though I am daily looking!" Becky snorted with laughter, then tapped the card. "That's my pa, God rest his soul. Hope you don't mind that I kept his name, but not everyone wants to hire a girl. And he taught me everything I know, after all."

"I don't mind at all. I have my father to thank for my . . . business too. So we have that in common."

The two young women shared a smile. Then Miss Morris went out to hang the sign near the side door, which the Miss Groves had decided would serve nicely as the library's separate entrance.

Her father's collection of books waited in crates and boxes, and after Becky left, Rachel worked to catalog them in the new ledger Jane had bought for her in Salisbury. She listed books by title and by author, and categorized them by genre. She pasted a library label within each book, and then Anna Kingsley helped her shelve them accordingly.

Rachel was just about to stop for the day, when Mrs. Barton from the Ladies Tea and Knitting Society plowed through the side door. She strode straight to Rachel's desk with a book in her hand.

"Are you accepting donations for credit toward borrowing books?"

"That's right, Mrs. Barton."

The dairywoman nodded briskly and plunked down a well-worn volume.

Rachel looked dubiously at the title. *The Care of Calves and Management of a Dairy*.

Would anyone else in Ivy Hill be interested in such a specific book? Rachel doubted it but said only, "Thank you, Mrs. Barton."

She dipped a quill and wrote the title in the appropriate column.

The woman bent to watch her write. "It's Bridget Barton, if you need my given name."

Rachel took a deep breath. "I should clarify that this book will become the property of the library. That is how things are done at the Fellows's Circulating Library in Salisbury, so I believe it is fair and common practice. But I wanted to make sure you were comfortable donating the book under these terms."

The woman hesitated. "Do you mean I can never have it back?"

"Well . . . if you change your mind, I suppose you might pay outright for whatever you borrowed, and then have it back."

Mrs. Barton chewed her lip. "Could I come here and . . . visit the book now and again? If I miss it?"

Rachel bit back a grin. "Yes, of course. Or you could borrow it at any time. But . . . this book is clearly important to you, Mrs. Barton, so if you want to reconsider, I will understand."

The dairywoman lifted a resolved chin. "No. . . . I already know it by heart, and someone else's cows should benefit from its instruction."

"Very well." Rachel finished filling out both ledger and card. "There you are."

"And the annual fee . . . Twenty shillings, was it?" Mrs. Barton paid for her subscription with coins extracted from her bodice.

Trying not to wrinkle her nose, Rachel accepted the warm coins and then gestured toward the many bookcases. "Would you like to select something to borrow now?"

"I would like a book, but the bossies will need milkin' again soon, so perhaps you could pick something for me? Something I'll enjoy?"

Rachel's stomach fell. "Oh . . . I would not know how to do that."

Mrs. Barton planted a hand on her hip. "Are you the librarian or aren't you?"

"I suppose I am. Though new and ill-qualified. Perhaps you could tell me what sort of books you like to read?"

"I don't know. I've had little opportunity to read for pleasure. And between you and me, I'm not the best reader—so nothing too difficult, if you please."

Rachel called to Anna Kingsley, still busy shelving books. "Anna? Would you please come here a moment? Mrs. Barton is looking for suggestions, and I know you are a great reader. Would you mind helping her find something?"

"Not at all." The young woman smiled at Mrs. Barton. "Do you like romances? I've just finished a gothic romance called *Fugitive of the Forest*. I could not sleep a wink all night."

"A romance, ey? What *would* Mr. Barton say?" The woman *tsk*ed, then gave a saucy grin. "Lead on, my girl."

Rachel watched them cross the room with a dizzying sense of awe. Her first patron. The Ashford Circulating Library had become a reality. She looked again at the money in her hand . . . the first she had earned in her life. Tentative excitement tingled through her. She might just support herself yet.

On her way home after posting letters, Mercy saw Mrs. Craddock walking up Potters Lane and caught up with her. The two women exchanged pleasantries about the beautiful weather before parting ways at the bakery.

Continuing toward Ivy Cottage, Mercy was taken aback to see Mr. Thomas, the glazier, standing at the front windows. Was he trying to catch a glimpse of his great-granddaughter?

Noticing Mercy, the old man ran gnarled fingers over a lower pane. "You ought to have this seen to. Hairline crack forming there."

Mercy approached, squinting at the window. "I don't see anything."

"Haven't got my trained eye, have'ee?"

"Apparently not."

He glanced down the street. Satisfied the baker's wife was out of earshot, he lowered his voice and said, "Could'ee come to our house? I've got to talk to thee."

"If you like. Or you could come in now, since you are here."

"No. Might raise questions."

"Mr. Thomas, would you like to see Alice?" Mercy glanced at her watch pin. "She is probably in the back garden now but will come inside any minute."

For a moment he seemed to consider it, then said, "No need."

"Shall I bring her with me when I come to call?"

"No. Definitely not."

Mercy sighed. "Very well. I have a class to teach soon, but I could come this evening around five, if that suits? Unless that will interrupt your dinner?"

He shook his head. "I eat at four most days. And the girl caring for Mrs. Thomas leaves for the day about then, so five will suit well."

"All right."

Mercy did not like secrets, but Mr. Thomas insisted he had his reasons for keeping Alice's connection to him and his wife private. He did not explain beyond that, leaving Mercy to come up with theories of her own.

She went inside and taught her class, feeling distracted. What did he want to talk with her about? Afterward, Mercy escorted the girls to their dinner. She left Ivy Cottage a few minutes before the hour, glad it was still light, although the autumn evenings were already beginning to shorten.

Mr. Thomas answered her knock and gestured her inside. The house was modest, simply furnished, and somewhat cluttered. But it had excellent windows.

He nodded toward one of two chairs near the fireplace.

She seated herself and looked at him warily. Was he going to confide something unsavory about Alice's background? Would he tell her he had decided to pull the child from Mercy's school? What?

He remained standing, evidently too fidgety to sit.

"Thank'ee for coming here, Miss Grove. My wife is not long for this world, and I don't wish to leave her longer than necessary."

Mercy said gently, "Now that Mrs. Thomas is so very ill, are you sure I should not bring Alice to see her just once? What peace it might give her."

"Peace?" His lip curled. "I doubt anything can bring her peace now." He glanced toward the back of the house to a door slightly ajar, then added more softly, "You think me heartless, I suppose."

"It is not my place to judge you, Mr. Thomas."

"But you think me cold to distance myself from the girl. You made that clear when I brought her to your school in the first place."

"I don't think you are heartless. But I do think you are depriving yourself and your wife of one of life's greatest blessings. Alice is a loving, affectionate child. What a comfort she might be to you both . . . especially now."

He shook his head. "Not after what her mother did. Mary-Alicia spurned our home and our protection to go her own way."

Mercy hesitated. "You did not . . . approve of her marriage to Mr. Smith?"

He scoffed. "Hardly. When she wrote years back with the news he'd been lost at sea, Mrs. Thomas wanted to ask her and the child to live with us, but I refused. That would have been condoning her behavior. You must see that."

"I understand that is how you viewed the situation. I do not have to agree."

"She wrote again late last year to tell us she were ill. Mrs. Thomas wanted to go to Bristol directly, but I were workin' on a greenhouse and couldn't leave 'til I'd finished. Commissions like that are few and far between. By the time I arrived, Mary-Alicia had passed."

He swallowed, and Mercy was relieved to see some sign of emotion cross his weathered face. "Her landlady gave me a sack of her things, handed over the child, and demanded her unpaid rent. I paid every farthing and brought the girl to you."

"That was . . . good of you, Mr. Thomas," Mercy allowed.

His sharp eyes bore into hers. "Have you and your aunt kept your word and not told anyone our connection to the girl?"

"We have. Though I have hated to keep secrets from my closest friends. Does Mrs. Thomas still not know her great-granddaughter is right here in Ivy Hill?"

He shook his head. "Mrs. Thomas was never good at keeping secrets even when in good health. How much more risky now that her mind is a slippery wheel and her tongue a loose gate?"

"Who is there?" a reedy voice called from the back room. "I hear someone. Is that our wee girl?"

Mr. Thomas shot Mercy a telling glance. "No, Mrs. Thomas. You forget. Mary-Alicia is gone. It is only Miss Grove, come to call."

"Miss Grove? Miss Grove, let me see you."

Ignoring a warning look from Mr. Thomas, Mercy rose, stepped to the door, and pushed it wide. A frail, elderly woman lay in bed, her silvery hair falling around her in untidy wisps, her eyes large and confused.

"Hello, Mrs. Thomas. It is good to see you. My Aunt Matilda and I think of you often, and pray for you."

"Pray for me? No, pray for our wee girl. She is very ill and far away. And Mr. Thomas says we cannot go to her!"

"Shh . . . Do not upset yourself, Mrs. Thomas." Mercy sat gingerly on the edge of the woman's bed and took her hand. "Mary-Alicia has gone to heaven and is safe and at peace. She would not want you to worry about her anymore."

"In heaven . . . ? Oh no. And her little child? Is she in heaven too?"

Mercy stole a glance at Mr. Thomas, in the doorway, but kept her expression even. "She is perfectly well, Mrs. Thomas, I promise you. She is healthy and happy and well cared for."

It was on the tip of Mercy's tongue to ask the poor woman if she wanted to see Alice, but she hesitated, knowing it would anger Mr. Thomas, and potentially upset young Alice as well. In the next moment, she was glad she had refrained, for Mrs. Thomas eased back against her pillows and murmured a relieved, "Thank God." A moment later, her eyelids fluttered closed.

"She'll sleep now, for several hours, most like." He gestured for Mercy to precede him back to the main room, closing the door most of the way behind them.

"You see I have my hands full here." Mr. Thomas jerked a thumb over his shoulder. "We are in no fit condition to care for a child."

"Yes, you explained that when you brought Alice to the school."

"And now all the more. My wife is dying, Miss Grove, and even were I able to overlook her mother's behavior, I am not a young man. You may judge me harshly, but I am not without feeling. I don't want the girl to be neglected or worse, should my wife and I both pass while she is still so young. That's why I've asked'ee here—I want you to become her guardian."

"Guardian?" Mercy's heart pounded.

"Yes. And she your ward."

"But why?"

"Why would'ee want to shoulder the burden?" he interjected. "And you an unmarried woman? I understand your hesitation, but appeal to your Christian charity."

Mercy had only meant to ask "Why me?" but did not correct him. She felt light-headed and her chest tight. She forced herself to take a deep breath, and to *think*.

When she said nothing, he went on. "I know I haven't contributed all I should toward her schooling, but I will make up for that now. I have been well paid for my work at the Fairmont."

"And if I agree?" Mercy asked. "I cannot become her legal guardian over a handshake. You would have to sign something—acknowledge your role as next of kin, to the lawyers at least."

"I will. Though I would still ask'ee not to spread it about the parish."

"Of course, but I would need to discuss the situation with my aunt, my parents, and my two closest friends."

He grimaced. "Very well, if you insist. Is your lawyer . . . ?"

"In Wishford."

He nodded. "Tell me where to be when, and I shall sign whatever is needed."

"Are you sure you will not change your mind? Raise Alice here?"

He shook his head. "Were my wife in good health, maybe. But as it is, no."

"Mr. Thomas, I will need some time to think this through and talk to my family before I formally agree."

He pulled a face. "Why? Do you not care for the girl? I realize you have other pupils to think of, but I have seen you with her out in the garden and after church. I thought you were fond of her."

He *had* been keeping an eye on his great-granddaughter after all.

Mercy nodded. "I do care, and I am very fond of her. But this is a serious step. One we would both do well to consider carefully before doing anything permanent and life changing."

"Very well. How long?"

Mercy stepped to the door. "I will let you know as soon as I can."

She walked back to Ivy Cottage, stomach stirring with conflicting emotions—surprise, uncertainty, hope. Had God answered her prayers? Was this His way of giving her the desire of her heart?

CHAPTER TEN

Later that evening, Mercy told her aunt about Mr. Thomas's request. She expected her to be pleased, but pleasure was not what she saw in Aunt Matty's expression.

"Really? Poor Marion." Matilda's eyes turned down at the corners. "I wish she could raise the dear girl herself, though I know she would approve of his choice were she able. I must say I am surprised the old codger thought of asking you. It is to his credit, but . . ."

"But what? You don't approve?"

"It is not that, Mercy. You know I am fond of Alice as are you. However . . . is Mr. Thomas certain she has no other family?"

"Not that he knows of. Do you remember Mrs. Thomas mentioning any other relatives who might step forward?"

"Not that I recall, though Marion was not acquainted with Mary-Alicia's husband or his family." Aunt Matty thought, then asked, "And what about our other girls? Might they feel slighted?"

"I think most of them would understand. Especially as they all have at least one parent living."

"True. Just . . . tread cautiously, my dear. And talk to Mr. Coine and your parents before you make any promises, all right?"

"Yes, I plan to."

"Good."

The next day, Mercy rode with Mrs. Burlingame into Wishford to speak to her family's lawyer, Mr. Coine. A few hours later, when the carter brought her back to Ivy Hill, Mercy stopped at The Bell to talk to Jane.

She found her at the desk. "I have news," Mercy announced.

"Oh? Good news?"

"I . . . think so."

"You don't sound too sure."

"My head is still spinning. May we talk in private?"

"Of course. Come out to the lodge."

Jane led her across the drive. She opened the door, pausing to bend and scratch the ears of her adopted stable cat, Kipper. When they were settled at Jane's small table, Mercy began, "You remember Alice, our youngest pupil?"

"Of course."

"I have been asked to become her legal guardian."

"Her guardian?"

Mercy nodded. "I have just been to see Mr. Coine in Wishford. He is your lawyer as well, I understand."

"Yes. But how did this come about?"

"I told you her mother recently died, and her father has been gone for years. Alice's great-grandparents are still living but feel unable to care for her."

"Who are they? Would I know them?"

"Mr. and Mrs. Thomas."

"The glazier? You never mentioned Alice had relatives in Ivy Hill."

"I know. Mr. Thomas asked me not to."

"Why?"

"I believe, among other things, he fears people would think poorly of him if they knew he was unwilling to take in his own great-granddaughter."

"Has Alice any other family?" Jane asked. "Distant relatives on one side or the other?"

"Not that Mr. Thomas knows of."

Jane squinted in thought. "So when I saw Mrs. Thomas in the churchyard, searching for a girl's grave, was she mourning her granddaughter—Alice's mother?"

"It's possible, since she died early this year. Though she is buried in Bristol, I understand."

"Poor Mrs. Thomas lost both her daughter and her granddaughter. . . ."

Mercy nodded. "Yes. It seems little wonder that her mind is tormented."

Jane asked, "Were you acquainted with Alice's mother?"

"Not really. Though I met Mary-Alicia once or twice when she was young. She spent a few summers here with her grandparents."

Jane tilted her head at that. "What was her surname?"

"Smith."

Jane nodded, chewing her lip. "You are a gifted teacher, Mercy. But for Mr. Thomas to give you their own great-grandchild . . ."

"I know. But Mrs. Thomas hasn't long on this earth, I'm afraid. And Mr. Thomas, well . . ." Mercy let the thought trail away unfinished.

"Has he no interest in the girl himself?"

"There was apparently a falling-out between him and Alice's mother years ago over something she did. He did not explain the particulars."

Jane's eyes flashed. "Well, whatever it was, it was not Alice's fault."

"I know, but I was unable to persuade him."

Jane looked off into the distance, still grappling with the news as Mercy herself had done. "So . . . he has asked you to become her guardian. To raise her after he and his wife are gone."

"Yes."

Jane returned her gaze to her. "You are basically doing that already, are you not? She is your pupil, she lives with you, you teach her, feed her, clothe her . . ."

"Yes, but this is not just for a few years of schooling. This is forever." Mercy gave a little laugh. "Or at least until she comes of age and wants to wash her hands of me."

"She would not. She is clearly attached to you already."

Mercy nodded. "And I her."

"So you've agreed?"

"Not yet. I told Mr. Thomas I needed to consider all the ramifications. Talk to my family, and our lawyer."

"What did Mr. Coine say?"

"He said because Mr. and Mrs. Thomas appear to be Alice's last living relatives, and there isn't a sizable inheritance at stake or anything like that, he does not think we'd need to involve the Court of Chancery. A signed agreement, just in case some other claimant challenges the decision later, is all he thinks we'll need to proceed."

"What does your aunt say?"

Mercy hesitated, brow furrowed as she thought back. "She isn't against the idea, but she cautioned me. Asked if I am certain Alice has no other family. She knows if I get too attached, losing her would break my heart."

"What about your parents? How will they feel about this?"

Mercy sighed. "They won't like it. They barely tolerate the school."

"Surely they would understand and not begrudge you this chance."

"I hope you are right. Oh, Jane. I want to be more to Alice than her teacher or guardian. I want to raise her as my own. The daughter I never had, and likely never will have otherwise."

Jane reached over and pressed her hand. "I understand."

Mercy met her friend's gaze and saw a faint sheen of tears shimmering there. "Oh, Jane, I'm sorry. I had not stopped to consider how this might make you feel."

Jane managed a tremulous smile. "I should hope not! Please, don't give my foolish feelings another thought. I may take five minutes to feel sorry for myself, but I am utterly and completely happy for you."

Mercy squeezed her hand. "Thank you."

The next day, Rachel sang to herself as she shelved more books. The side door to the library opened, and Rachel looked up, ready to greet another prospective patron.

Sir Timothy Brockwell entered, carrying a wooden crate. "Good day, Miss Ashford." A fond half smile warmed his handsome, aristocratic face. "A pleasure to hear you singing."

She flushed. "I didn't realize I was doing so loudly enough for anyone to hear."

"No need to be self-conscious. You have a lovely voice." He nodded at the crate in his hands. "I would like to be the first to add to your collection."

Her heart rate accelerated, but she kept her voice light. "You are too late, I'm afraid. Mrs. Barton has beaten you to it."

His smile fell, and he set the crate on the desk with a clunk. To her surprise, he looked sincerely disappointed.

She teased, "But if you like, you may be the first—and probably the last—to borrow the book she donated. I don't anticipate that it will be wildly popular."

She lifted it from the desk, where she had cataloged it and readied it to be shelved.

He read the title. "Actually, I might borrow this for my farm manager. He would find it useful."

"Really?" Rachel expelled a breath and shook her head. "I was only joking. Will I ever be able to gauge the sort of book a person might be interested in? So far I am not off to a promising start."

"You will no doubt learn to relish books as I do. As your father did. As must anyone of good sense." His dark eyes glimmered with humor. "And as you do, you will improve in your chosen vocation."

"I hope you are right." She regarded the crate. "In the meantime, you may donate books if you like, but I insist on crediting your account accordingly."

"No need. I am donating nothing. These books were my father's. Mamma had them crated up and stored in the attic. My father would like to see them shared, I think. So you may credit *his* account all you like, though he is no longer here to take advantage of it."

He grinned, and she was glad to see he could remember his father fondly without regret. Hopefully she would be able to do the same one day.

Rachel licked dry lips and explained the terms as she had to Mrs. Barton. Then she eyed his filled crate again. "But that many books is worth a great deal. So if you prefer to hold some back . . ."

He shook his head. "No. I understand the terms. The books are yours."

"Well, then, I accept with gratitude to both you and your father."

His gaze lingered on her face. "It is the least I can do."

She stilled at his words. Was he referring to their past? Or was it only the polite demur of a friend?

For a moment their gazes held, then his shifted. He surveyed the library and adjoining reading room. "How is everything coming along?"

"Well, I think. Mr. Kingsley is still adding more shelves and trim in the drawing room, but this room is ready. I officially open next week."

He withdrew a leather coin purse from his pocket and extracted a few coins. "Here is the subscription fee for myself and Justina. I am afraid Mamma is not much of a reader."

Rachel inhaled deeply and forced herself to hold out her hand. How strange it felt to take money from this man. She reminded herself she was providing a genteel service. It wasn't the same as, say, selling wares or being a fishmonger. Books were rather sophisticated, were they not? And she wasn't even selling them. Only lending them to subscribers. It was more like managing a club, really. She exhaled a little easier.

He asked, "Do I need to sign something?"

"Oh. Yes." She turned the registry toward him and watched as he signed. His hands looked strong. She supposed it was all the riding he did. She forced her attention back to her task, filling out the subscription cards.

The side door opened, and two men Rachel did not recognize entered, carrying boxes. Mr. Drake appeared behind them.

"Good day, Miss Ashford. Sir Timothy." He gestured to his men. "Right here on the floor, fellows. Unless you prefer them somewhere else, Miss Ashford?"

"No, the floor is fine."

The two workmen set down the boxes and quickly departed.

Mr. Drake explained, "These are books from the Fairmont. But don't worry, Jane has already sorted through them, kept those she wanted for herself, and has given her blessing on donating the rest."

Rachel smiled. "Thank you for doing that, Mr. Drake."

Sir Timothy stiffened. Offended by the man's familiarity with Jane, Rachel wondered, or what?

"My pleasure." James Drake looked around and into the adjoining room. "The shelves look well, I must say. Kingsley is doing an excellent job, as usual."

"I agree." She looked at Timothy and explained, "Mr. Drake contributed the bookcases from the former Fairmont House library."

"Mr. Drake is all generosity."

"Yes, he is. Thank you again, Mr. Drake." She chuckled. "At this rate, you shall have a free subscription for life."

"No, no. If you credit anyone, credit Jane. Well, I will let you get back to work." He bowed. "Good-bye."

Rachel bid him farewell, then turned back to Sir Timothy. "Now, where were we? Oh yes. Let's make a list of the books you've brought. . . ."

As Rachel sorted the books, Sir Timothy browsed the library shelves. She dipped a quill and began adding his father's books to her inventory ledger.

Daniel Defoe's *Robinson Crusoe*, as well as its sequel, *The Further Adventures of Robinson Crusoe. Waverley*. Johnson's dictionary. William Blake. Edmund Burke. And other names she did not recognize. And finally, several leather-bound volumes of Milton's *Paradise Lost and Other Stories*. She set about putting the volumes in order and frowned. One of the set was missing. She had only volumes two, three, and four. She looked through the other books in the crate, and even in the crates on the floor that Mr. Drake had brought just in case the volume had somehow fallen. It wasn't there.

The set would be more useful to readers and worth a great deal more if it were complete.

"Sir Timothy?"

"Hm?" He returned the volume he'd been flipping through to the shelf and rejoined her at the desk.

"Did you notice one of the volumes of Milton was missing?"

"No."

"You ought to keep the set together. If you would like these back, so you can put them with the first volume, you are welcome to do so."

His brow furrowed. "That's odd. I doubt Justina or Mamma were reading Milton. But I shall ask. I will also look again through Father's things, and ask the housekeeper to search as well."

"Only if it isn't too much trouble."

"Not at all. They should be reunited."

"Yes, they should."

He searched her face a moment, then cleared his throat. "That reminds me. Miss Ashford, I have wanted to talk with you about—"

Nicholas Ashford strode through the door, hesitating when he saw Sir Timothy at the desk.

Rachel's chest tightened. *Good heavens. Must everyone visit at once?*

Mr. Ashford looked around, then said, "And here I thought your library was not yet open for business."

"Not officially. Sir Timothy has only come to donate books."

"As have I." Nicholas lifted three volumes in his hand. His gaze fell on the crates, and his eyes dimmed. "Apparently, I need not have bothered."

"I felt the same way when Mr. Drake donated those two crates," Sir Timothy said kindly. "I brought only the one."

Rachel hurried to reassure the younger man. "I can always use more. Thank you, Mr. Ashford. That is very thoughtful. What have you brought?"

"Just a few *Waverley* novels. But I'll go. I can see you are busy."

"No, stay. We are almost finished here."

His gaze swung from Rachel to Sir Timothy standing nearby. "It doesn't look that way."

For a moment, an awkward silence hung in the air, then Sir Timothy drew himself up.

"No need to leave on my account, Mr. Ashford." He picked up his hat and gave the man a perfunctory smile. "I was on my way out."

Rachel stammered, "But . . . did you not want to . . . discuss something?"

Sir Timothy hesitated, pressing his lips together. "Another time, perhaps." He bowed and turned to go.

She watched him depart, her heartbeat loud in her ears. Then she turned to Nicholas.

He said, "It was rude of me to intrude like that. I am sorry."

It was better this way, she told herself. Nicholas was the man who wanted to marry her. She smiled warmly at him. "Not at all. You heard Sir Timothy. He will return another time."

Nicholas grinned. "In that case, how does a man go about getting a subscription to this fine establishment?"

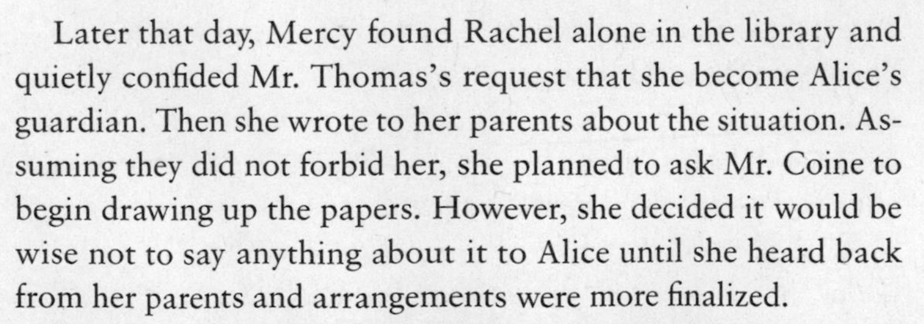

Later that day, Mercy found Rachel alone in the library and quietly confided Mr. Thomas's request that she become Alice's guardian. Then she wrote to her parents about the situation. Assuming they did not forbid her, she planned to ask Mr. Coine to begin drawing up the papers. However, she decided it would be wise not to say anything about it to Alice until she heard back from her parents and arrangements were more finalized.

On Sunday afternoon, Rachel offered to remain with the girls while Mercy and Aunt Matty visited the almshouse. After their visit, as they walked home together, Mercy looked up the road and was surprised to see Mr. Drake and the old glazier standing on the Thomases' doorstep.

Matilda followed her gaze. "That is Mr. Drake, is it not?"

"Yes," Mercy replied. "I wonder what he wants with Mr. Thomas."

"Windows for the Fairmont would be my guess."

"No doubt you're right," Mercy murmured, though she thought it strange to call at the man's house on a Sunday for a business reason.

Mr. Thomas abruptly slammed the door shut. Beside Mercy, her aunt gasped.

Mr. Drake stood there a moment, apparently stunned, then turned and walked away, striding in their direction.

He tipped his hat to them as he approached. Mercy would have nodded and walked on, but chatty Aunt Matty paused to wait for him.

"Hello, Mr. Drake."

"Good day, Miss Matilda. Miss Grove."

Matilda grinned. "I see Mr. Thomas was his usual hospitable self?"

"Yes," he wryly agreed. "Lost the skin off my nose when he slammed his door. Are you acquainted with him?"

"Of course. I know everyone in Ivy Hill. I've lived here all my life, after all, and I'm no April lamb."

"You could have fooled me."

Matilda chuckled, then sobered. "His wife and I were old friends. But lately, she doesn't seem to know who I am. So sad to get old. That's why I've decided to remain young." She smiled again, though sadly.

He said, "Mr. Thomas told me his wife was not well enough to receive visitors, and he was not willing to talk with me either."

Matilda nodded. "Private man. Suspicious and resentful too. I hope that isn't uncharitable to say. But life has given him cause, I own."

Mercy spoke up. "Surely if you wanted Mr. Thomas's services as a glazier, he would be happy to talk with you."

"As a matter of fact he has done work for me already. But this call was of a more personal nature."

"Oh?"

"Yes. I was told we might have an acquaintance in common, but when I asked him, all he would say was 'If you want windows repaired, I'm your man. If it's gossip you're after, go see Mrs. Craddock.'"

Aunt Matty chuckled again. "There's some truth there. Who is this acquaintance? Perhaps I would know him."

"It's nothing important. I had simply met a Miss Payne years ago and recently learned the Thomases were her grandparents. I was only curious about her and her husband."

Surprise flashed through Mercy. "You were acquainted with Mary-Alicia Smith?"

"Smith. Is that her husband's name? I heard she'd married but not her new surname."

Matilda nodded. "Yes. She married a Mr. Smith, a lieutenant of marines, if I remember correctly what Mrs. Thomas told me."

Mercy recalled her aunt previously describing him as a seaman on a merchant ship, but apparently she'd misheard, or her aunt was mistaken.

"Do you know the Smiths?" Mr. Drake asked.

"Not well," Matilda answered for them both. "I never met the husband. I did meet Mary-Alicia a few times, but that was years ago, when she was young. She spent time here with the Thomases as a girl."

"Yes, I recall her mentioning fond memories of her grandparents."

Matilda sighed. "Such a shame she has passed on."

Mr. Drake stiffened. "Passed on?"

Matilda laid a hand to her chest. "Oh, my dear sir! He did not tell you? Poor Mary-Alicia has been gone more than half a year."

His mouth went slack. "No . . . Mr. Thomas told me nothing."

"He's told almost no one apparently," Mercy said. "Mary-Alicia lived elsewhere most of her life, so most people here did not know her."

"I only knew because Mrs. Thomas told me," Matilda added. "And Mr. Smith died early in their marriage, I understand. Went down with his ship. I am sorry to be the bearer of such news."

"And I the hearer." He managed a mirthless smile. "But if I had to hear it, I am glad it was from you, kind lady. Still, what a shock. She was so young."

Matilda nodded her agreement. "Apparently she had been sickly for a long time. She had been laid low with—"

Afraid her aunt might break their promise to Mr. Thomas, Mercy squeezed her arm in warning. Matilda broke off mid-sentence, sending her an apologetic look.

"Come, Aunt Matilda," Mercy interjected. "We've delayed Mr. Drake long enough. And don't forget, we've left Miss Ashford on her own."

"Oh, only with a few girls. The rest have gone to visit their families. Rachel will manage perfectly well."

"Well, I won't keep you," Mr. Drake said, taking Mercy's cue. "By the way, Miss Grove. I received your letter and will be happy to talk with you about the charity school at some point, once things settle down at the Fairmont."

"Thank you, Mr. Drake. Just send word when you have time, and I will come to see you whenever it is convenient."

"I will do that." He bowed. "And now, I bid you good day, ladies."

He walked away, and Mercy turned to watch him go.

Her aunt patted her hand. "Well, that's good news, is it not?"

"Is it?" Mercy hoped something good would come of the man's interest.

CHAPTER ELEVEN

To celebrate the official opening of the circulating library, Miss Matilda insisted they serve cake. Rachel doubted the wisdom of putting sticky icing in the vicinity of all those fine leather books with gilt edges, but she accepted her offer graciously.

Several members of the Ladies Tea and Knitting Society arrived together in a show of support. Becky Morris, a twinkle in her eye, asked Rachel if she had any more romances like the one she had lent to Mrs. Barton. The other women chimed in, and Rachel feared the competition to borrow *Fugitive of the Forest* might devolve into fisticuffs. Thankfully, Anna Kingsley appeared with volumes of *The Nocturnal Visit* and *Northanger Abbey* and began extolling their gothic appeal as well.

Mrs. Klein asked if Rachel had multiple copies of any book, so a few of them might read the same title and later meet to discuss it in the reading room. Rachel provided volumes of *Waverley* for the purpose.

The Miss Cooks had come in a few days earlier to sign up for subscriptions, but now Judith asked if she could borrow a book without her subscription card.

Her sister frowned at her. "I thought you found your card, Judy."

"I did."

"You lost it again already?"

"It isn't lost. I put it somewhere special and shall recall where . . . by and by." She blinked her round blue eyes at Rachel. "I have never been a subscriber before. I was so proud of that card." Her powdered chin trembled.

"Don't worry. I shall give you a duplicate, Miss Cook."

Mrs. Barton patted her own bodice. "Keep it in your corset, Judy. That's where I keep my valuables."

Mrs. Burlingame sent her a sly glance. "No doubt Mr. Barton agrees."

"Phyllis!" the spinster sisters exclaimed, faces pruned in shocked indignation.

Miss Morris laughed until she snorted. "Please forgive us, Miss Ashford. And here we meant to be on our best behavior today."

When the women left, books in arms, Rachel sagged against the desk in relief. She was already exhausted, and it was not yet eleven!

After opening day, visits to the library slowed to a more steady pace, which was both a relief and a concern—Rachel still hoped for more subscribers.

A few mornings later, Rachel opened the library as usual, unlocking the side door and replacing the daily newspapers, which Miss Cook had asked her to save for her bird's cage.

Jane stopped in, borrowed a novel, and lingered to chat. When she left a short while later, Rachel slipped into the dining room for a cup of coffee. Returning to her desk, she dutifully opened one of her father's history tomes she was forcing herself to read. After all, how could she make informed book recommendations if she had not at least sampled all genres? Sliding her finger down the page and finding where she had left off, Rachel braced herself with a sip of coffee and forged on with the text.

Her coffee grew cold, and a long strand of hair escaped its coil as she bent over the volume, intent on untangling each sentence.

A shadow fell across her page, and startled, she jerked her head up. "Oh, Sir Timothy. I did not hear you come in." He had returned, she realized. As he said he would.

Hesitation flickered in his dark eyes, then he leaned close. His fingers brushed her temple as he tucked the unruly strand behind her ear.

Face flaming, Rachel closed the volume. "How . . . how may I help you?"

Timothy looked down to read the title, then cocked one eyebrow. "I did not take you for a historian, Miss Ashford."

"My father always said history was important—both our country's and our personal history." *Our personal history* echoed in her mind, the words seeming rife with unintentional innuendo.

Timothy's voice was quiet. "And do you agree with that?"

Throat suddenly dry, Rachel reached for her cold coffee and took a bitter sip. Should she ask him what he'd wanted to talk to her about on his last visit? Instead, she said, "Actually, this book is full of useful knowledge. Did you know the Dutch inventor Cornelius van Drebbel built the first submarine in 1620 from wood, greased leather, and pigskin bladders?"

A smile lifted his handsome features. "I am spellbound. Truly. Have you any other such engrossing books?"

She said wryly, "Yes, my father's collection has many others just as fascinating as this one."

"Lead on. And by the way, I was sorry to miss your grand opening, but duties kept me away. I hope it went well?"

"It did, thank you." The attentive way he looked at her made her pulse race. She gestured toward the history section. "Now, right this way."

After he'd chosen a book and thanked her, Timothy left and Rachel returned to her reading. Someone rapped on the library's side door but did not enter. Rachel looked up, surprised to see the Brockwells' butler standing outside the glass door as somber as a pallbearer, dressed in black from head to toe. Rachel waved for him to enter, but he either did not see the gesture or ignored it and knocked again with the head of his umbrella.

Rachel walked over to open the door for him. "Hello, Mr. Carville."

"Miss Ashford."

"Do come in. In fact, you may enter without knocking when the library is open. The Miss Groves have kindly consigned these rooms and this door for the library's particular use."

He lifted his pointed nose. "It is not my custom to enter a person's home unannounced."

"I see. Well. Welcome."

She gestured him forward, and he stepped tentatively inside.

Carville had seemed such a large, menacing presence when Rachel was a girl. Now the years had diminished him. His grey hair had thinned, his frame slightly bent so that he was not much taller than she was. Even so, he still possessed an air of grave authority that put Rachel on her guard.

"How may I help you?" Rachel clasped her hands and found them damp. Servant or not, Carville's years and high position with the parish's leading family gave him a certain standing and commanded respect.

He rested vein-wormed hands on the handle of his umbrella and surveyed the library.

Rachel swallowed a nervous lump. Heaven help her recommend a book to interest this man! "You are welcome to browse. Or are you looking for something in particular?"

"I am, yes. Sir Timothy Brockwell happened to mention that he donated some of his late father's books."

"Yes, he did. It was very kind of him."

"Perhaps. But if he had told me in advance what he planned to do, I would have gone through the books first, to make sure no important papers or keepsakes had been left among them."

"I did not see anything in the crate except the books, which I have already put on the shelves. But if you give me a few minutes, I could gather them for you."

She thought he might wave away her offer, but instead he nodded and said he would wait.

"Perhaps you would care to sit at the table? I shall bring the books to you there."

Again he gravely nodded and stepped to the table. But he did not sit, perhaps unwilling to do so in a lady's presence.

Rachel retrieved the heavy dictionary and placed it before him, then the poetry, politics, and novels, and finally the three volumes of Milton's *Paradise Lost and Other Stories*.

He gestured for her to sit, and when she accepted, he finally sat as well. He opened each book, peered at the fly leaves and title pages as though looking for an inscription. Then he flipped through the pages of each.

Finally satisfied, he asked, "Is this all of them?"

"Almost. Mrs. Klein has already borrowed *Waverley*, and I'm afraid the first volume of the Milton set is missing."

"Missing?" He frowned. "Sir Justin was never careless with his books. I wonder if Sir Timothy mislaid it. I shall have to speak to the staff."

"I did mention it to Sir Timothy, and he offered to ask his family and the housekeeper if anyone recalled borrowing the book or seeing it someplace it should not be."

"Someplace it should not be . . ." Carville repeated, eyes narrowed in thought. He traced a bony finger over a leather cover, then lifted his chin. "Ah."

Rachel watched him with interest. "Have you remembered where it might be?"

He looked at her as though just recalling she sat there. His thin mouth tightened. "I was only thinking. Sir Justin might have lent it to . . . some acquaintance or other, and after he died, the book was simply never returned. He was generous that way."

"Was he? I didn't know him well."

"Yes, much as his son has been generous with you."

Rachel frowned. "What do you mean?"

He looked at her askance. "Surely you knew about the game and other food he provided over the years, not to mention paying Thornvale's taxes when your father was unable to last year?"

Rachel stared, stunned. "No. I was not aware he did so."

"Perhaps I ought not to have mentioned it. Please do not repeat it." Mr. Carville rose. "Well, thank you, Miss Ashford. I will call at Mrs. Klein's and ask to see *Waverley*. If the missing book turns up, I shall let you know. I trust you will return the favor?"

"I shall."

The elderly man bowed and left. She stared after him, feeling more unsettled than when he'd arrived.

That evening, Mr. Kingsley returned to continue his work in the expanded library. Rachel had gone upstairs, so Mercy greeted him herself, then retreated to the sitting room across the corridor to carry on with her campaign efforts. Her wrist was growing tired from all her letter writing. She looked down at her ink-stained fingers with a rueful sigh, then began another appeal.

A short while later, she heard a grunt of pain and a muttered "Thunder and turf!"

Mercy frowned. That didn't sound good.

She walked to the drawing room door and peeked in, not wanting to interrupt if all was well. Instead, she saw Mr. Kingsley bent over in waistcoat and shirtsleeves, cradling his arm. His coat lay over a chair nearby.

"Are you all right?" She crossed the room to him, reminding herself that she had a brother and had seen a man in his shirtsleeves many times before.

"I will be," he replied between clenched teeth. "I've cut myself. Dashed foolish."

"Let me see." She reached for his arm, but he pulled away.

"No need."

"Let. Me. See," she repeated, in her authoritative, teacher's voice.

He fisted his hand, but she saw blood trickle between his fingers.

"Give me your hand before you bleed all over our best carpet."

At that, he grimaced and extended his hand, palm up, fingers cupped and bloody. An angry gash sliced his palm.

"Come with me. Hurry. Don't drip."

He stoically followed her across the vestibule and down the back passage to the scullery.

"Over the sink, if you please."

He complied.

She reached for his shirtsleeve. "I had better roll this up before it gets soaked."

"I'll do it."

"No, you'd get blood all over your white shirt." She rolled up the sleeve, trying not to notice the muscled forearm, blond hairs, and warm skin. Then she poured a pitcher of water over the wound to wash away the blood. The cut looked jagged but not too deep.

"I can do that." He tried to take the pitcher from her.

She ignored him. "Stay there." She returned a few moments later with a pot of ointment and strips of bandage. "I don't think you need a surgeon."

"Of course I don't. It's only a cut."

"But not a clean one."

"Dashed saw."

She took his large work-worn hand in hers and inspected the injury more closely. Her practical demeanor faltered as she realized she was holding a man's hand.

She drew a shaky breath and endeavored to remain officious. She wrapped and secured the bandage as best she could, though was frustrated to realize her own hands were not as sure and steady as usual.

"There. That should do it. You shall have to change the bandage often until the bleeding stops. Have you sufficient supplies at home, or would you like to take this roll?"

"I have all I need."

She looked up at him, disconcerted to find him looking not at his bandaged hand, but at her.

"Thank you, Miss Grove."

"Think nothing of it, Mr. Kingsley."

As she walked away, she repeated that sentiment to herself,

"Think nothing of it, Mercy Grove. For Mr. Kingsley certainly will not."

Mercy, however, would think of little else the rest of the night.

The next afternoon, while Rachel was relaxing with the Miss Groves in the sitting room, the vicar and his wife stopped by Ivy Cottage. They did not stay long. They had only come to let Matilda know that her old friend Mrs. Thomas had died in her sleep.

Matilda thanked Mr. and Mrs. Paley for telling her and promised to help with the funeral meal and anything else that was needed.

Rachel watched Miss Matty's expression with concern, and Mercy pressed her aunt's hand.

Matilda gave each a reassuring smile. "Don't worry about me, my dears. I am sad, of course, but not distraught. Marion Thomas is—was—a woman of faith who looked forward to eternity in heaven. I take comfort in that." She sighed. "And considering her state of mind and health these last several months, her passing is a blessing, though of course a difficult loss for her husband."

Rachel glanced at Mercy, wondering how the news might affect her and young Alice.

Mercy said, "At least her passing does not come as a shock—Mr. Thomas guessed his wife would soon pass. No wonder he set about getting their affairs in order."

Rachel nodded her agreement.

Later, Matilda went over to the Thomases' to take her turn sitting vigil with the deceased. She had feared Mr. Thomas might forbid anyone but the undertaker and his assistants from entering, but the glazier gave way to custom, and the women of Ivy Hill did what they did so well—they rallied around the bereft man, bringing meals and prayers and presence.

The morning of the burial, Matilda returned early to the Thomas home to help prepare the funeral meal, which the mourners would partake of after the service and committal.

Rachel and Mercy stood at the window, Mercy holding Alice's hand, when the funeral procession passed Ivy Cottage on its way to the churchyard. The bearers walked slowly, coffin held aloft. Several more men followed somberly behind—black crepe tied around their hats, long ends hanging down the back. Among them, Rachel saw Sir Timothy, Mr. Fothergill, and a few others she recognized.

After the procession had passed, Alice went upstairs with the other girls.

Rachel watched her go. "Did you tell her? Does she know it was her great-grandmother who died?"

Mercy shook her head. "It seemed strange to tell her, when she had never met the woman. Though she did recognize Mr. Thomas as the man who brought her here to Ivy Cottage."

"The whole situation is a little strange."

"I agree."

Rachel returned to the library. Some time later, she heard the church bells toll—the ringers sounding a peal, signaling the end of the interment.

Timothy Brockwell stopped by the library not long after, removing his hat as he entered. "Good day, Miss Ashford."

"Sir Timothy. I saw you pass by with the procession. How was the funeral?"

"Appropriately somber and hope-filled at once. Our vicar preached an excellent sermon."

"I am sure he did." Rachel recalled Mr. Paley's comforting words after her father's passing. "Were you well acquainted with Mrs. Thomas?"

"Not particularly, though I try to attend all the funerals of parishioners, when I can. To pay my respects."

"That is good of you. Did your father do the same?"

He shrugged. "He attended some, I believe. That reminds me. I asked my family about his book, and the housekeeper helped me search, but we have not yet found the missing volume of Milton."

"Thank you for trying. By the way, Carville came here a few days ago. He asked to go through the books you donated. Said he wanted to make sure no important papers or valuables were accidentally given away with the books."

Timothy nodded. "I happened to mention I'd donated them. You would have thought I'd given away the family jewels. Did he find anything?"

"No."

"Good, or the man would have scolded me as though I were still a misbehaving adolescent."

Rachel doubted Timothy Brockwell had ever misbehaved in his life. She thought of what Carville had said about the taxes and gifts of food. She was grateful but also embarrassed to realize they'd been recipients of Sir Timothy's benevolence. Recalling Carville's entreaty, she decided not to mention it.

Rachel drew herself up. "Well, I will keep the rest of the set for now. Hopefully volume one will turn up yet."

He nodded again, but made no move to leave.

Nervousness prickled through her. "Was there . . . something else?"

"Miss Ashford, you know that I have always . . ." He stopped, glancing at the black crepe around his hat brim as if recalling the solemn occasion. "Never mind. That is all for the present. And now I will bid you good day." He bowed and walked away.

Oh, Timothy, she thought wistfully. So skilled in restraint. A true, reserved Englishman, who believed in Shakespeare's adage "The better part of valour is discretion."

After he left, and Rachel was alone again, a silky ribbon of memory wove itself through her mind. . . .

Timothy had been away for several days, attending the quarter sessions with his father. Rachel went to Brockwell Court to spend the afternoon with Justina, who was lonely without him. Rachel had empathized.

They were outside playing battledore and shuttlecock when Timothy returned home, a day earlier than expected.

He walked out of the stables and drew up short, a smile breaking over his face. "Rachel, what a pleasant surprise."

"Justina asked me to visit since you were away. I hope you don't mind."

"Of course not."

Justina tossed down her racquet and ran to him. "Tim! We didn't expect you 'til tomorrow!"

He ruffled his little sister's hair. "Father sent me ahead. He returns tomorrow night."

"Guess what?" Justina clutched his arm. "I beat Rachel twice!"

Rachel nodded. "It's true, I'm afraid. Your sister is a dab-hand with a battledore. She has obviously played a great deal with her elder brother."

"Yes. Justina often asks to play, and I oblige her."

"Will you play now, Timothy?" the girl begged.

"Not now, poppet. I need to see how all goes on here at home. But first, shall we deliver Miss Ashford home in the curricle?"

"Oh yes! Let's do!" Justina turned to Rachel. "My brother promises to teach me to drive it when I am old enough. I *long* to drive. I shall be a crack whip with his bang-up pair. I know it!"

Timothy tucked his chin and raised his eyebrows. "Apparently someone has been spending too much time with her brother Richard." He and Rachel shared a smile over his sister's head.

Soon the three of them were crowded into the curricle, Timothy at the reins. He started the horses off at a sedate trot, but Justina begged, "Faster, faster!"

With an apologetic look at Rachel, he urged the horses to speed, turning the corner sharply. Justina tipped sideways, squealing in delight. Rachel held onto her hat.

As they drove up the High Street, Rachel was surprised to see her friend Jane Fairmont standing outside The Bell, talking to the handsome innkeeper they'd met in Bath. Jane lived nearer Wishford and rarely ventured into Ivy Hill unless in the company of Mercy, Timothy, or Rachel herself.

Following her gaze, Timothy glanced back over his shoulder, then looked again, his expression dulling with sheepishness, or perhaps guilt. But then he noticed Rachel watching him and managed a reassuring smile.

A few moments later, they reached Thornvale. Timothy handed the reins to his sister, who beamed in reply, and then he helped Rachel down.

He was quiet as he escorted her up the walkway, and Rachel feared that seeing Jane had left him with misgivings.

But at the door, he turned to her with a hopeful smile. "Shall we have our first riding lesson soon?"

"Yes. Please."

"Say, day after tomorrow, ten o'clock?"

Rachel nodded. "I shall look forward to it."

He pressed her hand, looking deep into her eyes. "As will I."

But the planned lesson had turned out to be nothing like she'd anticipated. Instead, it had been a hard lesson indeed.

CHAPTER TWELVE

Mercy thanked Alice for gathering the slates, then watched as she hurried to catch up with the other girls filing out of the schoolroom to wash before dinner. Mercy heard a man call a friendly greeting outside, and glanced out the window with interest. There came Mr. Kingsley walking up Church Street, toolbox in hand. He paused to talk with their neighbor a few moments before continuing to Ivy Cottage. Even though the circulating library had opened, Mr. Kingsley still came when he could to finish the detail work, adding trim and moulding around the installed bookcases.

Colin McFarland had arrived nearly an hour before to study with Anna, so Mercy went down to let him know Mr. Kingsley had come. But when she reached the sitting room and peeked inside, she saw Colin and Anna were still hard at work, their heads bent close together at the desk. The tip of Colin's tongue protruded as he concentrated on a column of figures.

He slid the paper toward Anna to review, then crossed his arms and chewed his lip while he waited.

Anna looked up and gave him an encouraging smile. "Almost. You summed the first two columns correctly but forgot to carry the four to the hundreds column here—see? You'll remember next time. Now, let's try multiplication. If a coach fare is seven shillings sixpence, and a family of four travels together, what will their total fare be?"

Colin stared down at the paper and sighed.

"It will get easier, Mr. McFarland. I promise. Come, I'll help you."

Mercy decided not to interrupt the lesson. Instead she stepped into the reading room to greet Mr. Kingsley and see if she might help him herself.

He glanced up when she entered, then looked again. "Oh. Evening, Miss Grove. Thought I heard Colin's voice."

She nodded. "He is . . . occupied at the moment but will be in soon, I trust. What are you working on tonight?"

"Miss Ashford asked me to build a partitioned stand to hold periodicals, like an oversized parlour Canterbury, if you've seen one. I've drawn a plan she likes, but I want to take a few more measurements. Make sure it will suit the available space." He took out a folding ruler from his toolbox and extended it.

Mercy offered, "May I hold one end for you?"

"Thank you—just there against the far wall."

She did so, and he measured, then wrote in a pocket notebook with a stubby pencil.

When he'd finished, she asked, "May I see your plan?"

"If you like. I'm no artist, mind." He turned back a few pages and showed her several views of the proposed cabinet.

"Very nice." She added on a chuckle, "I would selfishly suggest elongating the legs so taller people needn't bend so low."

She'd said it as a bit of a joke, but he looked from the drawing to the top of her head, a few inches below his.

"You're right. Taller people like us should not have to suffer cricks in our necks our entire lives." He grinned. "Excellent idea, Miss Grove."

Pleasure filled her at his praise, and she returned his grin.

Colin came in then, and Mercy was almost sorry to see him.

The next day, Rachel slept late, having stayed up past twelve reading the night before. When she awoke, she hurried to get washed and dressed and down to the library by the posted opening time of nine o'clock. She arrived downstairs as the tall case clock chimed the hour, so she proceeded directly into the library, forgoing breakfast. Her stomach rumbled its protest.

Miss Matilda entered the library through the drawing room, Mr. Basu on her heels with an old wicker basket.

"What is this?" Rachel asked.

"Books."

"More books? Who brought them?"

"We don't know. Mr. Basu found them on the doorstep this morning."

"Is there no name, or a note?"

Matilda shook her head. "Not that I can see."

"But how am I to credit someone if they don't give their name?"

"I suppose they wanted no credit."

"But I—"

"The books are heavy, my dear," Matilda interjected.

"Oh. Forgive me. Here on the desk, Mr. Basu, if you don't mind. Thank you."

He set down the basket and quickly exited. Matilda lingered.

"Did you see no one leaving?" Rachel looked out the library window.

"No."

Rachel sighed. "I will have to hope there is an inscription in one of them." She began pulling out books and stacking them on the desk.

The books themselves were a benign assortment: A cheaply bound Gothic romance, several women's magazines complete with fashion plates, a copy of *Steel's Navy List*, a few travelogues, a book of poetry, and another of sermons. She opened the covers, hoping for a dedication or name inscribed within. Nothing.

How frustrating!

Rachel frowned. "I don't like the idea of accepting books without giving proper credit."

"I know you don't." The older woman regarded her affectionately. "Do not be so proud, my dear. We've all needed help at one time or another. There is no shame in allowing friends and neighbors to bless us."

Rachel dipped her head, but Miss Matty raised it with a gentle finger. "You were once in a position to help others, Rachel Ashford. Now others are in a position to help you. Don't waste time feeling embarrassed. But when you are in that privileged position again someday, remember to return the favor."

A dry laugh escaped Rachel. "Will I ever be?"

"Yes, my dear, I think you will. And that is when you will be able to give 'credit' to those who need it. It is how village life works, at its best. At least here in Ivy Hill." She tenderly cupped Rachel's cheek. "All right? You'll remember?"

Rachel nodded, hope and doubt washing over her. "Thank you, Miss Matty. I will try."

Matilda left her, and Rachel ceased her search through the books and instead began adding the titles to her inventory list. When she'd finished, she glanced at the now-empty basket and noticed something lying at the bottom. She picked up the small rectangle of thick paper. A calling card.

James Drake
Proprietor
The Drake Arms, Southampton

So . . . the anonymous donation was not so anonymous after all. Why would Mr. Drake leave more books on her doorstep? The titles seemed too recent to be from the Fairmont attic and a few a bit feminine to be his personal property. She would have to ask him. Rachel decided to send him a note and invite him to call.

A few days later, as Mercy came downstairs, she noticed the door into the library stood open. As a general rule, they kept it closed during the day to keep the circulating library somewhat separate from the rest of the house and especially the school, giving them all a bit more privacy. Her aunt had probably forgotten and left the door open. Rachel had gone for a walk with Mr. Ashford, Mercy knew, and Aunt Matty had offered to watch over the library for her until she returned.

Mercy walked toward the door, intending to close it, but Aunt Matty appeared from around the shadowy corner and grasped her hand to halt her, a finger to her lips.

Taking in her aunt's stance and mischievous look, Mercy peered through the doorway to see what had caused her to hover there, listening. Inside the library, Mr. James Drake slowly strolled past each bookcase, hands casually clasped behind his back, surveying the shelves with an approving air, but not picking up a single book.

Matilda whispered, "I asked if I could help him, but he said he was just looking."

Mr. Drake sat down on one of the chairs, crossed his ankles, and leaned back—at his ease but reading nothing. Was he waiting, hoping to see Rachel? Probably. As pretty as Rachel was, it would be little wonder if the man had taken an interest in her. The only wonder was why no suitor had claimed her as his bride long before now.

Then Sir Timothy entered through the outside door, book tucked under his arm. The baronet had come to the circulating library before to donate books and to select a few to read. Now he drew up short at the sight of another male patron sitting there so casually.

"Mr. Drake."

"Good day, Sir Timothy."

Sir Timothy waved a gloved hand toward the shelves. "No luck finding something to interest you?"

"Not yet." Mr. Drake sent him a grin, but Sir Timothy did not return it.

"Mr. Drake, it seems to me I saw a lot of you at The Bell and now here at Ivy Cottage."

"I could say the same of you." If Mercy was not mistaken, a gleam of humor shone in Mr. Drake's eyes.

Sir Timothy looked not amused at all. "I am a subscriber and an avid reader. Are you?"

The hotel owner shook his head, lips pursed. "I am a subscriber, but books are not what bring me here."

A muscle in Sir Timothy's jaw twitched. "Mr. Drake, I don't know exactly what you are about, but may I remind you that it is not kind nor honorable to toy with women's affections."

Drake's mouth quirked. "Yet here we both are."

Sir Timothy frowned darkly, but Mr. Drake held up a conciliatory palm.

"Don't worry. I have no intention of toying with the affections of anyone in this house."

"Then what, may I ask, is your interest here?"

"You may well ask. But I am under no obligation to answer. However, your interest is perfectly obvious. And our young friend Mr. Ashford makes no pretense about his reasons for visiting Ivy Cottage either."

Sir Timothy crossed his arms. "So I've noticed."

The side door opened again, and Rachel stepped through, the door held for her by Mr. Ashford. Rachel's face was framed by a broad-brimmed bonnet, her cheeks pink with fresh air and exertion, and the bishop's blue spencer she wore brought out the color in her large, lovely eyes.

Her gaze landed on the two men, and she faltered. Stepping in behind her, Mr. Ashford drew up short to avoid colliding with her.

Mercy tapped her aunt's shoulder and gestured that they should move away, but Matilda remained glued where she was.

"Gentlemen," Rachel said a little breathlessly. "I hope you have not been waiting long. Are you here to find a book? Miss Matilda would have helped you—"

Mr. Drake waved away her concern. "Oh, she offered, never fear. But I am not here to look at books. You asked me to call, remember?" He slanted a smug look at Sir Timothy.

"Oh, yes. That's right. I forgot."

Rachel turned self-consciously to her companion. "Thank you for the stroll, Mr. Ashford. I enjoyed it."

"My pleasure. I did as well. Well, you have . . . em, patrons to attend to, so I will say good-bye for now." The young man bowed and took his leave.

Someone knocked on the front door of Ivy Cottage, startling Mercy. She was embarrassed to realize how long she and her aunt had been standing there observing the little drama before them. Mercy tugged her aunt's hand, pulling her reluctantly away from her listening post.

Before Mercy could reach the front door herself, Mr. Basu appeared from the kitchen and opened it. Mr. Kingsley and Colin McFarland stepped inside, carrying long pieces of trim, and talking companionably. With the two of them plus the men in the library . . . ? Good heavens!

Not since becoming a girls school had Ivy Cottage held so many men at once, Mercy thought. Too many men for comfort!

Rachel waited until the door closed behind Mr. Ashford, then turned back to the other two men.

"I did ask Mr. Drake to call, but may I help you with something first, Sir Timothy?"

"I can wait. Unless your business with Mr. Drake is . . . private?"

"Not really. I only wanted him to come in so I might credit him for his latest donation of books."

"Latest donation?" Mr. Drake's golden eyebrows rose.

"The basket of books you left on our doorstep?" Rachel gestured toward the empty wicker basket. "I assume you came when the library was closed and decided to leave them anyway."

"I left no basket."

"Are you being modest?"

Mr. Drake shook his head. "That is not in my nature, Miss Ashford. I would happily accept the gratitude of a pretty lady did I deserve it, but in this case, I do not. Why did you think the books were from me?" He grinned. "Besides my generous nature?"

"I found your card at the bottom of the basket."

"My card?" His brow furrowed.

"Yes. I have it here." She retrieved it from her desk drawer and handed it to him.

He studied it. "This is my old card, printed years ago, when I bought my first hotel. Strange that it should end in a basket of books here."

"Strange indeed."

"What sort of books were they, if I may ask?"

Rachel opened her inventory list and read the titles, including *Steel's Navy List* and a collection of sermons by Edward Cooper. She looked up at him. "Mean anything to you?"

"No." The frown line between his brows deepened. "Just someone I gave a card to long ago, most likely. Or someone who stayed at the Drake Arms. Not you, Brockwell, I take it? You once mentioned you'd been there."

"Yes, but I did not leave a basket of books."

Mr. Drake asked, "May I see the navy list?"

"Of course." She retrieved it and handed it to him.

He flipped through it, then tucked it under his arm. "Thank you. Add it to my account, please. And if you learn who the donor was, please let me know. Now I am curious."

"Yes. I will if I can."

After Mr. Drake left the library, Sir Timothy lingered.

Rachel turned her attention to him and noticed his distracted air. "Thank you for waiting."

"That's all right. I came to return a book and hoped to talk with you while I was here. We were interrupted before, and again today. You are—that is, your library is—rather popular."

"Which is a relief, I don't mind telling you. Did you . . . want to discuss anything in particular?"

He ran a finger over his mouth. "Are you . . . reading anything at present?"

"Yes, actually. A novel Matilda Grove recommended, called *Pride and Prejudice*. I am enjoying it far more than I would have guessed. In fact, I have been staying up late reading."

He grinned. "Did I not promise you would learn to enjoy reading? And far more quickly than I imagined."

She nodded. "And I've told several people how much I am enjoying the book, so I already have a waiting list to read it when I am finished."

His dark eyes glimmered with approval and something more. Admiration? Fondness? Pleasure and fear twisted through her in a single cord. *Careful*, Rachel warned herself. *Don't confuse a love of books with something more.*

If only her heart didn't still beat so when he was near.

The next day, Mercy received a letter postmarked London from her mother. She opened it with a sense of dread. This was the first reply she'd received from her parents since writing two letters to them: the first telling them about Rachel's circulating library, and the second more recently, about her plan to become legal guardian to one of her pupils. She doubted either piece of news would be well received.

Seeing her aunt and the almshouse matron, Mrs. Mennell, quilting together in the sitting room, Mercy carried the letter into the quiet drawing room and sat in one of the chairs. Taking a deep breath, she unfolded it and read.

Dear Mercy,

Your recent letters have us rather concerned. We have decided to come to Ivy Cottage for an overdue visit. You may expect us on the 3rd by four. I hope that will not be inconvenient for you or Matilda. In the meantime, we ask that you postpone any important decisions until our arrival.

We bring a guest with us, so do be prepared. Mr. Hollander is a friend of your father's—and your brother's tutor from his

Oxford days. You no doubt recall us speaking highly of him. He is ready to leave the bachelor-tutor life and would like to meet you. We have told him so many good things about you.

I know we can count on you to receive him with every kindness and accommodation. Perhaps Miss Ashford would be so good as to remove to the inn during our stay. We would be happy to take care of that expense, if necessary.

Until then,
Mother

"Oh bother!" Mercy exclaimed, barely resisting the urge to ball up the letter. Instead she slapped it onto her lap, then immediately picked it up again. "She cannot be serious. . . ."

Someone nearby cleared his throat. She looked up, chagrined to see Mr. Kingsley half hidden by the periodical cabinet he'd built for the library. She had not realized anyone was in the room.

He winced. "Sorry. Didn't mean to eavesdrop. I told Miss Ashford I'd deliver this today. Are you all right, Miss Grove?"

"No, I am not all right. All I did was write and tell my parents I've been asked to become Alice's guardian. And how do they respond? By arranging to bring a man to meet me. They have told him 'so many good things about me.' And only the good things, no doubt. He probably imagines me as intelligent as my father and as pretty as my mother. This man is in for a sore disappointment, and I the mortification of my life. No, not of my life, for they have put me through this before. I thought they had given up their matchmaking attempts and were resigned to allow me to stay on the shelf. But no!" She shook the letter in her hand, irritation coursing through her.

Suddenly she realized she was saying aloud her every thought without her usual self-control, embarrassing her listener and herself in the bargain. Her face heated. "Forgive me, Mr. Kingsley, for so abusing your ears. I am not usually so . . . indiscreet. I apologize."

"Nothing to apologize for. At least not to me."

Shame washed over her. "You are right; I should not speak so harshly of my parents."

"I didn't mean that. It's you who do yourself an injustice. I remember your parents, though I've not seen them in a few years. I'd say you have all their best traits and several more of your own."

Mercy stared at the man. Then she realized what he was doing. "You are kind to try to cheer me."

"I don't say it to cheer you. I say it because it's true."

Mercy felt her face heat anew.

He ducked his head. "Now I am the one rattling on. If you'll excuse me, Miss Grove, I'll get back to work."

Later that evening, Mercy shared the letter with her aunt, and the two sat commiserating when Rachel joined them in the sitting room.

Seeing their expressions, Rachel's face clouded. "What is it? What's wrong?"

Mercy sighed. "My parents are coming to visit in a fortnight, and they are bringing a guest. A man they want me to meet and clearly expect me to entertain a proposal from. Of course that is assuming this man will have any inclination to do so after he meets me." Mercy read from the letter: "'Mr. Hollander is a friend of your father's—and your brother's tutor from his Oxford days. You no doubt recall us speaking highly of him.' No, I don't remember. Not really. George did not last long at university. A friend of my father's? How old of a man is he? Do they expect me to marry a man my father's age?" Mercy's voice sounded unusually young and plaintive in her own ears. *Lord, give me patience!*

"He may not be so old, my dear," Aunt Matilda said gently. "But if he is, I shall marry him myself so you won't have to." She winked, but for once Mercy did not appreciate her aunt's humor.

Instead she groaned. She read aloud another excerpt for Rachel's benefit. "'He is ready to leave the bachelor-tutor life and would like to meet you. We have told him so many good things about you.' They probably exaggerated the good things, and left out the bad. And now they expect me to receive him with 'every kindness and accommodation.'"

Rachel squared her shoulders. "You need me to leave."

Mercy looked at her, stricken. "Oh, my dear Rachel . . . of course you must not go."

"You will need my room for your guest. Perhaps I might take a room at The Bell, or stay with Jane."

"Nonsense, Rachel. You live here now." Mercy looked at her aunt. "Perhaps I might share your room, Aunt Matty? You have a larger bed."

Matilda worried her lip. "I don't know that it would be quite proper to put the man in your bed, my dear. Might send the wrong message. But I can sleep in your room for a few nights, and we can give him my room. With all that lacework and purple bedclothes, he won't be eager to stay overlong." Again she winked at her niece. And this time, Mercy managed a small smile in reply.

"Good thinking, Aunt Matty."

CHAPTER THIRTEEN

Rachel walked listlessly into the butler's pantry to return the teacup she had taken into the library after breakfast. Then she wandered to the dining room windows and moved aside the curtain to look outside. What a grey day. Rain fell in steady, translucent streaks. In the house across the street, a neighbor pulled her shutters closed one by one, grumbling about her damp floors. Mrs. Mennell hurried by, a sack of day-old bread from Craddock's in one hand, a rickety umbrella in the other. The butcher's boy dashed past with a delivery, flat cap pulled low. In neighboring houses, more windows and shutters closed. The street emptied and quieted.

Now the only sounds were the pattering of rain and, from the schoolroom above, Mercy's muffled voice as she taught her lessons. Rachel sighed. Would anyone frequent her library on such a day? She was about to turn away when movement caught her eye. From around the corner of Church Street and Ebsbury Road, a dark figure appeared. A woman in a black hooded mantle walked as steadily as the rain, apparently unconcerned and unhurried by it. The hood was deep, shadowing her face within. Gloved hands clasped primly at her waist, a package of some sort tucked beneath her arm.

Who was it? Rachel wondered, and she watched until the woman walked past Ivy Cottage and out of view.

She let the curtain fall and started down the corridor toward the library. There must be some more dusting or organizing she could do. If not, she would ask Mr. Basu to build up the fire, and then she'd curl up in its most comfortable chair and continue reading *Pride and Prejudice*.

As she passed through the drawing room into the library, she heard a *thunk* from outside. Had someone knocked on the side door? She did not think she had locked it.

She crossed the room to the door, but no one stood waiting. Through the glass panels, she saw the woman in black disappear around the corner of the cottage. Rachel glimpsed a lace cap over dark blond curls and a long nose. Had she wanted to come into the library? Rachel opened the door, thinking to call after the woman and invite her in. But then she noticed a brown waxed-paper-wrapped package lying on the paving stones. With a flash of surprise and unease, Rachel picked it up and carried it inside.

Moving aside her ledger to avoid getting it wet, she dried the package with a clean dustcloth and peeled back the paper. The waxed paper had kept the contents dry.

A book. Of course it was. Rachel groaned. Why did people insist on donating books without staying long enough to receive proper credit? Recalling Matilda's admonition, Rachel knew she should simply be grateful, but—

Wait . . . She looked at the spine, surprise and confusion flaring anew. Then she opened the cover and read the title page to be certain.

Yes. Here was the missing volume of *Paradise Lost*.

A chill crept over her.

Only the damp, she told herself. *Only the rain*.

Rachel went to find Matilda Grove, who prided herself on knowing everyone in Ivy Hill.

She found her in the kitchen, rolling biscuit dough on the large worktable. At the corner stove, Mrs. Timmons skimmed a pot of soup.

"Miss Matty?"

"Hm?" She looked up from her rolling pin.

"Look what just arrived." Rachel held forth the volume.

Matilda reached toward it, but thought the better of her flour-encrusted hands and bent to peer at it instead.

Rachel explained, "It's the first volume of *Paradise Lost and Other Stories*. The one missing from the Brockwells' set."

"Sir Timothy found it after all?"

"No, it was left outside the library just now."

"In this weather? It might have been ruined!"

"It was wrapped in waxed paper."

"Who left it—did you see?"

"I don't know who it was. I saw a woman wearing a black mantle with a deep hood. I caught only the barest glimpse of her face, but I did not recognize her."

Matilda paused in her work, the furrow between her eyebrows deepening. "Did you see which direction she came from?"

"From the north, I think. I saw her walk around the house on the corner and turn up our street."

Matilda nodded, eyes distant. "Ah." She opened her mouth to say more, then with a glance at Mrs. Timmons, closed it again. She picked up a copper cutter and began pressing round shapes from the dough.

"Who do you think it was?" Rachel persisted. Was she about to get another lecture on pride and not insisting on crediting donations?

"Several farms and cottages up that way," Matilda said vaguely. "Difficult to tell."

"She was dressed in black—a recent widow, perhaps?"

"Oh, many women wear black capes in foul weather. Very practical, black is. Could have been anyone."

Mrs. Timmons spoke up. "I'll wager it was that witch. Would be like her, sneakin' out on a day like this, when she's less likely to be seen."

Confusion flared. "Witch? What are you talking about?"

"Never heard of the witch of Bramble Cottage?" the cook asked. "No, I don't suppose you would have, growing up in Thornvale."

"Who do you mean?"

Matilda frowned at the older woman. "Mrs. Timmons is only teasing you, Rachel. I am sure she would not say something so unkind about anyone."

Mrs. Timmons humphed and returned to her work.

Rachel looked down at the volume in her hand. "So I suppose it is unlikely that this book is even from the same set as the Brockwells'."

Matilda sent the cook a warning glance. "Milton was very popular. I imagine many people bought the first volume but could not afford to purchase the rest of the set as it was published."

Rachel nodded. "You are probably right. But what a coincidence, that it should be donated so soon after the Brockwells'."

Matilda's eyes glinted. "A coincidence indeed."

The rain continued. That night, lightning cracked outside Rachel's bedchamber window, and thunder like the beating of drums rumbled through Ivy Cottage.

Rachel lay in bed trying to read her novel. Distracted by the thunder, she set it aside and picked up a copy of *La Belle Assemblée* and looked at the fashion prints instead.

Just as she was about to set it aside and blow out her candle for the night, the door creaked open, startling her.

"Miss Rachel?" came Phoebe's shaky whisper.

"Yes?"

The door opened wider, revealing Phoebe and little Alice in their long white nightdresses.

"We saw light under your door. Everyone else is sleeping, but we can't sleep. Can we, Alice?"

The little girl solemnly shook her head.

"May we stay with you awhile? We're scared." Phoebe's eyes widened in appeal.

"Very well." Rachel set aside the magazine and patted the bedclothes.

The girls came forward eagerly, Phoebe climbing in on one side and Alice on the other. Rachel pulled the bedclothes over their legs.

"Will you tell us a story?" Phoebe asked.

"Hmm. What sort of story?"

Alice's gaze latched onto the large painting of Rachel and Ellen as young girls, posing with their mother. "Who are they?" she whispered.

"The littlest is me, that's my sister, Ellen, and the lady is our mother."

"My mamma died," Alice said, so quietly Rachel barely heard her.

She lowered her head closer to the little girl's and whispered back, "I know. I'm sorry. So did mine."

Alice took her hand and Rachel's heart warmed to the little girl, who rarely spoke to anyone except Mercy.

Thunder shook the windowpanes and the girls burrowed nearer Rachel's sides, cuddling close. Rachel searched her memory, but could think of no cheerful stories to tell. Her candle guttered, and Alice squeaked a little cry.

Rachel began talking, having no real idea of what she was going to say but determined to distract the girls from the storm.

"I cannot think of any stories about sisters, but I will tell you one about two friends. Once upon a time there were two girls. We will call them Lady Rose and Lady . . . Joan. They grew up near each other and were the best of friends. Lady Joan was everything good and amiable. She could ride a horse as well as any man. She could shoot and dance equally well. Joan was also kind and befriended Lady Rose even though Rose was a few years younger.

"Nearby, a young prince lived in the biggest and most beautiful house in the land. His mother, the icy queen, did not want him befriending the neighbor children, but the prince would sneak out to spend time with Joan anyway. He was kind to Rose as well but treated her like a little sister. Everyone knew he admired Joan.

"Rose went along when they walked into the village or through the woods. But she had never learned to ride. In fact, she was a little afraid of horses, so when the prince and Joan would go off riding together, they would leave Rose at home. Rose would stand at the gate and wave and watch until the two of them disappeared. She feared one day when they came back, they would be married and she would lose her best friends forever. Secretly Rose was in love with the prince, but she knew he loved Joan and would probably marry her."

Phoebe asked, "Was Rose angry with Joan? 'Cause the prince liked her better?"

"No, not angry. Sad maybe. But she loved them both and wanted them to be happy."

Rachel thought a moment, then continued, "As Rose grew older, she grew a little taller and her figure and complexion improved. Her father engaged a new lady's maid for her, who helped her select pretty gowns and knew how to arrange her hair in flattering styles.

"Finally, the day of her coming-out ball arrived. Rose had a new dress made for the occasion—a beautiful pink dress. She bathed in scented water, put on her new dress, and the new lady's maid curled her hair and fastened roses in it with white-beaded pins. When Rose looked in the mirror, for the first time in her life she saw a princess looking back at her. She felt beautiful. Happy. Full of excitement for the ball ahead.

"She floated down the stairs with a smile on her face, anticipating the reactions of her friends and family to her new dress, but what she had not anticipated was the prince's reaction. He was standing at the bottom of the stairs as she descended. He looked up at her, then looked again. For a moment it seemed as if he did not recognize her, and then his mouth fell open and his eyes widened. The prince looked at her not as a little girl, not as a little sister, but as a woman. An attractive woman. Rose felt as though she could fly!

"The prince told her she was beautiful and asked her to dance. They danced together and then again. Rose skipped and whirled through the figures until one of the roses fell from her hair. The prince asked to keep it as a memento. He tucked it into his pocket, close to his heart. . . ."

An ache formed and throbbed in Rachel's chest. She had to pause a moment, then took a deep breath and continued, "He danced with Joan and with other ladies as duty required, but all night, he only had eyes for her. Rose was not alone in noticing a change in how the prince looked at her and treated her. Joan noticed too."

"Was she angry?"

"I . . . am not certain."

Phoebe squinted up at her. "But it's your story."

"Yes . . . it is."

When she said no more for a moment, Phoebe prompted, "Did the prince marry Rose?"

"No."

"He married Joan anyway?"

"No. He married no one."

"Why?"

"I don't know."

Phoebe sighed. "This isn't a very good story."

"Shh." Alice gently hushed Phoebe.

Rachel injected a cheerful note into her voice. "But it is not a sad story. Not really. Rose was happy in many ways. She had a nice house to live in and was surrounded by good and kind friends."

Alice patted her hand at that and rested her head on Rachel's shoulder.

For a moment, Rachel remained silent, mind and stomach churning. Telling that tale had made her think. . . . Had she idealized that long ago night into a romantic fantasy instead of real life—a *Cendrillon* story of her own? Timothy was no more a prince than she a princess—they were both fallible human beings. It was time to get on with her life before it was too late.

Thunder boomed and again the windowpanes shuddered. Rachel said, "Shall I sing to you instead? Hopefully I am better at that than telling tales."

The girls nodded eagerly.

Rachel thought for a moment. Then she cleared her throat and sang, "'Come, thou fount of every blessing, tune my heart to sing thy grace; streams of mercy, never ceasing, call for songs of loudest praise. Teach me some melodious sonnet, sung by flaming tongues above'"—Lightning cracked the sky as if punctuating the words—"'Praise the mount I'm fixed upon it, mount of God's redeeming love . . .'"

The girls soon fell asleep, but Rachel lay there after the final notes faded away. How strange that a hymn her father had sung to her as a girl was the one that leapt to her mind and tongue. The last years of his life had been difficult for them both, but she was thankful for this reminder of better times in their past.

Rachel turned her head to look at one slumbering girl, then the other. Unexpected contentment warmed her. She never could have imagined lying here in a borrowed bed in Ivy Cottage singing to two girls not her own.

It is not a sad story at all.

CHAPTER FOURTEEN

A few days later, Mercy went downstairs after the day's classes were finished and passed Rachel coming up. "Library closed for the day?"

"Yes. My feet are tired."

"I imagine. Do you mind if I look for some books to use in tomorrow's literature class?"

"Of course not. You never have to ask—you know that."

"Thank you."

"By the way, your aunt is entertaining a caller in the reading room."

"Oh? Who?"

"See for yourself." Rachel's eyes sparkled with humor.

Entering the library a few moments later, Mercy heard a man's voice coming from the adjoining reading room, now and again punctuated by Aunt Matilda's cheerful tones.

She stepped nearer and glanced through the open doorway. James Drake and her aunt sat talking in the comfortable armchairs. Mr. Drake held a teacup and accepted one of Matilda's biscuits with a smile, nervy fellow. The two were the picture of old friends, though, granted, her aunt never met a stranger.

Matilda was clearly enjoying her conversation with the handsome gentleman, and Mercy did not want to interrupt. She walked to the literature section and began perusing the shelves. As she did, Mr. Drake's words registered.

"I stopped to offer my condolences to Mr. Thomas," he said. "Tried to, at any rate. He accepted the basket I brought, then slammed the door again."

"As you've gathered, Mr. Thomas keeps to himself," Matilda explained. "But I used to take tea with Mrs. Thomas every week or two, so I knew them a little better than most."

"Is that how you met Mary-Alicia?"

"Yes. I talked with her during a few of her visits."

"And what was your opinion of her?"

Matilda paused to consider. "She seemed quite ladylike and accomplished, especially considering her rather humble background. Her mother saw that she was educated and her manners genteel. But after her parents died . . . Well . . . not much supervision, you understand."

Mr. Drake apparently noticed Mercy in the adjacent room, for he stood and said, "Good afternoon, Miss Grove."

She looked over and raised a hand in greeting. "Hello. I am only here to choose a few books for class. Don't let me interrupt you."

"Very well." He resumed his seat.

Matilda added, "Join us when you're finished, Mercy."

Mercy nodded and continued her search. She thought their conversation might change course, but after sipping again, Mr. Drake asked Matilda, "Why did Miss Payne not come to live here permanently after her parents died?"

"The Thomases wanted her to, but she was . . . oh, sixteen or seventeen by that time and wanted her own way—as most of us do at that age. She replied to a newspaper advertisement and took a position as a lady's companion to a dowager with a taste for travel. After that, the Thomases barely heard from Mary-Alicia for nearly two years, save the occasional dashed-off note from some far-flung destination or other. I suppose you met Mary-Alicia during that period?"

"Yes, I met her in Brighton."

"I imagine she met Mr. Smith on the coast somewhere as well. She wrote to let her grandparents know she'd married an officer she'd met in the course of her travels. He had to ship out, so they'd eloped instead of returning to marry in the church here."

"Of course she married. A pretty girl like her."

Mercy glanced over at that and saw Aunt Matty nod.

She continued, "So Mary-Alicia lived alone in Bristol, awaiting her husband's brief leaves, apparently. Probably accustomed to such a life, growing up with a father in the navy."

"Do you recall Mr. Smith's given name?"

Matilda winced in concentration. "Marion told me once . . . I think it was something with an A. Adam or Alvin, or . . . oh, Alexander. That's it. As in, Alexander the Great."

"Alexander Smith," he repeated thoughtfully.

"Right. And months later, Mary-Alicia wrote again, to let her grandparents know she and her husband were expecting a child, and then again to announce the birth of a daughter. . . ."

Mercy wondered if she should interrupt their conversation as she had before on the street but decided rushing into the room to do so would be rude. Besides, she was curious to hear this part of Alice's background as well.

"Marion hoped her husband would finally allow their granddaughter to visit, as soon as her child was old enough to travel. Instead, Mary-Alicia wrote with the terrible news that her husband's ship had been lost at sea. The *Mesopotamia*, I believe it was. She had to remain in Bristol to await word of any survivors. None came. Again, Marion wanted to invite Mary-Alicia and her child to live with them here in Ivy Hill, but Mr. Thomas refused."

"Why? Was he still so upset about the elopement?"

Aunt Matty nodded again. "In his mind, she'd betrayed them, running off like that. And the man can hold a grudge like a prize bull. In any case, when Mary-Alicia fell so terribly ill, Marion was devastated. Her mind was already slipping by then, but even so she was distraught she'd not been able to help her, had not been with her at the end."

Mr. Drake's voice sounded deeper than usual. "She died in Bristol?"

"Yes. Buried there too." Matilda pressed his hand. "Again, I am sorry. Were you . . . good friends?"

"No." He quickly shook his head. "I had not seen her in years. I did not even remember the name Ivy Hill until I saw it in print recently and it struck a chord. Still, I am sad to learn of her fate."

"Apparently she had been laid low with childbed fever and never fully regained her strength."

"Did the child survive?"

Mercy held her breath. Would her aunt divulge Mr. Thomas's connection to Alice?

"Oh, yes." Matilda smiled. "Hearty and hale since the first time I clapped eyes on her."

"I saw no evidence of a child at the Thomases'."

"Why would you? She—" Her aunt's gaze darted toward Mercy. "That is, Mr. Thomas is a private man, as you've come to realize."

Mercy exhaled in relief.

Mr. Drake studied Matilda's face, speculation written in his expression. "I . . . see." He set down his cup. "Well, Miss Grove, I appreciate your filling me in on what I missed in Mary-Alicia's life. I am only sorry it ended so tragically."

He rose and bowed. "Thank you for the tea and conversation. Now, if you will excuse me, I had better get back to the Fairmont."

Matilda smiled. "You are very welcome, Mr. Drake. Good day."

He stepped into the library and greeted Mercy politely. "I came here with the intention of speaking to you about your charity school, not realizing you would still be busy teaching. Your aunt kindly invited me to take tea with her instead."

"We may talk now, if you like."

"Another time, if you don't mind. The day has got away from me."

"Of course. Another time."

He bowed again, and took his leave.

Mercy watched him go, wondering about Mr. Drake's connection to the former Miss Payne. There was more going on beneath that man's polished surface than he let on.

After the evensong service ended, people began to rise from their pews to greet one another or file out. Mercy remained with the schoolgirls, but Matilda walked over to talk to the Brockwells. Rachel stopped to speak to Jane and then the Ashfords. It was difficult to be friendly with Mrs. Ashford after her comments about the circulating library, but Rachel made an effort for Nicholas's sake.

From the corner of her eye, she noticed Sir Timothy stop in the aisle nearby, politely waiting for a lull in their conversation.

Mrs. Ashford noticed Sir Timothy as well and interrupted Rachel and Nicholas's exchange.

"Sir Timothy, how are you? A lovely service, was it not?"

"Indeed, ma'am."

Rachel and Nicholas turned toward him as well.

"Forgive the intrusion. I simply wanted a word with Miss Ashford, when she has a moment. No hurry."

Rachel said her farewells, noticing a hesitation on Nicholas's part, or perhaps disappointment. He had likely hoped to walk her home.

Sir Timothy stepped closer to her. "I am sorry your conversation was cut short on my account. Miss Matilda said you had something to show me?"

"Oh, yes. The prodigal has returned."

His brow furrowed, then cleared. "Do you mean the missing volume one?"

She nodded.

"Where did you find it?"

"Someone donated it yesterday."

His eyes widened. "You're joking. May I see it?"

"Of course."

"Then, may I walk you back to Ivy Cottage?"

"Yes, if you'd like." She reminded herself that it was only because he wanted to see the book.

He gestured for her to precede him down the aisle. Rachel caught Matilda's eye and signaled that they would go on ahead. Meanwhile, Sir Timothy paused to let his mother and sister know to take the carriage without him, saying that he would see them later at home. Lady Brockwell looked from him to Rachel with a slight frown but said nothing.

As the two descended the church steps together, Rachel saw Nicholas and his mother talking to Mr. and Mrs. Paley. He glanced over as she and Timothy walked by, then looked again, concern evident on his face. How to explain? She sent him a—hopefully—reassuring smile as they passed.

Reaching Ivy Cottage a few minutes later, Sir Timothy opened the front door for her and followed her inside. Rachel picked up a candle lamp from the vestibule table and carried it into the library, dim at this time of evening. There, she lit a second candle from the first, retrieved two books from the Milton set, and handed them to him.

He examined volume one at the desk, then said, "Let's compare the editions." He opened volume two and ran his finger over the publication information, pausing at the Roman numerals printed inside. "See here, both eighth editions and same year published." He looked at her. "What are the chances?"

Rachel shared Matilda Grove's theory that many more people bought the first volume than the rest of the set.

He nodded. "I suppose that makes sense. *Paradise Lost* is better known, whereas the later volumes contain the lesser-known *Paradise Regain'd* and other poems. I don't know if this particular edition was published serially or all at once. You don't know who donated it?"

Rachel shook her head. "I saw a woman pass Ivy Cottage with a bundle under her arm. It was likely her. She wore a hood, so I did not see her face very well. I believe she came down Ebsbury Road from the north. I am not acquainted with anyone who lives up there, as far as I know. Are you?"

He shook his head. "I am familiar with most people in the village, but not everyone beyond it. Especially if they have never appeared before the council or magistrates. I have met a few yeoman farmers who live out that way—the Millers, the Joneses . . ."

"Might your father have lent the book to one of them?"

He looked again at the first volume. "My father often encouraged my siblings and me to read his favorite books, so it is possible, I suppose."

Mrs. Timmons's remark about the "the witch of Bramble Cottage" went through Rachel's mind, but she decided not to repeat it. Instead she asked, "Is the book valuable?"

"It is not an early edition, but books like these are still expensive." Sir Timothy's dark brows knit.

"What is it?" she asked.

"Something about the houses up that way . . . I can't quite remember. Never mind, I shall ask Carville."

"By the way, would you mind letting him know the book has turned up? He asked to be informed."

"Of course."

Sir Timothy remained where he was, his previous distraction fading as he focused on her face. The flickering candle flames reflected in his brown eyes, turning them to warm caramel. Light and shadows played over his handsome face, accentuating his aquiline features.

Her gaze was drawn to his masculine mouth with its full lower lip, and not for the first time, she wondered what it would be like to kiss him. She was glad the darkness hid her blush—and that he could not read her thoughts!

He lowered his voice. "Rachel, may I ask if you and Mr. Ashford . . . That is, if you are not, I—"

Out in the vestibule, the front door opened and banged shut, and chattering voices reached them—the Miss Groves and their pupils returning from the evensong service.

He cleared his throat and stepped back. "Well, I won't keep you. If you find out any more about the person who donated volume one, let me know, will you? Just out of curiosity."

She nodded but didn't trust her voice to speak.

Flickers of that old hope rose in her heart, just as she'd felt awaiting his return to Thornvale for the promised riding lesson. She would be foolish to forget what had happened instead. . . .

Rachel had worn Ellen's riding habit and a new hat, though considering her father's financial problems, which he had just confided, she regretted the purchase. Even so, she was eager to spend time with Timothy again, doing something he loved. She hoped to learn to enjoy riding as well, and to spend many happy hours in his company in the future.

She went outside at the appointed hour, expecting him on horseback. He arrived on foot.

Still, she beamed at him. "Good morning, Timothy."

He did not return her smile.

"Miss Ashford. I am sorry. I said I would come to Thornvale this morning, so here I am, but I am afraid there has been a change of plans."

"Oh. Are you busy? No matter. We shall attempt my lesson another day." She smiled again, inwardly relieved to put off the frightening prospect a little longer.

Then she noticed his tight expression—the flared nostrils and pulsing jaw.

A groom passed by, and seeing him, Timothy gestured for her to precede him into the garden, away from listening ears.

Once there, he said, "I am afraid duties at home will keep me from that original plan. My days of pleasure riding must be curtailed; my time is not my own. I had looked forward to—" His voice hitched, and he pressed his lips together. "But I am not the one to teach you after all. I trust you will find someone else to do so. Someone better suited."

She stared at him, mind slowly freed from its ruts, the cogs beginning to turn, to click through his words—those spoken and those unspoken.

Please, no. . . . Her heart fisted. He was announcing not only the end of their riding lessons before they'd begun . . . but the end of everything else too.

What had happened? Had she done something wrong? Or had Sir Justin learned the news of her father's fall at the quarter sessions? If so, the Brockwells might want to distance themselves before the coming scandal. She could hardly blame them.

But would Timothy really reject her over it . . . ? An icicle pierced her chest, and all her happy buoyancy of minutes before drained away. She felt the tears fill her eyes but tried to blink them back.

He noticed anyway, and his eyes downturned. "Miss Ashford. Rachel." Expression stricken, he reached for her hand, then stopped himself. "I am deeply sorry. It is not what I want. However . . . " His Adam's apple rose and fell. "My father shan't live forever. He has decided it is time I begin learning all I need to know about managing the estate, his magistrate's duties, and everything else the baronetcy entails. He insists that should be my focus for now."

For now . . . ? She looked into his eyes once more, scouring them for any hope of a *later*, but he averted his gaze before she could look too deep.

He made a formal bow. "I wish you every happiness, Miss Ashford. If there is ever anything I can do to help you, please don't hesitate to ask."

Her heart ached, and her pride pricked her. She would be loath to ask Timothy Brockwell for help—not when she had hoped he was about to ask for her hand.

CHAPTER FIFTEEN

After the schoolgirls were in bed later that night, Rachel asked Mercy if she had any idea who the caped woman might be.

Mercy narrowed her eyes in thought. "A black mantle?"

"Yes. I believe she came down Ebsbury Road from the north."

Mercy slowly nodded. "I walk Fanny out that way on Sundays to visit her family. Their farm is just over the crest of the hill."

"Are you acquainted with any other women who live out there?"

"Only the Joneses and the Millers. But I have seen a woman who wears a black mantle in all weather. I had to reprove Fanny because she called the woman a witch."

"That seems harsh, even from Fanny. Though Mrs. Timmons said something similar."

"I agree, though between us, if you had seen how the woman looked in her front garden, stirring a cauldron over the fire with a long stick. And with that black cape, and rather pointed nose . . ."

"Mercy, I'm surprised at you!" Rachel teased. "What was she making—potions and poisons?"

"According to Fanny, yes. But judging by the smell, I would say soap. Not as diabolical, and far more practical."

"How old of a woman is she?"

Mercy shrugged. "Certainly not an old crone. Maybe . . . fifty?"

"What is her name, do you know? I'd like to offer her a subscription."

"I believe it is Mrs. Haverhill, though Aunt Matilda would know for sure."

"If she does, she did not tell me. Although I did ask her when Mrs. Timmons was in the room . . ." And their cook was not the most charitable or discreet person.

Mercy nodded again. "That might explain it."

"Have you not met the woman?"

"No. She keeps to herself, I understand. I don't know that I've ever seen her in Ivy Hill."

"How curious. Hmm." Rachel considered. "I wonder if she likes to read. . . ."

The next day, Rachel decided to walk up Ebsbury Road to see if she could spot this woman outside. If successful, she would try to strike up a conversation. Rachel took a few coins in her reticule, thinking she might ask to buy some soap before raising the topic of a subscription.

As she stepped out of Ivy Cottage, she saw Jane coming up Church Street.

Jane waved. "Rachel, where are you off to?"

Rachel met her at the gate. "To a Mrs. Haverhill's. Do you know her?"

"I have not met her, though I have heard of her. I understand she makes aromatic soaps and sells them at the Wishford market. In fact, I had planned to go out to her place at some point to ask if she might make some soap especially for The Bell."

"I want to offer her a subscription. She recently donated a book to the library. At least I think it was her. I only caught a glimpse of her face."

"Do you mind if I go with you?" Jane asked. "I'd like to meet her as well."

"Of course I don't mind. I would enjoy the company. And I'll feel less nervous about knocking on a stranger's door with you along. Let us hope she does not have a vicious dog."

Together the two friends walked up Ebsbury Road. They crossed Pudding Brook and passed a farmyard, the road narrowing as it ascended Ebsbury Hill. Near the top, they reached a charming cottage, surrounded by a low stone wall. In the large front garden, a cauldron lay tipped on the ground, its iron stand toppled beside the fire, embers still smoking. The garden gate hung open. A stone path led from it to the cottage's front door, which stood open as well. But Rachel saw no one about.

She and Jane exchanged concerned looks and walked tentatively up the path, stepping over a broken flowerpot. On the wall near the door hung a small plaque, partly covered by ivy. *Bramble Cottage.*

"Hello?" Rachel called. "Mrs. Haverhill?"

In reply, an orange tabby mewled and came padding to the open door.

Jane knocked on the frame and repeated more loudly, "Is anyone home?"

Rachel peeked over the threshold. She saw an end table overturned and desk drawers pulled wide, contents spilling forth like a burst seedpod.

What happened here? Instinctively, Rachel stepped back. Whoever had done this might still be near.

"Should we go in?" Jane whispered. "Make sure she isn't . . . hurt or something?"

Fear tightened Rachel's stomach at the thought of the two of them going inside. She looked over her shoulder, hoping to see someone to hail for help—a neighbor or field hand. She noticed a woman in black trudging toward the cottage from the opposite direction—the road that wound around the back way into Wishford. The woman carried a low market basket in her hands.

Looking up, she frowned, then strode forward purposely. "Yes? What do you want?" She stepped through the gate, fair eyes snapping with suspicion.

Rachel pointed. "The door was open when we arrived."

The woman glanced from the tipped cauldron to the broken blue-and-white flowerpot. Two identical pots stood near it, unscathed. Then she looked at the open door, and her mouth gaped in a dark maw. She dropped her basket and ran forward.

Jane and Rachel parted like curtains to let her pass between them and into the house.

Curious and concerned, they watched from the doorway as the woman turned a full circle in the room, surveying the overturned furniture and open drawers, then walked up the stairs, moaning, "No, no, no . . ."

A few moments later, she came back down, expression pained, a handkerchief pressed to her mouth.

She stood there, eyes distant. "The money I could understand, even the ring. But the lover's eye? The mourning locket? Knowing what they mean to me?" A thin, high wail escaped her. She pressed the handkerchief to her lips, her eyes, then held it beneath her nose, as though to stem a flood of emotion.

"Foolish, selfish, hurtful creature," she muttered.

"Mrs. Haverhill," Rachel gently began, "I am dreadfully sorry. Have you been robbed? Can we help you? Truly, you look very ill. May I make you some tea?"

The woman shook her head, her thoughts clearly elsewhere.

"Shall we . . . summon the constable, or the magistrate?" Jane asked. "So they can try to find out who did this?"

The woman looked over as if just recalling they were there. Her body stiffened, and a new emotion crossed her face. Fear?

"Oh. No, I . . . Thank you, but no. Please don't say anything to either the constable or Sir . . . the magistrate. This is my problem. I need no help to determine who did this. Who else knew just where to find everything of value? Who knew I hid a key in that particular flowerpot among those outside?"

"But if you know who did it," Rachel said, "surely you will want to bring that person to justice?"

"Justice?" She laughed bitterly. "Precious little of that in this world. No. There is nothing to be done. Please, don't say a word to anyone in authority, I beg of you. This is a . . . family matter, of a sort. And it must remain that way. Please. I must have your word. I could not live with myself if any harm came to . . . anyone, because of me."

Jane studied her anxious face. "Are you certain?"

"Yes. Perfectly." With one last wipe of her handkerchief, the woman assembled her composure and drew a long breath. "Now that's settled, what did you ladies wish to see me about? Or were you simply passing?"

Rachel regarded the woman more closely. Her nose was a bit prominent, especially red, as it was now, but her eyes were a lovely blue. Rachel said, "I am Miss Ashford. I believe you left a book for me at the new circulating library?"

A wary light shone in those blue eyes. "Is that a problem?"

"No! I appreciate every donation. In fact, I've come to offer you a credit toward borrowing another book, if you have any interest in a subscription." Rachel handed the woman a card with the credit noted.

Mrs. Haverhill accepted it reluctantly. "You needn't have done that. I wished nothing in return. I meant to leave the book anonymously, though obviously I failed. Still, I thank you."

Jane spoke up, "And I am Mrs. Bell. I had hoped to speak to you about possibly making some soap for the coaching inn, but we can discuss that another time."

Mrs. Haverhill nodded. "Yes. Another time I would be happy to speak to you. Perhaps next week. Would you mind returning then? I rarely venture into Ivy Hill."

"Of course. I don't mind at all. I shall stop by some afternoon soon." Jane turned.

Rachel held the woman's gaze. "Are you sure there's nothing we can do? It seems wrong to leave you to face this alone. The local magistrate is a friend of ours. He would want to help you, if he knew."

Mrs. Haverhill shook her head, eyes flat. "No, he would not. Now remember, not a word to him or to the constable."

Rachel blinked. "Very well, if you insist."

Jane took her arm. "Come, Rachel."

They walked away. At the gate, Rachel turned back and saw the woman still standing there, framed by the open doorway, a picture of betrayal and loss.

On the walk back into the village, Rachel slowly shook her head. "Why would she do nothing? Why insist the authorities not be told?"

Jane considered. "She mentioned it was a family matter 'of a sort,' whatever that means. She may not want to get some thieving relative into trouble."

"I suppose. If a prodigal son or daughter sneaked home and stole something to survive . . . She might not want her own child to be sent to prison, or transported."

"Sounds like whoever it was took far more than would be required for mere survival."

"Has she children?" Rachel asked.

"I have never heard of other Haverhills in the area, have you?"

"No. But I had not heard of Mrs. Haverhill until recently either. I know we promised not to report the theft, but do you think it would be all right if we asked Matilda Grove what she knows about Mrs. Haverhill?"

"I think that would be all right. If we don't mention the theft."

Rachel nodded her agreement.

Upon their return, they found Matilda Grove in the sitting room, sewing something.

"Hello, Rachel. And Jane—good to see you again, my dear."

"Hello, Miss Matty. What are you working on?"

She lifted a needle and wad of material. "Just a bit of mending."

Rachel said, "I could have done that—sewing is one of the few ways I can contribute."

"And no doubt you would do it better, but Mrs. Timmons asked me to mend a few aprons. I think she just wanted me out of *her* kitchen."

Jane and Rachel took seats near her, and Rachel began, "Miss Matty, how well do you know Mrs. Haverhill?"

"Ah. Was that who donated the book, after all?"

Rachel nodded, guessing Matilda had suspected as much all along.

"Forgive me for avoiding your questions earlier, but I did not want to mention Mrs. Haverhill in our cook's presence. She tends to say unkind things about her, as you heard. I barely know the woman, actually. I've only spoken to her a handful of times in all the years she has lived here. I took her a cake when she first moved into Bramble Cottage. A few other women tried to welcome her as well, but she invited none of us inside and made it clear she wanted her privacy. Some women were set against her because of it. Or for other reasons. I think Mrs. Snyder is the one who taught her to make soap in recent years, but beyond that she has always wanted to be left alone."

"Has she lived alone all this time?"

"Not exactly. She did have a maid-of-all-work. Bess Kurdle her name was, though she died last year. Bess would come into Ivy Hill on errands for her mistress now and again, but she was not well received—a bit of a troubled past, I gather. Both women preferred to do their shopping in Wishford."

"Yes, Mrs. Haverhill mentioned she rarely ventures into Ivy Hill."

Matilda nodded. "Bess Kurdle had a daughter. I believe she continued to work at Bramble Cottage after her mother passed on."

"How do you know that?"

"Mrs. Burlingame passes the cottage regularly on her route. She's mentioned seeing a younger woman working outside now and again. And apparently she sells Mrs. Haverhill's soap at the Wishford market."

Jane said, "She seemed upset about a . . . family matter. Has she children that you know of? I have never heard of a Mister or a Miss Haverhill, have you?"

Matilda shook her head. "No, there are no other Haverhills in

Ivy Hill. I don't know where she came from originally. London, maybe."

"Was she already a widow when she moved here?"

"Um . . . yes, I believe she was." Matilda rose, her chair scraping across the floor. "Why all these questions? Did you . . . hear something about her?"

"We met her today and are only curious."

"I suppose you offered her a library credit, and she turned it down?"

Rachel looked away. "Well, she took the card, though reluctantly."

Matilda laid a hand on Rachel's shoulder. "Remember what I told you, Rachel. Your chance to help someone in kind may arrive before you know it."

CHAPTER
SIXTEEN

Jane sat on the lodge steps, petting Kipper. Colin walked over, flipping through the day's post. "A letter for you, Mrs. Bell."

Jane accepted it. "Thank you, Colin. By the way, I tried to find you yesterday afternoon. Three post chaises arrived at once, and we needed help."

"Oh. Sorry, Mrs. Bell. I didn't think you'd need me then."

"I didn't either. I know you take a few hours of rest now and again, but do let me know when you leave the property so I know where you are if other unexpected needs arise."

"Very well, ma'am."

When he returned to the inn, Jane glanced at the letter and noticed the vaguely familiar handwriting. It was clearly and emphatically addressed to *Mrs. Jane Bell*. The first name underlined to differentiate from Mrs. Thora Bell, she guessed. From this detail, Jane concluded that the letter was from Hetty Piper. The former chambermaid would not know that Thora had since married and was now Mrs. Talbot.

Jane opened the seal and read:

Dear Mrs. Bell,

Believe me, I did try to find another place, armed with the fine character letter you wrote for me. But Goldie is de-

termined I shall work for no one in Epsom but her and has slandered my name all over town. So I've had no offers—respectable ones, that is.

Does your kind offer of a place at The Bell still stand? If the lioness forbids you to engage me, just say so and I shan't come. If I do come, I promise I shall do my best to keep my distance from her son. Heaven help me.

I must leave it to you to decide whether or not to mention the possibility of my return to Patrick Bell. Don't want him leaving the country again on my account.

I shall await your reply.

—Hetty

Jane had been sincere when she'd offered Hetty Piper a job at The Bell if she could find no decent situation in Epsom. And Thora—who'd sacked the girl when she'd worked there a few years ago—had moved to Angel Farm. So, the "lioness" was no longer involved with the day-to-day management of the inn. But Patrick was. . . .

Jane went looking for her brother-in-law and found him alone in the office. She stepped inside, shut the door behind her, and turned to face him.

He watched her with a raised brow. "That's an ominous beginning."

"I've had a letter that . . . concerns you." It might concern him very much indeed.

"How so?"

"When I was in Epsom a few months ago, I offered a situation to someone, and she has decided to accept."

His eyes narrowed. "Who are we talking about?"

"Hetty Piper."

He reared his head back and leaned hard against the chair. "Why on earth would you offer her a situation here? And why would she want one?"

"John had planned to help her before he died. Now I want to help her in his place. In your place."

"*My* place?"

"She was with child when she left here, Patrick. Do you deny you were . . . involved with her?"

He crossed his arms over his chest. "I don't deny it. I'm not proud of it, but I'm not solely to blame either." He frowned. "You will say I'm vain, but *she* pursued me. She was all eagerness at first, so I had few qualms about . . . proceeding."

He shifted his gaze to Jane. "I am not justifying my behavior, but that is the truth. Did she say otherwise?"

Jane shook her head. "No. She said it wasn't your fault. Not really."

Patrick nodded, visibly relieved. "There, you see? She kept her distance afterward, and I determined to do the same. I thought Mamma was none the wiser. But a few days later, I stepped out into the yard to see Hetty board the upline and disappear. Mamma had paid her fare and sent her packing. And, considering the awkwardness between us, I admit I thought it for the best."

"But she told me she wrote to you to let you know she was with child. Is that why you left the country?"

He threw up his hands. "Should I have married the chambermaid? Mamma would have loved that! I cared for Hetty, but I wasn't ready for that kind of responsibility. And besides, Hetty wasn't as innocent as she may have led you to believe."

"Has that any bearing on the situation?"

"I think it has. If she claims I am responsible. Where is the child now?"

"She said she had to give the child up to work—irrevocably, I assume. Especially when John failed to help her. He planned to. John read one of her letters and, in your absence, felt responsible to help. That was one of the reasons he went to Epsom that day—to meet Hetty. But he was struck down by a carriage before he reached her."

"And I suppose John's death is my fault too."

Jane shook her head. If Gabriel Locke was right, John was killed by the moneylender he failed to repay, though no one could prove it. She said, "No, Patrick. You are innocent where John is concerned, though not where Hetty is concerned." Jane lifted the letter in her hand. "Hetty says that if she returns, she will try to keep her distance from you. Can you say the same?"

"Yes, *Mother*," Patrick archly replied. "I have learned my lesson never fear."

The ire faded from his expression as rapidly as it had appeared, and he heaved a sigh. "I'm sorry, Jane. I behaved badly, I know. But are you sure you want to invite her back?"

"This isn't about what I want—it's about doing the right thing." Jane opened the door and looked back at him. "Don't make me regret it."

Jane returned to the lodge and wrote Hetty a letter of reply, inviting her to come to The Bell at her earliest convenience and enclosing a ticket for her fare.

After church the following Sunday, Mercy walked Sukey Mullins to her home between Ivy Hill and Wishford to spend the afternoon with her parents and brothers. Several of the girls had family near enough to visit, while a few others received calls from relatives in the Ivy Cottage drawing room on the Sabbath. Only two girls, Phoebe and Alice, were left out of this weekly ritual. Phoebe's father was a salesman who traveled a great deal, though at least he visited his daughter every month or so. As far as Alice knew, she was all alone in the world.

When Mercy returned from her escort duty, she was surprised to see a trio seated around the wrought-iron table in the narrow front garden: Aunt Matty, Alice, and Phoebe. The front garden bordered Church Street, with a low stone wall separating their little plot of lawn from the thoroughfare. The girls primarily played in the larger back garden, but Auntie liked to sit in her own little patch of peace on fine afternoons. She had likely felt sorry for the left-out girls and had invited them to join her in what was usually a "family" space.

Knowing it might lead to jealousy, Mercy generally tried to discourage any special attention among her pupils, and to hide her inordinate fondness for Alice from the others. But she could not blame her aunt for wanting to ease the girls' loneliness. Closer now, she noticed tea things as well as sketchpads and pots of paint before them. Matilda sipped tea and encouraged the girls as they painted pictures.

Seeing her approach, Aunt Matty waved. "Such a fine day. Join us!"

"I will—in a minute." Mercy went in the house to lay aside her reticule and fetch another teacup. She exchanged her somber church hat for a broad-brimmed straw bonnet, because the afternoon was quite sunny. Then she returned as promised. As she sat down beside Alice, she noticed Mr. Drake walking down the street.

Aunt Matilda lost no time in greeting him. "Good afternoon, Mr. Drake."

He tipped his hat. "Good afternoon, Miss Matilda. Miss Grove. Girls."

"Do come and join us, won't you?" her aunt offered. "We have an extra cup."

"Ah, you are very kind. But I don't want to intrude."

"Not at all. We like visitors. Don't we, girls?"

Phoebe nodded amiably, but Alice ducked her head, stealing glances at the man from beneath her own straw bonnet. Then she slid from her chair and climbed onto Mercy's lap as she often did.

"How thoughtful, my dear." Aunt Matty smiled at the girl, pulled out the vacated chair with a scrape, and patted its back. "We have a chair right here for you, Mr. Drake."

"Very well, for a few minutes. Thank you."

Mr. Drake entered the front garden and doffed his hat with extravagant flair. "Good day, m'ladies. James Drake, at your service."

The two girls giggled appreciatively.

"Miss Matilda, might you introduce your lovely companions?"

"With pleasure. You know Mercy, of course. But allow me to introduce Miss Phoebe."

"Hello, Miss Phoebe. A pleasure to meet you." He turned toward Alice, ready to greet her in the same manner, Mercy supposed, but his smile faltered as he stared at the little face within the bonnet.

Unaware, Matilda said, "And this is our youngest pupil, Miss Alice."

"Mary-Alicia . . ." he murmured.

The little girl shook her head. "Just Alice."

"Forgive me. I misheard."

Alice looked up at him shyly. "My mamma's name was Mary-Alicia."

"Mary-Alicia Payne—I mean, Smith?"

Alice nodded.

He lifted his chin in understanding. "Ah."

"That's right, Mr. Drake. . . ." Aunt Matty's eyes lit with interest. Mercy tried to nudge her beneath the table, but too late. "You have met Alice's mother. Does Alice resemble her in your view?"

He looked at her again. "Yes. A marked resemblance. That is, if my memory serves. But remember, our acquaintance was brief and many years ago now."

"My mamma died," Alice said, calm but somber.

"Yes, I learned of that sad fact only recently. I was sorry indeed to hear it."

Mr. Thomas would not like that Mr. Drake had unearthed his connection to Alice. But it could not be helped.

"My father died too," Alice added. "When I was a baby."

Mr. Drake nodded, expression grave. "I was sorry to hear that as well." He cleared his throat, then asked, "And how old are you girls?"

"I am ten," Phoebe replied. "And Alice is only eight."

"Good ages, the both of them. And don't worry, Miss Matilda." Mr. Drake winked at her. "I shall not ask you the same question." He turned to Alice again and smiled warmly. "Your mother was a kind and accomplished young woman. As no doubt you will become under Miss Grove's tutelage."

Phoebe's face puckered. "What's tute-ledge?"

Mercy chuckled. "Apparently I have a great deal more to teach."

He briefly returned her smile, then appeared to choose his next words carefully. "I am surprised you did not mention . . . these particular pupils . . . when last we spoke."

With a look at Mercy, Aunt Matty replied, "As I said, our glazier is a very private man."

"Apparently." He looked from girl to girl, his gaze lingering on Alice. "May I see your paintings, ladies?"

Phoebe proudly slid her page of pink and purple flowers toward him.

"Very nicely done," he praised.

Alice more reluctantly showed him her painting—a boat upon blue waves. "My papa's ship before it sunk. He was a brave officer, Mamma said."

"I am sure he was."

When he said nothing more for a few moments, Mercy asked, "Would you like to talk about the charity school while you're here, Mr. Drake?"

He hesitated. "Another time, if you don't mind. I don't wish to overstay my welcome."

"Not at all, Mr. Drake," Aunt Matty assured him. "We are always happy to see you."

He rose. "Thank you, Miss Matilda. Miss Grove. But for now I shall bid you ladies good day. Thank you for the agreeable visit. A pleasure to meet you, Miss Alice and Miss Phoebe." With another bow, he turned and walked away.

Had Mr. Drake once been in love with Miss Payne? Mercy wondered. If so, how strange it must be for him to meet her daughter now and hear about the man she had married instead.

The next day, Rachel returned to Bramble Cottage to check on Mrs. Haverhill. The cauldron was back over the fire, but the broken flowerpot still lay in pieces near the door. She saw no one about, but hearing a spade slicing earth, Rachel followed the sound to the side of the house. There she found Mrs. Haverhill working in a weedy kitchen garden, sparse at autumn's wane. She wore a soiled apron over a plain day dress—no black mantle today. Setting aside the spade, she knelt to rummage through the loosened soil. Extracting several small potatoes, she laid them in a basket next to a few scraggly turnips and one hairy carrot. She glanced up and gasped, pressing a hand to her heart.

"I'm sorry," Rachel said. "I didn't mean to startle you."

"For a moment I thought you were . . . someone else." The woman rose gingerly to her feet, kneading the small of her back. "I'm afraid I'm not exactly dressed for callers."

A scrawny hen bobbed by, pecking at the unearthed insects and clucking appreciatively. "You're welcome, Henrietta." The woman picked up her basket and started toward the front of the house. "What brings you back here today . . . Miss Ashford, was it?"

Rachel followed her. "Yes."

"As I said, you don't owe me anything. The book was not mine—only lent to me."

"Did . . . Sir Justin Brockwell loan it to you?"

The woman's eyes snapped to hers, warily searching Rachel's face. "Yes. Many years ago."

"I thought so. His son donated the other volumes a few weeks ago. I doubted the set would ever be reunited, but then, *voila*, you bring the missing book. What a fortunate coincidence."

The woman shrugged. "Sometimes things are given to us in this life that we think we can keep, only to realize we were wrong."

Chagrin swept over Rachel. "Mrs. Haverhill, I'm sorry. If the book means that much to you, I will return it."

"No, that particular book means little to me. And its return was no coincidence. Mr. Carville came by and asked me about the missing volume. I'd forgotten all about it."

She did not seem remorseful, Rachel noticed, for not returning it to the Brockwells years ago.

Before Rachel could ask another question, the rhythmic thunder of horse hooves reached them. Rachel glanced over and saw a rider approaching. Sir Timothy.

Rachel gestured. "Here comes Sir Justin's son now."

The woman stiffened and looked toward the cottage door as if about to flee. "Did you tell him to come?"

"No, I did not."

Timothy reined in his horse as he neared and tipped his hat. "Afternoon, ladies."

Rachel said politely, "Sir Timothy. Have you met Mrs. Haverhill?"

"I don't believe so. How do you do. I understand we have a mutual acquaintance."

The woman's eyebrows rose. "Yes, though I am surprised he told you."

"Only recently. I was reviewing some old papers and asked about Bramble Cottage. Thought I'd ride over this morning and remind myself what it looked like." He looked past the gate toward the cottage. "Carville mentioned you were lodging here. You and he are old friends, I take it."

"Mr. Carville?"

"Yes. Your landlord?" he added helpfully. "My family used to own this cottage, but my father left it to Carville. I'd all but forgotten."

The woman's face puckered. "What?"

"Don't worry. Carville assures me he has no plans to retire here for the foreseeable future. Which is good news for us both, as you shall keep the cottage and we the only butler Brockwell Court has known in my lifetime. Heaven help us when it comes time to replace him."

The woman's expression transformed from stupefaction to anger. "Sir Justin left this house to his . . . *butler*?"

"Yes. I thought you knew. Did Carville not tell you he owns the place now?"

Mrs. Haverhill's eyes flashed. "I have lived here for more than thirty years."

Confusion flickered over Timothy's face, but he said pleasantly, "Well. Nothing to worry about. Carville said he has no plans to change the current arrangement."

The woman huffed a sigh—in relief, or vexation?

It was on the tip of Rachel's tongue to tell Sir Timothy that it had been Mrs. Haverhill who donated the missing volume. But seeing the woman's expression, Rachel thought the better of it.

Sir Timothy remained a moment longer, perhaps awaiting an invitation to come inside—an invitation that was not forthcoming. "Well, a pleasure to meet you, Mrs. Haverhill. And to see you again, Miss Ashford. Enjoy your visit." He tipped his hat and rode away.

Rachel watched him go, then turned to find the woman staring after him, face pale.

"Are you all right, Mrs. Haverhill?"

She shook her head. "To meet him now of all times, wearing a ragged apron, my hands as black as dirt. And him so well turned out. He looks a great deal like his father."

"Do you think so?"

She nodded. "Don't you?"

"I confess I did not know Sir Justin well. Nor do I remember him very clearly."

"You fortunate girl."

Not knowing how to respond to that, Rachel asked gently, "Do you live alone here, Mrs. Haverhill?"

"I do now."

"Matilda Grove happened to mention your former maid died. I was sorry to hear it."

"Yes, I was sorry to lose her. She was more than a servant to me. She was a close friend."

"And she had a daughter?"

"You *are* well informed. Matilda Grove still has a busy tongue, I see. Yes, after Bess died, her daughter stayed on with me. Turned eighteen this summer. Then one day she went to market and never returned."

"Oh no. Did something happen to her? We should talk to the constable or . . ."

Mrs. Haverhill shook her head. "Something happened to her all right. But nothing illegal. Just so dreadfully foolish."

"What do you mean?"

"She fell in love with a man. Believed his promises."

"When was this?"

The woman shrugged. "Several weeks ago. She often went to the Wishford market to sell my soap and buy what we needed in exchange. That's where she first met the charming scoundrel. Apparently, he travels the southwest of England, selling wares at fairs and markets. He begged Molly to go away with him, promising to marry her. But first he had to persuade his family to accept her. I tried to warn her that men make promises they can't keep, even if they mean to at the time. I told her not to leave home with no guarantee—no vows, no license, no ring. She waved off my concerns. Said there would be time for all of that later. I hope she is right. But I doubt it."

"You've had no word?"

Mrs. Haverhill shook her head again. "I think I would have heard if she had married. I think she might even visit me. If for no other reason than to prove she'd been right and I'd been wrong. But I've heard nothing. Unless one counts . . . this." She gestured toward the pieces of broken pottery she had yet to discard.

"You think she did this?"

The woman winced. "She might have, if she were desperate enough. Hungry enough. Though my guess is that he did it. She trusted him and probably told him where I kept my key and few remaining valuables. I doubt I'll ever know for sure."

"I am sorry, Mrs. Haverhill. Is there anything I can do? Anything you need? I haven't much money, I'm afraid. But—"

"No, don't concern yourself, Miss Ashford. Thank you for your call, but I will be all right on my own."

Was the woman too proud to admit she needed help? Rachel could empathize with that but still wished there was something she could do.

CHAPTER SEVENTEEN

The next day, Mr. Basu led a gentleman into the sitting room.

Mercy looked up, surprised to see the man again so soon. "Mr. Drake."

"I've returned about the charity school you propose, since I had to rush off when last I was here."

"That is very kind of you. Please, be seated. You know I would have happily come to you at the Fairmont."

"That's all right." He took a chair near hers. "I thought I might better understand what you have in mind by seeing your present school. That is, if you don't object?"

"Not at all. Though what I propose is on a larger scale than my small private school here. As I wrote to you, I believe there is great need for a school that would educate both boys and girls, regardless of their ability to pay."

"Though someone must pay for it. Hence your letter to me and, I assume, to several others?"

"Yes, of course."

He leaned forward, his expression alert with friendly challenge. "I am a man of business, Miss Grove. How would you convince me that such an endeavor is a worthwhile investment?"

"An excellent question. I do not believe the school is merely selfless charity to the deserving poor. Investment is exactly what it is—you have hit upon it. An investment in the future of Ivy Hill. The children I hope to educate will become, in a few years' time, highly qualified potential staff for the Fairmont and other local businesses. And more broadly speaking, education will lead to better paying jobs and higher incomes for many families. Families who might then be able to afford a nice dinner at, say, a hotel, now and again."

He slowly shook his head, eyes alight. "You have missed your calling, Miss Grove. You ought to have been a politician. Or a revolutionist."

"I hope I am, in my small way. I believe every person should be able to read and write, understand the history of this great empire, and manage finances to better provide for one's family. I think education is vital, whether one works as a laborer, or in service, or anything else. We are not brute beasts. We are created in the image of God with intelligence and creativity, to do good on this earth for our fellow man."

His mouth quirked in . . . amusement?

Defensiveness pricked her. "You are laughing at me."

He raised his hands. "No, not at all. I am impressed. I rarely see such passion—it is rather affecting, honestly. Now, why don't you show me your school here and describe how you envision the proposed charity school."

"Very well." She rose, and he followed suit.

She led him up the stairs. "The girls are outside at present, so I will take you up to the dormitory first." She showed him the sleeping quarters, the tidy narrow beds, dressing chests, and communal washstands, then took him down to the large and bright schoolroom, pointing out the desks, slates, wall maps, globes, primers, and other books.

"An excellent room. Far better than the dim, musty boarding school I attended as a lad."

"Oh?" She watched his profile with interest. "Not a good experience, I take it?"

He shook his head. "I still have the advertisement that convinced my father. '*Adamthwaite Academy offers liberal instruction with domestic comfort, suitable for gentlemen or men of business. No holidays.*'" He smirked. "Liberal discipline, more like. Dreadful place. We were not allowed to return home to keep us from telling what life was really like there."

"Could you not write to your parents?"

"I did. Once. My father wrote back and said my complaints only proved I was weak and needed a firm hand to guide me. He said discipline would be the making of me."

Pity and indignation filled Mercy. "Dreadful is right. Rest assured there will be no mistreatment allowed in the charity school. Nor is anyone ill-used here—you may ask the pupils yourself, if you like. Here parents are free to visit, and most of the girls spend Sunday afternoons with their families and are, for the most part, eager to return."

"But not Miss Phoebe or Miss Alice?"

She was impressed he remembered both their names. "Phoebe's father travels a great deal for his work but visits when he can. And Alice is . . ."

"On her own," he supplied.

"Well, she has me." Mercy smiled self-consciously, then hastened to add, "And Aunt Matty and the other girls, of course. She is not alone."

He nodded thoughtfully, and the two returned downstairs. She led him to the back window and gestured to the garden where the girls played. "The pupils spend time outside daily, when the weather allows. I believe fresh air, play, and exercise do a world of good for body and mind."

"I agree."

Shepherded by Anna, the girls came dashing in, and most darted curious looks at Mr. Drake as they passed. Phoebe and Alice brought up the rear. Mercy saw recognition cross Alice's face, and Phoebe greeted him.

"Good day, Mr. Drake."

"Miss Phoebe, a pleasure to see you again. And Miss Alice."

The girls bobbed curtsies, then hurried away to stow their

bonnets and gloves. Alice looked over her shoulder at the man before turning the corner.

"What polite young ladies. Well done, Miss Grove."

"Thank you. Now, have you any other questions I may answer for you?"

A short while later, he took his leave, armed with a copy of the detailed plan and projected expenses she had prepared for Lord Winspear. He promised to review the information but felt confident she could count on his support.

So why did she feel illogically troubled?

Later that day, Rachel looked out the library window. A smart-looking curricle pulled by matched bays drew up in front of Ivy Cottage, Justina Brockwell at the reins, her brother beside her, and a young groom on the back. With a little ache, Rachel recalled again her last ride with this pair.

Sir Timothy gave his sister a hand down, handed the reins to the groom, and strode to open the library door.

Justina entered, beaming. "Hello, Rachel. Timothy brought me a subscription card, but I had to see this for myself. A circulating library? How novel!" The girl's dimples blazed. "I have been waiting to use that quip ever since I heard!"

Rachel grinned. "You are most welcome, Justina. Please make yourself comfortable and browse all you like."

"Perhaps you might direct me to the romances?" Justina waggled her eyebrows.

"Of course. Those shelves there."

Justina stepped away to look, but Sir Timothy lingered near the desk.

"By the way," he began, "I was surprised to see you paying a call at Bramble Cottage. Have you known Mrs. Haverhill long?"

"No, I met her only recently. She . . . came to the library," Rachel hedged, not sure she wanted to be the one to raise suspicions in his mind. "I was surprised to see you there as well."

He nodded. "You mentioned Ebsbury Road when we talked. Later, I went home and searched through my father's papers. I remembered something in his will about a property out that way, but I had so much to deal with when he died, that I didn't question it at the time. It is not unusual to leave some small bequest to a loyal old retainer, but to leave Carville a house and plot of land—one not even on our own estate? It seemed somewhat strange to me."

"Perhaps he has some family connection to the cottage, and that is why your father left it to him?"

"If so, he didn't mention it to me."

"Miss Ashford?" Justina called. "Have you anything by Mrs. Roche?"

Rachel excused herself to help Justina locate novels by that author and returned to the desk a few moments later. The library door opened again, and she and Timothy both turned as a man entered—Carville himself.

"Hello, Carville," Sir Timothy said. "What brings you here?"

"I saw the curricle outside and presumed one of the family must be here."

"Excellent timing. We were just talking about you."

"Indeed, sir?"

"Yes. Miss Ashford and I stopped by Bramble Cottage recently and met your lodger."

"Why on earth would you do that, sir?" The older man's face stretched with incredulity.

"Simple curiosity. Miss Ashford was just asking if you had some boyhood connection to Bramble Cottage?"

"No, sir."

"I notice we still pay taxes on the place. I assume you receive rent from Mrs. Haverhill?"

"Not as such. She hasn't much and . . ." With a glance at Justina across the room, he lowered his voice. "That is, she is an . . . old friend. In her debt, so to speak."

"Ah . . ." Timothy murmured, but his brow remained furrowed.

Carville shifted uncomfortably and looked at Rachel. "I understand the missing volume has been returned?"

"Yes, it has. Thank you."

The old man grimaced. "My fault. I loaned her the book years ago and failed to see to its return before now."

"Her? It was Mrs. Haverhill who donated the book?" Sir Timothy looked at Rachel in surprise.

"Mm-hm." Guilt pricking her, she did not quite meet his gaze.

He watched her a moment longer. "Well, I suppose there is no harm done. At least the volumes are now reunited."

The butler turned to Rachel. "May I see it?"

She gave the book to him, and he flipped through the pages. "Yes, all is as it should be." He closed the cover. "Then, if you will excuse me. Duty calls."

"Can we offer you a lift, Carville?" Timothy offered. "Though you would have to share the groom's seat."

"No, thank you, sir." The butler's raised nose indicated such a position would be beneath his dignity.

Timothy watched him go. Then, glancing at Justina to be sure she was occupied, he said quietly, "I wonder if this Mrs. Haverhill is Carville's . . . well, a woman he might have married if he were not required to live in Brockwell Court to carry out his duties. Or perhaps a poor relation, living on his charity, and ours, as it turns out. Because when I went through the accounts more closely, I found that we have not only been paying taxes, but also for coal and candles for years."

A different conclusion whispered itself in Rachel's mind, but she kept it to herself. A look at Timothy's set jaw told her he was not ready to hear it.

CHAPTER EIGHTEEN

The temperature had grown unexpectedly warm that late autumn afternoon, almost uncomfortably so. Jane opened The Bell's ground-floor doors, hoping a little air circulation would cool off the interior.

As she propped open the front door, she saw Thora and Talbot rattling up the High Street in their cart. Jane waved, her heart lifting to see them. She hoped they would have time to stop and talk.

Talbot slowed his horse and halted nearby.

"Hello, Mr. and Mrs. Talbot." Jane grinned with teasing relish. "And how is the newly wedded couple?"

Thora bit back a smile. "Still getting used to that name, though I admit I like hearing it."

Talbot said, "Thought we'd visit, if you have time. Perhaps over tea?"

"Of course! I would enjoy that."

"Good. We'll just take Gert here into the yard and join you shortly."

"Wonderful. I'll let Patrick know you are here."

"Walk on," Talbot called to his old horse, and the cart moved forward, turned through the tall carriage archway, and disappeared into the courtyard.

Jane walked back inside the inn. She poked her head into the office to let Patrick know his mother and Talbot were there, then crossed to the side window, watching as ostlers Tall Ted and old Tuffy hurried forward, all smiles, to greet the couple and take charge of their horse and cart.

Jane didn't see Colin McFarland anywhere about, which worried her. He had been scarce lately—preoccupied. Was he sneaking off again to help at his parents' farm? Or was it something else that kept him from his duties? She would have to broach the subject with him soon, though she didn't look forward to the confrontation. For now, she would enjoy a visit with her mother-in-law and her new husband, the inn's former manager turned gentleman farmer.

A short while later, the four of them were seated together in the coffee room at Jane's favorite table near the front window.

"How are things here?" Thora began. "Everything all right?"

"Yes. I think so." Jane glanced at Patrick for confirmation.

He obliged with a nod. "Revenue is up. So that's a good thing. And we've hired a farrier."

"Oh?" Thora looked at Jane. "No word from Mr. Locke?"

Jane shook her head. Gabriel Locke had gone back to his uncle's horse farm, and she had given up hope he might return.

She said, "You know Jake Fuller had been filling in. His grown son, Tom, recently married a local girl and moved back to Ivy Hill, so we have hired him on."

"How is that going?"

"Good. Everyone likes Tom."

Everyone except Athena, Jane thought. Hopefully her horse would get used to the new man in time.

Jane added, "The Kingsleys have finished their work in the dining parlour. You'll have to take a look before you go. But they'll be back, hopefully soon, to work on the stables. Mr. Kingsley plans to start on that after he finishes his current projects at the Fairmont and Ivy Cottage."

"Ivy Cottage? What is he doing there?"

Jane described Rachel's new circulating library, and the old Fairmont bookcases Kingsley had refit for her. Jane was relieved to find she felt no bitterness, but was instead glad that her father's library shelves were being put to such a good use—to hold Sir William's books. The two men had been friends, and her father would like that, she thought.

"Yes, we heard about the library." Talbot nodded approvingly. "Good for her."

Thora asked, "How much longer will the work at the Fairmont take? I thought it would be completed by now."

"Mr. Drake thought so as well. But everything is taking longer than anticipated."

Patrick *tsk*ed. "What a pity."

"That is often the case," Talbot said. "Especially with a big project like that, and on such an old building."

Jane nodded. "He says every time they try to move a wall or add on, they find underlying structural problems, rot, water damage, or something else to repair before they can continue."

"Bad news for him, but good news for us—or rather for you," Thora clarified. "Don't worry—I realize the inn isn't my concern any longer."

Jane held her gaze. "I know you will always care about The Bell, Thora. And I'm glad of it."

"I did not see Colin McFarland when we arrived," Thora said. "Any improvement there?"

Jane exchanged a quick look with Patrick, then shifted. "He is doing well, Thora. Thanks for asking. But let's not talk about business now. I want to hear all about your wedding trip."

Thora waved a dismissive hand. "Oh, it wasn't anything extravagant. First we spent several days with my sister and her husband in Bath. Talbot had never been."

Jane noticed Thora still called him Talbot, as most everyone did. She supposed after working together so long, the habit was deeply ingrained.

He nodded. "Beautiful city."

"Then we toured the Somerset countryside and ended at the coast. I have always wanted to see the coast."

"Sounds lovely," Jane agreed.

"We couldn't stay away from the farm too long," Talbot explained. "But the hired men watched over things for us, and Sadie came in to cook for them and help out as needed so we could get away."

"Did you enjoy yourselves, I hope?"

"I liked having Thora to myself, away from chores and our daily responsibilities." Talbot looked at his wife. "I hope you enjoyed it as well?"

"I did. Though it seemed strange to be idle, and not to be here in Ivy Hill. But I liked showing Talbot around Bath and exploring the countryside and coast together. But oh, the state of some of the inns we stayed in! We could have taught them a thing or two."

Talbot winked. "But we resisted, didn't we."

"Barely."

Thora smiled at Talbot, and Jane was touched to see the warm fondness shining in her eyes.

"Yes, we had a lovely time together," Thora said. "But I for one am glad to be home. In my new home." She clasped Talbot's hand where it rested on the table, and tears bit Jane's eyes at the rare display of affection from her stoic mother-in-law.

Patrick had been strangely quiet during the meal, and Jane wondered why. Was he worried about something—about Hetty? Afraid Jane would mention the maid in his mother's presence? Jane decided not to raise the subject, not on Thora's first visit back to The Bell in several weeks.

Thora seemed to notice Patrick's reserve as well and directed her curious gaze at her son. "And you, Patrick? Anything new with you?"

From the corner of her eye, Jane noticed a woman walk past the window and hesitate at the inn's open front door.

She rose. "Excuse me a moment. I think someone is coming in."

"I'll go, Jane," Patrick offered.

"No, you stay and fill your mother in on all she has missed. Don't forget the one-man band and the family of ten who insisted on sharing one room."

Leaving Patrick to describe the interesting guests they'd hosted recently, Jane walked to the front desk to greet the prospective customer.

The woman, wearing a black hooded mantle, stepped into the entry hall. How hot she must be in all that dark material on the unseasonably warm day. She lowered the hood and Jane recognized Mrs. Haverhill. Jane had not seen the woman since she and Rachel visited Bramble Cottage. On that day, Mrs. Haverhill had been distressed and agitated after the theft, hurrying about to inspect her losses. Today, she possessed a quiet determination. Her complexion was more pale than Jane recalled, and she looked sad and almost . . . desperate as she approached the booking desk.

"Good day, Mrs. Haverhill," Jane began. "Things have been busy here, and I haven't had a chance to return about the soap. So thank you for coming to see me."

"That is not why I've come."

"Oh. Then how may I help you?"

The woman winced and pressed a hand to her temple.

"Are you all right, Mrs. Haverhill?"

"Just a touch of headache. The sun . . ."

"Yes, a warm day for autumn." Jane eyed the woman's layers of black clothing. "You are in mourning, I take it? I hope you don't mind my asking. I am a widow as well and wore bombazine myself until recently, so I empathize."

"Yes, I am in mourning," she replied briskly. "Tell me, how much is the fare to London?"

Jane shifted into her professional role. "Well . . . you have two main options—stage or mail." She gathered the appropriate printed timetables and laid them on the desk. "Here are the schedules and corresponding fares. You can see that going by Royal Mail coach is the fastest. But it is more expensive as well."

"My goodness," Mrs. Haverhill breathed. "Fares have certainly risen since last I traveled."

"Oh, and when was that?"

"Thirty years ago."

"Yes, I suppose prices are shocking, then. Though I am happy to report the roads and the coach springs have improved greatly in thirty years as well."

Mrs. Haverhill took a step back. "It was probably a foolish notion anyway."

"Did you *need* to go to London for some reason?" Jane asked. "If there is a family emergency or illness, perhaps you might . . . pay me as you can?"

The woman shook her head. "I have no family. At least, none who would receive me. I have a brother I thought might . . . But no. It was probably an unrealistic idea. Be glad you are a widow, Mrs. Bell."

Jane looked at her in confusion. "I don't understand."

"Never mind. Thank you for your kind offer, but I have changed my mind."

"Are you certain? Do let me know if you reconsider."

The woman's pale countenance took on a grey pallor, and she seemed to sway.

Jane stepped around the desk. "Mrs. Haverhill, are you unwell? Why do you not sit down a moment?"

"I have troubled you long enough. Good day."

She turned and walked unsteadily across the entry hall. One moment she was framed in the open doorway, the next, she crumpled to the ground.

"Mrs. Haverhill!"

At her cry of alarm, Thora, Talbot, and Patrick came rushing out of the coffee room.

Jane called, "Quick, go find Dr. Burton!"

Thora knelt beside the woman. "I think she has only fainted. Patrick, run to Fothergill's for some salts. That will be quicker. If he thinks she needs a physician, you can ride for him then."

Already the woman shifted, her face contorting and eyelids fluttering. "No doctor," she muttered. "Don't have the . . . Don't need one."

"Shh . . . lie still," Thora soothed. "Everything's all right."

A few minutes later, Patrick returned, the apothecary on his heels.

Mr. Fothergill knelt at the woman's other side and swept a vial beneath her nose. Her face wrinkled, and she pushed it away.

Thora rolled her eyes. "She's already come to, Mr. Fothergill, but thank you."

Jane said, "Add the salts to our account, if you please. We will keep some on hand, just in case."

"I should still examine her."

Thora rose to her feet. "Then, let's carry her into a private parlour. No need to make her a spectacle."

Talbot and Patrick carried the woman, who protested at being lifted, and laid her on a padded bench in the private parlour. There Mr. Fothergill felt her pulse, looked into her eyes, and asked her questions about her symptoms. After a few minutes, he decided she was in no imminent danger but said she should not be alone for a few days, until she felt herself again. Rest, fluids, and wholesome meals were his prescription. And if she was still not well after that, Dr. Burton should be consulted.

"You will stay here," Jane said, recalling the woman lived alone and had no family nearby.

Mrs. Haverhill shook her head. "I could not."

"Of course you can. You heard Mr. Fothergill. You are not to be on your own. And don't worry. We have a few rooms open at present, so you are welcome to stay at no charge."

"Why are you being kind to me? You won't be, not when you hear . . ."

Hear what? Jane thought but said only, "Shh. We'll talk later." She shot Thora a questioning look, but Thora's expression told her nothing.

Mrs. Haverhill was able to get to her feet with help, and Thora and Talbot each took an arm and helped her up the stairs. Jane led the way and opened the door to the first empty room. There Talbot excused himself and said he would ask Mrs. Rooke to send up an invalid tray.

"First, let's get you out of these heavy clothes," Thora said. "You must be sweltering. No wonder you fainted. And a cool bath, I think."

"Good idea." Jane had noticed that Mrs. Haverhill, though genteel in appearance, carried a less than fresh odor. "I'll ask Alwena and Ned to bring the tub."

A short while later, the bath had been delivered and filled, and the chambermaid and potboy had gone, though not without casting curious looks at their unusual guest. Privacy restored, Jane and Thora helped Mrs. Haverhill off with her dress and petticoat. As they began unlacing her long stays, Thora hesitated and met Jane's gaze with a long look of concern. The woman's skin was deeply creased from the boning, even through the thin fabric of her shift.

"Mrs. Haverhill," Thora asked, "how long have you been wearing these?"

The woman hung her head, clearly embarrassed. "Since my young maid left. I couldn't get out of them myself."

"When was that?"

"Several weeks ago now."

"You poor thing," Jane murmured.

They helped the woman bathe, wash her hair, and slip into an old nightdress left by a guest weeks ago, laundered but not reclaimed. "This will do for now," Thora said. "It's clean at least."

Jane offered, "I can ride out to your house later, Mrs. Haverhill, and fetch some of your own clothes, if you like."

The woman hesitated. "I am afraid I have fallen behind in washing my things. I am still learning to do for myself."

"I understand," Jane said. "Mrs. Snyder launders all my clothes. I would be lost without her."

They got the woman into bed and insisted she drink the broth and eat the custard Alwena brought up. Finally, Mrs. Haverhill nodded off.

Leaving the woman to sleep, they tiptoed out of the room, and found Alwena hovering in the corridor.

"What is it, Alwena?" Jane asked.

The maid's eyes were large. "Mrs. Rooke put up a fuss. Said she did not want to cook for 'her sort.' What did she mean? Is that woman a . . ." She mouthed the taboo word *prostitute*. "You could lose your license!"

Thora frowned. "Mrs. Haverhill is our guest, Alwena. That is all you or Mrs. Rooke need concern yourselves with. But I will tell you right now that she is not . . . that . . . and never has been. I will tell Mrs. Rooke the same before I go. I know I speak for Mrs. Bell as well when I say that we—*she*—will brook no such slander of anyone under her roof."

"Very true." Jane nodded, though inwardly her thoughts whirled. If Lord Winspear heard a known woman of ill-repute was lodging in The Bell, he would not hesitate to summon her on charges of keeping a disorderly house.

"Go on, Alwena. Back to work. The dining parlour will not sweep itself." Jane waited until the girl had trudged down the stairs before turning to Thora, eyebrows high.

Thora took her arm and led her down the passage, out of earshot of their new guest or anyone eavesdropping at the bottom of the stairs.

"Thora . . ." Anxiety filled Jane. "What is it? Do you know more than you've said? Are you acquainted with her?"

"Not really. She has always kept to herself. But I don't want you to be ignorant, Jane."

"She isn't . . . what Alwena said, is she?"

"No. Not as far as I know. But you may have to defend your decision to invite her to stay here. There were rumors about her when she first moved here some thirty years ago. And people have long memories."

"What sort of rumors?"

"Oh, you know how people gossip. An attractive woman living on her own, and young at the time. How could she afford it? And why was a certain man from Brockwell Court seen going up Ebsbury Road more often than before? She didn't help her case, refusing invitations, being aloof to those who called and tried to befriend her."

Jane wanted to ask who the man was, but didn't want to appear the gossip. Instead she said, "That is not a crime."

"In Ivy Hill it is," Thora snapped. "You know I have never joined the charity guild or the Ladies Tea and Knitting Society, so I am not privy to all the village gossip. But if even *I* heard speculation about the woman . . . well, I just want you to be prepared. I think you did a kind and Christian thing in offering to care for her for a few days. I just don't want you to be caught unaware if others grumble."

"Thank you, Thora." Jane thought of something. "Would you and Talbot do me a favor?"

"Of course."

"Would you mind stopping by Ivy Cottage on your way home and discreetly letting Rachel Ashford know Mrs. Haverhill is here? We called on her together, and I think she would want to know."

"Happily. It is barely out of our way at all events. Would you like to write a note, or shall I work out a way to talk to her in private?"

"You may simply call in to see her new library. Perhaps even become a subscriber while you're there."

"I know Talbot plans to." Thora straightened. "We shall take our leave as soon as I have a word with Mrs. Rooke. That is, if you don't mind?"

"No, please do."

Thora nodded. "Send Colin or one of the ostlers out to the farm if you need help with Mrs. Haverhill. Or anything else."

"Thank you, Thora. I will."

Jane hoped she would not regret asking Mrs. Haverhill to stay.

CHAPTER NINETEEN

The library door opened, and Rachel looked up from her desk. Nicholas stepped inside, a vase of flowers in his hands.

"Good afternoon, Miss Ashford." He gave her a rueful smile and handed her the flowers. "I remembered a vase this time."

"That was not necessary, but very thoughtful. Thank you."

She set it on the desk and positioned it to best effect while he selected a periodical.

"I've come to read the newspapers—and to see you in the bargain, if you don't mind."

"Of course not. You are very welcome."

He smiled at her, then sat down nearby with the latest copy of the *Salisbury Journal*.

In the adjacent reading room, members of the Ladies Tea and Knitting Society were engaged in a heated debate over *Waverley*, the novel they had all read. Rachel watched the proceedings through the open doorway.

Charlotte Cook shut her copy with a snap. "I found the main character insufferable—an insipid young man. And the narrator rattles on and on."

Judith Cook nodded. "Yes, I am quite of your opinion."

Mrs. Barton shook her head in disgust. "All those strange spellings for dialect. I could barely make out a word. I tried reading it aloud to my bossies, and their milk curdled on the spot!"

Rachel suppressed a laugh. She met Nicholas's gaze over the newspaper and found him grinning.

"Might you be exaggerating a little, Bridget?" Mrs. O'Brien asked.

"A very little."

Mrs. Klein pressed a hand to her heart. "Oh, but when the author describes the picturesque Highlands and bonny Flora playing the Scottish harp near a waterfall . . . I was completely transported." She sighed. "It was all so delightfully romantic."

Judith Cook nodded. "Yes, I am quite of your opinion."

Nicholas and Rachel shared another smile.

He set aside the newspaper and joined her at the desk. "Miss Ashford, will you come to Thornvale tonight and have dinner with us?"

Rachel hesitated. She would enjoy visiting dear Thornvale again, though being there would be bittersweet—especially with Mrs. Ashford on hand to remind her she was no longer its mistress.

"Thank you for the invitation, Nicholas. I—"

The door opened, and Mr. and Mrs. Talbot entered.

"Excuse me a moment."

Jane's mother-in-law took her aside and told her about Mrs. Haverhill's collapse. Rachel thanked her, promising to visit later that afternoon. Mr. and Mrs. Talbot both signed up for subscriptions while they were there, and she thanked them for that as well.

When they left, Rachel approached Nicholas. "I am sorry, but the Talbots brought news—I am needed at the inn this evening. Perhaps another time?"

"Of course. I will hold you to it."

As soon as she closed the library that day, Rachel put on bonnet and gloves and walked to The Bell.

Jane greeted her warmly. "Thank you for coming, Rachel. We are busy this afternoon, and I can't spend as much time with her as I'd like."

She led Rachel up to the woman's room. Jane knocked and poked her head inside. "Mrs. Haverhill? Rachel Ashford has come to see you, all right?"

"Yes. Of course."

Rachel stepped inside, and Jane closed the door gently behind her.

Mrs. Haverhill looked tidier than when Rachel had last seen her dirty and perspiring in her garden. But she looked markedly peaked.

"Miss Ashford. How good of you to come. My, my, your third call on me in a week's time. I don't know why you and Mrs. Bell are so kind to me, but I am grateful. Although it is difficult for me to . . . accept charity."

"That I understand." Rachel smiled and sat in a chair beside the bed. "Are you feeling better? I was sorry to hear you fell ill."

"I suppose everyone knows . . . and is spreading the news of my mortification."

"Not at all. Jane simply sent word through her mother-in-law. I believe Thora was on hand when you . . . when the incident occurred?"

"Yes. She was kind as well. Surprisingly so. I've heard enough about Thora Bell over the years to expect a harsh taskmaster, but I suppose I should know better than anyone not to believe everything one hears about someone."

"Thora does have a stern reputation." Rachel glanced around the room—it was much nicer than she would have guessed. "Would you like me to let anyone know where you are?"

"No."

"You have no way to reach your young maid? Perhaps if she knew you were ill . . ."

"No. I don't have her direction. Nor do I believe Molly would come back. Not now."

"I am sorry. Is Molly's father gone as well?"

"He's long gone. He was sent to prison for poaching and died before the year was out. Bess had just given birth to Molly and was bound for the workhouse. A terrible fate, especially for a mother. Thankfully one of the magistrates took pity on her and spared her. Asked me to take Bess on as my maid-of-all-work. I agreed. An unusual situation, but it suited us. Little Molly grew up in Bramble Cottage, on her mother's hip as she cooked. Or playing with her few homemade toys on the floor . . ." Tears filled the woman's eyes, and she swiped at them with the back of her hand.

Mrs. Haverhill sucked in a breath. "Oh no!" She looked earnestly at Rachel and sat up straight. "You have been to my house. You know what happened there. I must ask you to do me a favor."

Rachel hesitated. Would she regret agreeing? The woman seemed a bit unstable. She swallowed. "If I can."

Mrs. Haverhill grasped Rachel's hand. "Would you go to my cottage and see to Mr. Nesbitt, make sure he is all right?"

Rachel blinked. "Mr. Nesbitt?"

"He'll try to escape, but don't let him."

"Mr. Nesbitt is your . . . ?"

"My cat. Mrs. Bell is so busy, I hate to ask her. But he has never been left alone so long before."

Rachel smiled in relief. "I will be happy to do that."

A knock sounded, and Jane nudged the door open with a tray. "I've brought you two some tea."

"Thank you, Mrs. Bell. Very thoughtful." Mrs. Haverhill settled back against her pillows. "And your friend Miss Ashford is a godsend. She has offered to go to Bramble Cottage and check on my cat for me. I'm afraid he will be out of food, but if he has enough water, he'll be all right for another day or two . . . hopefully."

Jane set down the tray on the bedside table. "Do you know, I have a cat myself. I've been saving some kipper for him, but he's so overfed, he can go without tonight. Rachel, you take it for . . . ?"

"Mr. Nesbitt," Rachel supplied.

Mrs. Haverhill sighed. "Thank you, Mrs. Bell, that is a worry off my mind."

Rachel asked, "Is there anything else you need me to bring back for you while I'm there? Brush, tooth powder? Or a book, perhaps?"

"Mrs. Bell has generously provided all I need. Just make sure my cat is looked after. That's all I ask."

"May I have the key?"

"It is in another blue-and-white pot. I placed it where the broken one stood."

"You put the key back where it was?" Rachel blinked in disbelief. "After someone who knew where it was used it to break in?"

The woman shrugged and avoided their gazes, not attempting to explain. Rachel's heart twisted to see how much the lonely woman hoped young Molly would return. Mrs. Haverhill would clearly welcome her with open arms. Even now.

Rachel stayed long enough to take tea with the woman, keeping the conversation light after that, and then excused herself. Downstairs, she found Jane in the office.

Jane handed over a wrapped dish of the promised kipper and walked Rachel out.

"We're expecting a large party shortly, or I would go to Bramble Cottage with you. But don't go alone, all right? Take Mercy or Mr. Basu—just in case whoever broke in the first time decides to come back."

Rachel shivered. "I admit the prospect of going in alone is a little daunting."

Jane held the door for her. "No wonder, seeing the state of the place. Ah. There's Timothy. I am sure he will help you on your mission of mercy."

Rachel looked over sharply. Sure enough, there came Sir Timothy toward them, only steps away.

"Mission of mercy?" he echoed, looking from Jane to Rachel. "Of course I would be happy to help, if I am needed."

"That is all right," Rachel demurred. "You needn't come with me."

"I think it would be a good idea," Jane insisted. "An empty house and all."

"An empty house?" His face puckered in confusion.

"She is going to Bramble Cottage to bring a gift to Mr. Nesbitt." Jane tapped the dish for emphasis.

"Who?"

Rachel gave him an apologetic look. "I shall explain on the way."

Together they walked up Ebsbury Road until they reached the cottage. There, Rachel found the key in the pot, unlocked the door, and opened it. She had expected the sour smell of cat or worse, but instead a pleasant aroma of dried flowers and spices greeted them.

Rachel was relieved to see Mrs. Haverhill had restored some order to the room, at least picking things off the floor and righting the furniture, though a pile of papers still lay in a jumble on the sofa, a few drawers remained open, and an old wardrobe, apparently used as a coat closet, stood ajar, a wad of cloaks, shawls, and muffs shoved back inside and not quite closing. Rachel did not explain the disarray. She would not incriminate young Molly Kurdle and betray Mrs. Haverhill in the process.

"Rather cluttered," he observed, hands clasped behind his back. "Looks like she was trying to find something in a hurry."

Rachel murmured a noncommittal "Mm-hm."

They walked slowly, quietly, around the ground level, ostensibly looking for the cat. The main room held a fireplace, sofa, and armchair on one side, and on the other, a modest dining table, chairs, and sideboard. A mourning wreath hung on the wall.

Rachel noticed a pair of masculine spectacles on an end table beside a thick book, though perhaps they were Mrs. Haverhill's. In one of the open drawers, Rachel saw a finely carved pipe. In another, a single leather glove that looked too large to be a woman's. Following the direction of her gaze, Timothy asked, "And what do we know about Mr. Haverhill?"

"I did not ask. I believe she has been on her own for a long time."

She waited, but he said nothing further. She wondered if he still suspected she might be Carville's paramour.

At the back of the cottage they found a small kitchen and larder.

Rachel noticed a bowl on the floor containing dregs of water and an empty dish next to it. But still no sign of the cat.

She replenished the water, then looked into the adjoining room. The servants' bedchamber, Rachel assumed, for inside were two narrow beds, neatly made. An old doll sat propped on one, and several childish drawings, now yellowed and curling, were tacked to the walls.

Beside her, Timothy's gaze lingered on the drawings. "Has she children?"

"Not that I know of. She mentioned her former maid had a daughter and that they both lived here for many years."

"Where are they now?"

"The mother, Bess Kurdle, died last year. Her daughter left only recently. Fell in love with the wrong man, apparently. The old story."

His head snapped toward her at that, but she kept her gaze on the doll, and whispered a prayer for Molly Kurdle, wherever she was.

He said, "Bess Kurdle . . . I know that name. But how?"

She glanced over, saw his brows furrowed in thought. She explained what Mrs. Haverhill had told her, about one of the magistrates sparing a widowed Mrs. Kurdle the workhouse and arranging the position for her here at Bramble Cottage.

"Ah . . ." He lifted his chin in recollection. "I remember hearing that story. Lord Winspear wanted to take a hard line as he had with her husband. A poacher, was he? But Father took pity on her."

"Yes. Very kind of him," Rachel murmured, her own thoughts in a tangle. She wondered about Sir Justin's motives but did not want to cast doubt on his father's memory.

They returned to the main room, where a narrow stairway led to the upper story—to Mrs. Haverhill's bedchamber, she guessed. It would feel like an invasion of privacy to ascend those stairs, Rachel decided, so she did not. Instead she called, "Mr. Nesbitt?"

She felt foolish calling for a cat by a man's name, but it was effective. The cat came padding down the stairs at last, groggy from a nap, or shy at the sound of strangers in his abode. Rachel unwrapped the dish of kipper and set it on the floor. His reserve dissolved, and he ate greedily.

Straightening, Rachel noticed a framed miniature portrait on the side table and picked it up. "It's Mrs. Haverhill. How young she is in this. How lovely."

She held it out for Timothy to see. He gave it a cursory glance and nodded his agreement.

"It is easy to see why Carville might admire her."

"Or any man," she added, still not believing Mrs. Haverhill had ever felt anything but disdain for Mr. Carville.

She replaced the portrait, and his eyes lit upon a book beside it.

"I remember this book." A soft smile lifted his face. "My father had a well-worn copy. Byron's first book of poetry. It was not well received, but he liked it." He ran his finger over the cover, that nostalgic smile lingering on his mouth. Then he picked up the book, as if recalling the weight and feel of the volume in his hands.

"Now, here is a book you ought to have in your library." He handed it to her. "Do you?"

She returned his smile. "I don't know, I shall have to check."

She idly opened the cover . . . and felt her smile fall away. For a moment she stood there, staring down at the flyleaf.

To Georgiana. With love always, J.

J could be almost anyone, she told herself, wanting to protect Timothy, and herself. She would not be the one to show him this.

Noticing her stillness, he asked, "What is it?"

"Hmm? Oh, nothing." She closed the book and set it back down. "I will review my inventory as soon as I get back."

Apparently satisfied, he looked again around the small but well-furnished cottage, taking in the quality upholstery and fine glassware and china displayed in a corner cupboard. At least the thief or thieves had not smashed or stolen those as well.

Was he wondering who had paid for it all?

Rachel mused, "Apparently, Mrs. Haverhill was once well-off.

But I don't believe that is the case any longer. She has taken to making and selling soap in the Wishford market. And I think hunger, as well as fatigue, played a role in her collapse."

He nodded. "Thankfully, she has you and Jane to help her." He cleared his throat. "Speaking of hunger . . . have you eaten?"

She shook her head and glanced at the mantel clock. "I have missed dinner at Ivy Cottage—we eat early. But I shall sneak something from the kitchen when Mrs. Timmons isn't looking, never fear."

"Then come to Brockwell Court for dinner tonight."

She blinked up at him in surprise.

Her reluctance must have shown, for he said, "I know you were not as warmly received last time as you deserve, but Justina is eager to see you. And I would enjoy your company as well."

"But your mother . . ."

"Leave her to me."

Rachel glanced down at her walking dress. "I would have to change."

"We can stop by Ivy Cottage on the way."

Hope and dread knotted her stomach at once. *Foolish creature*, she thought irritably, reminding herself to keep her expectations low. "Very well."

He smiled at Rachel as though she had given him some great gift, and gestured for her to precede him out the door.

CHAPTER TWENTY

"Rachel!" Justina squealed and threw her arms around her. "How lovely to see you again. You are staying for dinner this time, I insist. I shall not take no for an answer."

"Your brother has invited me, so yes."

"Has he indeed? Well done, Timothy." She cast a dubious glance over his blue coat and tan trousers. "You had better go and change before Mamma sees you. I shall keep Rachel company in the meantime, never fear."

"Very well. Don't abuse her ears while I'm gone, Justina."

"No promises."

He ascended the stairs, and Justina led Rachel into the drawing room. "Come and tell me everything."

The two sat and talked, Rachel describing all she was learning about books, managing a business, and the many Ivy Hill residents she was becoming acquainted with through the library.

Justina's eyes sparkled. "May I ask about Mr. Ashford, or would that be prying?"

"Oh no." Rachel shook her head. "I have been talking for the last ten minutes at least. It is your turn. What was your mother hinting about when last I was here? About your being marriageable and needing your own lady's maid now?"

Justina blushed and shifted. "Mamma pretends I am as good

as engaged, but as I said, nothing is settled. I am, however, being encouraged to accept a certain man."

"And do you like this man?"

The girl shrugged. "I hardly know. He does not seem a bad man. It would be easier to protest if he were rude or ill-favored. But he is not."

"What is his name, if I may ask? Would I know him?"

"I don't think so. His name is Sir Cyril Awdry."

The name rang a faint bell in Rachel's memory. She recalled a cheerful, sporting man who talked too much and laughed too loud. A man of good character but a little too much of the rattle.

Justina went on, "I think he's too old for me—perhaps five and thirty. Though he is boyish in his way, so he seems younger."

"Has he proposed?"

"Not formally. Timothy has convinced him I am too young and to wait until my next birthday."

"Good. Then you shall have time to allow your acquaintance to deepen before you must decide."

Justina nodded, her eyes downturned. "Oh, Rachel, I miss you. You were like a big sister to me. I once thought you or Jane would marry Timothy and be my sister forever."

Rachel ducked her head, immediately self-conscious. *As did I.*

Justina took her hand. "What happened, Rachel? I have always wondered. I was only eight or nine at the time, so I wasn't privy to all the details."

"I was not either, so don't ask me." Rachel forced a smile. "Now, that is enough about the ancient past."

Lady Brockwell swept into the room, regal in an emerald-green dinner dress, and drew up short at the sight of Rachel there.

"Miss Ashford, I . . . did not know we were expecting you."

Sir Timothy entered after her, and Rachel's heartbeat quickened. No man wore evening clothes like he did. The well-tailored coat emphasized broad shoulders and narrow waist. The high white shirt collar accentuated a masculine jawline and cleft chin. His dark hair and side-whiskers drew her gaze to his strong cheekbones and thickly lashed eyes. Eyes that held hers in warm reassurance before turning to his mother.

"Mamma, I asked Miss Ashford to join us for dinner. I know you will make her welcome. She is my guest."

Lady Brockwell's gaze swept over Rachel's simple but appropriate attire. "Of course I will. But you ought to have asked me first, Timothy. You forget we may be expecting visitors this evening."

"If you mean the Awdrys, Sir Cyril simply mentioned he might call on his way to the Salisbury races. The man is a horse-racing enthusiast. His will only be an informal visit, if it happens at all."

"Nonsense, Timothy; you particularly invited him to come shooting with you."

"That was *you*, Mamma," Justina interjected. "You said, 'Do come to Brockwell Court and shoot as many birds as you please.'"

"Justina, I do not appreciate being mocked."

"I am sorry, Mamma," the girl placated. "But please don't be cross. If he does come, I would like Rachel to meet him."

Lady Brockwell lifted a stony chin. "I am not cross, merely reminding you of a previous engagement."

"That is all right, Justina," Rachel demurred, growing increasingly uncomfortable. "I am sure I shall meet him at some point, when . . . all the villagers do."

Carville entered and announced, "Sir Cyril and Miss Awdry."

Lady Brockwell shot Timothy a look, then turned to smile at the newcomers.

The man who entered was slim and of average height, with wavy brown hair, bright eyes, and a ready smile in his tanned, boyish face.

The woman beside him matched his height but was large boned, with none of his fine, almost delicate, features. She stood, her frock a few inches too short, her half boots showing beneath her hem, shoulder-width apart in mannish stance.

The gentleman bowed and beamed at Lady Brockwell. "A thousand apologies, madam, for appearing unannounced at such an hour. I see that you are already dressed for dinner and looking uncommonly well, I must say. I hope you will forgive us for taking the liberty. We had hoped to arrive earlier, but Mr. Bingley invited us to call. Pleasant fellow and so obliging. He showed us his new hunting rifle. Excellent gun. You are acquainted with the Bingleys?"

"We are, yes. These many years."

"Right. Excellent." He turned toward Justina and bowed once more. "Miss Brockwell. A pleasure to see you again."

She curtsied in reply. "Sir Cyril."

His gaze shifted away as quickly as it had landed, like a nervous butterfly. "Allow me to introduce my sister, Miss Penelope Awdry."

Lady Brockwell faltered. "But . . . we met your sister in London. A . . . different sister."

"That was our younger sister, Arabella."

"Ah." Lady Brockwell sent Timothy another meaningful glance. "I was looking forward to seeing her again."

"Arabella does not enjoy the sporting life. She's at home with our mother."

"A pity."

"But of course we are pleased to make your acquaintance, Miss Awdry," Justina added politely, and then she introduced Rachel to them.

Rachel had briefly met the man in the past, but he did not acknowledge the acquaintance, so neither did she.

Sir Cyril grinned at Lady Brockwell. "You may see Arabella again soon, if you wish, ma'am. For as I stand here, invitations are on their way to you via post. We are hosting a concert at Broadmere."

"Then we shall look forward to that, won't we?" She looked from son to daughter, who both dutifully nodded and expressed their thanks.

Sir Cyril turned to Timothy. "Now, you did offer to take me shooting, Brockwell, did you not?" He rubbed his hands together in gleeful anticipation.

"We did, yes."

"I have brought my new fowling piece, and Pen has hers. She'll best us both, if we are not careful." He laughed, a bit more boisterously than the comment required.

He looked up at his host expectantly. Did the man think they would go shooting then and there?

"Tomorrow, perhaps," Lady Brockwell suggested. "I am sure you would like to change and have dinner first. You will stay the night, I trust?"

"Yes, if not an imposition. I do apologize for taking the liberty of arriving at Brockwell Court so—"

"Nonsense. You have already apologized, and there is no need. We did extend a general invitation for you to call when next you were in the area."

"Very kind of you, madam. Exceedingly kind. Is she not kind, Pen?"

His sister solemnly nodded.

"Carville will show you to your rooms and see your bags delivered," Lady Brockwell said. "My son's valet will attend you, Sir Cyril. And my daughter's lady's maid will help you change, Miss Awdry."

The woman looked down at her dress, and Rachel's heart went out to her. She hoped Miss Awdry had brought another.

Half an hour later, they were all seated around the long table in the high-ceilinged dining room with its silver candelabra, gleaming domed dishes, and a dazzling array of forks, knives, and spoons for various courses. Rachel had eaten alone and simply at Thornvale since her father's illness. And meals at Ivy Cottage were informal affairs. But sitting there in an out-of-fashion evening dress and having to make light conversation with the Brockwells and their guests was altogether different. Eight years ago, she had been a part of their set, of this life. Did she still belong? Did she want to?

Across the table, Sir Cyril regaled the company with an enthusiastic account of his sister's victory at a recent archery tournament.

He paused to ask, "How many rounds did you win, Pen—nine out of the ten?"

"Seven."

He laughed heartily. "Seven. I began to feel sorry for the other competitors." His smiling gaze landed on Justina, then shifted to Timothy. "I look forward to a good day of shooting tomorrow."

"I hope to oblige you, though if it storms, as the sky suggests, I cannot guarantee it."

"If that be the case, a set-to of rat hunting in the barn will serve as an excellent alternative."

Lady Brockwell's expression curdled at the mention of rats at the dinner table, and she said abruptly, "Your father was much older than your mother when they married—is that not so?"

Sir Cyril smiled at her, apparently not taken aback by the change of topic or prying question. "Indeed he was, God rest his soul. But hopefully Mamma will be with us for many years to come." He turned to his sister for confirmation.

Miss Awdry obliged him. "She is in excellent health."

"And had your parents been long acquainted before they married?" Lady Brockwell asked.

"Yes! They grew up together." Sir Cyril's boyish face glowed with memory. "She was like a little sister to him for years, but then she blossomed before his eyes and stole his heart, or so he always told us. Quite the romantic, Papa was."

Timothy glanced at Rachel over the rim of his glass. For a moment she held his gaze, then looked away first.

"Ah. Well. How quaint," Lady Brockwell allowed. It was clearly not the answer she'd wanted. "However, sometimes romance comes before marriage and sometimes it is the other way around." She paused and waited until the next course was laid before continuing.

"Consider Sir Justin and me. We barely knew each other when we became engaged. In fact, he was courting another woman when we first met. A completely unsuitable woman, as he later came to understand. But he remembered his duty to his family and to this estate, and he married me instead. It was not a love match at first. But we grew to love and respect each other. And we were happy, in our way."

She glanced at Timothy and Justina in turns. "And I am certain that if your father were here today, he would support what I say, and assure you he never regretted that decision."

Rachel noticed Justina blush. Was this lecture directed solely at her, encouraging her to accept Sir Cyril? Or was it also directed at Timothy, warning him against *her*? Rachel felt her neck heat at the thought.

Lady Brockwell gestured toward a formal portrait of Sir Justin on the wall and began extolling her late husband's valor in serving as magistrate and militia captain. "Sir Justin was away from home a great deal. He often missed dinner with his family, going out even in the foulest weather for a council meeting or petty session, or to attend the assizes out of town. So dedicated was he."

She shifted her glance to Timothy. "My son is dedicated as well, though he seems to somehow manage most of his duties from his office here at home. Sir Justin, however, preferred to go to the people, not make them come to him."

Timothy acknowledged her words with an unconvincing smile, the corners of his mouth pinched deep.

Later, when the meal concluded, Lady Brockwell signaled that it was time for the ladies to withdraw. She rose and led the way out of the room, leaving the men to talk racing and hunting over cigars and port while the females awaited them in the drawing room.

As the four women filed out, Miss Awdry glanced longingly over her shoulder, as though she dearly wished to remain with the men. Rachel could not blame her. The beginnings of a headache were tightening her temples.

In the drawing room, Lady Brockwell held court, continuing her lecture on the true value of marriage, and how the romantics had it all wrong. Rachel found herself thinking of Mrs. Haverhill. What exactly was the truth there?

Lady Brockwell's little pug dog padded through the open door, sniffed Miss Awdry's hem, and then sat at her feet. He stubbornly refused to go to his mistress for all her cajoling.

She gave up with a dismissive wave of her hand. "Ungrateful creature."

Miss Awdry said, "Probably smells the stables on my shoes."

Lady Brockwell grimaced and asked Rachel how the Miss Groves fared.

Rachel answered politely, then shifted the conversation to include Miss Awdry, asking what other sports she enjoyed, which turned out to be a rather long list—fishing, crude and fly, riding, jumping, hunting, fowling, and archery, to name a few. But Lady Brockwell soon turned the conversation to Miss Awdry's younger sister, asking about her accomplishments and doing a little fishing of her own—dangling questions about prospective suitors, and praising Sir Timothy's superior qualities.

Rachel's head began to throb. She stood. "Pray forgive me, Lady Brockwell. I've felt a headache coming on all evening, and it has worsened." *Perfectly true.* "I am afraid if I don't have an early bedtime, I shall be useless in the morning."

"And you have your little library to open at the crack of dawn—that's right." Lady Brockwell turned to her guest. "Miss Ashford here is quite the woman of business." Her tone was not complimentary.

"That is very impressive, Miss Ashford. I applaud you."

"Thank you, Miss Awdry. It has been a sincere pleasure to make your acquaintance. But now I must bid you all good night." *Before I say something I will regret.*

Justina rose to embrace her, and Lady Brockwell halfheartedly offered to call for a carriage, but Rachel insisted the fresh air and the walk back to Ivy Cottage would do her good. Lady Brockwell did not press her, though Rachel knew she would never allow her daughter, or even Miss Awdry, to walk home alone at night. Then again, Miss Awdry likely had a pistol in her reticule and would be perfectly safe on her own.

As Rachel crossed the hall toward the front door, Sir Timothy stepped out of the dining room.

"You are not leaving already?"

"I am."

"Has Mamma sent for the carriage?"

"No, I insisted I would walk. It isn't far."

"Then at least allow me to walk you home. It is after dark. I insist."

"If you like. Though I would be perfectly all right on my own."

He turned, his gaze pinning hers. "Yes, I believe you would be, Rachel Ashford. You and Jane . . . independent women, the both of you."

She looked at him in surprise. "Is that a bad thing?"

"I meant it as a compliment."

"Oh. Well then, thank you."

He helped her on with her shawl and opened the door for her. They descended the steps and started down the drive.

"I am sorry you had to sit through one of Mamma's lectures. I am used to them. It has been ingrained into me since I was old enough to understand—probably earlier—that romantic love is fleeting. But marry the right person for the family's sake, and love will come in time." He sent her a sidelong glance. "Forgive me. That was a thoughtless thing to say."

Rachel looked over at him while they walked—his handsome profile illuminated by a hunter's moon.

She took a deep breath and ventured, "They wanted you to marry Jane."

He met her gaze. "They were once . . . resigned to that idea."

"And now Miss Arabella Awdry is the favorite."

He shrugged. "With Mamma, perhaps, but not with me."

Dare I? Rachel thought. She had wanted to know for so long. Emboldened by the darkness, she asked, "Was I ever the right person for your family's sake?"

For a moment he did not answer. The only sounds were the

crunching of their shoes over the pea-gravel drive. Then he said, his voice rumbling low in his chest, "You were to me."

She swallowed. "Do you mean, until my father lost everything and had his name dragged through the papers?"

He winced. "I would not say it so harshly, but I can't deny its effect. Though even before that, my parents had their concerns."

"Concerns? Why? Because your father was a baronet and mine only a knight? I am still a gentleman's daughter."

"Your father's behavior called that distinction into question." He waited until they had passed the lamplighter, then added, "And your grandfather's reputation was not without blemish either. His gambling debts were the reason your father had to go out and make his own fortune."

Rachel felt herself growing angry but marshaled her self-control. "It all boiled down to money, I suppose? My father lost his fortune and my dowry, rendering me unsuitable?"

They passed the public house, and he lowered his voice. "There was more to it than that, you must allow. There was the very real scandal caused by your father's questionable business dealings. It was only due to the help of some highly placed friends that he did not end in bankruptcy or worse."

"So you washed your hands of me."

"No. That was not what I wanted. I thought I would let things lie for a time. The scandal would die down eventually, and people would forget—hopefully my parents among them. But then my father died, sending me into mourning. And afterward, I was overwhelmed, striving to take his place on the estate, in the parish, among the JPs. . . ."

When they reached Ivy Cottage, he stopped at the gate and sighed. "I know you have long been expecting a proposal, and I . . . I am sorry."

"Don't be." Rachel's head pounded and indignation flared. "After tonight, I think I am fortunate to have escaped that particular noose." She jerked open the gate.

"Rachel!" he breathed, offense and hurt in his tone. He grasped her hand to keep her from storming off. "Wait."

Rachel pulled away, shaking her head. "And you are wrong, Sir Timothy. I may have once hoped for a proposal from you, but no longer. You may leave here with your conscience clear. No need to offer out of charity."

"I was not—" Agitation tightened his every feature. "Very well. Forgive me for raising such a distasteful prospect, Miss Ashford. And accept my best wishes for your health and happiness."

With that, he turned on his heel and stalked away, disappearing into the night.

CHAPTER TWENTY-ONE

Mr. Kingsley arrived unexpectedly just before their dinnertime the next evening. Mr. Basu was busy in the kitchen, so Mercy opened the door for him herself.

"Mr. Kingsley. Come in out of the rain."

"Foul weather." He stomped his boots and tipped the water from his hat before stepping inside. "Sorry to arrive so late. Had to finish up a few things at the Fairmont first."

"No matter. I did not realize you were coming this evening."

"I've only come to take a few measurements for a raised library desk I've proposed to Miss Ashford—a larger one at a more comfortable standing height."

"Excellent idea—like a shopkeeper's counter."

His mouth quirked, and his eyes shone with subtle humor. "Well . . . I would not describe it that way—not to Miss Ashford."

She grinned. "Ah. Wise man."

Aunt Matilda joined them in the vestibule. "Mr. Kingsley, what a pleasure. Have you eaten? We are having hot soup and fresh bread. Just the thing on a night like this."

"No, thank you. I usually have something on the way over, but I can wait 'til I get home."

"Why not join us? Mrs. Timmons always makes plenty. The

girls have already eaten, but Mercy and I were just about to sit down. Miss Rachel won't be joining us. She is . . . not feeling well."

Mercy and her aunt had overheard bits of her argument with Sir Timothy the night before, and Rachel had truly felt ill all day.

Mr. Kingsley said, "I'm sorry to hear it."

"Only heartsick," Aunt Matty clarified. "She'll be all right, by and by. But do please join us."

"I don't want to be an imposition."

"Imposition!" Matilda scoffed. "When you have worked long hours here out of the goodness of your heart? It is the least we can do."

He hesitated. "It isn't customary."

"Surely once would not hurt? It's only a humble bacon and cabbage soup, but no one makes it better than our Mrs. Timmons."

He slowly shook his head. "Miss Grove, you do know how to tempt a man. I am afraid I am powerless to resist bacon."

"Wonderful! I will fetch another bowl!"

"May I wash my hands first?"

"Of course," Matilda said. "I'll show you to the scullery."

"I know where it is." He looked at Mercy from beneath a fall of sandy blond hair.

Mercy guessed he was remembering the day she'd helped him clean and bandage his cut. Her face warmed at the memory.

A few minutes later, the three of them sat down in the dining room, and Mr. Kingsley smiled apologetically. "I'm afraid my table manners aren't equal to such fine company as you ladies."

"We shall not be giving an examination, Mr. Kingsley," Mercy assured him. "You are among friends."

Matilda spread her serviette on her lap. "We see all sorts of manners and lack thereof at this table and have survived perfectly well." She looked at him expectantly. "Would you like to say grace?"

"Oh. Of course." He cleared his throat. "For what we are about to receive, may the Lord make us truly grateful, amen."

"Amen."

Mr. Kingsley placed his own table napkin on his lap. They ate without speaking for several minutes, Mr. Kingsley surreptitiously watching how Matilda spooned her soup and attempting to imitate her genteel motions. The soup spoon looked small in his large, work-worn hands. He slurped once, winced, and reddened.

Mercy quickly tried to think of something to say to fill the slurp-revealing silence.

"The Egyptians highly esteemed the cabbage," she blurted. "Even raised altars to them. The Greeks and Romans ascribed to them great healing powers."

He looked over at her, soup spoon dripping, halfway to his mouth.

She swallowed. "But we did not cultivate them here until well after the reign of King Henry the Eighth. Nor carrots, nor radishes, nor other vegetables of like nature."

"Is that so?"

Her aunt pressed her lips together and handed her the bread basket.

Mercy felt her face heat in embarrassment. "Forgive me. I did not mean to give a lecture."

Mr. Kingsley broke off a piece of bread. "Not at all. Quite interesting."

Mercy sipped her soup, then tried again. "Anna mentioned that you live over the Kingsley Brothers' workshop?"

"That's right. I often go down and do a bit of carving or what-not after my regular day's work. Very convenient. Also, we think it a wise precaution what with all the tools we keep downstairs."

"I see."

He scraped the bottom of his bowl. "Delicious soup."

Mercy reached toward the tureen. "Would you like more?"

"No, thank you. I've had plenty."

"Do you do your own cooking, Mr. Kingsley?" Matilda asked, and Mercy felt embarrassed at the leading question.

"Such as it is, yes. Though my brothers' wives often invite me over, so I don't starve, as you can see." He patted his midsection, then reddened again. "Sorry."

Mercy had already noticed his lean midsection, in masculine contrast to his broad shoulders, and saw nothing to apologize for in the least.

Rachel reviewed the argument in her mind and could not help but cringe at the memory—her questions, Timothy's unflattering answers, and the harsh words she'd said in reply. He had injured her pride and she'd struck back, more forcefully than she'd intended. He had told her the truth—a truth that embarrassed her, though she could not refute it. And she had punished him for it. Now guilt and remorse were punishing her.

Oh, her stubborn pride and untamed tongue! She could hear her mother's voice, gently admonishing her and Ellen not to provoke each other into heated arguments. "Remember, girls—a gentle answer turns away wrath, but harsh words stir up anger." If only she had heeded that advice.

Why had she asked—what had she expected? Rachel pressed her eyes closed against the image of Timothy's stricken face. At least now she knew for certain. Her family's scandal and financial ruin had not changed. If anything the marks against her had worsened since becoming a humble boarder in Ivy Cottage, and now one who worked for a living as well. She could still hear Lady Brockwell's sour tone when she'd described Rachel as "*quite* the woman of business."

Rachel sighed. This was for the best, she told herself. Now she could stop wondering *why* and stop wondering *if* . . . and focus on the suitor she had.

The next morning, Rachel washed, dressed, and shook off her malaise, determined to put aside self-reproach and join the others. Her stomach growled as she walked downstairs—she was hungry after forgoing dinner the night before. Entering the dining room, she gave Mercy and Matilda reassuring smiles. *I am well. No need to worry.* Then she sat down and consumed a convincingly large breakfast. As they ate, Mercy reminded them that her parents and guest were due at four that afternoon.

Mr. Basu brought in the mail. An invitation had arrived, addressed vaguely to *Miss Grove*. Matilda read it, then handed it to her niece. "I think it must be for you, my dear. It is from the Awdrys."

"The Awdrys? Then it is more likely for you." Mercy read the invitation, then looked up. "I don't believe I will go. But Aunt Matty, you would enjoy such an evening, I know."

"I would indeed. But Broadmere is a long way from here, and without a carriage . . . No, I will send our regrets."

Rachel was surprised Matilda did not try to persuade her niece to attend. Then she remembered. Many years ago, Sir Cyril had paid Mercy marked attention, which she had not reciprocated. Rachel supposed it might be awkward to be a guest in his house now. Rachel recalled her own discomfiture at Brockwell Court. Her argument with Timothy echoed through her mind again, but she quickly banished the memory. She thought of Nicholas instead. Would things be terribly awkward between them in future, if they did not marry? She hoped not. For she sincerely liked the man.

Later that afternoon, Nicholas came to visit her in the library, a bright smile on his face.

Her heart lightened, and she smiled in turn. "You seem in good spirits."

"I am. At the prospect of spending time with you."

"Oh?"

"We received an invitation to a concert at the home of Sir Cyril Awdry—are you acquainted with him?"

"A little."

"We are to hear an Italian singer. Come with us."

She ducked her head. "I was not invited."

"I am not so sure. The invitation was addressed simply to *The Ashfords, Ivy Hill, Wiltshire*. Are you not an Ashford of Ivy Hill?" He grinned. "I would not be surprised if this invitation was meant for you in the first place, especially as we have never even met the man."

"I don't know . . ."

"Please say yes, Miss Ashford. I promise my mother will be on her best behavior."

"She cannot want me to come."

"But I very much do. How can I enjoy that long journey without your company? Perhaps Miss Grove might come with us. We have room for four in our carriage, though we shall be snug."

"I don't think the Miss Groves plan to go, though they received a vaguely addressed invitation as well."

"Then let's convince them."

Rachel could not resist his boyish enthusiasm. Together they walked into the sitting room and relayed Nicholas's offer.

Mercy smiled softly. "Thank you, Mr. Ashford. That is very kind of you. I will not attend, but my aunt would enjoy the outing very much. In fact, I was sorry that it seemed she would have to miss out."

Matilda said, "Are you sure you won't change your mind, Mercy?"

"I am. But you go, Aunt Matty, and have a wonderful time."

"Then I shall indeed. Thankfully, I have not yet posted my regrets." Matilda winked. "Sometimes procrastination pays."

The sound of a carriage and four on rather narrow Church Street was a rare occurrence, drawing Mercy to the dining room window to investigate. A hired chaise and four post horses arrived. Anxiety rippled through her. Her parents were early. Rachel was occupied in the library, and Aunt Matilda and the girls were still in the schoolroom, though perhaps that was for the best.

The carriage door opened, and her father unfolded himself from within, straightening to his full height, and then held out his hand to help her mother alight.

After her, a third occupant emerged—the tutor, the man they wanted her to meet. He was not as tall as her father, and not as old. From this distance, that was about all she could tell. Mercy took a deep breath and told herself to remain calm.

Mr. Basu padded past her toward the front door, but before he reached it, her parents let themselves in without knocking. *Why should they?* Mercy reminded herself. It had been their house long before she began to think of it as her own.

She gave her cheeks a quick pinch, knowing it would take far more than that to make herself comely but hoping to minimize the disappointment she would likely see on the man's face.

She entered the vestibule wearing a determined smile.

Her father's hair and side-whiskers held a bit more silver than she remembered. And in his long homely face, she saw the unfortunate resemblance to her own.

Her mother looked lovely as always, if a bit more plump. She wore a fashionable carriage dress and velvet-collared cloak that made Mercy feel shabby as she stood there in her plain day dress.

"Hello, my dear. Here we are." She glanced at Mercy's dress and bestowed the smile she wore when saying something unpleasant. "I realize we are a bit earlier than we wrote, and no doubt that is why you have not yet changed. But oh well. We're all here now. And this is our guest we wanted you to meet." She turned to the man still standing on the doorstep.

Her father turned to him as well. "Come in, my good fellow. Come in. My dear, allow me to present Mr. Norbert Hollander. Mr. Hollander, my daughter, Miss Grove."

He stepped inside and bowed. "How do you do?" He was stately looking and somewhat taller than she was. That was a point in his favor.

Mercy curtsied. "Mr. Hollander, a pleasure to meet you."

"Mr. Hollander is a tutor and lecturer of Worcester College," her father said. "He taught George during his Oxford days."

"Yes." Mercy injected a cheerful note into her voice. "So you mentioned in your letter."

She glanced at the man again, trying to judge his age. Considering he had been George's tutor, he must be at least forty or forty-five, though he could pass for several years younger. He had a pleasant, ordinary face with a straight nose, placid blue-grey eyes, and lips as thin as her own. His light brown hair was receding slightly at the front and a bit longish in the back. He was not handsome, but then, neither was she.

He wore a traditional frock coat in sensible grey. His striped waistcoat puckered slightly over his mildly stout middle. His shirt collar was not as pristine as it might have been, and his wrinkled cravat was haphazardly tied—evidence not of poverty, she surmised, but of a bachelor's neglect.

He stood stiff and somber, clutching his hat. Mr. Basu, hovering nearby, finally yanked it from him and took her father's as well.

"Oh. Thank you," he murmured.

Mercy smiled, hoping to put him at his ease. "Welcome, Mr. Hollander. Please do come in. You must be tired and thirsty after your journey. Why don't you go into the sitting room, and I shall see about tea."

"The family sitting room, my dear?" Her mother gave another of her false smiles. "I think, with a guest, the drawing room might be more appropriate."

"You forget, Mamma. The drawing room is now part of the circulating library. I wrote to you about it, remember?"

"Just as I wrote to you about . . . several things, which you don't seem to recall either. But . . . very well."

They crossed the vestibule, and Mercy gestured them through the open sitting room door. "Do be seated—anywhere you like. I will just step into the kitchen and ask Mrs. Timmons to make tea."

At the door, Mercy laid a hand on her mother's arm. "Mamma, perhaps you would help me a moment?"

"Help you ring for tea? I hardly think . . ." Seeing her daughter's expression, she relented. "Oh, very well."

The men continued inside, but Mrs. Grove allowed her daughter to lead her several yards down the passage. "What is it, Mercy?"

"I thought we should discuss sleeping arrangements."

"I assume you are putting him in George's old room? Unless

you have relocated your schoolroom to the attic, as I suggested long ago?"

"No, Mamma. The girls' dormitory is up there. Aunt Matty has offered her room. You know Rachel Ashford has been living in George's old room for some time now. It seemed wrong to put her out for a stranger."

"He is not a stranger. George and your father have known him for years. And I trust he shall not be a stranger to you for long either." Her eyes sparkled.

"Mamma, don't get your hopes up."

"My hopes would be higher were not Rachel Ashford under the same roof. Pray do not be offended, my dear, but a side-by-side comparison with her is not to your advantage. That is why I had hoped Miss Ashford would have gone elsewhere before we arrived. Could she not remove to the inn for a few days?"

Mercy felt hurt and offended on her friend's behalf.

Rachel stepped out of the library nearby, and Mercy was mortified to realize she had overheard the exchange. "I would not mind at all, Mrs. Grove. I did offer to leave, but you know Mercy—she was too kind to accept. I will pack my things and be out of your way in no time. I shall need to return to oversee the library, but I will keep to those two rooms."

Her mother sighed. "In that case, never mind, Miss Ashford. If you are going to be here anyway, there is no point in sleeping elsewhere. Stay. We shall make the best of it."

"Very well," Rachel agreed and retreated back into the library.

"Thank you, Mamma," Mercy said dutifully. "Now, why do you not rejoin the men. I will be there as soon as I speak to Mrs. Timmons."

"All right. Don't be long."

Mercy kept a smile on her face as she walked away. But when she entered the privacy of the butler's pantry, she stopped and leaned against the counter. Closing her eyes, she drew a deep breath. She asked God to give her kindness, patience, self-control, and anything else that would help her through this awkward visit without dishonoring her parents or being inhospitable to their guest.

A short while later, as the four of them took tea, they discussed impersonal topics like the tedium of the journey on dusty roads and debated the improvements of the turnpikes. Afterward, Mr. Basu appeared to show Mr. Hollander to his room. The weary travelers would have an hour to rest, wash, and change before dinner.

Mercy was glad for the respite as well and used it to gather her composure. She also gathered the girls to ask them to be especially quiet and polite during the next few days, and to heed Miss Ashford and of course her aunt while Mercy was busy with her guests.

Mercy had barely made it to her bedchamber when her mother knocked once and let herself in. Behind her, Mr. Basu carried several boxes. "There on the bed, if you please." Mr. Basu set down the boxes and quickly departed.

"I brought you a new walking dress, spencer, and bonnet." She kept her voice low, since Mr. Hollander was on the other side of the wall in Matilda's room.

"Thank you, Mamma."

"But for now, do change into something pretty for dinner. What about that rose-colored evening gown I had made for you?" She stepped to Mercy's closet and began pulling out gown drawers.

"I think that one is too young for me."

"Nonsense."

"Perhaps the ivory, instead?"

"Oh, very well. For tonight . . . We don't want to appear to be trying too hard. But the rose one tomorrow."

Mrs. Grove looked over her shoulder. "Where is that upstairs maid of yours? She should be here helping you change. Helping us both."

"She is no doubt busy helping Mrs. Timmons and Mr. Basu prepare dinner. You know we have only a small staff. And that is all we need . . . usually."

Her mother sighed. "I knew I should have brought along my maid, but with Mr. Hollander in the chaise, we were cramped as it is, and Martine would leave me for the dowager next door if I forced her to ride outside all the way from London."

"We will make do," Mercy assured her.

Her mother helped Mercy dress and then brushed and pinned her daughter's hair herself. As she did, Mercy was taken back to her childhood when her mother had often done the same. They had not been so fine as to need a lady's maid in those days. And even though their former housemaid used to attend Mrs. Grove, her mother had often tried to do "something" with Mercy's hair before church or a social event. Mercy's fine, straight hair had rarely cooperated, and her mother had yanked out strands more than once in her impatience to comb through the tangled length.

Sitting there now, Mercy felt a bittersweet lump rise in her throat. She could not even relish the pleasure of having someone brush her hair, because she anticipated a painful tug or criticism at any moment. She felt herself shrink on the seat, until she was that young girl again—a girl who avoided meeting the gaze of the plain spinster staring back at her.

CHAPTER
TWENTY-TWO

Later that evening, after the girls had eaten, the Groves and their guest gathered around the long table in the dining room, Rachel included and perfunctorily introduced. The meal began in reserved silence, save for the clink of serving dishes and cutlery. It reminded Mercy of their recent dinner with Mr. Kingsley.

Mercy subtly observed Mr. Hollander while he ate. His table manners were good, she decided, though he ate a bit too fast. If he were one of her girls, she would admonish him to slow down to avoid a stomachache.

Mercy tried to think of pleasant, innocuous conversation, but she felt nervous. Every question that flitted through her mind seemed too forward or leading. She did not want to give the impression she was interviewing the man as a prospective husband.

Was she?

Mercy sent a look of appeal to her loquacious aunt, but even Matilda remained subdued in her sister-in-law's presence.

As Mr. Hollander bent with relish over his meal, her mother jerked her head toward him, signaling Mercy to engage him in conversation. What to say? His family—she could ask about his family.

Before she got the words out, Mr. Hollander filled the uneasy silence himself. "What delicious turnips and roast chicken. I like good, plain food, well prepared. Far better than the fare one gets at Worcester College." He glanced at Mercy. "May I compliment you, Miss Grove, on the excellence of the cooking?"

Her mother coughed, but Mercy kept her expression even. "I am afraid not, Mr. Hollander. Our cook, Mrs. Timmons, gets all the credit."

"Ah. I did not wish to assume ladies living alone could . . . well. Excellent meal, all the same."

"Really, Mr. Hollander." Her mother smiled, though clearly embarrassed. "We are perfectly able to keep a cook for Ivy Cottage. As well as our own in London, of course. Mr. Grove is not so miserly as to leave his daughter and sister to shift for themselves."

"And we are grateful for your generosity, Papa," Mercy said. "Though the school does bring in a little income. A very little."

"Please no talk of that at dinner, Mercy," her mother bid with a stilted little laugh.

Aunt Matilda spoke up at last. "I have a fondness for baking, Mr. Hollander. Cakes and biscuits are my specialty. Though Mercy insisted Mrs. Timmons be allowed to make our dessert tonight, along with the rest of her excellent meal."

Mr. Hollander smiled at her. "I shall hope to have the pleasure of your fine baking another time during my visit, Miss Grove."

"Then, indeed you shall, Mr. Hollander." Aunt Matty's eyes twinkled.

Mrs. Grove coughed again, and Mercy bit her lip. She glanced over and found Rachel hiding a smile behind her water glass.

Their visitor looked around the dining room. "What a superbly featured room. It reminds me of the provost's dining parlour, though smaller, of course."

Her mother nudged her under the table.

"Thank you," Mercy said. "We are fond of it."

Her father added proudly, "Ivy Cottage has been in the Grove family for generations, though it has been expanded over the years."

Mrs. Grove nodded. "It is a sweet, snug house, I will allow. Excellent for a young family. Though now, of course, Mr. Grove and I prefer to live in London. And you, Mr. Hollander? Might you enjoy village life after so many years in Oxford?"

Mercy choked on a turnip.

Mr. Hollander did not seem embarrassed by the leading question. He answered thoughtfully. "Indeed I might. For Oxford is rather like a collection of small villages, now I think on it, with its separate colleges, communal greens, and secluded courtyards. Yes, I find the prospect of village life charming."

"Would you not miss academia?" Mercy moved her foot to avoid another nudge from her mother.

"Some aspects, yes. But surrounded by my books and intelligent company, I should do very well anywhere, I think. As Sheldon says, good books are the most reliable of friends, though they often spur us to self-reflection, when we might prefer to pass the time thus untroubled." He chuckled.

He had a sense of humor, at any rate, Mercy allowed. "Sheldon? Is that an author?"

"Oh, no, forgive me. Professor Sheldon. I forget you don't know him."

"Ah." Mercy's mind sought another topic. "And . . . have you a favorite author?"

He grimaced. "I do detest that question. How can one answer? How can one choose a favorite from among one's very confidants and mentors? I am not a youth with my arm slung around the shoulder of one chum to the exclusion of others. Each suits at a different time. A different season . . ." He paused, glancing from abashed face to abashed face. "Pray, do not be offended. I meant no disrespect. I forget I am not in a debate with my peers."

Mercy hesitated. "We are not your peers?"

"I only meant . . . with other tutors and lecturers. We are accustomed to regular and heated debates on such topics." He grinned. "The academic equivalent of the public house brawl."

Mrs. Grove cleared her throat at the inappropriate reference.

With a glance at Mercy, Matilda offered, "I am fond of Anne Radcliffe myself."

Mr. Hollander looked at her gratefully. "I am not familiar with that name. Is she a . . . poet?"

"A novel writer."

"Awful, gothic stuff, I gather." Mr. Grove made a face. "Not to the taste of learned men like us, Hollander. I am a Wordsworth man myself, but you know that."

Mr. Grove turned to Rachel. "Have you any Wordsworth in that circulating library of yours?"

"Yes, I believe so."

Her father explained, "Miss Ashford here has filled our library and drawing room with her late father's books. An impressive collection, if memory serves."

"I can think of no better use of space." For a moment Mr. Hollander's gaze lingered on Rachel's face. "Are you a great reader, Miss Ashford?"

Was that a hint of admiration in his eyes for her pretty friend or simple curiosity? Mercy could not be certain.

"I am afraid not, Mr. Hollander," Rachel replied. "I have only recently begun to appreciate books."

"Oh . . ." Mr. Hollander's brow furrowed at the foreign thought. Any hint of admiration Mercy had seen—real or imagined—faded.

Mrs. Grove interjected, "But Mercy is a great reader."

Mercy thought this praise ironic, when her mother had long disapproved of her studious ways.

Her father nodded thoughtfully. "Yes, she always has been. Far more so than George ever was. It is one of the reasons I insisted she be educated alongside her brother when the two were young. That is, of course, until George went off to Oxford." He looked expectantly at Mr. Hollander.

The tutor faltered. "Em, yes, George was a very . . . likable young man. Very popular with his fellow students."

He abruptly turned to Mercy. "And you keep a girls school, I understand, Miss Grove?"

She noticed her mother slant her father an anxious look, but Mercy kept her focus on Mr. Hollander. "Yes, I do."

"I once thought I should like to keep a boys school when I retire from Oxford. The idea of being a headmaster to younger lads, while their minds are still developing, less cynical, open to ideas . . . Or, if not a school per se, perhaps I might take a few pupils into my home for private tutoring."

"Have you a home, Mr. Hollander?" Matilda asked, eyes innocently wide. She ignored her sister-in-law's glare.

"Only a few rented rooms. Living at the college does not allow the luxury of a private house. But now that I am leaving that life, I desire to have a home of my own."

"You say you *once* thought of keeping a boys school," Mercy said. "You have changed your mind?"

"Perhaps one day I shall. However, I have long desired to write a book, though the time to do so has eluded me. Once I retire, that shall be my first objective." Here he glanced at Mercy. "Or perhaps, my second."

Mercy felt her cheeks heat, and noticed her parents exchange silent smiles of triumph.

After dinner, her mother said to her, "Why don't you take Mr. Hollander for a turn about Ivy Green, Mercy?"

"Of course. If he likes."

The man nodded amiably. "I would like that, yes."

Matilda rose. "Shall I go with you?"

"Yes, do come, Aunt Matty."

Her mother frowned. "Matilda, I don't think they need a chaperone for a simple walk around the green. It is not even dark yet."

Matilda sat back down. "Only trying to be helpful."

Instead, her aunt and Rachel volunteered to oversee the girls' evening prayers and bedtime so Mercy could spend time with Mr. Hollander.

He donned his greatcoat and hat, while Mercy went to slip a long-sleeved redingote over her dress to ward off the autumn evening's chill and tied a bonnet under her chin. Mercy led him out the rear door, through the walled back garden, and out the gate onto the village green.

The trees bordering the broad grassy rectangle were beginning to mellow into golden hues. The ivy climbing some walls remained evergreen, while other varieties festooned cottages with swaths of orangey-red leaves.

Across the green, a father and son practiced with cricket bat, and a group of lads kicked a ball about, stretching twilight as long as they could until their mothers called them home.

Mr. Hollander grasped his lapels and surveyed the scene. "This reminds me of the Worcester quadrangle, although that is situated along a canal."

"This is Ivy Green, which has always seemed like an extension of our back garden." Mercy looked around with nostalgic fondness. "I have spent many pleasant hours here, picking wildflowers, sketching, reading, watching George and his friends kick, bat, and pitch balls in one game or another. They all rather looked the same to me, I confess. I have never been athletic."

"Nor I. Which got me trounced at school more than once, I can tell you."

She slanted him an empathetic grin.

He returned it. "And what subjects do you teach your pupils, Miss Grove?"

"You will not be impressed. I'm afraid they have little use for the classics or philosophy."

"Though you could teach those subjects, from what your father says."

"Not well. I have been away from them too long."

"But you do teach literature? History? Mathematics?"

"Literature, yes. The girls read a great deal. And British and world history. And basic mathematics, but nothing too advanced."

"What books do you require them to read?"

Mercy told him, and he nodded along approvingly. "I am familiar with Richardson and Cowper, but not Burney. Perhaps you might recommend a specific title I could read by way of introduction?"

"With pleasure."

As they walked on, Mercy explained, "The girls are from modest backgrounds. If they don't marry, they will likely become servants or shopkeepers, so we also teach sewing, manners, and basic etiquette."

"Watercolors? Dancing?"

"No, we have not included those to date, though pleasant diversions, I grant you."

He smiled, eyes softly focused in memory, and she noticed deep creases at the corners. "If I remember correctly, George was far more interested in dancing and poetry than history. Anything that might impress the ladies."

She returned his smile. "That sounds like my brother."

His gaze lingered on her face. "You have a lovely smile, Miss Grove. I hope you don't mind my saying so."

"Thank you, Mr. Hollander. That is very kind."

His gaze slid to the top of her bonnet and narrowed in a measuring fashion. "You are a tall woman, Miss Grove."

"As I am aware." Mercy dipped her head, feeling self-conscious under his scrutiny. She recalled Mr. Kingsley looking at the top of her head in a similar fashion, saying, *"Taller people like us . . ."* She asked, "Is . . . that a problem?"

"No. Merely an observation—I hope not an inappropriate one. I have not had those lessons in manners your pupils have, and fear my social skills are painfully lacking."

"Not at all, Mr. Hollander."

They walked on around Ivy Green, hands behind respective backs, Mercy feeling unsettled and conflicted. She had expected, almost hoped, to instantly dislike the man and for the feeling to be mutual. But life, she realized, was rarely that simple.

Mercy dressed with care the next morning, donning an embroidered, belted overdress over her usual plain day dress. She left her bedchamber just as Mr. Hollander stepped out of Aunt Matty's room. From the floor above came the rumble of eight pairs of shoes as the herd of girls, shepherded by Rachel and the maid, Agnes, descended the stairs in a rush, eager for their breakfast. They streamed past the man, catching him up in their giggling wake and nearly bowling him over. He stepped out from among them in an ungainly little twirl.

Mercy smiled at him, and he smiled back.

"Good morning, Mr. Hollander. I see you have met my pupils."

"In a manner of speaking."

"You are up early."

"Yes. It is my habit."

"Mine as well. Come, let's go down to breakfast, and you can meet the girls properly."

He hesitated only a moment. "Very well."

Was he daunted by the prospect? She hoped the girls would remember to be on their best behavior.

Instead, breakfast that morning turned out to be a clamorous and chaotic pass-the-butter affair, accompanied by more noise and less decorum than usual. Or perhaps Mercy was simply more aware with their guest at the table. Spoons clattered, elbows on the table reprimanded, tea sloshed, and serving dishes passed and passed again.

Thankfully her father was not an early riser and her mother took her breakfast on a tray in her room. So Mercy, Matilda, Rachel, and Mr. Hollander were the only adults there to witness the tumult.

Fanny asked, with her mouth full, "Are boys easier to teach, Mr. Hollander?"

"Perhaps . . . quieter."

"Do you like our teacher?"

"Fanny!" Mercy's neck heated.

His expression remained unperturbed. "I do, yes. Do you?"

"Of course." Around the table, heads nodded. Little Alice's especially.

"Then you are just as intelligent as Miss Grove said you were."

That earned him a smile from the girls and from Mercy as well.

When the girls finished eating, Rachel offered to go up with them to the schoolroom for morning prayers, so the two Miss Groves could linger with their guest.

"Thank you, Rachel."

When they had gone, peaceful quiet reigned.

Mercy sighed. "That is more like it. I apologize. The girls are in unusually high spirits this morning."

"I thought it invigorating. Rather like dining with freshmen after a football match."

Mercy chuckled appreciatively. "More tea, Mr. Hollander?"

He nodded, and she poured.

Her aunt held out her cup as well. "You mentioned wishing to write a book," Matilda began. "A noble venture, to be sure, but would that not require a great deal of time and effort without remuneration for years, if ever? How do you intend to support yourself?"

Mercy had rarely heard her sweet aunt speak so pointedly. She supposed she felt protective of her only niece.

Again, Mr. Hollander took no umbrage. "A valid question. I recently received a modest inheritance from a late uncle that will allow me to pursue writing for a time, rather than income, if money is not an indelicate subject to raise among ladies."

"Not at all." Matilda's eyes shone with mischief. "We like money, don't we, Mercy."

Mercy bit back a grin. "And what topic do you propose to write about?"

"A Gothic novel, I hope?" Matilda teased.

"I was thinking of a treatise on education" came his solemn reply.

"Ah." Mercy considered how best to respond. "That is a . . . broad subject."

"Agreed. I have yet to determine the scope. Do I include the history of formal education back to the ancient Greeks, or limit myself to Great Britain? Or do I narrow the scope further yet to the insights gained during my years at Oxford?"

"I suppose it depends on the particular readers you wish to reach."

"Why, everyone."

Mercy hesitated, then said gently, "If only everyone were as interested in education as we might like, Mr. Hollander. But—"

"You think I overestimate my book's appeal?"

"I don't mean to discourage you in the least. But only consider, for example, someone like me. I am very interested in education, and buy books when I am able, but I don't know that what you will write would be applicable to someone in my situation—a teacher in a girls school. And if a person is not involved in education at all . . ." She let the thought drift away on a shrug.

"Why not applicable?" A worry line deepened between his eyebrows.

"I am only suggesting that you might want to formulate broader applications for the experiences and methods you've honed over the years, so the book might be of help to more people. Or you could simply write specifically for other university tutors and professors. That in itself would be a lofty ambition."

"Though not one destined to sell many copies."

"Not as many, no."

An awkward silence descended.

When it had lingered a bit too long, her aunt interjected, "How delightful that you two have so much in common, so much to talk about."

"I quite agree, Miss Grove."

Mercy heard more politeness than warmth in his words and noticed the man's eyes had dulled. She regretted discouraging his dream.

Matilda added, "Perhaps Mercy might assist you in writing your book, Mr. Hollander. She is extremely clever."

"Aunt Matty! I am sure Mr. Hollander does not want or need my help."

"On the contrary." Mr. Hollander's eyes warmed again. "I think that an excellent idea."

After church on Sunday, Mercy decided it was time to introduce Alice to her parents.

Feeling as nervous as the little girl looked, Mercy led Alice by the hand into the sitting room where her parents waited. Rachel had arranged the girl's blond hair for her, and Mercy thought she looked even more charming than usual.

"Mamma. Papa. This is Alice. The pupil I . . . wrote to you about."

Her father nodded and smiled down at the girl. "A pleasure to meet you, Alice."

Her mother inspected the child as though she were a mackerel of doubtful freshness.

Mercy touched Alice's shoulder. "Can you greet Mr. and Mrs. Grove, Alice?"

"Good d-day," she managed, meeting their gazes for a fleeting second.

"And how old are you, Alice?" her father asked.

"Eight, sir."

"Eight. Yes. A good age for schooling. And are you a good pupil, Alice?"

"I . . ." The girl shrugged.

"She is," Mercy assured them. "She reads as well as students several years older."

Her father nodded. "Excellent."

"She is lovely," her mother allowed.

"I agree. Well. Thank you, Alice. You may rejoin the others now."

Alice bobbed a curtsy and all but dashed from the room.

Her mother watched her go. "Is she always so timid?"

"She is shy."

"Are you sure about this, Mercy?" Her father studied her face.

"I am. Do you . . . object?"

Her mother shifted. "That depends on Mr. Hollander. You must admit it is a lot to ask of a prospective husband. Are you sure she is worth the risk?"

"I am."

"Then let us hope Mr. Hollander is an understanding man."

CHAPTER TWENTY-THREE

Rachel walked back to The Bell on Monday afternoon—the day Mrs. Haverhill planned to return to Bramble Cottage. Even though Mrs. Haverhill was much recovered she still felt a little weak, and Jane insisted on sending her home in the inn's gig. Jane drove it herself, and Rachel squeezed onto the bench beside them. A basket of things packed for her from The Bell's kitchen rode in the back.

They soon left the cobbled village streets behind, crossed Pudding Brook, and jostled their way up the rutted road ascending Ebsbury Hill. When they reached Bramble Cottage, Jane halted the horse, climbed nimbly down, and tied the old nag to a fence post.

Mrs. Haverhill gasped.

Rachel looked toward the house in alarm, fearing signs of another theft. Instead, the door was closed, but the cottage walls were splattered with bright bursts of yellow egg, orange squash, and rotten red tomatoes, with pinkish smears trailing to the ground.

"Nooo," Mrs. Haverhill groaned. "Not again."

"What on earth . . ." Jane muttered.

Rachel helped the woman down. "Has this happened before?"

"Yes. Though never this bad." Mrs. Haverhill crossed to the henhouse, its door swinging listlessly on its hinge. Pain flashed across her face. "Henrietta is gone."

Jane planted her hands on her hips. "Mrs. Haverhill, I want

you to promise me you will not try to clean this up yourself. Do you hear me? We don't want you collapsing again. I will bring help from the inn . . . though it will have to be tomorrow. Today is one of our busiest days, and with Patrick in bed with a cold, I cannot spare anyone. But this muck isn't going anywhere before then. Promise me you'll leave it?"

Rachel squinted in thought. "I have another idea."

That evening, Rachel sat, heart pounding and palms damp, at the Monday night meeting of the Ladies Tea and Knitting Society. Jane could not get away, but she promised Rachel she would be praying for her. Mercy had excused herself from their guest to attend, which did not please Mrs. Grove, though Rachel was glad she was there. Even so, without Jane by her side, Rachel's confidence flagged. Who was she to say anything to these women? She had never been like her mother, caring about her less fortunate neighbors, taking baskets of food or visiting the sick. But people could change, could they not?

Before she could find the courage to speak up, the carter, Mrs. Burlingame, raised the topic herself.

"I rode past Bramble Cottage on my way into town. What a sight! Someone—or several someones, by the look of things—threw eggs and rotten vegetables again."

"Serves her right," Mrs. Barton grumbled.

Julia Featherstone frowned at her. "No one deserves that. Eggs are devilish hard to clean. Not to mention expensive. What a waste."

Mercy looked at the others. "Some of you may not know she recently fainted on the High Street. . . ."

"The High Street? What was she doing there? I thought she never ventured into the village, unless in the dead of night."

"The point is, she is not well," Mercy said, "and should not have to clean that herself."

Mrs. Barton sniffed. "I hope you are not suggesting we do it."

"Why not?" Miss Cook challenged. "It was probably someone's son in this very room who did it."

"Why are you looking at me?" Mrs. Barton glared. "I hope you are not accusing one of my boys, Charlotte Cook."

Charlotte humphed.

Mrs. Barton continued, "Why should we help her? She has spurned every attempt we made to befriend her when she moved here."

Mrs. Snyder threw up her hands. "That was thirty years ago!"

"A woman like her can't expect help from decent people."

The vicar's wife sighed. "My boys and I will do it."

Poor Mrs. Paley. She felt duty bound to do everything no one else wanted to do. For the first time, Rachel noticed how weary the woman looked.

Rachel stood. "No, Mrs. Paley, you do too much as it is." She looked around at the assembled women, some surprised and some annoyed that she would speak when she was such a new member. She searched for the right words and began.

"I don't know the whole story, but even if the rumors are true, haven't we all made mistakes? I certainly have. And you all know my father did. Whatever the case, she is on her own now, as many of us are. Left to fend for herself. You know her longtime maid and friend died. And recently that woman's daughter left as well. And now her house has been vandalized. She has been living off a few scrubby vegetables from her garden and the eggs from her last hen, which was either let out of its pen or stolen.

"She has never even dared to offer her soap at the market here in Ivy Hill. She imagines she would be shunned, perhaps hit with rotten eggs again. And she probably would be, unless we do something—unless we make it known we support her. We are the women of Ivy Hill, and we wield influence in our community. Can we not influence our community for the good? For the good of one woman, one neighbor, one of *us*?"

Rachel stopped speaking and drew in a long breath. Around the room, the women stared at her, expressions inscrutable. Face burning, Rachel sat down. Had she made a fool of herself? Probably.

The silence stretched. Even Mercy remained quiet. Even Mrs. Paley. Had she overstepped? Spewed righteous indignation and made things worse? She hoped not.

Rachel swallowed, clasped her hands, and waited.

Finally Mrs. Barton said, "Goodness me, what speechmaking. We shall have to bring in more chairs at this rate."

Was she criticizing or complimenting? It did not sound like a compliment.

Then Mrs. Barton gave a decisive nod. "Well, I can be there at eight. Have to milk my bossies first, but we rise early at the dairy."

"I will join you," Mrs. O'Brien said.

Mrs. Snyder nodded. "Me too."

"I will bring buckets and rags in my cart," offered Mrs. Burlingame. She looked at the young sign painter. "Becky, could we borrow your ladder?"

"Of course."

"I can spare a hen," Miss Featherstone offered.

"And I . . ." Mrs. Klein pronounced, like a benediction, "shall bring the tea."

Rachel expelled a breath she barely realized she'd been holding. Beside her, Mercy took her hand and gave a gentle squeeze.

Mr. and Mrs. Grove insisted their daughter stay home the following day with Mr. Hollander, so Mercy offered to watch over the library while Rachel helped at Mrs. Haverhill's.

Rachel, Matilda Grove, and the schoolgirls left Ivy Cottage together the next morning, wearing old gloves and gardening aprons over their clothes. Matilda carried a plate of biscuits.

Even though Mercy had to remain behind, she thought it would be a good lesson for the girls—not only in helping a neighbor but in showing them Mrs. Haverhill was not the witch some of them imagined her to be.

When the ladies of Ivy Cottage reached Ebsbury Road, they met up with Julia Featherstone, who held a clucking but otherwise docile hen under her arm. Mrs. Burlingame rumbled up in her cart. Mrs. Klein sat in back, steadying the urns of tea nestled there, while Miss Morris sat beside her, holding onto a ladder.

When they reached Bramble Cottage, they discovered Mrs. Snyder had arrived earlier and already had some of Mrs. Haverhill's clothes laundered and hanging on the clothesline beside the house.

Mrs. Barton was there as well, scrubbing away at the walls with short but powerful arms. One of her adolescent sons worked beside her, while another lad hauled the buckets Mrs. Bushby filled at the well.

They all pitched in, scrubbing, dumping water, sharing the ladder or finding crates to stand on to reach higher places, and gathering the vegetable fragments, which could be fed to the McFarlands' pig.

Mrs. Haverhill poured tea and replenished food on a small table they'd set up for the purpose. They had Matty's biscuits, Mrs. Bushby's plums, and a basket of individual chicken-and-leek pies Jane had sent over from The Bell.

Mrs. Haverhill began the morning stiff and wary, on her guard for cruel comments or anyone who'd come only to peek inside private Bramble Cottage at last. But she warmed as the morning progressed and all were kind to her—save for a few scowling adolescent boys. But even their scowls dissolved upon the arrival of the schoolgirls. Soon the tension began to visibly ease from Mrs. Haverhill's frame.

She provided soap and towels for the helpers to wash their hands before eating. And she sent each one home with her gratitude and a small bar of sweet-smelling soap she had made from Mrs. Snyder's recipe. Later, as the cleaning "party" drew to a close and people began to depart, Matilda took Rachel aside.

"Well done, my girl. Your mother would have been proud of you. I know I am."

Tears stung Rachel's eyes at her tender praise, and she squeezed the woman's hand. "Thank you."

Matilda and the pupils left to return to the schoolroom, but

Rachel remained behind to help tidy up. Mrs. Haverhill put the kettle on, asking Rachel to stay and talk over the day before she left as well.

As Rachel stepped back outside to gather the few remaining cups and utensils, she was surprised to see Timothy Brockwell walking up the path, his black horse tethered at the gate.

"Miss Ashford," he said formally and bowed.

She instantly felt the tension between them and stood there awkwardly, unsure what to do, what to say.

"Sir Timothy."

He held up his palm. "Don't worry, I have not come to continue our last conversation, which so upset you. I have only come to call on Mrs. Haverhill, to see how she recovers."

Rachel dropped a spoon and bent clumsily to retrieve it. "That's all right. I can be out of your way in a few minutes."

From behind her, Mrs. Haverhill said, "Rachel, would you mind staying?"

She glanced over her shoulder to where Mrs. Haverhill stood in the open doorway. "I . . . don't know that Sir Timothy wants me—"

"Well, I do," Mrs. Haverhill insisted.

"I don't mind at all if Miss Ashford remains," Timothy said.

Rachel pressed a hand to her prickly stomach. "Very well." She preceded him back into the cottage.

As they entered, Mrs. Haverhill looked warily up at the newcomer. "Good afternoon, Sir Timothy."

"How goes your recovery, Mrs. Haverhill? I hope you are in good health?"

"I feel much better, thank you. Due in large part to Miss Ashford here, as well as Mrs. Bell."

His gaze flickered to Rachel, then away. "Excellent friends to have, I agree." He cleared his throat. "I would like to ask you a few questions, if I may?"

"You may, though I should warn you—you may not like my answers." Her eyes held a shimmer of sadness.

She and Rachel sat on the sofa together, and he took the chair opposite.

Mrs. Haverhill folded her hands in her lap. "What would you like to know?"

He held her gaze. "The truth."

"Very well. Ask what you like."

"You mentioned you have lived here for thirty years," he began. "You came here when you were very young, then."

"I was young all right—not yet four and twenty."

"You moved to Ivy Hill after . . . Mr. Haverhill died?"

She sighed. "There was no Mr. Haverhill. I never married. Only in my heart. We thought *Mrs.* would grant me an air of respectability."

His mouth tightened at that. "Were you and Mr. Carville acquainted before you came to Ivy Hill?"

"No. Wait, that's not exactly true. I believe I saw him in London once or twice. He went up with your family for the season back then."

"You were . . . friends, Carville tells me."

"Mr. Carville and I? No. He has never liked me. And in those days, I was not accustomed to keeping company with servants. I was a lady, if you can believe it. Not a rich one, but a lady all the same."

"But he told me you were an old friend, and that was why you paid no rent here."

"Tim . . ." She shook her head, her tone indulgently maternal. "Do you really still not know? I have never paid rent for this place, even before Carville inherited it from your father." She looked at Rachel, eyebrows high in question.

Rachel opened her mouth to answer but closed it again. What could she say? She doubted Timothy would have believed her even had she tried to tell him what she suspected.

Mrs. Haverhill sighed heavily. "I am so weary of secrets. I think almost everyone in Ivy Hill—probably even Wishford—knows, except for those the truth most affects. The gossip stopped short of Thornvale, Fairmont House, and Brockwell Court—at least abovestairs."

"What are you saying?" Sir Timothy's jaw tensed, and Rachel saw dark suspicions glinting in his eyes. He guessed, or at least feared, more than he let on.

"Bring the tea, will you, Rachel?" Mrs. Haverhill asked. "I hear the kettle. I have a feeling my throat will be dry before my tale is told."

"Of course." Rachel rose and stepped into the kitchen. She poured water into the teapot already on the tray, added a third cup, and returned.

Mrs. Haverhill watched her cross the room, and her gaze fell on the miniature portrait on the table. She picked it up and began.

"This is what I looked like when I met Sir Justin. Though he wasn't Sir Justin then, as his father was yet living. My mother scraped together all the money she could to give me a London season, determined to help me find a suitable husband before she passed. My brother, a barrister, served as my chaperone. When I met Justin, I thought our financial worries were over. Don't mistake me. I was not drawn to his wealth alone. I loved him, and he fell in love with me and wanted to marry me. I was never so happy in my life, before or since.

"He said he needed to talk to his parents first, before formally asking my brother for my hand. I understood that he needed to convince them and anticipated a fight. I was a gentleman's daughter but had little in the way of connections or dowry. He assured me they would come round to the idea, given time and persuasion.

"When the season ended, his parents insisted Justin return to Ivy Hill with them, and away from me. He went, promising to return as soon as he'd persuaded them. I waited but, in all honesty, steeled myself for disappointment, sure I had seen the last of him.

"Then one day, he unexpectedly showed up at our house, urging me to pack quickly, for he had a carriage waiting outside. I thought he meant we should elope, scandal though that would be. Oh! If only we had! Instead, he told me he was taking me to Brockwell Court, where he would make his parents see reason. Once they knew me better, he said, they could not refuse."

Mrs. Haverhill sadly shook her head. "I was young and foolish.

I left my brother's protection to travel without a chaperone with a man not my husband. Socially, I was ruined as soon as the carriage pulled away from our house. Yet I truly believed Justin would marry me, and when he did, no one would remember a night or two on the road unaccounted for."

Rachel kept her gaze on Mrs. Haverhill but from the corner of her eye noticed Sir Timothy clench his hands.

"But as we entered Wiltshire, I could see his bravado waning. He was more anxious than I had ever seen him. In the end, he had the coachman divert to Salisbury and secured a room for me at the Red Lion there. He decided he would talk to his parents alone first."

Again she shook her head. "He returned to Brockwell Court only to discover that they had all but arranged a match for him while he'd been away. To your mother."

"We ran up quite a tally at the Red Lion while he tried to negotiate with his parents. Finally he announced that he had acquired a cottage for me not far from Brockwell Court. He'd bought it quietly from an aging widower going to live with his son. He promised to refurbish it and provide a servant. It would only be temporary, he said. Until he talked his parents out of trying to force him to marry a stranger he did not love.

"In the end, as you know, he gave in to their urgings and married your mother. I was devastated, yet deep down, a part of me had always known it would happen. Of course the decision was not as difficult as it might have been, since he convinced me it didn't have to mean the end for us."

She shrugged. "Justin thought he could have it all—eat his cake, yet keep it too. The marriage his parents wanted to a suitable, wealthy wife. A proper heir to follow in his footsteps. And me, whenever he grew bored or lonely."

Mrs. Haverhill glanced at Timothy. "You might be tempted to conclude he intended to make me his mistress all along. But I honestly don't believe he meant to deceive me, though perhaps he had deceived himself into thinking he could ever gain his parents' blessing. Oh, the compelling promises he uttered. The idyllic pictures he painted of our secret life. And I abandoned reason and let myself be persuaded."

Tears brightened her eyes. "And I was happy for a time, or at least content, living here with Bess and young Molly. Of course, eventually, my precarious situation could not fail to erode my confidence . . . and my conscience. But what could I do? I could not go back to my brother's house unmarried. He could not have sheltered a ruined woman without losing every client he had, and the society of every friend of any moral standard. Besides, I was too ashamed to go back. So I remained."

She inhaled deeply. "When Sir Justin died, the monthly allowance that supplied our household died with him. The last several years have been difficult, financially and emotionally. Wearing mourning has not been a ruse. I suppose you will say I am getting my just deserts. Suffering the consequences I deserve and always knew would come one day."

She sipped her tea before continuing. "I lived in fear for months that the cottage would be taken away as well, and I would be out on my ear without a penny and nowhere to go. Instead, Mr. Carville came and coolly told me that I was to be allowed to live here, and the taxes and heating would be paid, but that from then on I was on my own for the rest. I gather Sir Justin insisted on his deathbed, or I am sure Mr. Carville would have enjoyed putting me out. He is clearly still determined to protect Sir Justin's reputation and the Brockwell name. I am the wicked woman who led his perfect master into sin, and he will never believe otherwise."

Mrs. Haverhill looked at Timothy, eyes pensive and weary. "I suppose you will refuse to believe it as well."

Sir Timothy crossed his arms over his chest. "I don't know what to believe. Carville insists you are just another unfortunate woman my father met during the course of his magisterial duties, another poor widow like Mrs. Kurdle whom he felt sorry for and decided to help out of his great generosity."

Mrs. Haverhill looked at him, expression full of pity. "You believe that if you need to, Tim. If it helps you sleep at night."

"Why do you call me Tim?" he snapped. "That is rather presumptuous."

"Pray do not be offended. It is an old habit. It is how your father referred to you when we spoke of you."

His jaw tensed. "It is a familiar name you have no right to use."

At his harsh tone, Rachel protested, "Timothy, please."

He ran an agitated hand over his face. "Can you prove any of this?"

"I could. I have the letters he wrote to me, though they are personal and I'd rather you didn't read them. I would show you the ring he gave me and other mementos I had of him, but they . . . have gone missing."

Instead she picked up the book of poetry Timothy had noticed when he and Rachel came to feed her cat—the one with the inscription Rachel had seen but Timothy had not. Mrs. Haverhill opened it to the signed page and laid it on the table between them.

Rachel held her breath.

He stared at the inscription, face white. He looked . . . thunderstruck.

Concern washed over her. "Timothy?"

He snapped the book shut. It felt like a slap.

Rachel didn't know what to do, what to say.

He looked at her, betrayal written on his face. "You saw this the other day, didn't you."

"I did, but I thought . . . *J* could be anyone."

He shook his head, a bitter twist to his lips. "I recognize my father's handwriting. I know it almost as well as my own."

Timothy turned to Mrs. Haverhill. "He might have given you that book before he married my mother."

Mrs. Haverhill opened the book again and pointed to the publication date. "That would be a trick, as this book was published within the last fifteen years."

Sir Timothy's nostrils flared. He pushed the book away, rose, and stalked out of the cottage.

Rachel looked at Mrs. Haverhill. "I'm sorry. He's upset."

"Of course he is."

"Excuse me." Rachel grabbed her shawl off the peg and followed Timothy outside, jogging up the path to catch up with him.

He glanced at her then stared straight ahead. "I apologize for leaving without saying good-bye. If I had stayed, I would have said something worse."

"I understand, and so does she."

He stopped at the gate, where his horse waited, and grasped the post. "When Mrs. Haverhill began weaving her tale, suggesting my father loved her, I thought she was deluded. That she had mistaken his pity for admiration or affection. But now . . ."

He shook his head, over and over again, eyes flashing. "I am an idiot. Carville indeed. He lied to protect the Brockwell name, and I believed him. I have been so willfully blind. All my life Father drilled the primacy of family honor and duty into me. Into Richard and Justina as well, but mostly to me as eldest and heir. Everything else—personal desires, dreams, love—was to be subjugated beneath what was best for the future of the Brockwells.

"All the while, he was not honoring his family, his wife, or his vows before God. All the while, besmirching the Brockwell name and his own integrity. And to think how he and my mother looked down on your father when he . . . made mistakes that are, at least in my view, nothing to this. What a hypocrite. And what proud hypocrites he made of us all."

Rachel had never seen him so angry.

He looked at her warily, eyes veiled. "Go on. This is your chance. Scoff at us. Shun us. We deserve it. I deserve it."

She saw the raw grief etched into his face, and compassion filled her. His image of his father had been shattered, much as her image of her own father had been. Rachel shook her head. "I would never do that."

"Why not? We all turned our backs on you and your family, except Justina. Too young to understand or to 'know better,' as Mamma would say."

Again Rachel shook her head. "I will not," she repeated. "It is not your fault. You didn't even know. Does your mother, do you think?"

"If she knew, she hid it well." He ran a hand through his thick hair. "You heard Mamma at dinner. She boasted about how Father was courting another woman but remembered his duty to his family and married her instead. I am certain she believed that former relationship ended then. I confess I never considered what became of the other woman."

He tipped his head back. "Now I see. . . . Father left the cottage to Carville, because he did not want to list his mistress in his will and thereby alert us to the woman's existence. He didn't devise a contingency for expenses after he died. Probably assumed he would live for a long time to come. Instead, he left her with the use of a house without the means to feed and clothe herself."

He looked over his shoulder at the cottage. "I am tempted to feel sorry for her, but how can I, when she and my father betrayed my mother? Betrayed us all."

"I realize she wasn't an innocent party. Yet I do feel sorry for her." Rachel recalled Mrs. Haverhill's devastation over the theft. *"The money I could understand, even the ring. But the lover's eye? The mourning locket? Knowing what they mean to me?"* "Wrong though it was, when she came to Ivy Hill, she really believed he loved her and would marry her."

Rachel felt sorry for Timothy as well. She also felt guilty for the part she had played in dredging all this up, and for trying to protect him instead of being fully honest with him.

He jerked the rein off the post and struck off down the road, leading his horse. Rachel walked beside him, lengthening her stride to keep up.

Irony sharpened his tone. "The *selfless* public servant, serving his fellow man with long hours, late nights, and nights away from home to fulfill his onerous duties. . . . Ha! Mamma belittling me for devoting fewer hours, and for working from home when *Sir Justin* went out to the people. If only she knew where he spent those hours, and who benefited from his attention! My whole life is based on lies. Every decision I've made to do something or not do something. All I thought I was and stood for . . . a sham."

"No, Timothy," Rachel tried to soothe him. "Not everything. You are not your father."

But her words did not seem to penetrate.

He looked at her, his demeanor suddenly officious. "I hope I can count on you to not spread this about?"

"Of course." Indignation flared at his tone. As if she were the village gossip! "I have never breathed a word against the Brockwells for their dealings with women, unfair or otherwise."

"What does that mean?"

She lifted her chin but said no more, fearing she might cry if she did.

"Forgive me." He ran an agitated hand over his face. "You have been hurt by all this as well. You were right when you said you had escaped the noose of marriage to a Brockwell."

Oh, how she regretted those words! "Timothy, I . . ."

"I have to go." He mounted his horse and galloped away.

Rachel watched him go, anxiety twisting her stomach. What had she done by bringing Mrs. Haverhill to his notice? And what would he do, now that the truth had come to light?

CHAPTER TWENTY-FOUR

While Rachel and the girls were busy at Mrs. Haverhill's, Mercy busied herself in the library, and Mr. Hollander kept her company. Her mother tarried upstairs, but eventually her father joined them, perusing the bookshelves and talking in low tones with the tutor. Then the two men settled themselves in the family sitting room with their selections. The time passed pleasantly, and Mercy enjoyed greeting those who came in and answering their questions, though the library was quieter than usual with so many Ivy Hill women busy elsewhere.

Midmorning, Mercy stepped out of the library for a short while to bring the men coffee and cake, then returned to find several people had entered during her brief absence. She signed up a new subscriber—a traveler staying at The Bell—and directed Mr. Paley to the theology books. Then voices from the adjoining room drew her attention.

Stepping to the doorway, she was surprised to see her mother seated in the drawing room turned reading room, talking animatedly with one of her old friends, Mrs. Bingley.

And there, near the bookcases, stood Mr. Kingsley. Not working for once but looking at a book. He nodded to her, and she smiled back, but as her mother's words registered, her smile faded and embarrassment washed over her.

"I tell you, Mrs. Bingley, Mr. Hollander is perfect for Mercy.

A great reader, a learned professor, and a tidy inheritance in the bargain. And such ambition. Mercy is going to help him write his masterwork, which will make him famous and—"

"Mamma!" Mercy interrupted. Walking over to them, she said brightly, "You did not tell me Mrs. Bingley had called."

"She has not." Her mother lifted her chin. "She is only here to visit the circulating library."

"Had I known you were in town, my dear," Mrs. Bingley soothed, "I would have paid a call sooner."

"Well then," Mercy said, "what a happy coincidence that Rachel's library brought you here today, Mrs. Bingley. How is the family—in good health, I trust? And Miss Bingley? So grown up the last time I saw her, I almost didn't know her."

From the corner of her eye, she saw Mr. Kingsley return the book to the shelf. He nodded again to Mercy on his way out and left empty-handed.

At dinner that evening, her mother was all smiles. Genuine smiles, Mercy noticed.

"We received a letter today from your brother—forwarded here from London." She beamed at her husband. "It is as we hoped, my dear. He is engaged to marry Miss Maddox!"

"That is excellent news."

"It is . . . mostly." Her mother's elation dimmed, and a worry line appeared between her brows. "If only her family did not live so far away. Ah well. We shall worry about that later."

Aunt Matilda lifted her glass. "To George."

Mr. Hollander lifted his as well. "To the happy couple."

Mercy joined the toast, pleased to see her mother looking so jubilant.

She held her husband's gaze. "Life is certainly looking up, my dear."

Her father grinned slyly at Mercy and Mr. Hollander. "Yes, a time of good news all around."

After they had eaten, Mrs. Grove looked significantly at her husband. When he failed to notice, she turned to Mr. Hollander and forged ahead. "What a filling dinner. You will certainly want to take another stroll after that. I understand Mercy showed you only the green last time. And of course you saw the church on Sunday."

"And a lovely church it is."

She shifted her gaze to Mercy. "Perhaps tonight, you might show him more of the village and the charms of life here in Ivy Hill."

"I . . . of course. If Mr. Hollander would like to walk?"

"Indeed I would."

Mercy rose, feeling self-conscious under her family's expectant gazes. They gathered hats and gloves and this time left by the front door.

"I apologize about my parents," Mercy began as they started east along Church Street.

"Apologize for them? Why?"

"They are being rather . . . overt."

"I don't mind. Subtlety is not one of my strengths."

Nor Mamma's, Mercy thought.

He added, "I prefer to be clear about what we are doing here."

Mercy felt a little breathless. "And what is that, Mr. Hollander?"

"Only the obvious. Your parents brought me here to meet you. They tell me you are amenable to marriage, and so am I."

Mercy swallowed. "But we have only just met. We are a long way from deciding whether or not we might suit."

"Are we? Well, that's cold coffee. I take pleasure in administering tests, I admit, but don't like taking them myself. Too much pressure to perform."

"You needn't perform for me, Mr. Hollander. Just be natural. And we shall . . . see."

"Be natural? Do any of us reveal our true natures to a new acquaintance, especially one of the opposite sex? Do men not bathe and put on cologne, and endeavor to squelch all inappropriate topics and bodily sounds? Nor am I ready to see you in paper curlers, with cream on your face. Not yet. I don't think anyone really means it when they say to 'act naturally.'"

Mercy's face heated. "I see your point."

She led him past the bakery toward the public house. Then they walked down Potters Lane. At its end, she gestured toward The Bell, mentioning her friend Jane, then pointed out businesses along the High Street.

She told him about her campaign to build a charity school in Ivy Hill, and her lack of success so far. She thought he might offer to help teach in this future school she dreamt of, but he only nodded, taking it all in.

They returned by way of Ivy Green. Across its expanse, a group of lads played. They tackled their tallest member, jumping in a pile, laughing and jostling for the ball.

Mercy winced. "They will injure one other."

"Oh, that's just how boys play," he assured her.

"If so, then I am glad I teach girls."

The ball squirted out of the pile and rolled toward them. Mr. Hollander bent and picked it up.

The boys rolled off one another, looking around for the ball. One noticed and called, "Throw it back, sir. Will ya?"

Instead, Mr. Hollander walked toward them, ball in hand, and Mercy hurried to catch up with him.

From the bottom of the pile of lads, a man appeared—Joseph Kingsley. He sat up and rubbed his head, a boyish grin on his face. "You lot weigh more than a load of granite." His grin faltered when he saw the two adults standing there.

He rose to his feet, dusting off his trousers. He was dressed in shirtsleeves and braces, his hair askew, grass stains on his knees.

He nodded to her, expression sheepish. "Evening, Miss Grove."

"Mr. Kingsley. From a distance, I thought you were another boy. Though a tall one."

"Aw, just having a bit of fun with the lads. Tom and Frank there are my nephews. They needed another player for their team."

"And who won?"

"Not I, by the looks of it. You'll have to forgive my appearance." He brushed ineffectually at a dirt smear on his sleeve.

Mr. Hollander tossed the ball to one of the boys, and they ran off with it, leaving the adults to talk. Mercy stood there silently, feeling ill at ease.

When she failed to introduce the two men, Mr. Kingsley nodded toward her companion. "Is this your . . . guest?"

"Oh. Forgive me. Yes, this is Mr. Hollander. A friend of my parents, visiting from Oxford."

"Not just a friend of your parents', I hope," the tutor mildly objected.

Embarrassed, she continued, "Mr. Hollander, this is Joseph Kingsley, the local builder, who so capably fitted out Miss Ashford's library."

Joseph wiped his hand on his trouser leg and offered it to the man. Mr. Hollander hesitated only a moment before shaking it.

A blond woman appeared on the edge of the green—short, petite, beautiful. She wore a fitted red spencer over her gown and a bright smile. Mercy did not recognize her.

"Joseph!" She waved vigorously.

He looked over, and a matching smile split his face. "Esther!" He glanced back at them. "Excuse me, Miss Grove, Mr. Hollander. Nice meeting you."

"Likewise."

Mr. Kingsley bounded across the grass and picked up the woman in a playful hug. She squealed—just as you'd expect a little woman would.

"Is that his wife?" Mr. Hollander asked.

Mercy shook her head. "I don't know who she is." Mercy did not think the blonde was one of his brothers' wives either.

Joseph called to his nephews, and they ran to join them. The tall man, the petite woman, and the two lads walked off together, Mr. Kingsley laying an affectionate hand on one of the boy's shoulders. They looked like a family. A perfect, happy family.

Mercy turned to Mr. Hollander and smiled bravely. "Shall we?"

CHAPTER TWENTY-FIVE

Crossing The Bell entry hall the next morning, Jane drew up short at the sight of Thora and Talbot in the coffee room. She looked at the tall case clock and her stomach pinched. Normally, Jane would be happy to see her mother-in-law. But Hetty Piper was due to arrive soon.

Jane's formerly tense relationship with Thora had transformed into one of mutual respect and fondness. Even so, Jane had not quite mustered the courage to tell her about Hetty's imminent arrival. Thora Bell Talbot was still an intimidating figure, a woman of strong opinions, not easily changed. She had been the one to give Hetty the sack because she disapproved of the girl. How would she react to learning Jane had hired her again at the inn Thora had once ruled like an all-powerful monarch?

Jane took a deep breath and pasted on a smile. "Thora. Talbot. Good morning."

"Morning, Jane," Thora greeted.

Kind Walter Talbot rose and pulled out a chair. "Can you join us, or are you busy?"

Jane hesitated. "Thank you. I would enjoy that. I have a . . . few minutes."

"Oh?" Thora's tone grew mildly curious. "What is happening in a few minutes?"

Alwena came over to pour her a cup of tea, and Jane was grateful for the interruption. "Thank you, Alwena. And just toast this morning, when you have a chance?"

Jane sipped her tea, hoping it would ease her nervous stomach. She wondered if there was some polite way to hurry Thora out of the inn before Hetty's coach arrived. She said, "You need not wait for me, if you two have already eaten? I'm sure the farm keeps you very busy, Talbot."

"Indeed it does. But we've taken on an extra hand to help with the animals, and that frees us up quite a bit."

Here was her opening. Jane set down her teacup. "Speaking of extra hands, I have engaged another chambermaid. We are busier than before, thankfully, so the timing seemed good."

"Who have you hired?" Thora asked. "Has she any experience?"

Jane licked dry lips, longing for another sip of tea. "Yes. As a matter of fact, she has worked here before."

"Who do you mean?"

"Hetty Piper."

Thora's eyes flashed, and Jane hurried on. "Now, Thora. I know you may not approve, but I have good reason."

"That girl has experience all right, but not the kind to help The Bell."

Talbot laid a hand on Thora's, though his gaze remained on Jane. "I remember Hetty. A sweet girl and a hard worker."

"She turned every man's head, including Patrick's. Or do you forget it?"

"That wasn't her fault."

"Was it not? She certainly didn't discourage the attention. It is why I dismissed her. Why on earth would you offer her a place now, after all this time?"

Jane took a breath. "Do you remember my telling you what I learned when I went to Epsom?"

Thora stilled, her expression softening in memory. "That's right. You said John went to help her, for some reason."

Jane nodded. "It was one of the reasons he went to Epsom."

Though the horse races were probably the primary reason, she added to herself.

"Hetty had a difficult time finding a respectable situation after she left here." Jane did not mention Thora's refusal to give the girl a character reference.

Thora shifted in her chair. "Do I want to ask why John felt duty bound to help this girl, and now you do as well? You told me there was nothing improper between her and John, did you not?"

"I did. And no, there wasn't. Not between her and John . . ."

She let the words drift away and sink in. Talbot and Thora exchanged a look, and then both sat back in their chairs.

"Ah," Talbot replied for them both.

Face grim, Thora asked, "Does Patrick know she's coming?"

"Yes, though not that she arrives today."

Thora lowered her voice. "Was there . . . a child?"

Jane nodded. "Gone. She gave it up."

Thora winced. "Where is Patrick, by the way? I did not see him in the office when we arrived. Tell me he has not already left the country again."

"No, I sent him to Wishford on some errands. I could have sent Colin, but I thought I would let Hetty settle in first."

Talbot nodded. "Very considerate, Jane."

Thora's lip curled. "And why you were trying to get rid of us."

"Not rid of you, Thora. But . . . Hetty has reason to be uneasy in your presence, you can't deny."

Talbot grinned. "She used to call you the lioness, I recall." He chuckled. "Rather apt."

Thora did not return his grin but nudged his arm. "You have to live with this lioness, so be careful."

"Beware your bite, you mean. I know." He patted her hand and regarded her fondly. "I shall spend the rest of my days trying to tame you. Shall I succeed, do you think?"

Jane expected a sharp retort, but instead Thora's eyes softened. "You have made a good start already."

My goodness, Jane thought, feeling suddenly as awkward as a third person on a wedding trip.

Alwena arrived with Jane's breakfast, and for the second instance that morning, Jane was grateful for the maid's timely appearance.

Jane had nibbled only a few bites when the southbound coach rumbled up the road, its arrival heralded by a sharp horn blast from its guard as the coach turned the corner.

She folded her napkin and rose. "If you will excuse me, I will go and greet Hetty myself. Assuming she hasn't changed her mind about coming."

Talbot again nodded, and to Jane's relief, Thora made no move to follow.

Jane went out into the yard as the ostlers, Tall Ted and Tuffy, hurried forward to meet the coach and take charge of the horses. The coachman greeted them and asked them to check the hooves of the leader.

Jane waited, wondering how Hetty's fellow passengers had treated a poor, coarsely dressed maid. Hopefully no one had harassed her.

The guard stowed his horn and hopped down from the back. He opened the coach door and let down the step. From inside, two gentlemen jostled to assist a lady within, arguing over which would carry her valise. One alighted first, elbowing the guard out of the way and offering his hand to the woman now framed in the open coach door.

Hetty Piper.

Hetty shook her head at their antics, smiling sweetly all the while. She extended a gloved hand and allowed the first gentleman to help her down.

She looked even prettier than when Jane had last seen her. Gone were the maid's plain dress, apron, and mobcap. In their place, she wore a green spencer over a carriage dress of gold and ivory stripes. A high-brimmed bonnet perched on the crown of her head like a straw halo, its ribbons tied under her chin, her dark red hair framing her cherubic face in charming spirals.

Then Hetty's gaze alighted on Jane, and her smile dimmed. "Hello, Mrs. Bell."

"Hetty." Should she have called her Miss Piper instead? At the moment, she certainly looked the part of a fashionable young lady. "Welcome," Jane added.

A small voice called, and Hetty turned back to the carriage door. Little arms reached out and wrapped themselves around Hetty's neck. Hetty scooped up a little girl of one or two and hoisted her on her hip.

Jane stood there, dumbly. What in the world? Did the child belong to a fellow passenger? But the toddler's tousled locks were nearly as ginger as Hetty's.

The second gentleman passenger handed Hetty's valise to Colin, who'd come out to assist, all of the men no doubt thinking Hetty a well-heeled guest and not a chambermaid. Jane was relieved to notice, however, that Colin did not stare at Hetty or her significant bosom, as the other men did.

Hetty's pretty face crinkled in an apologetic smile as she walked toward Jane. Closer now, it was clear her gown was old, likely secondhand, though of good material.

"I'm sorry I didn't tell you about my . . . traveling companion here," Hetty began. "I was afraid you would change your mind about letting me come."

Jane whispered, "Is this your child, Hetty?"

"She is." Hetty glanced back at the departing gentlemen. "They assume I am a young widow. Treated me like a princess."

"But you told me you had no child. That you'd had to give her up."

Hetty winced and looked down. "I didn't say she'd . . . died or anything. I said she was gone, and she was. I had to leave her with a wet nurse with two other babes in her care, so I could work. Goldie was the only one who would hire me, and she didn't even allow talk of babies, let alone anyone who worked for her to acknowledge having one. Bad for business. You caught me off guard, coming to the Gilded Lily like that with no warning. The words were out of my mouth before I could think better of them. Keeping her a secret had become second nature to me. I didn't mean to lie to you, but I let you believe I'd given up my child permanent-like, and I apologize."

"You didn't mention her in your recent letters either."

"I know. I'm sorry. Would you have let me come anyway?"

Jane hesitated. Would she have? How could Hetty work as a maid with a child to take care of? Was this Patrick's child? If so, he should be offering to marry her, not offering her a job.

The little girl stared at her, two fingers in her mouth, blue eyes round and fastened on Jane's face. "Is she . . ." Jane began, then stopped. She probably shouldn't ask about the girl's paternity right in front of her. Even though the girl was far too young to understand, the public, bustling stable yard was not the place for such a question.

But Hetty likely guessed what she'd been about to ask, for she looked away, then said quietly, "I did not come here with the intention of blaming anyone, or of asking for anything more than a situation."

"But you have . . . ?"

"Betsey."

"Betsey, to take care of."

"I know, but I'll think of something. I did before. There must be someone in the village who would be willing to watch her for a share of my wages. She eats anything now, though not too much, honest."

Jane sighed. "I don't see how this will work, Hetty."

"But you said you'd help me."

Fear shone in the young woman's wide eyes, and Jane hurried to reassure her. "And I will. But let me think what is best to be done."

Hetty glanced over Jane's shoulder and stiffened. Jane felt a prickle of foreboding and guessed who must be standing behind her.

She looked over. Sure enough, there stood Thora.

Talbot stood several paces behind, his thin face a grimace of apology. "I tried to stop her."

Hetty took a shaky breath. "Hello, Mrs. Bell. Mr. Talbot."

Thora just stared, but Talbot managed a nod. "Hetty, good to see you again."

Jane forced a smile. "I don't think I told you when I wrote, Hetty. But Thora and Talbot have recently married. She is Mrs. Talbot now."

"Oh . . ." Hetty breathed.

Thora gave her a pointed look. "But still a lioness."

Talbot's grimace deepened.

Hetty looked at Jane with betrayal in her expression, but Talbot lifted a hand. "Don't blame Jane, Hetty. I'm afraid I let the nickname slip. I thought it rather fitting. At the time."

Thora gave him a sour glance before turning back to Hetty. "And who is this?" She nodded toward the child.

Hetty squared her shoulders. "My daughter, Betsey."

Thora opened her mouth to . . . what? To ask Hetty who the father was? To condemn her? To demand to know how she expected to work with a child in arms? But the seconds ticked by and Thora said nothing.

"Of course she is." Talbot chuckled uneasily. "With that ginger hair and blue eyes, who else's daughter could she be?"

"I wonder . . ." Thora murmured. "How old is she—a year and a half?"

"Give or take."

Thora lifted her chin, her eyes distant in thought, or perhaps calculation. "Ah."

"It isn't what you think, Mrs. Bell—er, Mrs. Talbot. I have only come to work in a respectable place. I couldn't let Betsey grow up with a mother who worked in a . . . a place such as I was working—as a maid, mind. Only a maid."

Thora shot Jane a look. "You neglected to mention that part."

"It's not *her* fault. You're the one who . . ." Hetty broke off, thinking better of accusing the *lioness*.

"I'm the one who did not give you a character," Thora herself supplied. "I remember. I didn't think you deserved one at the time, but perhaps I was wrong. If so, I apologize."

Hetty stared at the woman as if she'd sprouted wings.

Jane did as well, though she had an inkling why Thora may have apologized.

And here came that reason now, striding through the carriage archway and across the courtyard. He lifted a hand in greeting. "Hello, Mamma. Talbot. Didn't expect to see you this—Oh!" He stopped midstride, and Colin, coming by with a small trunk for a departing guest, nearly collided with him.

"Hetty." Patrick's expression sobered. "So today is the day of your arrival." He sent Jane a knowing look that reminded her very much of Thora's. "And no doubt the reason Jane dispatched me to Wishford this morning."

"You are back sooner than I expected."

"That's because you sent me on a wild goose chase. There was no soap maker at the market today."

Jane frowned. "I am sorry. I thought Mrs. Haverhill might have returned by now."

Patrick's gaze shifted back to Hetty, and from Hetty to the child in her arms. His brow furrowed.

Hetty inhaled and lifted her chin. "Hello, Patrick."

Reluctantly, he asked, "And this is your . . . ?"

"My daughter. Betsey."

He opened his mouth to ask . . . something, then closed it again, perhaps deciding he might not like her answer.

Instead, he studied the little girl's face. The girl was all Hetty, as far as Jane could tell. She saw no obvious resemblance to handsome, dark-haired Patrick, though their blue eyes were similar. Then again, Hetty had blue eyes as well.

Jane had not known Patrick as a boy. She glanced at Thora, wondering what she saw when she looked at the child.

She did not know what to do. Did she give Hetty an apron and cap and set her to work? Or did she give her a guest room until they figured out some plan?

Hetty looked tentatively from face to face, up at the inn, then out the archway. "If I am to stay and work, I had better see about finding someone to watch Betsey—"

"I shall watch her," Thora said abruptly. "That is, if you don't mind, Talbot." Her gaze shifted from him to Hetty. "And if you can countenance a lioness caring for your cub."

Hetty stared and stammered, "Mrs. Bell, no. It's too much to ask. You have no reason to—no obligation to us, to her. I know I should not have turned up with her like this, but please believe me, I never meant to hint that you should . . . or to presume—not in a thousand years."

"I did raise two boys, you know. I am not incompetent, I assure you."

"But you have your own work, surely."

Thora waved a dismissive hand. "Oh, I help Sadie with the housework and Talbot with the accounts and whatever else I can find around the farm to keep me busy, but I'm bored senseless many days, truth be told."

Talbot's eyes downturned. "I thought you were happy."

"I am happy. With you. But I miss . . . being busy. I like having responsibilities. New challenges. I would be happy to watch over Betsey while you work, Hetty. If you would not mind."

"It is not that I would mind the help, Mrs. . . . Talbot, but I would not want to give you the wrong idea, or think that I am implying that Betsey is your . . . responsibility."

Thora frowned. "Enough excuses, Hetty. I realize I am not your favorite person and not your first choice to care for your child." She looked at Jane. "Who else might have an extra hand to spare? She won't be able to pay much."

"Perhaps Mrs. McFarland might like the extra income?"

"Eileen McFarland has her hands full as it is! And although I've come around to Colin, would you really want to put this child under his father's roof?"

Jane sighed. "I suppose not. I could ask the Ladies Tea and Knitting Society, see if one of them might be willing. We don't meet for several days, but I could begin asking around."

Thora looked pointedly at her son. "Unless you have a better idea?"

"I, um, no. No better idea."

"Well, let's not stand out here all day." Thora fell into her former take-charge role. "Tongues will be wagging as it is."

Talbot smiled at Hetty. "And I am sure you must want to rest after your journey."

She shook her head. "I feel perfectly well, truly. I've come to work, not rest. I don't want Mrs. Rooke to box my ears my first day back."

"Leave Bertha Rooke to me." Thora looked at Jane. "That is, if you don't mind my having a word with her, Jane?"

"Be my guest." Jane had already dreaded explaining Hetty's return to the staff, but now, with a child in tow?

"Mrs. Talbot," Hetty began soberly. "If you are willing to watch Betsey for a few days until I can find a long-term situation, I would be much obliged. I will pay you—"

"No, you won't."

Hetty blinked, and Jane saw tears in her eyes. Her voice quavered. "May I . . . please?"

For a moment the two women locked gazes, Thora clearly surprised at the fear in Hetty's plea. Jane was as well.

Talbot spoke up. "Don't worry, Hetty. We will work out an arrangement that will be comfortable for everyone, all right?"

Hetty nodded, but anxiety lingered in her eyes.

CHAPTER TWENTY-SIX

Hetty had insisted that she would walk Betsey out to the farm herself the next morning, so Thora was surprised when the carter's wagon came rumbling up the lane, Mrs. Burlingame at the reins, Hetty and the child beside her.

"Morning, Thora."

"Phyllis. Kind of you to give them a ride."

The carter shrugged. "Saw them walking. Your farm is not far off my usual route. It's no trouble to give these two a ride in the mornings."

Hetty climbed down, shifting the child to her other arm. "I appreciate that. Betsey here is heavier than she looks."

"See you tomorrow, then." Mrs. Burlingame nodded and commanded her horse to walk on.

Hetty looked at Thora. "Thank you again for offering to watch Betsey while I work." She pulled a scrap of paper from her apron pocket. "I've written down a few things, in case it's helpful—when she usually naps and what she likes to eat. If she fusses, a biscuit usually helps. She is partial to them."

Hetty handed over Betsey and the list of instructions. Thora was pleased to see Hetty wrote with a legible, if childish, hand and rather good spelling.

"And here is a blanket I made. It's pitiful, I know. But it will help her fall asleep."

"We shall get on perfectly well." Thora accepted it. "And Talbot and I will bring her to the inn this evening so you don't have to walk back. Now, go."

With many thanks, Hetty hurried off on foot to return to The Bell for her first day of work.

As soon as Hetty disappeared, Betsey began to cry.

"Come now, no one's pinching you." Thora carried the girl inside and into the bedchamber she and Talbot shared, looking for something to distract the child. Snagging something shiny off her dressing table, she carried the child back into the sitting room and sat on the sofa.

Thora looked at the toddler with her ginger curls and round, wet blue eyes and felt her heart crack open a bit. She lifted the gold chain before the girl's face, hoping to amuse away her tears. The bracelet had been a gift from Frank, her first husband. Shortly before she died, Nan—her friend and Talbot's sister-in-law—had encouraged Thora to bring her blue heart out of hiding. Now Thora dangled the enamel pendant before Betsey's tear-streaked face. The girl fell silent, watching it, entranced, and Thora congratulated herself on her quick thinking.

A second later, the little fist shot out and grabbed the heart, yanking it off the chain.

Thora gasped. "No, now, give that back."

The adorable imp refused, clutching it as if it were life itself . . . or a biscuit.

Thora didn't want her to choke on the thing. "Come on, my girl, hand it over."

As Betsey stubbornly refused to yield, Thora saw her first indication that the girl might be related to her after all.

Thankfully, Talbot came in from the barn with a kitten to show Betsey, and the blue heart was released at last.

Now if only the toddler did not choke the kitten.

When it was time to go outside for recess that day, Mercy donned the bonnet her mother had brought. It had a soft crown of floral printed cotton, which complemented the new Pomona-green dress and matching spencer. Glancing in the mirror as she tied the ribbons, Mercy was pleasantly surprised by her reflection. She felt almost pretty in the becoming attire.

Mr. Hollander came out into the back garden to keep Mercy company, while Matilda stood talking over the garden gate with Mrs. Shabner, Ivy Hill's dressmaker.

For a few minutes, Mercy and Mr. Hollander sat on the bench together and simply watched the girls play. Alice and Phoebe took turns on the swing while Anna pushed them. Sukey sat on a rug beneath the tree, reading as she often did. Two other girls played with a neighbor's cat that had leapt atop the garden wall.

"How old are they?" Mr. Hollander looked from pupil to pupil. "I have no experience with girls to gauge their ages."

"They range from eight to almost eighteen at present. Though Anna, the eldest, is more helper than pupil at this point. She will make an excellent teacher one day. In fact, she is already tutoring one young man in arithmetic."

Mercy's gaze returned to Alice. She took a deep breath and prayed for the right words. "Mr. Hollander. I need to tell you something. Something very important to me. Do you see the little girl there, on the swing? That is Alice, my youngest pupil. Her great-grandfather, her last living relative, has asked me to become her legal guardian. My lawyer is even now drawing up the documents."

His brows rose. "Guardian? That is a great deal to ask of you, is it not?"

"Not in this case. I want to do it. As I have no children, it would be a blessing to raise Alice as my own."

"But . . . you might yet have your own children."

"If so, then I would be doubly blessed. But I am thirty years old. Not *too* old, but, well, there are no guarantees, are there?"

"This is a complication I had not foreseen, Miss Grove. Your parents made no mention of a child."

"It is recent news to them as well. They wanted to meet Alice before saying anything one way or another, and now they have."

"I see. May I ask what became of the girl's parents?"

"Her father died years ago. Lost at sea. Her mother died only recently, though she had been sickly since Alice's birth."

"But Alice herself is in good health?"

"Yes, perfectly."

"Her parents were . . . married?"

Mercy hesitated. Was it only the objectionable elopement that caused Mr. Thomas to disown his granddaughter? Mercy sensed there might be more to it than that, but she wasn't sure. "Yes, as far as I know."

"Forgive me, but is there something wrong with the girl . . . that her grandfather wants to be rid of her?"

Mercy winced at his wording but calmly clarified, "It is her great-grandfather. His wife recently died, and he wants to make sure Alice will be taken care of when they are both gone. There is nothing wrong with that, and nothing wrong with her either."

"Pray, do not be offended, Miss Grove. I am only asking. Have I not the right to know?"

Had he? Did she want him to have that right? Mercy was not certain. "Why do you not talk with Alice and judge for yourself?"

"Talk with her? I would have no idea what to say to an eight-year-old girl."

"You get on well with the girls at breakfast. And you talk to young people all the time in your work."

"As a teacher, yes, but not as a prospective parent."

"You would learn. That is, had you the need to."

He ran an agitated hand over his face. "I think it only fair to remind you that I have been a bachelor for a long time, Miss Grove. Marriage itself will be an immense change. But to parent someone else's child in the bargain? I can learn the one, but the other, at the same time? I don't know—that would be an advanced course of study indeed."

Mercy clasped her hands. "I realize it is a great deal to ask. Do not make yourself uneasy, Mr. Hollander. I understand your reservations. I was asked to serve as Alice's guardian before I met you. At the time, I did not think it would affect anyone else, at least directly."

"But you will not change your mind now? Surely he would understand if you must reconsider?"

"I don't want to reconsider. I was fond of Alice before he asked, and now all the more."

"I see. Well, that shows me where I fall in your list of priorities."

Mercy's stomach knotted. She'd offended him. . . .

But he quickly lifted a palm. "Which, if I am honest, is a relief to discover. I admit I feared you might be . . . overeager to wed."

He'd meant *desperate*, Mercy supposed, but she was glad he'd not articulated the word. "No. I am not bent on leaving my single state. Teaching has given my life purpose and fulfillment."

"But if you were to marry, you would not have need to continue teaching."

She looked at him in astonishment. "My need to teach goes deeper than financial gain. It is my calling. My purpose."

"But would not being a wife—your husband's helpmeet—be your new purpose?" Again he held up a hand. "Miss Grove, I don't mean that in a condescending manner, truly. I understand that a woman of your intelligence and education would want to do more than plan menus and write laundry lists or whatever it is that wives do when they have servants to cook and clean."

Aunt Matty waved good-bye to Mrs. Shabner, then looked in their direction. Seeing them in deep conversation, Matilda called to the pupils, "Let's go in, girls. Time has got away from us."

As her aunt shepherded the girls inside, Mercy turned on the bench to better see Mr. Hollander's face. "Then what are you suggesting I do?"

"That you take all that passion for education and help me write my book, as your aunt proposed. A book that will improve the lives of not just a few pupils, but if all goes well, many hundreds more. Thousands, even."

"How could I help? I am a teacher, not a writer."

He thought for a moment. "You could . . . compile my notes

and devise those broader applications you suggested. Edit and proofread and write fair copies and whatever else needs doing. Your help would be invaluable, don't you see? Your experience as a teacher would not be wasted. With your assistance, I could complete the book more quickly, and I know it will be a great success."

"And if it is not?" Mercy asked, thinking, *You have not written a single word yet!* It seemed like quite a leap to depend on it for his future livelihood.

"And if it is not," he answered calmly, "then I will pursue my former plan of opening a boys school or becoming a private tutor."

"But I already have a school."

"Yes, with six girls of humble birth who pay, what, a few pounds a year? Without your father's support, you could not live on that. You know a boys school, especially a prestigious one with an Oxford man at the helm, would command a far greater income."

It would; she could not deny it.

He added gently, "Would not caring for the boys, acting as the school's matron, be a reasonably satisfying substitute?"

Mercy felt flustered. "Substitute for what—for pupils of my own, or children of my own?"

"Both, if need be. As you say, there is no guarantee of future offspring."

"I am not sure. . . . What about Alice?"

"I will have to think about that," he replied.

"And so will I."

That afternoon, Jane found the office empty and wondered where Patrick was. When she rounded the booking desk, she saw a foreign sight: Patrick carrying two large water cans up the passage from the scullery.

Hetty met him as she came down the stairs. "You didn't have to do that, Mr. Bell. I'll take those up from here."

"You should have Ned or Colin carry them for you."

"They're busy. Besides, I did all the hauling at Goldie's."

"You're not at Goldie's any longer, thank God. And here, the male staff help with the bath water."

"I don't mind. I am as strong as they come." She playfully flexed an arm muscle. "See?"

His gaze remained on her face. "Yes, I do see. And if you are half as strong as you are pretty, heaven help us all."

She gave him a charming smile at that, and he stood there smiling back like a besotted schoolboy.

"Patrick?" When he didn't respond or even seem to hear her, Jane repeated more loudly. "Patrick!"

He jerked around, water sloshing on the floor. "Hm? Oh, Jane, sorry."

Jane rolled her eyes. "Haven't you something more productive to do than flirt with our new maid?"

He lifted the water cans. "I was helping her."

"Um-hm."

"And now I had better deliver these before the water cools." He gave Hetty another smile and carried both cans effortlessly up the stairs.

With a guilty glance at Jane, Hetty bent to wipe up the spill with a cleaning rag. "Sorry, Mrs. Bell."

"That's all right, Hetty. Not your fault."

The door opened, and Jane turned. There came Talbot and Thora, Betsey in arms. Seeing her mother, the little girl all but launched herself out of Thora's clasp.

"Ma, Ma!"

"Hello, my love!" Hetty rose, wiped her hands on her apron, and picked up the child, hugging and kissing her. "I missed you. How was she? Any trouble?"

Thora shot Talbot a look. "No trouble at all."

With Betsey returned to her mother's care, Thora went to the kitchen to greet Mrs. Rooke while Talbot talked to Colin at the front desk.

The cook grumbled about the returning chambermaid having a child sleep in her room. Scandalous and unheard of!

"Am I cooking for a baby farm now rather than a renowned coaching inn?" Bertha Rooke's eyes flashed. "It would never have been allowed in your father's day. Or yours."

"Perhaps not. But you do know I am caring for the child so Hetty can work here?"

"I heard that but could not credit it. Are you not the one who gave her the sack in the first place?"

"I was. But people change."

"Her or you?"

"Both, hopefully. Or perhaps I was wrong about her."

Mrs. Rooke humphed. "Love has softened your brains."

Thora chuckled. "You're probably right about that."

Mrs. Rooke was likely not the only one raising eyebrows over the situation—probably gossiping about it as well. Let them. Thora decided she did not care.

Talbot was still talking to Colin at the desk, so Thora sought out Patrick. She found him alone in the office, massaging his shoulder muscles.

"Patrick, I want to talk to you."

He slouched in the chair, mouth quirked. "How that tone does take me back. Something tells me I shall not like what you have to say."

"Look at me and answer honestly. Were you and Hetty . . . involved . . . when she worked here before?"

"Yes—though only very briefly."

"So it is possible the child is yours?"

He shrugged. "I suppose it is, yes."

Thora shook her head. "When I sent Hetty away, I thought I could prevent the worst from happening. I did not know I was already too late. I was trying to protect you. Now I see I should have been trying to protect her."

Patrick sent her a swift glance, and in it she saw a depth of hurt that surprised her.

"I am not a lecher, Mamma. She came to me. But thank you for that sterling summary of my character."

Regret and concern twisted Thora's stomach. "I am sorry. But can you blame me, after . . . everything?" She reached out and cupped his chin. "Let's not waste time on past regrets, Patrick. It's what we do now that matters."

CHAPTER
TWENTY-SEVEN

The next morning, when Mercy went downstairs for breakfast, she was surprised to see Mr. Hollander in the vestibule, valise in hand.

Her stomach sank. "Mr. Hollander, you're leaving? I thought you planned to stay longer."

"I had. But I have decided to travel back early on my own. I have been to The Bell and secured a place on an Oxford-bound stage."

She walked nearer, heart pounding dully. Her mother would not be pleased. "Do my parents know?"

"I told your father late last night. Your mother had already gone to bed. I asked him to pass along my gratitude for introducing us."

"I did not intend to offend you, Mr. Hollander."

"You did not." He patted her hand and looked at her earnestly. "I don't go away angry, Miss Grove. I go away . . . hopeful. You know where I stand, but I will not pressure you. I will leave you to consider what you want for the future. I think you and I could have a good life together. Not everything you want, perhaps, but I believe we could be happy. I have read enough on the subject to glean that some compromise is required in marriage—some sacrifice of personal preference—and I am willing to do so where Alice is concerned."

That was a relief. Or was it? If only he were willing to compromise on her school as well!

"But I shall not oversell my charms, which are not legion, I realize." He handed her a card. "Please do write if you think of any further questions, or when you reach your decision. I move out of my rooms after Christmas, so if you could let me know by then?"

"I will, thank you. I appreciate your patience." Outwardly, Mercy remained calm, but her heart and mind were not. Should she ask him to stay longer, or give him an answer now? If only she knew what the answer should be.

After breakfast with the girls, Mercy returned to her bedchamber. Her mother came in, hair still in paper curlers, dressing gown over her nightdress, expression pained.

"Your father just told me." She closed the door. "Mr. Hollander has gone back to Oxford?"

"Yes."

"Why? Don't tell me you refused him already."

"He is giving me time to decide without pressuring me. I hope you will do the same, Mamma."

Catherine DeLong Grove heaved a sigh. "Mercy, I see now that we have made your life here too comfortable. Allowed you to believe that you would have Ivy Cottage to yourself with no obligation to the rest of the family—save your aunt, of course. But that was never our intention. This house was never meant to be a girls school, subscription library, or whatever notion strikes you next. It is a family home. Meant for a married couple and their children. You and George grew up here. Before that, your father and Matilda.

"I had hoped you would marry long before now. I have tried, heaven knows, to help you over the years, to improve your chances and introduce you to the right sort of men. Not all were interested, but a few were. However, none of them were good enough for you. This one wasn't tall enough or had enough clever conversation. That one was too much the rattle or sportsman."

Defensiveness flared. "I never said they were not good enough."

"But you didn't marry them either, did you? Do you know Sir Cyril Awdry is now courting young Miss Brockwell?"

Yes, Mercy had heard. "They weren't right for me, Mamma."

"Now we bring Mr. Hollander to you on a silver platter. Taller than you, intelligent, well-read, and a professor, for goodness' sake, and still you despise him."

"I don't despise him. I never said a critical word about him."

"Of course not. Everyone knows Mercy Grove is too kind and gentle to say an unkind word about anyone. How weary I am of hearing the saintliness of my only daughter extolled."

The words pricked her. "I am not a saint, Mamma. And I cannot claim to never say anything I shouldn't."

"Yes, about your mother, no doubt. Who is so horrid as to try to see you well married and happy!"

"I am happy. Or I was."

Her mother stepped closer and looked into her face. The anger fell away and in its place, her direct scrutiny seemed to strip Mercy bare. Her mother might not always empathize, but she knew her daughter very well.

"Look me in the eye and tell me the absolute truth. Can you tell me, before God, that you are never lonely? Never hope for a husband to love you, comfort you, and show you affection? Never wish for children to love and teach and pray for?"

In her mother's expression Mercy saw not belligerence but earnest question. Tears and pain brightening her eyes, she repeated, "Can you?"

Mercy lifted her chin. She did not believe all women needed a husband or children to be fulfilled. To be complete and whole and happy. She opened her mouth to say so, but the words stuck there. She swallowed and shook her head. If only she were one of those women.

Her mother grasped her hand. "You see, my dear? You may not approve of our bringing Mr. Hollander here, but you must allow we are only trying to help you. I don't want you to be alone all your life. Now, will you marry the man or not?"

"I . . . don't know if I can, Mamma."

Her mother sighed. "Then you leave me no choice, Mercy.

George and his new bride will need a place to live. As I said, Ivy Cottage is a family home. A Grove family home, meant for a married couple. If you refuse to marry Mr. Hollander, we will offer the home to George and his soon-to-be wife."

Mercy sucked in a breath. "But . . . George has had no interest in Ivy Cottage, Ivy Hill, or England, for that matter, for two decades. Perhaps you never said the house was mine and Aunt Matty's forever—but with you and Papa living in London and George out of the country all these years . . . yes, I did see this place as my house. I do. This is my home. It isn't right you should give it to someone else if I simply choose not to marry a man I don't love."

"Please don't be melodramatic, Mercy. George has as much right to live here as you do. More, now, as he will soon have a wife to provide for and, one day soon, God willing . . . children."

Mercy's heart beat hard. "And what are Aunt Matilda and I supposed to do? And what about Alice?"

"Calm yourself, Mercy. Heavens, I have never seen you so upset. No one is putting you out on the street. Matilda will live out her days here with George's family. And if you choose that fate for you and your ward as well, so be it."

"But what about my school? My other pupils?"

"They must go. The schoolroom will be returned to its original purpose, as will the drawing room. All those extra bookcases must go."

This could not be happening. "And Rachel?"

Catherine Grove sighed again. "The Ashfords were old friends. If their daughter needs a place to stay, and you are willing to share your bedchamber with her, I shall not object. Though I don't know that our new daughter-in-law will feel the same way. Or you might live in London with us, if you prefer."

Mercy shook her head. "No, Mamma. Ivy Hill is my home. I don't wish to leave it."

"Then marry Mr. Hollander and raise his children here. The decision is yours." Her mother squeezed her hand and departed, leaving Mercy alone to ponder her fate.

That evening, Mercy sat through a tense and quiet dinner in a daze of disbelief. Rachel and Aunt Matilda kept looking at her in concern, but how could Mercy reassure them all was well when it was not?

After the meal, her father called her into the sitting room and closed the door behind them. "If it helps at all, Mercy, I am sorry. I feel I must support your mother in this, but I take no pleasure in it."

He led her to a chair and sat down opposite her. "I still hope it will work out between you and Mr. Hollander. Because I really can't deny that your brother and his wife will need a home to begin married life. If you both married, I suppose we might have to justify buying a second house for George, but if not, you can all live here."

Mercy stared glumly at her hands. "But no school."

"You can understand that, can't you? George and Helena will need the room for their children and her parents, when they visit."

"How do you know they will even want to live here?"

"George hinted at it. In his last letter."

Mercy winced. "And Mother is eager to oblige him."

"I don't say I approve of your mother's methods—of attempting to force your hand—but please try to understand. These last years have been trying for her—physically and emotionally. Women her age often go through . . . changes, I gather. Her physician says it is quite normal, though perhaps more noticeable in your mother's case."

"Why?"

"Because life has disappointed her."

Mercy's heart thudded. "I have disappointed her, I think you mean."

"Oh, Mercy, you are not alone in that. I have disappointed her as well. She had such lofty aspirations for me. I was supposed to distinguish myself somehow. Write a great treatise or run for political office or some such. Why do you think she has wanted to live in London all these years? So I could rub shoulders with the right sort of people. I have never been ambitious enough for her."

He rose and began pacing the room. "George disappointed her as well. Disappointed us both, truth be told. Determined to go to India against our wishes—I blame Winston Fairmont for that. How else would a boy raised in landlocked Wiltshire develop such a strong desire to cross the ocean? But even that venture proved a disappointment. He never became the success—financially or otherwise—we'd hoped. Otherwise, he might be in a position to buy his own house.

"And of course your mother has long wished you would marry and have children. It's only natural she should. You can't blame her for that. Nor can I deny that grandchildren would have been a pleasant diversion these last few years.

"And now George is engaged at last. She has something to look forward to, and pour her great energies into planning—setting up housekeeping for the new couple. The dream of grandchildren is in her grasp at long last. Miss Maddox, however, is from the north, near York. Your mother fears that if we don't provide an appealing living situation for them, then she will prevail upon her family to provide a house in the north, where we would very rarely see any future grandchildren.

"But with them here in Ivy Cottage, we would be within relatively easy traveling distance and have rooms to stay in whenever we like. You can see the attraction of the plan."

He sat back down with a sigh. "I know your mother can be . . . difficult. More so these last few years. I hope it is not disloyal to say so, but I want you to understand, to find it in your heart to give her extra patience and gentle forbearance."

"I will try, Papa."

"I know you will, my dear aptly named daughter. You do recall that it was my idea to name you Mercy?"

She nodded. She had heard the story before.

"Your mother wanted to name you Gertrude or Ophelia or

some such nonsense. But I insisted. And I was right—you have lived up to that name."

"Thank you, Papa."

He looked at her fondly. "Can you not like Mr. Hollander? Or at least respect him enough to consider him as a potential husband? I don't say he is a perfect man, but you must admire his education and love of books, if nothing else!"

"I do."

"Then give him a chance. But know that either way you will always have a home—with George here or with us in London, if you prefer."

"But my school, Papa."

"I know you will miss your school. But you might yet have your own children. Then could you not pour your talents into raising and teaching them? If nothing else, you might help educate George's children one day. They'll need their keen aunt to guide them. Heaven knows it will be beyond George." He winked at her, and she managed a small grin in return.

"You have given me much to think about, Papa." She rose. "So if you will excuse me . . ."

"Of course." He rose as well and pressed a kiss to her forehead. "It will be all right, my dear. You'll see."

Mercy managed a wobbly smile and turned from the room. She walked upstairs to the schoolroom, quiet this late in the day. There she shut the door, and the tears she'd fought so hard to contain filled her eyes and ran down her cheeks. Mercy leaned back against the wall slate, heedless of the chalk sure to mar her gown.

She closed her eyes tight, squeezing every muscle of her face, her hands, her body, trying to restrain the loud cry building within and threatening to burst forth.

Nearby, a book clapped closed, and Mercy's eyes flew open. There sat little Alice in the window seat, half hidden behind the curtain. The little girl set down the book and walked over to her, steady green eyes latched onto Mercy's face, a wrinkle of confusion between her brows.

"Are you crying, miss?"

Mercy wiped a hand over her eyes. "A little."

"I have never seen you cry before."

"Everyone cries sometimes. Even me." And something told Mercy her crying days were just beginning.

Alice held out her hand to her. It was a sweet gesture, something Mercy had offered to her so many times.

Mercy took Alice's hand in her own. "Thank you."

"Shall I sit with you awhile? It always makes me feel better when you sit with me."

"Yes," Mercy whispered, throat tight. "I would like that very much indeed."

CHAPTER TWENTY-EIGHT

Seeing little Betsey with Hetty, Jane felt a stirring of self-pity she recognized but did not like in herself. Why was it that women like Hetty bore perfectly healthy babies when they didn't want any, while she who had so desperately longed for one remained childless?

Memories of her losses flashed in her mind, but she squeezed her eyes shut, trying to keep them at bay.

Jane excused herself and escaped to her little lodge—which only brought the past closer. She sat down heavily on the bed she and John had shared, and where those awful scenes had taken place. Alone there, she felt powerless to stop the memories, especially of the most recent and most painful time.

After John had died, she carried that final babe longer than any of the others. And she had allowed herself to hope that God would spare the child, since He had taken John.

But He had not.

When the bleeding had started that night—too early! Not again!—Jane had sent a maid no longer in their employ to fetch the midwife. Mrs. Henning had understood Jane's desire to keep her pregnancies private—not to raise anyone's hopes when she had lost one child after another. So she had come to the lodge now and again to check on Jane discreetly, ostensibly for a social call, should anyone see her or ask.

That night, Mrs. Henning had brought the physician with her, her own confidence flagging after so many failed births. Yet both were powerless to do anything to stop Jane's child from coming into the world too soon.

Jane had wanted to see the baby more closely but was afraid to, should he not be whole. But then she decided she didn't care. She wanted to hold her son. But Dr. Burton said it would only make things harder.

He gave her laudanum or something to calm her. It made her feel drowsy. Disconnected. She heard him say in a low voice to the midwife that he would take care of the remains.

Jane had wanted to shout at him. *He is not "remains." He is my son. That is his body. The body I carried within mine and came to love.* But none of it came out, at least not sensibly.

Mrs. Henning noticed her distress and told the doctor she would take care of the child herself.

When Jane awoke from a heavy sleep, Mrs. Henning was there at her bedside. She did her best to reassure Jane. She said she had wrapped his little body in clean cloth and laid him in a small wooden box made by the joiner and kept on hand for just such occurrences. Jane had been grateful to know he would be protected that way.

The midwife went on to tell her she had delivered her sad burden to the church for burial, reminding her that no markers were used in such cases.

At the time, it was enough to know he'd been buried properly. Jane had not wanted to ask questions and spread her tale of woe.

But now? Logical or not, she longed to know where her children were—to have a place to grieve, to mark, and to remember.

Jane walked to St. Anne's first thing the next morning.

The vicar was just stepping out of the church as she arrived. "Morning, Jane. Good to see you. I am expected at the almshouse in ten minutes, but—"

"That's all right, Mr. Paley. I am here to see Mr. Beachum, actually. Is he here?"

He pursed his lips. "Really? I'm afraid I don't know. The man has been here for more years than I have and sets his own hours. He wasn't in the vestry just now, but he also keeps a private office downstairs. Do you know the way?"

"I will find it. Don't let me keep you."

"Very well, good-bye." Mr. Paley started down the church path, and Jane went inside and down the narrow stairs that led to the crypt and storage room. Nestled between them, she found a closed door bearing a small placard: *Parish Clerk*.

Jane knocked, and a voice called, "Come."

She entered the dim, cave-like chamber. Inside, an elderly man hunched over a paper-strewn desk.

"Mr. Beachum?"

"Yes?" He looked at her over the tops of his spectacles. "Ah, Mrs. Bell. Are you lost? I rarely receive visitors down here."

"No. I am here to see you."

"Oh? Is something the matter?" Hope sparked in his eyes. "Have you a complaint to lodge against the vicar?"

"No, nothing like that. I was only wondering if you could tell me the location of a certain grave. A few graves, actually."

"Of course." He pulled out a broad sheet of paper folded like a map and spread it out on his cluttered desk. "I have the whole churchyard plan right here. Who are we looking for?"

Jane swallowed. "My children."

"Your . . . Ah." He refolded the plan and laced his fingers over it. "Mrs. Bell, if you are referring to premature or still births, they are not on this diagram. As you know, the cemetery proper is reserved for church members and those baptized."

"But—"

"Such things are kept quiet for privacy's sake, Mrs. Bell. It is a sensitive matter, these poor creatures born too soon or passed on before baptism."

"I understand it is a private matter for many women. It was for me. But why can I not know myself?"

"It is not a matter of public record."

"But you do record it?"

He shook his head. "Only the general area used for such burials over various time periods, not specific plots by name."

"Why?"

"That is the way it has always been done here."

"But you are responsible for the parish burials?"

"Under the churchwardens' authority, yes. Just as my father was before me. Though the sexton digs the graves. And he, as everyone knows, is a bit daft."

Jane frowned, stretching out her hands in supplication. "Is it so much to ask? I only want to know where my children are buried."

"As I said, I cannot help you. The records are still in disorder from Mr. Bingley's last term as churchwarden. It would take days to unearth even the general location. And as you see I am busy, so . . ."

Jane turned and walked out. She did not thank him or wish him good day. She only wanted to escape that dank room and heartless man before he saw her cry.

Longing to confide in Jane, Mercy walked to The Bell. On her way, she passed the Kingsley Brothers' workshop, a brick building with an extended roof over an open-sided work area on one side, and double doors to an enclosed workroom on the other. The sign above read:

Kingsley Bros.
Masons, Builders & Carpenters
Plans Made & Estimates Given

The broad double doors were open, and inside Joseph Kingsley worked. Mercy stopped to watch him. Scraper in hand, he smoothed a wooden rocking horse poised atop two sawhorses. She noticed sawdust in his side-whiskers and in the fine hairs on the backs of his hands.

He glanced up and paused in his work. "Miss Grove."

"Good day, Mr. Kingsley. How are you?"

"Well enough. How are things at Ivy Cottage? With your . . . suitor?"

She looked at him in surprise.

"I was there when you received your parents' letter, remember? You told me you feared the man would expect you to be as clever as your father and as pretty as your mother."

"That's right." She averted her gaze, embarrassed to recall all she had said to him in the agitation of the moment.

"He was not disappointed, was he?"

She shook her head, surprised anew to realize it was true.

He resumed his smoothing. "I told you he would not be."

Mercy darted a look at the man, but he kept his focus on the wood. He set down his scraper and picked up a piece of dried sharkskin instead.

She asked, "Is that a new commission?"

"No. A gift for a niece."

"How thoughtful."

He shrugged. "I always make something from oak for each new member of the family."

"Why oak?"

"I like working with it." His low voice was accompanied by rhythmic swishing as he polished the wood. "It's hard yet beautiful. Lasting."

Mercy stepped closer, running her hand over the smooth surface. "Your niece is a lucky girl."

He flashed her a small smile. "So the visit went well?"

Mercy considered how best to respond. "In some ways better than I expected, and in some ways far worse."

He glanced up. "How so?"

Again she paused, her stomach churning to think of her parents' ultimatum.

His expression sobered. "You needn't tell me anything, Miss Grove. I should not have pried."

"I don't mind. I just don't know how much to say. I don't want to abuse your ears again."

"I did ask."

"Then I will say that he . . . made his willingness clear, but I told him I needed more time to consider. We have only just met."

"Sometimes attraction is immediate, Miss Grove."

"Attraction, maybe, but mutual respect and affection? Love? How long does that take? At all events, he asked for my answer by Christmas."

"I heard your mother when I visited the library. She is obviously in favor of the match—made him sound perfect for you. Educated, well-read, a professor of all things. Writing a book together, I think she said?"

Mercy ducked her head. "I would only assist." She changed the subject. "What brought you to the library? Did you forget a tool or something?"

"No." Now he averted his gaze. "I went thinking I'd find a book to read. But most of them were over my head."

"I am sure that is not the case. You are clearly intelligent and capable."

Again he looked up to study her face.

She found his eye contact deliciously disconcerting and dragged her focus to his hands instead. "Your work is lovely, by the way."

"Thank you."

Mercy pressed her lips together and took a deep breath. "When Mr. Hollander and I saw you on the green with your nephews, he asked me if that charming blond woman was your wife. I said I did not know who she was. I did not recognize her, so . . ."

"Esther? No. She is not my wife."

Something in his tone made her stomach cramp.

Mercy licked dry lips. "You are . . . a widower?"

He darted another look at her, then averted his gaze, brushing shavings and grit from the horse's withers. "Yes."

"I . . . don't believe I ever met your wife."

"No, you wouldn't have. I married Naomi years ago, when I lived in Basingstoke, working on a long-term commission there."

Naomi . . . "What happened?"

His face twisted. "She died in childbirth, a year after we wed, our only child with her. I don't talk about it—to anyone, usually."

What a selfish fool Mercy felt now for her prying questions. "I'm sorry."

He nodded. "Me too."

He did not, she noticed, explain who the pretty blond woman was.

She swallowed. "Well. Good day, Mr. Kingsley."

"Good-bye, Miss Grove."

How final that sounded.

Mercy continued on to The Bell to talk to Jane. She found her in the entry hall, just returned from some errand, pulling off her bonnet and gloves.

Taking one look at her face, Jane hurried to her side. "Mercy, what is it? Here, let us go to the lodge and talk in private." She called into the office for Patrick to oversee the desk, then linked her arm through Mercy's and led her across the drive.

In the keeper's lodge, Jane pulled out a chair for her at the small table, and took the seat across from her.

"Tell me."

Mercy took a deep breath and told her all about Mr. Hollander's visit and her parents' ultimatum.

"There I was, campaigning for a larger school, when I should have been more thankful for the one I had. Now I am losing my school, and George and his wife will have Ivy Cottage unless I marry."

Jane's eyes widened. "Oh, Mercy, no."

Mercy nodded. "Mr. Hollander is not a bad man, Jane. I enjoyed discussing books with him and sharing a few meals, but that does not mean I am ready to share my life with him. My . . . bed. No." She shuddered.

Jane pressed her lips together, then said gently, "I know it can be an unsettling prospect at first. I remember . . . well, vaguely." She chuckled. "It is natural to be nervous. But are you certain you would not feel that way about *any* man?"

Mercy looked away, feeling her face flush.

Jane's eyebrows rose high. "Oh, Mercy!" she exclaimed, astounded and chagrined. "I am sorry. I had no idea there was someone else. I hope I did not hurt your feelings by teasing you. How thoughtless of me."

"There is *not* anyone else," Mercy insisted. "In terms of . . . actual possibility. No one else is courting me or anything like that. But there is someone I . . . like. And the thought of sharing *his* life and his bed . . ." Her sentence trailed away, and again her face heated.

Jane studied her. "Not as unappealing?"

"Not unappealing at all."

"Good heavens. I don't suppose you will tell me who it is?"

Mercy shook her head. "I had better not. Especially with Mr. Hollander awaiting his answer."

"Does this man you like . . . whoever he is . . . know about Mr. Hollander? That he has basically proposed and given you 'til Christmas to decide?"

Mercy sighed. "He knows."

Jane winced. "And he said nothing? No hint that it . . . bothered him?"

"I don't think so. I am no expert in reading men, of course, but he seems to agree with my parents that Mr. Hollander and I are well matched. Both educated and well-read. Both teachers."

"And this other man is not?"

Mercy crossed her arms. "He isn't very book educated, that is true. But he is capable and intelligent, generous and hardworking . . ."

"Goodness, you do like him. Does he like you?"

Mercy shrugged and considered. "I think he likes me well enough—at least as a friend. We talk easily. He admires my knowledge and teaching ability as I admire his strength and skill."

"That is a start."

Mercy shook her head. "No, it isn't. I saw him embrace a beautiful woman the other day. My complete opposite—petite, blond, pretty, charming . . ."

Jane blinked in surprise. "Rachel?"

"No, someone even prettier, if you can imagine. You should have seen how he smiled at her! He embraced her right there on the green. Besides, he seems to be encouraging me to accept Mr. Hollander. How could he communicate more clearly that he has no romantic interest in me himself? Apparently only Mr. Hollander is thus afflicted."

"Oh, Mercy, what will you do?"

"I don't know. I will lose my school either way. Should I give up my independence too—in exchange for a husband and possibly children of my own?" She looked at Jane. "You gave up your former way of life to marry. Was it worth it?"

"Oh, Mercy, our situations are so different. I was attracted to John from the beginning. And although I had my reservations about marrying him, I never doubted he loved me."

"Did you love him?"

"I came to, yes. Not the all-consuming love of novels and poetry, but yes. And after romantic love waned, I still cared for him." Jane laid her hand over hers. "Could you come to care for this Mr. Hollander?"

"Care for him, yes. Love him? Desire him?" Mercy shook her head. "I don't know."

"What does Rachel say about it?"

"I haven't discussed it with her yet. Her future is at stake too. I think I could sway Mr. Hollander to keep the library, but if I don't marry him, it will definitely have to close. I can't bear to tell her she might lose her library so soon. I don't want to worry her unnecessarily."

"You can't marry a man you don't love just to save Rachel's library."

"I know. But I feel terrible about it."

Jane squeezed her hand. "She will understand. And what about Alice? What has Mr. Hollander said about her?"

"He finds the idea of becoming an instant parent daunting, but he is willing to do so for me."

"Good. That is to his credit."

Mercy studied her friend's face. "Is something wrong, Jane? You look sad. I have been so wrapped up in my own concerns, I failed to ask how you are?"

Jane looked down, and Mercy doubted she would tell her.

For a moment Jane pressed her lips together, and then she said, "In all honesty, I am feeling sorry for myself. We have a child about the place now, and it has reminded me of those I lost. But it shall pass." Jane smiled bravely. "I am determined not to be ruled by self-pity."

Mercy squeezed her hand, and held on a little longer than usual. "I admire you, Jane. And I will try to do the same."

That evening, Thora noticed how gloomy Jane seemed and asked what was bothering her.

"Hm? Oh, I am just tired. We had a difficult guest last night. A Lady something or other and her suspicious lady's maid. She demanded to inspect the bedclothes and watched while Hetty changed the perfectly clean sheets yet again. And poor Mrs. Rooke had the meals she'd prepared sent back thrice."

"Poor Mrs. Rooke? Those are words I never thought to hear you utter."

Jane did not even grin.

"Jane," Thora insisted, "what is it?"

Finally, her daughter-in-law confided her unsatisfying visit to Mr. Beachum and the reason for it.

Jane managed a sheepish smile. "You will probably think me very foolish. It is an impractical desire to know. I realize I should give it up."

Thora shook her head. "Never liked that man."

Thora said nothing more and made no promises. But she determined to call on Mr. Beachum herself as soon as she had the opportunity.

CHAPTER TWENTY-NINE

The looming loss of her school throbbed in Mercy's chest like a broken rib. Her mind struggled to believe it. There must be something she could do. Might she relocate the school somewhere else, like the church? But what about her boarding pupils? Or did God want her to give up the school for some reason she could not fathom? Was she supposed to accept this, or fight it? If only discerning His will was easier.

Longing for direction and comfort, Mercy selected a book from Rachel's library—a book of sermons.

Rachel marked it down in the ledger, then glanced again at its spine. "This is one of the books donated anonymously. You are the first to borrow it." She grinned up at Mercy. "I hope it proves more interesting than it looks."

Mercy thanked her and took it up to her room.

Reading the sermons in bed that night made her drowsy, which was a comfort, of a kind. She soon fell asleep, book to her chest, waking only long enough to blow out the bedside candle before closing her eyes once more.

In the morning, Mercy awoke to find the book still in bed with her. Hoping she had not bent its pages, she carefully lifted and closed it, only to find something sticking out. *Oh no*. Had she torn a page? She carefully extracted the piece of paper, surprised to find it folded in thirds. A letter—its seal broken and the direction smeared illegible.

Curious, she opened it, and read:

Dear Grandmother,

Please don't fret. That you still love me and pray for me is such a balm, I cannot tell you. I know it distresses you that you cannot come here to help me, nor invite me to live with you there. But it is not your fault. Grandfather feels to do so would be condoning my sin. If just for me, I would not mind so much. But I do worry about my daughter. My health worsens by the day. My biggest worry is what will happen to her if I were to die here, alone, where no one really knows or cares about me.

So I must beg one more favor and apologize for having to ask you to keep another secret from Grandfather. The last one—I promise.

There is only one person I can think of who might help my daughter if I don't survive. I met him years ago when I worked for Lady Carlock. I did not have his permanent direction until much more recently, when I happened into Lady Carlock in Bristol. She told me she had seen the man again on one of her recent travels. In fact, she had his card in her reticule and gave it to me. I enclose it herein.

He was a kind and generous man, as I recall. If the worst happens as I fear, please post the enclosed letter to him per the address on the card.

All my love and gratitude forever,

M.A.

Mercy frowned, her mind rapidly sifting through thoughts. *M.A.* . . . A letter from Mary-Alicia, written to her grandmother before she died? Mercy glanced at the book again. If so, Mr. Thomas must have donated this book after his wife's death. Who was the "generous man" mentioned in the letter?

She thought immediately of James Drake, who met Mary-Alicia in Brighton. But she had traveled with that lady for nearly two years and had surely met many people. Mercy told herself not to jump to conclusions.

She opened the book again and flipped through the pages. Nothing. Where was the second letter M.A. mentioned? It was not enclosed, nor a card. Had Mrs. Thomas posted it, as requested? It seemed likely. Unless . . . had the elderly woman already been confused when the letter arrived?

A knock sounded, and Mercy jumped, sliding the letter under the book.

Her mother popped her head in. "Still in bed? Come on, sleepy girl, time to get dressed for church. And we leave tomorrow, remember, so I may need help packing. Will you do these up for me? Then I will help you." She turned around, so Mercy could reach her corset strings beneath her unfastened gown.

Mercy scrambled out of bed to oblige her. "Of course."

The letter, and her questions, would have to wait.

After church, Mercy's parents lingered to chat with Lady Brockwell and a few other old friends, saying their farewells. Murmuring that she would see them at home, Mercy followed her aunt and the girls as they filed out of the nave. Rachel, she noticed, had been taken aside by Mr. Carville, the Brockwells' butler. She wondered what the two of them had to talk about.

Aunt Matilda and Mrs. Shabner strolled arm in arm, as usual, down Church Street, and Alice and Phoebe followed their example in miniature behind them. The other girls walked ahead, talking and giggling in a little cluster.

As they passed the public house, Mr. Drake strode up Potters Lane. Phoebe waved energetically, while Alice made do with a shy smile.

"Good morning, Alice. Miss Phoebe." He fell into step beside Mercy. "Good day, Miss Grove."

"Hello, Mr. Drake. I did not see you in church."

"I am not much of a churchgoer, I'm afraid."

Mercy thought. "Actually, we have not seen you at all in some time."

"I took a trip down to Portsmouth."

"Oh? Any particular reason?"

"Curiosity. Your aunt mentioned that Alice's father died on the *Mesopotamia*, is that right?"

"I believe that is what Mrs. Thomas told her. Though that was years ago. Why?"

"After we last spoke, I consulted a complete collection of *Steel's Navy Lists*—which include Royal Marines—hoping to find confirmation of Mr. Smith's service and details of his death. Do you know what I found instead?"

Mercy shook her head, unease filling her.

"I learned that no lieutenant named Alexander Smith was listed among the missing and presumed dead of the *Mesopotamia*. Nor had any such man even served aboard that ill-fated ship."

"Perhaps his rank had changed, or my aunt misheard or misremembered his given name. Smith is a very common surname, you must allow."

"True. However, I did find an Alexander Smith, a lieutenant of marines, listed in several older editions, among the crew of another ship."

He watched her reaction, then added, "I also found the name Alexander Smith circled in the copy of *Steel's Navy Lists* donated anonymously to Miss Ashford's library."

Mercy wasn't sure she wanted to ask what Mr. Drake was suggesting.

Reaching Ivy Cottage, Matilda and the girls went indoors, while the two of them lingered near the gate.

He continued, "So I tracked down that Alexander Smith and found him living on half pay in Portsmouth. Very much alive and having never met a Mary-Alicia in his life."

Surprise and suspicion twisted Mercy's stomach. She studied his face. Why would Mr. Drake take time away from his hotel to look for Mr. Smith? Why was he so interested? She thought again of the "generous man" mentioned in the letter and asked, "How did you meet Miss Payne again?"

"I met her at a Brighton resort, while she was traveling with an older woman as her companion."

Mercy's heart began to pound dully. "How long ago was that?"

"About nine years."

"She must have married soon after," Mercy said, but the words sounded hollow in her ears.

"I think Mr. Thomas has his doubts about that." Mr. Drake crossed his arms. "And that is why he refuses to talk about his own granddaughter or acknowledge his great-granddaughter."

Quite possibly, Mercy thought, again recalling M.A.'s letter. She lowered her voice. "That is a theory better kept to yourself, Mr. Drake. Such a rumor could only harm an innocent young girl like Alice."

"I am not spreading rumors, Miss Grove. I am speaking to you in confidence. I simply want to learn the truth."

"Even if the truth hurts Alice?"

"I have no intention of hurting her."

"I hope not. With Mary-Alicia gone, as well as the grandmother she confided in, I doubt we shall ever know the full truth. And that may be for the best."

Mercy's parents came strolling up Church Street arm in arm. She did not want to discuss this in front of them.

"Please excuse me, Mr. Drake."

"As you wish." He nodded and walked away, tipping his hat to Mrs. Grove as he passed.

Her parents followed her inside Ivy Cottage.

Her mother's face brightened with interest. "Who was that man, Mercy?"

"Oh . . . just a friend of Jane's. He owns Fairmont House now."

"Does he indeed?" Her mother eyed her carefully. "Anything else we should know about him?"

Mercy shook her head. "No. Definitely not."

When the service ended that Sunday, Rachel was surprised when Mr. Carville sought her out.

He took her aside and said, "I am worried about Sir Timothy. He left without telling me his plans. Have you spoken with him?"

"No. Not in some time." Rachel had not seen him since he rode off, upset, from Mrs. Haverhill's.

"He seemed rather agitated. Do you know where he went?"

"I don't."

Carville looked around, then lowered his voice. "Did he learn the truth about that woman?"

Rachel held his gaze and did not pretend ignorance of what he was asking. "Yes."

"And he blames me, I suppose."

"No. His father."

"Him? What about her?"

"She is part of it, of course, but learning of his father's deception shocked and deeply disappointed him."

"But he knows I . . . lied to him." A sheen of fear shone in the old man's eyes.

"Yes." She gentled her voice. "But he also knows you were trying to protect the family."

He nodded. "I was. You don't think Sir Timothy intends to do anything . . . rash, do you?"

"Of course not," Rachel replied with more confidence than she felt. "Sir Timothy can be depended upon to act responsibly."

Yet, was not riding off on an unexplained absence already rash, Rachel wondered—at least for him?

"I am sure you are right, miss," the butler said. "At least I hope you are."

When Rachel returned to Ivy Cottage a short while later, she found Mercy waiting for her in the vestibule.

"Rachel, I know it is Sunday, but could you do something for me?"

"Of course, anything."

"Has Mr. Drake returned that edition of *Steel's Navy List* he borrowed?"

"Not yet."

"Then I'd like to see everything else given by the same person who donated the book of sermons I borrowed yesterday."

"Of course. Just give me a few minutes." Rachel looked at Mercy again, noting her disturbed expression. "Is something wrong?"

"I don't know for certain. Hopefully not." Mercy hesitated, glancing at the library door. "Shall I help you?"

"No need." Rachel nodded toward little Alice, lingering near the stairs, book in arms. "I see Alice is waiting for you to read with her. I will do this."

Mercy looked over, her expression immediately softening. "Very well. Thank you."

Mercy walked away, hand extended to Alice, and Rachel stepped inside the library. She opened her inventory ledger, referenced her list, and began gathering the books that had been donated in the same basket with *Steel's Navy Lists* and that particular book of sermons: a Gothic romance, women's magazines, a few travelogues, and a book of poetry. She opened the covers looking for any inscription, as she had started to do before Matilda urged her to accept donations without seeking to credit the donor. She saw nothing. What was Mercy hoping to find?

She stacked the books on the desk for Mercy to look at when she came back, and closed her ledger. Then something caught her eye. She regarded the stack of books from the side. From this angle, she noticed a slightly widened gap in one of the book's otherwise tightly bound pages. Had several pages become folded over, or was something stuck inside? She picked up the romance and opened it to that spot.

Inside, she found a folded rectangle. Not sealed, nor addressed. Should she open it, or wait for Mercy? Hoping to discover the donor's identity, Rachel unfolded the paper and read.

Dear JD,

Do you even remember me? More likely my face is but a blur in your memory. But I have never forgotten you.

Even had I tried, I could not. For I have a daily reminder. And in her small face and soft green eyes, I often catch a glimpse of yours. It draws me up short and stills my thoughts, and just for a moment I allow my mind to travel back and relive those days that are probably far more vivid in my mind than in yours.

We had planned to stay another week in Brighton, as did you, or so you said. But Lady Carlock is an impetuous woman and decided late in the night that we must away the following day. I don't know if she had learned of our relationship, or if her desire to see Wales immediately was real and genuine. Whatever the case, we left early the next morning.

I wrote a note, intending to leave it for you at the front desk. Imagine my surprise when the clerk told me you had already quit your rooms and departed. No, you had left no forwarding address, nor a note for me.

Did you fear this very thing and leave before I could demand anything of you? That is what I have often imagined. Though now and again, I allowed myself to wonder if you might change your mind and try to find me. I considered writing to you, but I did not have your direction at the time. I thought we had shared so much, yet in hindsight I realized how little of your life you had actually shared with me.

After spending some weeks in Wales, I left Lady Carlock and took lodgings in Bristol, where I eventually had a child in secret. I wrote letters to my grandparents, fictionalizing a whirlwind romance and elopement to a marine whose name I picked from a navy list. I did not initially tell them where I was living, afraid they would seek me out and discover the truth. I had a little money saved and supported myself as best I could by taking in sewing for a milliner.

When my daughter was several months old, I thought

it would be safe to let my grandparents know where I was. When I read news of a ship lost at sea, I wrote again to say that my husband had been on that ship and was now missing and presumed dead. I thought they would invite me to live with them, but they did not. My grandmother would have, I know. But my grandfather forbade it. Apparently, he never believed my story. He knew or at least suspected I had lied and despised me for it.

My health since giving birth has not been good. I contracted a fever from which I never fully recovered. All these years of hand-to-mouth living in damp Bristol have no doubt taken their toll. Whatever the case, the apothecary offers me many elixirs but little hope.

My grandparents are quite elderly, and I'm not sure they would be equal to raising a child, even were my grandfather willing to take her in. And so I write to you.

Should the worst happen, as I dread, I have decided I must let you know the truth now that I have your direction (I happened to see Lady Carlock not long ago, and she gave me your card). I will send this letter to my grandmother for safekeeping, with instructions to post it to you after I am gone.

This is my last will and testament, of sorts. I have scant worldly goods to bequeath, but I have one most precious possession, and I would do anything to protect her.

Her name is Alice. She is your daughter. I have kept that fact secret from her. She believes she is the daughter of Alexander Smith, who died at sea. She is seven years old at the time of this writing and has your eyes.

At the bottom of this letter, I will add both my landlady's address in Bristol, as well as my grandparents' direction in Ivy Hill, Wiltshire. Hopefully you can find Alice through one of them.

May God bless you for any help you might give her.

Sincerely,
Mary-Alicia (Payne) Smith

Rachel pressed a hand to her chest, realizing it was beating too hard and too fast. Footsteps approached, and Rachel instinctively turned, hiding the letter behind her back. From the corridor, she heard cheerful voices. She looked through the doorway in time to see Mercy and Alice appear, hand in hand, chatting companionably.

Noticing her, Mercy began, "We thought tea and biscuits might be in order after our reading. . . ."

Taking in Rachel's expression, the smile on her face fell. "Rachel? What is it? What's wrong?"

"If you want me to burn it, I shall."

"Burn what? What is it?"

Rachel hesitated, looking meaningfully at Alice.

Mercy bent and gently told the little girl to go upstairs and play with Phoebe.

When they were alone, Mercy walked near, her face puckered in concern.

With a shaky hand, Rachel handed her the letter.

Rachel barely breathed as Mercy bent over the page, her brow furrowing as she read.

Mercy murmured, "This must be the letter Mary-Alicia enclosed when she wrote to Mrs. Thomas. . . ." She read a little longer, then sucked in a gasp, pressing long fingers to her mouth.

Rachel reached up, bracketing Mercy's shoulders, and felt her tremble. She yanked a chair across the floor and positioned it behind Mercy, who looked unsteady on her feet.

"Here, my dear. Sit." She gently guided her into the chair. "There. Can I bring you something for your present relief? Tea? A sip of sherry?"

Mercy shook her head, face pale.

Rachel knelt before her friend, pressing her knees with all the assurance she could muster. "Mercy, it does not have to change anything. Or at least not everything. Apparently no one posted the letter, and neither must we. We don't even know who the JD referenced there is. Only initials. And the card she mentioned enclosing isn't here now. Oh! The card . . ." Rachel let the words drift away as the implication struck her.

Mercy's eyes dulled. "We don't need to post the letter, Rachel."

Rachel nodded. "That's right. There's no need."

"Because he's right here in Ivy Hill. It's James Drake."

Rachel bit her lip, then admitted, "I did find an old calling card of his in the basket that held these books. At the time, I thought he had donated them, but he insisted he did not."

Mercy nodded. "You see? No wonder he has been loitering about the place. Asking questions about Miss Payne and Mr. Smith and Alice. He must know he is Alice's father. Or at least suspects."

"Even if he does, it doesn't mean he will want to take responsibility for her. The letter only asks him to help Alice in some way. It says nothing about acknowledging her or housing her or . . ."

Tears filled Mercy's eyes. The sight was so rare and so heartrending that tears filled Rachel's eyes in reply.

Rachel tried to comfort her. "If he failed to do his duty by Mary-Alicia all those years ago, why would he make an effort now, after she is gone? Please don't cry. We don't have to do anything with this letter. Or . . . we could return it to Mr. Thomas. You know he would be the last person to share this with Mr. Drake or anyone else for that matter."

"It isn't right."

"I know, my dear, I know. You and Alice are like mother and daughter already. You have cared for her and sheltered her all these months, and—"

"No. I mean, it isn't right to keep it from him."

"Mercy, you owe Mr. Drake nothing. He is all but a stranger to Alice."

"I am not thinking of him, at least not alone." Mercy met her gaze. "She has a father."

"But do you think it will help Alice in the long term to learn that her mother was not married? That she lied to her about who her father was?"

"I don't know." Mercy dropped the letter into her lap and tented her hands over her eyes. "Oh, Rachel! What am I to do? I am losing everything I love."

Chilly autumn wind howled at the Ivy Cottage windows as Mercy climbed the stairs, letter in hand. With a surge of gratitude, she saw that Mr. Basu had already lit a fire in her bedchamber. She closed the door behind herself and sank into the armchair near the hearth, where she often read the Scriptures in the morning or a favorite book in the evening after a long day of teaching or campaigning.

Mercy sat there, staring into the flames as they charred and chewed the kindling and started in on the coal. She lurched to her feet and stretched the letter toward the fire, ready to offer it another course. Perhaps Rachel was right. This was old news and need not be devastating. Mr. Drake had not laid eyes on Alice's mother in nearly nine years. He had not offered to marry her, nor apparently tried to find her. Why would he make some grand gesture now? Jane spoke highly of him, true. He had been generous in offering advice and support to her when The Bell was struggling, and had helped Rachel with her library. So he *might* offer to help Alice as well. Perhaps with financial support or a stipend to ease his conscience—a nod to doing his duty better late than never. Or would he do more?

But Mr. Drake was not even married. He was a man of business with a hotel in Southampton and working hard to open another in Ivy Hill—and who knew where next? Would he want the responsibility of a child? If Alice were a boy, maybe. Men seemed to romanticize the notion of passing along skills and property to a son. Less so to a daughter, in her experience. Though certainly her own father had taken pains to educate her. . . .

Stop it, she told herself. Rachel was right. She was overreacting.

Mercy sat back down. *This letter is not mine to burn*, she reminded herself. *I am an honest person. It would be unfair to Alice and to Mr. Drake.*

If Alice were older, Mercy might confide in her first—see if she had any interest in a relationship of some sort with the man before she went to Mr. Drake. But Alice was young and might not understand. Or worse, she might expect this man to suddenly lay aside his own plans and concerns to take up hers, to make her the center of his universe and shower her with affection and gifts. And if he instead ignored or rejected her? Mercy's heart cramped at the thought. She might selfishly wish Mr. Drake would want little to do with Alice. But for Alice's sake, she could not hope for such an outcome.

There was nothing for it. She would have to show him the letter privately. Assure him she was making no demands on Alice's behalf, and that she was ready and willing to raise Alice herself. Though considering her own state of upheaval where Ivy Cottage was concerned, she could not state the latter as confidently as she might once have.

CHAPTER THIRTY

Lady Brockwell came to the library the next day, wearing a somber grey pelisse trimmed with chinchilla. She closed and locked the door behind her. Rachel blinked in surprise.

"So we are not interrupted." Lady Brockwell nodded toward the reading room. "Is anyone else here?"

"Not at the moment."

"Good." She stepped nearer. "I am here to ask about Timothy. I am concerned. I understand he rode off in a pique, and we have not seen him in a week's time. It is very unlike him."

"I agree. But as I told Carville yesterday, I don't know where he is."

"Did the two of you argue?"

"Perhaps, but he did not leave on my account."

"Then what has upset him?"

Rachel replied evenly, "That is for him to tell you—or not, as he deems best." She supposed Lady Brockwell was the wronged wife and she should feel sorry for her, but that was not what Rachel felt.

"What are you not telling me?" The woman narrowed her eyes. "I insist you tell me everything."

"I would not insist, if I were you. For you shall not like my answer."

"What does that mean? Don't play games with me, Miss Ashford. Tell me the truth. You owe me that much."

Hot anger washed over Rachel. "You are wrong, Lady Brockwell. I owe you nothing. You are not my mother to command me. Nor my mother-in-law. You made quite sure of that."

"Is that what this temper tantrum is about? You are angry I wanted more for my son than to be linked to a family plagued by financial ruin and scandal?"

Rachel barely resisted the urge to shout, *Scandal? You are in no position to condemn my family for a scandal!*

Lady Brockwell waved a dismissive hand. "Could you expect us to rejoice at the prospect? To delight in the hope of such relations?"

Rachel held her tongue by a supreme effort of self-control.

"I may not be your relative." The woman leaned close and had the gall to grasp her wrist. "But I am still your elder, and a person deserving of respect. I demand you tell me what has upset Timothy."

Rachel took a deep breath. "I realize you are worried about him, but you have no right to demand anything where I am concerned. Now, please release me."

Rachel jerked her arm free and turned. She unlocked the door and held it open until Lady Brockwell lifted her imperious chin and stalked out. Rachel shut the door behind her none too softly, but her fleeting triumph quickly transformed into guilt. She had never spoken in so cutting a manner to anyone in her life. And certainly never dreamed of doing so to Sir Timothy's mother. Rachel had likely alienated the woman forever. And probably her son as well.

"Oh, God, forgive me," she whispered. "And please protect Timothy, wherever he is."

Leaving Betsey with Sadie and Talbot on Monday, Thora walked into town. If Beachum tried to put her off as he had Jane, Thora was armed for battle.

She strode purposefully up Church Street, basket in hand.

Reaching St. Anne's, she made her way down to the crypt, knocked once on the parish clerk's door, and opened it.

"I am busy. If—" The man's protest broke off as Thora strode inside uninvited.

"Ah, Mrs. Bell. The second Mrs. Bell to grace my office in recent days. I am surprised."

"It is Mrs. Talbot now, remember. And you must know why I am here. My daughter-in-law came to you to learn where her children are buried. She is still waiting."

"As I told Mrs. Bell, I am a busy man. I cannot in good conscience set aside my pressing parish duties to search through old records for no official reason."

Thora looked around the cluttered office with its stacks of papers and open books. "Yes, I see how organized and productive you are. Well, you go on and see to those pressing matters. I shall wait." She moved a pile of old newspapers from the only extra chair and set them on the floor.

"Wait? There's no need. I will send word when I have time."

"I doubt I shall live that long." Thora swiped a handkerchief over the dusty chair and sat down. "No, you continue on, and I will sit here quiet as a mouse."

"You would be bored indeed." He gestured to the stack of correspondence before him. "This might take hours."

She nodded. "So I anticipated. Never fear." She lifted her basket and began removing items from it. She set a candle lamp on the small table beside her, and pulled out her needlework and the spectacles she wore for close work.

"I brought my own tallow candle because tapers can be so expensive, and I would not want to be a burden on the parish funds."

"Good heavens, you are certainly prepared."

"I am. I am prepared to wait as long as it takes." She slid on her spectacles.

"Mrs. Bell, I don't have time to entertain you—"

She held up her palm. "Then, please don't attempt it. I have no desire to converse with you, Lesley, I assure you."

He frowned at that and returned to his pile of correspondence.

Thora picked up her needlework. A moment later, she rose. "May I trouble you for a light?" She nodded toward his burning lamp.

"Of course."

She removed the globe with a clang of glass against brass, dipped her candle into its flame, and returned the globe with another clang. "Sorry."

He winced, and both resumed their work.

The cheap tallow began smoking, filling the air with an odoriferous haze. She'd bought the cheapest, oldest stub the chandler could find.

He wrinkled his long nose at the smell of burning mutton fat but made no comment as he turned a page.

Next Thora crinkled open a brown paper sack. She pulled out an overcooked biscuit and offered it to him.

"No, thank you."

She began chewing the crunchy treat. Loudly.

He sighed and returned his quill to its holder. "You have always been a stubborn woman, Thora Stonehouse."

She smiled. "And that is one of my better qualities."

The Kingsley brothers arrived at The Bell on Monday afternoon, and Patrick took them out to the stables to show them the areas that needed repair.

So Jane was alone in the office when Thora appeared. She had not expected to see her until the end of the day, when she brought Betsey back.

Thora laid a small piece of paper on the desk. "I am sorry, Jane. I was able to get the general area from Beachum but not the exact place."

Jane's pulse pounded. "That is more than I wrested from him. Thank you, Thora."

"They are along the outside of the east wall, here. I hope you can decipher the sketch."

Jane studied the scrap of paper. "I can. Thank you."

"Could you not choose a spot and claim it for them?" Thora's voice was unusually soft. "Might that be close enough?"

Jane managed a nod. "I hope so."

"Shall I go with you, or would you rather go alone?"

"Alone, I think. But I appreciate the offer." Jane pressed a hand to Thora's arm, and Thora covered it with her own.

"I hope it helps."

"Me too."

Jane had put off widow's weeds, and her heart was almost ready to follow suit. If only she could get past this last grief—the babies she had lost. And with them, her hope of ever bearing a child who would live.

Autumn flowers clasped low at her waist, Jane walked through the churchyard the next day. Reaching the east side, she lifted a low branch bearing orangey-brown leaves and stepped out a small gate. Walking along the stone wall, she felt self-conscious about intruding, fearing the disapproving Mr. Beachum might see her and order her to leave. Or passersby might wonder what she was doing. In the next moment, she decided she did not care. She needed to do this.

Jane surveyed the strip of land—a long grassy expanse eight or ten feet wide and maybe a hundred feet long between the churchyard wall and a farmer's field. Dainty red campion blossoms and a few clusters of creamy common dropwort waved in the breeze. Fallen acorns and chestnuts dotted the ground, but no crosses or stone markers. Perhaps Thora was right. Jane may not know the exact location, but now that she knew the general area, she could pick a place and make it hers. Theirs.

She walked a few yards farther along the wall, then stopped to squat low and lay her little bunch of flowers on the ground. As Jane hunched there, a shadow fell over her. Was it the parish clerk come to tell her to leave, to remind her such things were private and best forgotten?

She glanced up. Mr. Ainsworth, the old sexton, stood there.

Jane winced. "I know it isn't done. But please leave me be. I just need a place to put my flowers and remember. Is that so wrong?"

Instead Mr. Ainsworth bent and gathered up her flowers with his shabby gloves.

Anger and violation swept over her, and she resisted the urge to yank the flowers from his soiled grasp. *How dare he!* There was no law against laying flowers.

He turned and ambled away. Jane lurched to her feet and started after him.

Then she stopped in her tracks.

He had walked only five or six feet. He bent and laid one flower, then a handbreadth away, another, then another. "Here, missus."

Jane sucked in a breath, then walked slowly forward. Did it mean . . . Did he really know?

Throat burning, she whispered, "They are . . . here?"

"Aye, missus. Laid them here myself, I did. Ever so gentle and careful-like."

Her heart hitched.

He pointed to the stone wall, and for the first time Jane noticed the small markings scratched there: *JB IIIII*.

He laid the final flower. "Here's the place for your posies."

Jane's chest tightened until she could barely draw breath.

He straightened gingerly, removed his hat, and laid it over his heart.

For a moment she stood beside him, tears filling her eyes. "Thank you," she managed.

He nodded and hobbled away.

Jane felt her knees begin to tremble. Then her chin followed suit.

She waited as long as she could. But he had barely passed through the gate when she crumpled to her knees, heedless of her gown. Tears coursed down her cheeks. She pulled off her gloves, pressed her bare palms to the earth, and cried all her secret losses and pent-up pain into that hallowed ground.

CHAPTER
THIRTY-ONE

On Tuesday afternoon, Rachel looked up from the library desk, and her heart lurched. "Timothy!"

"Hello, Rachel." He stood there in greatcoat, top hat in hand. His face looked lean and a little weary after his week away. His boots were in need of a polish and his tousled hair in need of a trim. He had never looked better.

She rose and hurried forward, stopping short of touching him. "I have been so worried. Your mother too. She came to see me."

"I know. She told me when I arrived home late last night."

Rachel ducked her head, ashamed to think of all she had said to her. "She wanted to know why you were upset. I did not tell her anything, but I spoke to her unkindly, and I am sorry for it."

"She has certainly given you cause, which is what I told her when she described how she confronted you, not to mention all the rest."

"Did you tell her about . . . Bramble Cottage?"

"No. I considered doing so but decided against it. She feels Father's loss keenly as it is. I did not want to strip away her whole perception of her husband and her marriage. It seemed too cruel."

"I understand. I . . . hope you don't blame me for unearthing all this."

"Blame you? It isn't your fault."

"But if I had never started the library, accepted donations, brought Mrs. Haverhill into our lives . . ."

He shook his head. "The truth always comes out in the end. And now we must pray that something good will come of it."

Rachel nodded, her eyes lingering on his. "May I ask where you went?"

"I needed to get away—to think. I also went on a mission of sorts."

"Mission? What do you mean?"

"Come to Bramble Cottage with me, will you? Then I can tell you and Mrs. Haverhill the news at once."

"Very well. Let me just ask Miss Matty to watch over the library for me."

He agreed, and she hurried to find Matilda and to don a cape and bonnet.

Sir Timothy was quiet on the way, refusing to give any hint of his news. So as they walked, Rachel told him instead about her conversation with Carville at church.

When they reached Bramble Cottage, Mrs. Haverhill opened the door and invited them inside, her graciousness not fully masking her surprise at Sir Timothy's return. She offered to make tea, but he declined.

"Please, may we sit and talk?"

"Of course."

She and Rachel sat on the sofa, while he took the armchair facing them, a low table between.

From his inner coat pocket, he withdrew a small parcel—a rectangle of folded plush velvet. He laid it on the table between them and pulled back the corners of fabric to reveal its contents: a ring, a locket, and a lover's eye brooch.

Mrs. Haverhill sucked in a breath, clapping a hand over her mouth. She looked at him with wide eyes, then tentatively reached out and picked up the locket and then the brooch.

"I never thought I'd see these again."

She tilted the brooch toward Rachel, and she saw it held a small framed portrait of a man's eye framed with tiny pearls. Then she lifted the gold ring with a single emerald. "I never wore this while making soap or gardening. I kept it hidden away. Or so I'd thought. How did you . . . ?"

"I wish I could claim some heroic feat," he said. "But the fact is, I was contacted by a Bristol pawnbroker who recognized the family insignia carved inside the band and contacted me hoping for a reward. He guessed the ring must have been stolen but did not notice the insignia when he first bought it from a young man who gave his name as Kurtz. Does that name mean anything to you?"

Mrs. Haverhill shook her head.

"Probably a false name, at all events. The dealer bought the pin and locket from the same man, so I guessed they might be your missing mementos. He had already sold the locket but kept a record of who bought it. Took some time, but I was able to track down the person and buy it back."

Rachel's heart warmed. "That was good of you."

Mrs. Haverhill nodded. She again looked down at the ring, made as though to slip it on, then stopped, holding it awkwardly suspended.

Her eyes flashed to his. "Your father gave this to me, but I suppose you want it back."

"No. I searched the inventory records and found a note that this particular family ring had been 'gifted to a special friend' years ago." He nodded toward it. "It's yours."

She slid it on her finger, the fit a bit loose in her current state of health.

"There's more." He pulled a long folded envelope from the same pocket and handed it to her.

"Here is the deed to Bramble Cottage—it's yours outright to live in or sell or let as you see fit. And with it is a bank draft, sufficient, I believe, to keep you in comfort. I hope you understand that I deemed it better to give you a lump sum rather than ongoing support."

"Yes, better to make a clean break of it. I understand. And it is exceedingly kind of you, Tim . . . Sir Timothy."

He shook his head. "Not kind. Responsible. My father made you his responsibility, and he would never want to see you suffer deprivation. Nor do I."

"What about Carville?" Mrs. Haverhill asked. "He has a claim to the cottage too."

Sir Timothy lifted an unconcerned shrug. "He will be rewarded for his long service in other ways. He signed over the deed without complaint. He knew he was left the property only as a guise to hide Father's relationship with you."

She studied his face. "I suppose you hate me."

He hesitated. "And I suppose you bitterly resent us, his family."

She shook her head. "I don't blame you. Any of you. Sir Justin made his own mistakes, and I made mine."

She rose and stood at the hall mirror to pin on the brooch. "I gather your parents' marriage was not . . . without its tension and conflict. Over the years, I have often thought I should leave. If I had not been so dashed dependent on him for every necessity of life, I might have done. Even so, guilt plagued me. If I had not been here, to compare to, to divert him . . . might he have given his marriage a fair effort and loved his wife in time?"

"I cannot pretend to approve of any of this," Timothy said. "Though I know my parents' relationship would not have been ideal even without your influence, lies and adultery must have a detrimental effect on any marriage. I don't say that to injure you, but you must own the truth of it."

She turned. "How could I deny it? I share the blame—of course I do."

"I blame my father." Nostrils flared, Sir Timothy shook his head, jaw tense.

Mrs. Haverhill walked slowly toward his chair. Standing before him, she reached down, slipped a finger beneath his chin, and lifted it. He looked at her in surprise, and she earnestly held his gaze.

"Your father failed in many ways, and he knew it. But he also knew he had done all right where you were concerned. Oh, he realized he had to share the credit with your mother and with God for your excellent natural character, but he was very proud of you. He thought the world of you, Tim. And someday when you're not so angry and are able to forgive him, I hope you will remember that and treasure it. For though your father was far from perfect, he was still a man of worth. A man whose esteem meant something."

For a moment longer, their gazes remained locked, and then she released his chin and stepped back.

He inhaled, gave a small nod, and rose.

Rachel stood as well, and together she and Sir Timothy took their leave.

They walked back into the village side by side, hands behind their backs.

"That was generous of you, Timothy. I am impressed."

He shook his head. "I felt it my duty. And a way to make peace with an unhappy chapter of my family's past." He looked at her. "Although I realize some wrongs can never truly be righted, and certainly not by a few tokens and a piece of paper."

Rachel looked up at him, gauging his meaning. He held her gaze a moment, then looked away across the field. He picked up a stick and struck at nettles in the hedgerow. "I hear you will be moving your father's books out of Ivy Cottage." His Adam's apple rose and fell. "Back to Thornvale, I assume?"

Rachel gaped at him. "Where did you hear that?"

"My mother talked to Mrs. Grove when she was here. Something she said led Mamma to believe you would be moving your belongings back to Thornvale. And since you told me yourself of Nicholas Ashford's proposal, it seemed a credible report."

Rachel's thoughts spun. Surely a simple misunderstanding—the women assuming that if Mr. Ashford was pursuing her, it was only a matter of time until she and her books returned to Thornvale. Or was something else afoot? Fear trickled through her.

As they turned the corner onto Church Street, she said, "I have no fixed plan at present. If Mrs. Grove said I would be removing the books, then she knows something I don't."

"I am sorry to distress you. I should not have repeated it." He tossed away the stick and looked at her. "Then . . . you have not become engaged while I was away?"

"No."

His expression brightened. "In that case, would you attend a concert with us at the Awdrys' tomorrow?"

"Oh." Rachel felt suddenly winded. Why would he ask her? After their fight. After . . . everything? She swallowed, avoiding his gaze. "Thank you, but I have already agreed to attend with Matilda Grove and . . . the Ashfords." She felt herself flush in embarrassment. Especially when she had just denied the rumor about her and Nicholas.

She stole a glance at him and saw his eyes dull. "I am sorry."

"Don't be. You have nothing to apologize for, Miss Ashford. It is my own fault." He smiled faintly. "He who hesitates is lost."

The Kingsley brothers rumbled into The Bell stable yard in force the next morning, their wagon loaded with tools, lumber, and men. Jane was relieved they were finally able to turn their attention to the stables, which needed repair before winter.

She asked Mrs. Rooke to prepare a meal for them, and Cadi and Alwena spent more time ogling the men out the window than working.

Cadi blinked wide, innocent eyes at Jane. "I could take them some tea or lemonade—just to be helpful."

Jane sent her a knowing look. "I think I will let Mrs. Rooke do that, Cadi, but thank you."

The ostlers let the horses out into the paddock during the construction, but Athena did not get along well with the carriage horses, kicking and shying when they neared. So they kept her separate—tethered in the yard to keep her out of the way of the long planks, dust, and debris.

Even so, the loud hammering and the strange men coming and going set Athena more on edge than usual. The horse had always been spirited, and lately more skittish. She was clearly not acclimating well to all the changes she'd experienced over the last few months: moving here to The Bell under Gabriel Locke's care, then Gabriel leaving, then Jake Fuller filling in for a time, and now Jake's son, Tom.

Jane retrieved a carrot from the kitchen, planning to go out and try to comfort her horse. As she passed through the corridor, she saw Hetty on the stairway. Patrick stood on the half landing above, stretching up with a feather duster to reach the candle chandelier for her.

Good gracious. Patrick cleaning something of his own free will? He must be smitten indeed.

Coming back inside after visiting Athena, Jane found Hetty and Patrick standing near one another in the office, Patrick pointing out a series of marks on the wall.

"See here? This is the year I passed John in height, although he was older. He did not like that, I can tell you."

Hetty traced her fingers over the marks. "You are so blessed to have grown up here, Patrick, in one place your whole life. Knowing everyone in town . . ."

"It had its blessings, I own, and its drawbacks."

"Like what?"

"Like being in one place your whole life. Knowing everyone and everyone knowing your business."

Hetty smiled thoughtfully. "It all depends on your perspective, I suppose."

"I suppose you're right. And where did you grow up?"

"Oh, here and there. We moved around a great deal—never in one place very long." She sent him a wry look. "Rather like you these last few years."

"Touché." Patrick leaned near and pulled something from her hair. "Just a cobweb." His fingers lingered, caressing the red tendril.

Jane cleared her throat. "Hello, you two. I hope you are behaving yourselves."

"Oh! We are." Hetty blushed. "In fact, I was just telling Mr. Bell I need to get back to work upstairs."

"She was, Jane. My fault—I was distracting her."

Hetty gathered her housemaid's box and marched purposefully up the stairs.

Patrick watched her go. "I'd almost forgotten how pretty she was. How sweet and clever. How she makes me laugh."

"Careful, Patrick. You begin to sound like a man besotted."

"Hm? Oh, well, yes. But nothing to worry about, Jane."

Jane was not reassured.

She picked up a basket of clean linens from the passageway and carried it upstairs. She found Hetty plunked down on the bed she was supposed to be making, hands pressed to her cheeks.

"Oh, Mrs. Bell, I should never have come back here. What was I thinking? He is so handsome and so devilish charming, it makes it nigh unto impossible to think clearly—to remember my promise to keep him at arm's length."

Jane sighed. "Do be careful, Hetty. Remember he's abandoned you once before. I care for my brother-in-law—don't mistake me—but you know what he's like. I'd hate to see you get hurt again."

"I know, and you're right. But he seems different now. He still flirts with me, but he's thoughtful and kind too. He hasn't done anything improper, though I confess that if he tried to kiss me, I'd take him in my arms and kiss him back."

"Then keep your arms busy," Jane advised and thrust the laundry basket into her hands.

CHAPTER THIRTY-TWO

The morning of the Awdrys' concert, Nicholas sent a trio of small peach-colored silk roses, arranged to wear pinned to one's bodice. How thoughtful. Rachel knew it was too late in the season for fresh roses this color, but these made a lovely substitute.

Later, when dressed for the occasion, Rachel pinned the flowers to the bodice of her ivory evening gown. She checked her reflection in the mirror and was satisfied the gift was suitably displayed.

When the Ashfords' traveling chariot stopped in front of Ivy Cottage early that evening, Rachel stood waiting in the vestibule. She could see Mrs. Ashford's profile through the carriage window. Nicholas let himself out and came to the door alone.

Rachel invited him inside. "Matilda will be down in a moment. She went back upstairs for a fan."

He nodded. "That's all right. We have plenty of time." His gaze roamed her form and face with obvious pleasure, then fixed on the silk roses. "Those look well on you. You are so beautiful."

Rachel felt her cheeks warm. "Thank you."

He stepped nearer. "Miss Ashford. Rachel, I—"

"Here I am, here I am . . ." Matilda bustled into the vestibule, reticule and folded fan in hand. "Sorry to keep you waiting, Mr. Ashford."

"Not at all."

Matilda smiled at him. "Perhaps you might help Rachel on with her shawl?"

"With pleasure."

Rachel handed him her kashmir shawl, and he settled it around her shoulders. Then he opened the door and escorted the ladies to the waiting carriage.

As promised, Mrs. Ashford was polite and even cordial, although most of her warmth was directed toward Matilda rather than herself. That was fine with Rachel. She was relieved the woman's attention was pleasantly engaged elsewhere. As the two older women talked, Rachel felt herself relax against the cushions, lulled into a sleepy state by the carriage's constant motion. Now and again, she looked over and found Nicholas watching her. His mouth would curve into a small smile, and she returned it.

When they finally reached stately Broadmere and entered the fortress-like hall, Rachel was struck by the many mounted animal heads on the walls—not her favorite decoration.

Sir Cyril Awdry greeted them with a toothy grin. "Welcome, welcome, one and all."

Rachel thanked him, though she had the distinct impression that he did not recall who she was.

People milled in the antechamber, while others proceeded into the large ballroom to find a seat among the rows of chairs.

Rachel saw Justina Brockwell and Miss Bingley, and excused herself to greet them.

Justina beamed. "Rachel! I am happy to see you. You came with the Ashfords, I see."

"Yes, and Miss Grove."

"I know you met Sir Cyril and his sister Penelope at our house, but have you met his younger sister, Arabella?"

"I have not."

Justina turned to survey the crowd. "There she is. Talking with Timothy."

Rachel followed her gaze, easily picking out Timothy's tall masculine form, handsome in evening dress. He stood talking to a pretty, willowy young woman dressed in a striking white gown. Its wide neckline exposed much of her shoulders and delicate collarbones without an immodest display of bosom. A blue silk tunic wrapped around her tiny waist, clasped with a jeweled brooch. It must be the latest style, Rachel thought, quite unlike her own gown, with its lower neckline and less distinct waist. The young woman's honey-colored hair was ornamented with a sophisticated bandeau and ostrich plume. Rachel's silk roses and simple coiffure suddenly felt too girlish for her seven and twenty years.

"She is lovely," Rachel observed.

"As are you." Justina pressed her hand. "Do sit near us. Promise?"

Rachel nodded. "I will if I can."

A few minutes later, she walked with the Ashfords into the ballroom lit with wall sconces and tall candelabra stands. Mrs. Ashford selected a chair in the same row as the Brockwells, so Rachel was able to sit near Justina after all. Timothy, however, ended up one row back, next to Arabella Awdry. Rachel felt self-conscious with him behind her.

When the appointed hour for the concert had come and gone without fanfare, people began to look around in restless curiosity.

Sir Cyril walked to the front of the room, clasped and unclasped his hands. "Thank you all for coming. Goodness. Such a lot of people." He smiled, put a hand on his hip, and then lowered it again. "I know you have come expecting music, and music we shall have. Hopefully—eventually. Our songbird has just arrived, after some unexplained delay, and needs time to prepare and warm her voice—whatever that means. Personally I find tossing back a brandy is all that's needed to warm my throat, but I am uninitiated in these matters."

He chuckled to himself, then went on. "I have been told that many ladies and gentleman go in for this sort of thing. Personally, I detest Italian singing. There is no understanding a word of it. But I am vastly happy to oblige all of you."

He grinned, and again the awkward hand rose to his hip, and then back down to his side. "I hope you will enjoy Signora Maltese.

I prefer a good folk song, myself. Or whistling as I strike across a field, gun in hand, pointer at my side, birdsong filling the air. Now *that* is music to my ears—that is, until I blast them down." Again he chuckled, then cast his anxious gaze over the room. He looked at the clock, rocked on his heels, and adjusted his cravat. "I could whistle for you now . . . ?"

Lady Awdry stood. "Perhaps a few of the young ladies might be prevailed upon to play for us? Until the signora is able to join us?"

He beamed and blew out a breath. "Excellent idea, Mother." He gestured about him. "We have a pianoforte, a harp, and sheet music by the score." He cast about the room again. "Now, who will fill the gap? Stand in the breech? Help a fellow out?" His gaze landed on his tall sister. "Penelope looks about to flee the room."

Rachel glanced over and noticed the elder Miss Awdry looking decidedly ill at ease. What she lacked in obvious femininity, someone had tried to compensate for with too many ruffles and flounces, and the feathered turban on her head was an unfortunate choice, as it made her the tallest person in the crowd.

"Don't worry, Pen," Sir Cyril assured her. "I shan't ask you to play, unless it is a game of cricket!" He tittered and rocked on his heels again. Then his eyes sought his younger sister. "But Arabella will play, will you not? Unless someone else wishes to go first?"

Nearby, Mrs. Bingley nudged her daughter, clearly eager to display her accomplishments to advantage.

"But, Mamma," Miss Bingley whispered, "I am not out yet."

"Close enough, my dear. The invitations to your ball go out next week."

Lady Brockwell looked expectantly at Justina, but the girl shook her head, alarm pinching her pretty features.

Rachel watched the two young women with sympathy. It was clear neither felt inclined to play.

Miss Bingley rose with resignation, clearly accustomed to being prodded to perform. She sat at the pianoforte and launched into an ambitious Irish air. She played reasonably well, though perfunctorily, with little pleasure for herself or her hearers.

When she finished, polite applause escorted her back to her chair.

Then Arabella Awdry walked forward and situated herself at the harp.

Watching her regal posture and skilled fingers as she plucked sweet music from the strings, Rachel felt reluctant admiration for the favored young woman.

When she finished to much applause, Sir Cyril announced a five-minute intermission while he went to see how the signora progressed.

Lady Brockwell turned toward her. "Do you play an instrument, Rachel?"

She shook her head. "I am afraid not."

"I am surprised."

Sir Timothy leaned forward from behind them. "But Miss Ashford possesses a lovely singing voice. Well I remember hearing it."

Rachel felt warm gratitude at his gallantry.

"Excellent idea, Timothy." Justina turned to her, all eagerness. "Rachel, you sing while I play. Everyone will be so enthralled by your performance, they shall not notice how imperfectly I play."

Rachel was too old to be displaying her accomplishments. She shook her head. "I don't think so, Justina. I have not sung publicly in ages, outside of church. No one wants to hear me—"

"Please, Rachel. I won't be half so frightened if you go up with me."

Rachel glanced over her shoulder at Timothy, but his concerned gaze remained on his sister. "Justina, you needn't play if it makes you uneasy."

"It is only a case of nerves," Lady Brockwell said. "She ought to oblige Sir Cyril in this instance, in a show of support. Prove her ability as an excellent hostess, managing well the little problems that inevitably arise at such events."

Sir Cyril returned to the front of the room, rubbing his hands together. "A few more minutes yet, I am afraid. Who else will oblige us?" He glanced hopefully at Miss Brockwell.

In turn, Justina widened her eyes at Rachel in urgent plea.

Rachel's singing voice had been complimented in the past, but she'd had no formal training. She felt her only true talents were embroidery and other fine needlework—neither of which would help Justina at the moment.

She sighed. "Very well, Justina. If you truly want me to."

"I do." Justina took her hand, led her to the pianoforte, and quickly sifted through the music.

Sir Cyril beamed. "Excellent, a duo next. Thank you, Miss Brockwell. And Miss . . . ?"

"Miss Ashford," Justina supplied, then selected a piece of sheet music from the pile. "This one looks simple enough." She looked to Rachel for approval. "All right?"

Rachel glanced at it, nervous under so many expectant eyes watching them.

"I think I remember that one, though I shall have to look on now and again."

Justina gave her a crooked grin. "Well, I shall be looking every second, and even then making mistakes, so just do the best you can." The girl flexed her fingers and played the introduction.

Rachel inhaled a fortifying breath and began to sing:

> "Oh, ne'er can I the joys forget
> of many a vanish'd year,
> they blossom in my mem'ry yet,
> as lovely and as dear:
>
> Like roses in a wilderness
> my lonely heart their beauties bless,
> and seem a fragrant chain to be,
> which binds that heart, my love to thee . . ."

Oh, why had she agreed to sing this song? Rachel silently lamented. The poignant melody, the words that quickly moved from joy to vanished years, aching memories, roses, and a heart bound to an old love?

Rachel mustered all the composure she had learned at her dear mother's knee and even at her sickbed. She sang on, hoping the waver of her voice was not noticeable. She felt tears prick her eyes and prayed that if anyone noticed, they would think it a trick of the candlelight and nothing more.

She felt Timothy's gaze on her and shifted slightly toward him. There he sat, his eyes sparking with some strong emotion, or perhaps they only reflected flame from a nearby sconce.

She glanced at Nicholas and found him watching her as well, as if transfixed with wonder.

Noticing her gaze move to Mr. Ashford, Timothy's eyes dulled and his shoulders slumped. Finally, the last verse was sung, and Justina played the concluding notes.

For a moment the chords echoed in stillness, fading, fading. Then applause broke out, begun by a beaming Matilda Grove. Others joined in, and Rachel turned toward Justina to divert the embarrassing attention toward her young accompanist, who dimpled and curtsied.

Sir Cyril came to the front, bowed over Justina's hand, and smiled at Rachel. "Well, well, well. Very nicely done. Ah, I see the footman gesturing that Signora is ready. Let us hope she does not disappoint after such fine performances, or sings overlong to make up for her tardiness—for punch and a good supper await us at the conclusion of her program to reward your patience."

Signora Maltese came forward in a swirling silk gown, her accompanist sat at the pianoforte, and the concert began. She performed Italian arias fit for a London opera. Her trilling soprano was impressive in range, if occasionally jarring at its highest reaches. Rachel was certainly relieved not to have to sing after her.

After several pieces, the regal-looking woman with black hair and snapping eyes addressed her host in accented English. "I hear, my *discerning* sir, that you prefer folk songs to my music."

He grinned and opened his mouth to reply in the affirmative, but his mother nudged him, and replied in his stead. "He was only jesting, Signora."

"If you say so, my lady. Still, my mother was born in Ireland. So this is for you, Sir Cyril." She broke into a jaunty folk song with spirit and toe-tapping good humor. The company roared with approval, and Rachel's former melancholy was swept away on its tide.

After the singer had taken her final bow, her appreciative audience began to rise and cluster around her with congratulations and gratitude.

Rachel rose as well, glad to stand after sitting so long.

In a moment, Nicholas was there before her, his eyes shining with admiration.

"You sing like an angel, Miss Ashford. Truly, you have been blessed with a fine voice."

She felt herself blush. "Thank you, but I am afraid it was obvious I've had no training and little practice in years."

"Your voice has a pure, natural quality that I found quite affecting."

"You are very generous. But enough of me. Had you not better sing the signora's praises?"

"I had rather sing yours."

Sir Timothy approached and nodded to Nicholas. "Mr. Ashford." Then he turned to her. "Thank you, Miss Ashford, for kindly agreeing to sing for my sister's sake. I know you would rather not have done so." His mouth quirked. "And I hope you shall forgive *me* for suggesting you sing in the first place."

Nicholas turned to him with a little frown. "Why should you apologize for suggesting Miss Ashford sing? She sings beautifully."

"I agree. Even more beautifully than I remembered." He studied her face carefully. "Did . . . Justina choose that particular song?"

She hoped he didn't think she'd selected that song with him in mind. Embarrassment singed her ears, but she forced herself to meet his gaze. "Yes. I let Justina pick."

He inhaled deeply. "That is as I thought. Well. Thank you again, and now I shall intrude no longer. Good evening." He bowed and walked away.

Nicholas, however, remained by her side until his mother insisted he compliment Miss Bingley's and Miss Brockwell's performances as well. Over the crowd, Rachel noticed Sir Timothy thank the signora and then cross the room to talk with tall Penelope Awdry, who stood alone against the far wall. Arabella walked over to join them, and he greeted her with a smile.

Timothy had acknowledged Arabella was his mother's current favorite, though not his. Had he changed his mind? If so, Rachel could not blame him, not when she had declared she no longer wanted a proposal from him, and continued to see Mr. Ashford.

Rachel turned from the disheartening sight and nearly ran into Mr. Bingley.

"Ah, Miss Ashford. How goes the library?"

"It is going well, I think."

"You have Sir Timothy to thank for that, you know. Lord Winspear did not want to approve a second business operating out of the same residence, but Sir Timothy used all his powers of persuasion until he wore the man down and got his way. I went along with it, of course. Seemed harmless enough to me."

Rachel's heart pounded. "No, I did not know. Thank you, Mr. Bingley."

Timothy had said nothing to her about any obstacles. Just silently helped her. Pulse racing, Rachel looked across the room at him once more. He met her gaze a moment over the crowd, then returned his attention to the Miss Awdrys, nodding politely at something Arabella said. Standing near a wall sconce as they were, the feather in Penelope's turban fluttered dangerously close to a candle flame. With a gentle hand to her elbow, Sir Timothy directed her out of harm's way. Penelope stammered an embarrassed thank-you, while her pretty sister beamed up at him. Unconsciously, Rachel laid a hand to her aching heart, and felt silk roses instead.

During the carriage ride home, Mrs. Ashford chatted eagerly, dominating the conversation. This was fine with Rachel, for she was in no mood to talk.

"Lady Brockwell was in excellent spirits. She is usually so reserved, I find, but was quite animated tonight. Happy to see Sir Cyril pursuing her daughter, and her son so attentive to the younger Miss Awdry. Such particular attention. Did you notice? And Miss Awdry seemed to admire him as well, if my eyes did not deceive me. Ah yes, Lady Brockwell could barely suppress a smile all evening. No doubt pleased at the thought of such excellent matches for her children. I can only imagine how she must feel. . . ."

Rachel felt Matilda's concerned look, but she kept her gaze trained out the window at the passing moonlit countryside.

Mrs. Ashford went on, "It is a wonder Sir Timothy has not married before now. He must be thirty, at least, though men of his rank have the liberty to marry later in life, unlike us poor females. I wonder what has kept him from it? A gentleman of leisure like him—what else has he to do with his time than find a wife!" She chuckled at her little joke.

Rachel spoke up. "Sir Timothy is not idle, ma'am. He has many responsibilities around his estate and the parish. He sits on the board of governors for the almshouse, leads the village council, and serves as magistrate besides."

Mrs. Ashford waved a dismissive hand. "Yes, yes. No doubt works his gloved fingers to the bone, riding, hunting, traveling to town, and whatever else gentlemen do with their time."

"Mrs. Ashford, you—"

Matilda pressed a warning elbow into Rachel's side. Rachel changed tack. "You are right that he enjoys those things as well." She turned her attention to Nicholas. "And what about you, Mr. Ashford? Do you ride and hunt and visit London?"

"None of those, really. Though I look forward to becoming more involved in parish affairs. Mr. Paley tells me I shall soon be asked to serve a term as churchwarden, and I assured him I will be happy to help however I can."

"That is very good of you."

Mrs. Ashford's voice reverberated with pride. "It is his right and responsibility as master of Thornvale."

Rachel was relieved to feel no bitterness at the thought. "And he will do a creditable job, I don't doubt for a moment."

His mother nodded. "Now that is something we agree on, Miss Ashford."

Even in the dim carriage, Rachel could see Nicholas's eyes glow warmly as he looked at her.

"Thank you, Miss Ashford. Your confidence means a great deal."

The look should have given her pleasure, but guilt pricked her instead.

CHAPTER

THIRTY-THREE

Clutching her gloved hands in her lap and praying silently, Mercy sat across the desk from Mr. Drake in his office at the Fairmont. She barely resisted the urge to fidget as he read Mary-Alicia's letter. His golden eyebrows bunched together as he read, and then his expression cleared.

He sat back hard against his chair, expelling a long breath. "I have wondered ever since I met Alice—her looks, her age . . ." He shook his head, fingers pressed to parted lips. "Poor Mary-Alicia. If only I had found her."

"May I begin, Mr. Drake, by assuring you that I did not come here to try to compel you to do anything about this. I simply thought you had the right to see the letter. I realize that your . . . acquaintance with Miss Payne was years ago and not of long duration. You are under no obligation to—"

"Of course I am."

Mercy squeezed her hands until her knuckles ached. "I want you to know that Mr. Thomas has asked me to act as Alice's guardian. My lawyer is already drawing up the papers. So she will be well taken care of, no matter what."

His focus returned to the letter, regret pulling at his features. Had he even heard Mercy speak?

"She was wrong. I never forgot her. Nor did I leave that resort to avoid her. I'd received an urgent message that my mother was ill. I thought Mary-Alicia would be there another week at least." He grimaced. "I should have left her a note. My permanent address. Something. But I left in such a hurry.

"This was just before I bought my first hotel. I doubt I mentioned where my parents lived, even though that was still my official residence at the time. I have made a point of distancing myself from the Hain-Drakes. Determined to make my own way in the world. I never dreamed that decision would bring such consequences."

"Your hotel . . . exactly. Mr. Drake, you have a fledgling business to think of, as well as your hotel in Southampton, which must consume a great deal of your attention. So I will understand if you don't have time for the added responsibility of an eight-year-old." Could he hear the desperation in her calmly phrased arguments? She hoped not. "I think all Miss Payne wanted was someone to protect Alice. To provide for her. I am in a position to do that."

"So am I."

"I know you are a generous man, Mr. Drake. Jane Bell is a close friend of mine and speaks highly of your helpful nature. If you would like to provide some sort of stipend for Alice's upkeep, or a trust fund for when she comes of age . . ."

"Comes of age? She is only eight years old, Miss Grove. That is a lifetime away. I want to be involved now, and not only financially."

Mercy's stomach dropped. Even as the words came out of her mouth, she knew she was grasping at straws. "Mr. Drake, you are not even married."

"Neither are you."

"No, but Alice has lived with me these many months. She is fond of me, trusts me . . ."

"I am her father."

Mercy felt her world spinning out of control. This was not going at all as planned. She drew a shaky breath. "I suggest we both take time to think this through. And I will need to talk with Mr. Thomas."

She reached for the letter, but he snatched it from her grasp, eyes like green glass.

"I had better keep this. It is written to me after all. I wouldn't want anyone to be tempted to extort anything from me for its return."

Her mouth fell open. "I would never—!"

"What else am I to think? You bring this here, then try to take it back, after all this talk of my hotels and hinting that offers of money would be acceptable?"

She gasped. "For Alice! Not for me. You misunderstood. I only want what is best for her."

"And you believe you are the best judge of that? You are not her mother, Miss Grove."

Indignation and mortification washed over her. "I know that."

He clenched his hand. "This is my rightful God-given responsibility, not yours."

"You believe in God, Mr. Drake?" Irony tinged her voice.

"I do now." His mouth twisted. "And as far as Mr. Thomas—the grandfather who disowned Mary-Alicia and left her to die in poverty? I don't care a whit what he wants. His wishes are immaterial."

"If you don't care about his wishes, think of Alice. She has grown up believing herself the daughter of Alexander Smith, who married her mother and died at sea. And most everyone else believes that too. Will you expose this innocent child as illegitimate? You can pretend it won't affect her reputation, her happiness, and future marriage prospects, but you would be fooling yourself."

"Dashed gossipmongers! Then it will be our secret—at least until Alice is older and decides how she wants to deal with the issue."

Mercy feared she might be ill. "Do you really mean to raise her as your daughter? How will you explain that without revealing the truth?"

He spread his hands, a cool smile on his face. "I am an old friend of the Smiths'. Nothing could be more natural than their closest friend should feel responsible to care for their daughter, now they're gone, especially as her great-grandfather is unwilling to do so."

"That is a lie. You never met Mr. Smith."

"Actually, I did—in Portsmouth. Gregarious fellow, especially when someone else is buying. I was a much closer friend of Mary-Alicia, though for Alice's sake, we may not want to trumpet that fact about. And since you seem to have a low opinion of my character, it will not shock you to learn that I will happily lie to protect Alice. Though I would prefer to make my true role known, I will first consider how best to proceed. Talk to a lawyer myself."

But Mercy had not been willing to lie to protect Alice. *Oh, God, have I made a terrible mistake?*

Temples pounding, Mercy rose. "I hope you will take time to reflect carefully before you do anything hasty, Mr. Drake. Consider what is best for Alice long term."

She exited his office in a fog of disbelief. What had she done by antagonizing the man who held Alice's future in his hands? A future Mercy would likely have no part in after this.

To get Athena away from the construction, Jane had tried taking her out to Angel Farm, but the unfamiliar surroundings and animals agitated her more than the noise at The Bell. Jane thought about the Fairmont but discounted it since that place, too, was crawling with workmen. So she returned Athena to the inn, hoping the horse would eventually calm down.

A cold rain fell the next day, so instead of tethering Athena in the yard, the horsemen put her in the high-sided stall at one end of the stable, where she seemed to feel more secure than out in the open. They left her there the following day as well, but every time a loud noise erupted—a dropped hammer or a curse shouted by a careless workman—Athena would rear up or kick. Jane feared she would injure herself, and sure enough, when she went out with an apple that afternoon, she was sorry to see a gash on one of Athena's rear legs and went to ask Tom Fuller to look at it.

Tom entered Athena's stall to examine her injury, but Athena whinnied and reared up, her hooves coming dangerously close to Tom's head, scaring them both. Tom slipped out of the stall, defeated, and shut the gate behind him

"I can't do it, Mrs. Bell. I'm sorry. And she shouldn't be ridden until her hooves are trimmed and re-shod and that cut treated. But you see how she is—she won't let me near her. She's gone wild, I tell ya. That's racehorse blood for ya. Unpredictable, jumpy creatures. I've had my fill. Hate to say so, but I give up on your mare."

"Tom, no. She needs someone to care for her. She's high-spirited, I know, but she has been out of sorts since Mr. Locke left, and now all the construction and noise. She'll settle down, eventually. Get used to life here again."

"I doubt it, ma'am. And meanwhile I'm not willing to get kicked in the head until she settles. I've got a wife to think of now and a child on the way."

"I . . . understand, Tom, of course."

After he left, Jane lingered, trying in vain to soothe her horse.

"I know, girl. I know," she whispered. "I miss him too."

The former gifts she'd offered Athena—carrots or a slice of apple—no longer appealed to the thoroughbred. She was off her feed, and Jane's worry grew.

Should she write to Gabriel Locke and ask him to come and see Athena? Or at least ask his advice? Yes, she decided, she would. For Athena's sake. And for her own.

Dear Gabriel,

Athena isn't herself without you. She is unhappy and unsettled. She kicks and shies away from your replacement. She nips at other horses and is disrupting the whole stable yard. She has already injured herself by rearing up inside her stall. And she will let no one near her, except me, and I don't know how to help her.

I am sure you are busy with your uncle's horses, but if you

might send along any advice or instructions our new farrier might try, we—I—would be most appreciative.

Sincerely,
Jane Bell

Would he respond? Jane thought of the argument they'd had before the coach contest. She had been so angry when she learned John had gambled away the loan money and put The Bell in jeopardy, and angry with Mr. Locke for keeping the truth from her. Before that discovery, she'd been on the cusp of trusting Gabriel. The harsh words she'd thrown at him repeated themselves in her mind, and she winced to recall all she had said in the heat of anger. . . .

"You should have told me the truth. Instead you lied and pretended to be someone you're not. A simple farrier with his own Thoroughbred, a fine watch, and a bank account in Wishford? . . . I don't want a man I can't trust living on my doorstep."

He'd ridden away after that, but she had gone after him to apologize. She had not been prepared to fully trust the man, but she had hoped that would change, given time. Instead, he left again after helping The Bell's team win the coach contest—although they had parted amicably, she'd thought.

Would he help her now? She hoped so. Because she and Athena needed someone they could trust.

After her meeting with Mr. Drake, Mercy remained in a state of disconnected denial for a few days, as though nothing had changed in her plans to become Alice's guardian. It was wishful thinking, of course, but it allowed her to teach her classes and get through the days until she could get away and inform Mr. Coine of recent developments. Now she could put off reality no longer.

She rode into Wishford again with the carter and planned to walk back when she finished, assuming the clouds on the horizon did not portend a storm.

Mrs. Burlingame sent her a few curious glances as they rode along, but Mercy did not explain the reason for her trip.

When they arrived on the High Street, Mercy thanked the woman, smoothed her skirts, and walked into the law office.

Mr. Coine's usual smile was absent. "Miss Grove. I meant to drive over to see you later today. You have saved me a trip." He led her into his office and closed the door. "I am afraid another claimant has come forward in the case of young Alice."

"Already? That is what I came to discuss with you."

"I'm sorry. No doubt it's a shock. Though less than it might have been, as I gather you and Mr. Drake have already discussed this."

"Only . . . a preliminary discussion. No specifics have been decided."

"You know he claims to be Alice's natural father. He presents compelling evidence, including the fact that no Alexander Smith is listed among the crew of the downed ship Alice's mother claimed took her husband's life. But of course most convincing is the letter, written by Mary-Alicia Payne herself, referring to her daughter's father as JD. When paired with other correspondence he provided in which several people address him by those initials, I believe most would find it sufficient evidence. He told me he is prepared to take his case to the Court of Chancery, if need be."

"I see." Did Mr. Drake really want Alice, Mercy wondered, or had she unintentionally created a competition with a man who could not resist a challenge? She inwardly groaned at the thought. *Oh, Lord, please protect Alice.*

She asked, "Just out of curiosity, what if I had never found that letter?"

"His claim would have been more difficult to prove. But with him a respectable, successful man of business able to summon character witnesses, if need be . . . ? The end result might have been the same."

"What about Mr. Thomas's wishes?"

"If there was no evidence for Mr. Drake's paternity claim, Mr.

Thomas's wishes, as verifiable next of kin, would be paramount. But a father has a stronger claim than a great-grandfather."

Mercy exhaled a sigh.

He studied her face. "Have you some reason to be concerned about the man's character or intentions?"

Had she? Or was she only disappointed for herself? Mercy shook her head. "No. Not really."

"Then for the girl's sake, might not this be good news? Though a blow for you, to be sure. I am sorry, Miss Grove. I blame myself for not warning you to guard your heart against the possibility of another claimant. But even her own great-grandfather had no inkling. Who could have guessed?"

Mercy rose, a false smile fixed to her face. "Who could have guessed, indeed. Thank you for your time, Mr. Coine. And do send your bill. You spent time on this even if it didn't turn out as we'd hoped."

"I would not think of it."

"As you wish. Good day." She turned, willing her tears to wait. The time for denial had passed.

She made it to the street, on legs of melting wax. She grasped the side of a parked wagon for support. *Please help me accept this, God. Your will be done. . . .*

Without warning, Joseph Kingsley appeared, one strong arm bracing her back, the other holding her hand.

"Miss Grove! What is it? Are you ill? You look very ill. Shall I find a doctor?"

She shook her head, not trusting her voice.

He guided her down the street to a stair-stepped mounting block. She sat, and he lowered himself to his haunches before her, looking up into her face with concern.

"What's happened?"

"I have had distressing news. I can bear losing the school, if I must. But Alice too?"

"I am sorry. Her kin changed her mind?"

Mercy hesitated, tears filling her eyes. "Another . . . relative . . . came forward."

He winced and took her hand in his. "Is there nothing to be done?"

Mercy shook her head, chin trembling. She became aware of passersby staring at them and ducked her head.

Mr. Kingsley seemed to realize it at the same time. "Come, let's get you home. Did you walk here?"

"No, but I planned to walk home."

"My cart is just there, at the livery."

Helping her up, he tucked her arm through his, held it close to his side as they walked, and led her through a narrow door into the livery—the rear door apparently, for she encountered no one except several bored-looking horses in their stalls.

"You wait here. I'll be right back." He pressed her hand, and his gentle care only fueled her tears all the more.

He made to release her arm, but for a moment she held fast. "Th-thank you, Mr. Kingsley."

He took a step nearer and reached out his free hand, perhaps to offer a consolatory pat, she guessed. Instead, he wrapped both arms around her shoulders and held her close.

For a moment Mercy stood in stiff surprise. Then she leaned slightly into his embrace, relishing the warm comfort of being held. She was in the arms of a man for the first time in her life—a man she admired. A tingle of pleasure rose amid her sadness, but like a fragile flower in the wind, it quickly bowed. A horse stomped a hoof, and a door rumbled open on the opposite end, breaking the sweet spell.

She pulled slowly away, digging into her reticule for her handkerchief and avoiding his eyes. "Again, thank you, Mr. Kingsley. You are very kind."

"I did nothing. I wish I could help you somehow."

She managed a watery smile. "You *have* helped me. More than you know."

CHAPTER THIRTY-FOUR

Later that day, Mercy walked to The Bell to confide in Jane. When she arrived, she saw Colin McFarland at the desk.

She managed a smile for the young man. "Hello, Colin. How are things here? The lessons helping?"

Colin darted a look toward the office. "Shh . . ."

Mercy stared at him in disbelief. "You mean you haven't told Jane yet?"

Colin shook his head.

"Told me what?" Jane asked, stepping out of the office to greet her.

Mercy gave the clerk a pointed look.

Sheepishly, Colin explained, "I have been going to Ivy Cottage for tutoring in arithmetic."

"Ahh. So that's where you've been. I wondered. You should have told me."

"I know. I meant to. I was . . . embarrassed."

"No need. And you have improved so much already. Patrick and I have both noticed."

"Thank you, ma'am. I appreciate your understanding. And your patience."

Jane turned to her and teased, "Well, Mercy, what other secrets are you going to divulge today?"

Mercy did not smile in return.

"Uh oh." Jane's smile faded. "Shall we go to the lodge again?"

"If you can get away."

"Colin has things in hand here. Don't you, Colin?"

"I do, indeed. Finally."

Jane led her to the keeper's lodge, and once seated, Mercy told her about Alice and Mr. Drake.

Jane's eyes grew wide. "Mr. Drake? Good heavens . . ."

"Well, the letter we found was addressed only to a *JD*, but apparently some people refer to him by his initials."

Jane nodded and said gently, "Yes. In fact, when Mr. Drake first arrived here and signed the inn register, he wrote his name as JD. He told me that was what most of his friends called him. Friends who would no doubt attest to that, if need be."

"That is what Mr. Coine concluded as well." Mercy looked up at Jane. "I was not sure if I should tell you. I know you and he are friends. But I needed to talk to you."

"Of course you did; and I am glad you told me. I wonder if Miss Payne is what brought him to Ivy Hill in the first place? That would explain so much. But oh, Mercy, what a disappointment for you. I am somewhat surprised he wants to raise Alice. He recently told me he did not think he was cut out to be a father."

"Evidently, he has changed his mind." Mercy looked down. "I have been asking God why all this is happening to me. If I did something to deserve it, or . . . if there is something I need to learn from this. If so, I want to learn it quickly and be done. I never want to feel like this again. Or lose someone so dear to me."

"*If* there is a lesson to be learned, then you would, of course, be the first to learn it and learn it well, but you are the last person to deserve something like this."

Mercy shook her head. "No, Jane. I have my weaknesses. I was proud. Proud to be from the oldest family in Ivy Hill. Proud to be independent—mistress of my own school and home, or so I thought."

"I am so sorry," Jane repeated.

"I am sorry too. Sorry for myself, but now . . . I will stop." Mercy sniffed and managed a wobbly smile. "Forgive me, Jane."

Jane squeezed her hand. "There is nothing to forgive. I only wish there was something I could do."

Jane paused, then added, "Mercy, I know you don't want to hear this, but if Mr. Drake is Alice's father, it is good that he wants to be a part of her life. It would be one thing if she never knew, if you let her believe for the rest of her life in a fictitious father who died at sea. But, Mercy . . . You are the most honest person I know. And you would have told her the truth, eventually."

"I would have, yes. When she was old enough to understand. And then it would be up to her whether she wished to invite him into her life or not."

Jane shook her head. "After how many lost years? She would resent him for abandoning her, and you for keeping him from her. It would be a different matter if Mr. Drake were unwilling or uninterested or some vile character. But he is none of those things."

Mercy looked at her closely. "Do you still miss your father, Jane? Wish him back in your life?"

Tears sprang to Jane's eyes, and Mercy instantly regretted the question.

Jane opened her mouth, closed it, and then said, "We are not talking about me. I was already grown when my father departed. Too old to feel . . . abandoned."

It was not very convincing. Mercy didn't know all the details about why Mr. Fairmont left, and Jane almost never talked about him.

Jane swiped at her eyes and changed the subject. "By the way, have you told Rachel her library is in jeopardy?"

Mercy grimaced. "No. But I must. I have put it off too long as it is."

Rachel was preparing for bed that night when Mercy knocked on her door. Rachel invited her in, immediately noticing how somber she looked.

"What is it, Mercy?"

"Rachel, I have to tell you something. I should have told you before now. You remember hearing that George is engaged?"

"Yes."

"My parents are going to offer Ivy Cottage to him and his new wife, unless . . ."

"Unless what?"

"I marry Mr. Hollander."

"Oh, Mercy."

She raised her hand. "I don't want you to worry about a place to live. You will have a place with me for as long as you want one. But your library . . ."

Rachel blinked. "I see." So what Timothy heard from his mother and Mrs. Grove had not been rumor or supposition after all. "And what about your school?"

Mercy shook her head.

"Oh no." Rachel's stomach sank.

"I am sorry, Rachel. You have only had your library for a short while. I feel terrible. I don't think my parents will change their minds. Nor do I think George would agree to keep it here. If I marry Mr. Hollander, he might be amenable, but I have not yet decided what to do about him, and I felt it only right to give you fair warning that, after Christmas, the library may have to close."

"Mercy, don't you dare marry a man to save my library. I would never forgive myself. Truly. You decide what is best for you. Promise me."

"I have been trying to decide what is best. I even made a list. What I would gain by marrying Mr. Hollander—a husband, possibly children, remaining mistress of Ivy Cottage—far outweighs what I'd give up. On paper the decision is an easy equation, simple to solve. But in here . . ." She pressed a hand to her heart and slowly shook her head. "Not simple."

"I understand." *All too well*, Rachel thought and gently squeezed her hand. "Thank you for telling me."

"We have our next meeting Monday night," Mercy reminded her. "Perhaps the ladies might help us solve both our problems?"

Rachel managed a smile. "This may be beyond even the Ladies Tea and Knitting Society."

Mercy returned her smile and left the room, closing the door behind her.

Rachel stood there, doubts and fear descending. How was she to support herself now? A prayer sprang to her lips but wilted there unspoken. Was she still too proud to ask God for help?

She thought again of Nicholas Ashford. Should she accept his offer of marriage? Especially now, when she was about to lose her livelihood?

Rachel picked up the silk nosegay Nicholas had given her before the concert. From a distance, it looked lovely. Almost real. The flowers carried with them a poignant reminder of her mother, and her beloved rose garden at Thornvale. It could be Rachel's rose garden if she married Nicholas. . . .

Of long habit, she brought the flowers to her nose but smelled only the vague scent of ironed linen. Close up, the artificial petals were less realistic. Lifeless. But the silk bouquet would not fade or wilt like the real thing.

She opened her mother's Bible and extracted the single rose she had pressed between its pages—saved from the bouquet Timothy Brockwell had given her eight years ago, a week after her coming-out ball. The petals, once peach-colored, had dried and darkened to a sherry hue.

Which was better, she asked herself. One real, glorious rose, long faded but never forgotten? Or a tempting substitute that promised to last forever?

Saturday nights at The Bell were usually slow, so the ostlers sat in the stable yard playing music together as they often did when their duties allowed. Tall Ted played his fiddle, and Tuffy, his old mandolin. The two tried to cajole Colin to join them on his pipe, but he mumbled an apology and said he had an errand to run. Even though Colin had finally confessed to Jane that he was being tutored by Anna Kingsley, he was still not eager for the other fellows to find out.

Jane went out to the stables to look in on Athena, then lingered outside to listen to the men play.

The side door opened and Hetty tentatively stepped out of the inn, a pipe in her hand and Betsey on her hip. "May I join you?"

Tuffy raised his shaggy eyebrows in surprise. "'Course you can."

Hetty looked at Jane. "That is . . . if you don't mind, Mrs. Bell?"

"Not at all. You've been working hard, Hetty—you deserve a little leisure. But I didn't know you could play."

The girl shrugged. "It's been a long time, so don't expect too much."

Jane reached out her hands to hold Betsey for her. The little girl settled into her arms without complaint, and Jane relished the warm comfort of holding the sweet-smelling toddler.

Hetty sat beside Tuffy. Ted played a familiar old folk melody on his fiddle while Tuffy strummed along on his mandolin. After a few sharp notes, Hetty began drawing a sweet harmony from the pipe, adding depth to the tune. They finished the song, and Jane and Betsey applauded.

"Well done, lass." Tuffy nodded in approval. "You play as well as Colin, and are a sight prettier. But don't tell him I said so." He winked.

"Do ya know this one?" Ted launched into another tune.

Patrick came out to join them, taking Betsey in his arms and bouncing her about in a little jig. Seeing it, a bittersweet lump rose in Jane's throat. For a moment in the fading twilight, Patrick looked so much like John that she could imagine it was him, dancing with their own child in The Bell yard.

Soon after, a post chaise arrived, pulling the ostlers from their music. Hetty thanked them for including her, then held out her arms to Betsey, taking her back from Patrick.

He looked at her, clearly impressed. "Where did you learn to play like that?"

"My father taught me as a girl."

"Is he a musician?" Jane asked.

"Not really. He dabbles in this and that."

"Do you play other instruments as well?"

"No, though he did. The tenor serpent was his favorite. He wanted us all to play something. Playing together passed the time and, em, people seemed to like it."

"A musical family," Jane mused. "How delightful."

Patrick joked, "A regular family music troupe, were you? The Pipers perform on their pipes . . ."

"I did not say we were a music troupe," Hetty snapped. "What an idea."

"I was only teasing."

"Oh. Sorry," Hetty murmured, chagrined over her reaction.

"Where is your family now?" Jane asked gently.

"I don't know. That is . . . I have not been in contact with them, since . . . since Betsey was born."

"They must worry about you."

"I did write. To tell them I was well. And not to worry."

"Good. But you must miss them."

"I do. Especially my sister."

"Your sister?" Patrick blinked in surprise. "You never mentioned a sister."

"Did I not? I suppose it's because I . . . haven't seen her in a long time. But it's for the best this way."

Patrick's brow furrowed. "Why?"

"Goodness. It's past Betsey's bedtime. She'll be peevish for Thora tomorrow, and we don't want that. Come, my lamb. Time for bed. Good night, Patrick, Mrs. Bell."

"Good night." Patrick reached out and smoothed a ginger curl from Betsey's brow, then watched mother and child disappear inside.

Jane observed him with interest. "Patrick, you are clearly fond of Hetty, as well as Betsey. Why don't you marry her?"

"I am tempted, believe me. She is more . . . everything . . . than I remembered or realized. She is well-read too. Shakespeare especially. Not what one would expect."

"She wasn't always in service, apparently. What did she do before she first came to The Bell—do you know?"

"No."

"Where was she from originally?"

He shrugged. "You heard her dodge your questions. She doesn't like to talk about her background or her family."

"Yes, so I've gathered."

He shook his head. "I've thought of proposing, but what kind of life could I offer her? When I am your, what . . . assistant? And she a chambermaid?"

"Perhaps she wouldn't have to work if you two married."

"Then what—she and Betsey would live in my dank little room belowstairs?"

"Perhaps we might give you one of the two-room apartments, like the one your mother used to occupy?"

"And lose income? We're at capacity a lot more often now than we used to be."

"Hmm. I'd have to think about it, but perhaps you could move into the lodge, and I could—"

"No, Jane. Absolutely not. I will not put you out of your home."

She looked up at him from beneath her lashes. "Did you not try to do that very thing not so long ago?"

"Not your home. Just the inn itself. Besides"—he winked—"I've matured a lot since then."

CHAPTER THIRTY-FIVE

On Sunday, Rachel sat through the church service in a bit of a daze, reciting the responses and prayers by rote, her mind distracted and conflicted as she thought of her recent conversation with Mercy, and the conversation to come with Nicholas Ashford.

Partway through the sermon, Mr. Paley's words broke through her fog and began to register.

"God offers every fallen human an incredible gift. He offers salvation and eternal happiness freely through Christ, by faith in Him, if we will but receive it. Grace costs us nothing, but it was purchased with an incalculable sacrifice, the Son of God himself, who appeased God's justice in our place. We can never deserve or repay this gift. We can only accept with praise and thanksgiving. . . ."

The service continued with a prayer of thanksgiving, but Rachel's heart beat hard, muffling the words. *Never deserve or repay it?* It sounded too easy. It sounded like . . . charity. Something she had resisted all her life.

Nicholas walked Rachel home from church. He clearly noticed her subdued manner and sent her worried, sidelong glances.

She led him into the library, empty on a Sunday. There, Rachel swallowed and forced herself to meet his gaze.

"I am sorry, Mr. Ashford. But I think it is only fair to release you."

"You refuse my offer?" He blinked. "You don't want more time?"

The pain in his eyes lanced her heart.

"I am fond of you. And I am glad to count you as friend as well as family. I sincerely hoped we might be more than that. . . ." She shook her head, throat burning. "But my heart will not be swayed."

He looked down, turning his hat brim in his long pale fingers. "I think I've known what your answer would be for some time now. It still hurts though."

A lump rose in her throat. "I am truly sorry."

He winced. "Please stop apologizing, Miss Ashford." He swallowed. "Has Sir . . . Has someone else made you an offer?"

A strangled little laugh escaped her at that.

"You are not engaged?" he asked.

"No."

"Is it because of my mother?"

Rachel thought of Lady Brockwell. She could endure the most difficult mother-in-law for the right man. "No."

His nostrils flared. "Apparently 'no' is your answer to all my questions."

Guilt flooded Rachel, but she bit back another unwanted apology.

"Well." He cleared his throat and avoided her gaze. "I wish you happy, Miss Ashford."

"And I you, Mr. Ashford." Rachel's voice trembled. Her chest ached with the pain of hurting a fellow human being—one she cared about.

He left, leaving Rachel with a knotted stomach. Foolish or not, her heart was tied up with old affections and hopes, and she guessed it always would be.

Mercy remained after the service to talk with Mr. Paley. She lingered in the nave until the pews emptied and the vicar stepped out of the vestry after removing his cleric's gown. Within a matter of minutes, he had given Mercy the latest and none too encouraging report about her request to use the church building to house her charity school. Then he walked out with her.

He opened the door and paused on the steps to bid her farewell. "Again, I am sorry the churchwardens refused your request, Miss Grove. I think they might eventually authorize use of St. Anne's for Sunday school classes, but a charity school for general education?" He shook his head. "We have our work cut out for us there, I'm afraid. A noble goal, however. I applaud you."

Mercy's heart felt heavy, but she managed a smile for the kind man. "Thank you for trying, Mr. Paley."

"At least you have your girls school, ey? That is something."

"Actually . . . only through the end of the year."

"Oh? I am sorry to hear it. Though now you mention it, your mother hinted about changes coming to Ivy Cottage. I don't recall the particulars, but she seemed pleased."

"Yes, well, I . . . "

Something in the churchyard caught the vicar's attention, and his face brightened. "Mr. Drake, hello!"

Mercy looked over, stomach falling. James Drake stood on the path nearby. It was the first time she had seen him since that ugly scene over the letter. What was he doing in the churchyard? Had he overheard their conversation? She felt embarrassed to have her failures discussed before this particular man.

Mr. Paley whispered in an eager aside, "You must excuse me, Miss Grove, but I have been most anxious to deepen my acquaintance with our new neighbor."

Mercy nodded. "Of course."

He hurried down the steps. As the clergyman approached, Mr. Drake looked uncomfortable.

"I was, em, just having a look around."

"You are very welcome, sir! We have not had the pleasure of your attendance in divine services, I don't believe. I do hope you will join us next Sunday?"

As the men talked, Mercy walked away, but she felt—or at least imagined—Mr. Drake's gaze on the back of her neck.

The next day turned chilly, and Thora and Betsey spent a fair amount of time sitting together in the old armchair drawn close to the fire. The little girl liked to be read to, and Thora was glad for an excuse to catch up on some reading that interested her as well. They read several pages of *The Care of Calves and Management of a Dairy* she'd borrowed from the circulating library and then turned their attention to the newspaper.

Little Betsey on her lap, Thora read in a sweet voice, "'A man has been tried at the county assizes for stealing a silver spoon, which he pretended to have carried off in a joke. The jury, however, happened to be too dull to understand such jokes, and the wit was sentenced to be transported.'"

Thora *tsk*ed. "Naughty man, ey, Betsey? You know, perhaps I shall buy you a silver spoon yet, my girl." It was, after all, a traditional gift for a child, as well as practical.

She adjusted the paper and read another story. "'A singular shooting match took place between Mr. Bingley of Stapleford and Sir Cyril Awdry of Broadmere, for five gold sovereigns, to shoot at twenty-five potatoes thrown up in the air, which were all hit by the sportsmen, and the wager consequently not decided.'" Thora shook her head. "And the nobility wonder why the people revolt."

Talbot stepped in from the other room and looked at her aghast. "What on earth are you reading to the girl, Thora?"

She looked at him over the tops of her spectacles. "Oh, she doesn't know the difference at her age. She just likes to be read to."

"You know, we could find more appropriate reading material for her. Perhaps Miss Ashford has some at her library."

"Maybe. That reminds me. I saved a few children's books, along with some of the boys' baby clothes and toys, and stored them in the inn's attic. I think I'll go and fetch them this afternoon."

"Shall I go along to help you?"

"No, I'll manage, if I may have the cart."

"Of course you may." He kissed the tip of her nose. "You, my love, may have anything you want."

She playfully pushed him away. "Go on with you, you old Romeo."

He smiled, then looked from her to Betsey and sobered. He pulled the chain with its blue heart from his pocket. "By the way, I fixed this. I reinforced the link so she can't pull it off again. I think it's too big for her to choke on, but just in case. . . ."

He laid it in her palm.

"Thank you, Talbot. I plan to give it to Hetty for Betsey to have when she is older."

"Thora . . ."

He looked down, considering his words before speaking, she guessed, and tensed in anticipation.

"Don't mistake me, please," he began. "I enjoy seeing you with Betsey. I see how much pleasure she gives you—even when she gives you headaches and wears thin your patience. You are good with her. And she likes you. But . . . guard your heart. At least a little. We don't know how long she'll be here. How long Hetty will be at The Bell. And when, or even if, Patrick will ever . . ."

"You don't think he'll marry her," Thora realized. "You think he'll run off again instead of taking responsibility."

"I don't know. I hope not. I hope for the best, as you do. But we can't ignore the past, or make assumptions about the future. I would never tell you to withhold affection from the girl. Just . . . be careful." He placed his hand over hers, closing her fingers over the chain. "I would hate to see you get hurt."

Thora took Sadie into town with her because she was eager to get supplies from Prater's and the greengrocers. Thora drove the cart while Sadie held Betsey on her lap, pointing out the cows and sheep as they passed.

They delivered Betsey to her mother early. Hetty beamed at

the girl, kissed her profusely, and thanked Thora for caring for her angel.

There is an angel in The Angel once again, Thora thought wistfully, thinking of the inn's former name and her father's old pet name for her. How strange that at one and fifty she missed her parents more than ever.

Jane looked up from the desk and greeted her with a smile. "Good day, Thora."

"Hello, Jane. Do you mind if I go up into the attic? I stored some things up there and thought I would take them back to the farm with me."

"Of course I don't mind. What sort of things? Clothes and such?"

"Yes. And . . . such."

"Make yourself at home. I hope that goes without saying. I have to finish these orders, but if you need someone to carry things down, I could ask Colin."

"No need. I'll manage on my own."

Thora went upstairs and then up the narrow, ladderlike steps into the attic. Weak autumn sunshine streaming through small windows on either end of the garret illuminated the musty space.

She found the trunk and opened the dusty lid, wanting to review the contents before deciding whether to take the entire trunk or merely select a few things. The interior was a shadowy cavern, so she dragged the trunk toward a rickety bench near a window. There Thora sat in a shaft of sunlight and began sorting through the items inside.

On her lap, she laid articles that might be useful for Betsey. Some the girl had already outgrown, like baby booties and a christening gown. Still Thora fingered the fine fabric and tiny stitches, feeling an ache in her chest for her infant sons, both long gone one way or another. Tears stung her eyes. What she wouldn't give to cradle their small soft bodies once more. To see their gummy smiles and the unconditional love shining in their innocent little eyes . . .

Feeling foolish, she sniffed and set the booties aside and thought of Jane. Here Thora was, crying when she'd had her chance to raise two boys to adulthood, since she had not lost John until past thirty. Poor Jane had lost all of her babies. Had never even had the chance to hold them once . . . Thora's heart twisted anew for her daughter-in-law.

Something near the bottom of the trunk caught her eye, and Thora bent and pulled out a bundle wrapped in tissue. Unfolding it, she was surprised to find a silver spoon with a ribbon around its handle. Who had put it there? She had not.

A scuffle step brought Thora's head up. Jane appeared at the top of the stairs, candle lamp in hand.

"Oh, Jane, you startled me."

"Sorry. I thought I would see if you needed any help. Find what you were looking for?"

Thora was tempted to slam the lid, to hide the spoon, knitted caps, and telltale booties, but she had never been one to hide from uncomfortable scenes.

"Yes. I thought I might find some things for Betsey among John and Patrick's old things."

Jane glanced down and surveyed the assortment on her lap and in the open trunk: miniature articles of clothing, a set of wooden blocks, and a few children's books.

"Ohhh . . ." Jane expelled a long breath and sank onto the bench beside her.

Thora handed her the silver spoon. "Did you put this in here?"

"No. I have never seen it before."

"Nor I."

Jane held it up to the light, revealing an engraved *B* on its handle.

Seeing the inscription, Thora's throat tightened. "John must have purchased it. When you were expecting."

Jane's eyes flashed to hers, then returned to the spoon, glistening by candlelight. "Do you think so?"

Thora nodded. "Probably meant it to be a surprise."

Jane considered. "He must have hidden it up here . . . after."

For a moment, they both looked at the silver spoon, remembering John. Then Thora cleared the lump from her throat and selected something else.

"You might like to see this." She held up a lock of hair tied with ribbon. "Saved from John's first haircut. I wanted to wait longer, but Frank said no boy of his would look like a girl. 'Bad enough we put boys in dresses until breeching, as it is.'"

Jane managed a halfhearted chuckle. "Sounds like Frank." She touched the soft lock of baby hair and traced a finger over one of the caps and painfully tiny booties. "I did not realize you had stored away John's and Patrick's baby things. I thought you would have given everything away by now."

"I gave away many things. Held on to only some special keepsakes I couldn't bear to part with. Like this christening gown."

"Saving them for your grandchildren, I suppose."

"Yes, I suppose I was." Thora looked at her daughter-in-law. "Jane, I hope this doesn't make you feel too sad."

"No. Well, maybe a little. I am better now that I have a place to mourn. Truly. I am happy for you. Betsey is like the grandchild you never had. I am . . . happy for you both." Jane's chin trembled, but she went on breezily, "And goodness knows we have all despaired of Patrick ever settling down. This might be the answer to your prayers. Seeing you with Betsey now . . . Well, it's a relief. You have a grandchild at last."

"She isn't my grandchild, Jane. Not . . . officially."

"I know, but I have seen Patrick and Hetty together. How he looks at her. How he helps her and how well he treats her. I think—or at least hope—that it is only a matter of time."

Thora nodded. "I do too."

Thora went to talk to Patrick before heading back to the farm. She found him leaning against the doorframe, watching with a soft smile as Hetty entertained Cadi and Alwena with an amusing impersonation of the difficult lady and her snappish maid who'd recently stayed at the inn, slipping from the maid's Irish accent to her mistress's tonnish voice with ease.

Thora regarded her son, then took him by the arm and led him into the office. "Come, Patrick. I am not blind. You can barely keep your eyes off her—or your hands, I'd wager."

"Mamma, I have been a perfect gentleman. This time."

"I believe you. And that gives me hope that you really do care for her. That you could be happy together."

"I do care for her, Mamma. It surprises me how much I do."

"Well then, what are you waiting for? I know I discouraged you from pursuing her in the past. But now . . . Do you not think you should do your duty by her?"

He raised his hands. "Mamma, you astound me. Tell me honestly—if not for the child, would you say the same thing?"

"How can I know? You and Hetty are joined now . . . in a way I might not have chosen. But now you have a second chance to make it right. Don't run away from your responsibility, Patrick. Not again."

He crossed his arms. "I have shown responsibility. Staying on here to help Jane, even after my own aspirations were thwarted."

Thora studied his face. Why was it so hard to believe he had changed? That he would settle down and stay with inn keeping. Stay with one woman as well. *Oh, God, help Patrick to be the man you want him to be. And help me have faith in my own son!*

"I have noticed, Patrick. So has Jane. And I am . . . glad." She wanted to say she was proud of him, but the words curled and died on her tongue. Instead, she tilted her head to one side and regarded her handsome second son. "Patrick, how old are you?"

"Almost nine and twenty, as you know very well."

"Nine and twenty." She shook her head in wonder. "You know, nothing matures a man like having someone else to be responsible for. A wife and child to look after. To love and protect. It would do you a world of good."

"You make it sound so romantic," he dryly replied.

"There is more to marriage than romance."

"And this from a woman barely returned from her wedding trip. Poor Talbot."

She swatted his arm. "I didn't say there was no romance, I said there was *more* than that. There is making a decision to love someone no matter what. To stand by that person and love him or her more than your own life. To put his or her needs and well-being above your own."

"Sounds . . . terrifying."

Thora nodded slowly. "It is. But when the other person is doing the same, it's something altogether . . . good."

CHAPTER THIRTY-SIX

On Monday evening, Rachel settled into a chair as Mercy called to order that night's meeting of the Ladies Tea and Knitting Society. Jane was not in attendance, Rachel noticed, nor the dairywoman, Mrs. Barton, who had become one of her library's more frequent patrons.

Among the other items on the agenda, she knew Mercy planned to solicit ideas for alternate locations for both a school and library, should they become necessary.

Mercy began with an update of her charity school campaign, reporting that the churchwardens might consider allowing use of the church building for religious instruction—if parents provided funds for the materials—but not for general education.

A few women groaned in response, while others nodded their understanding.

Miss Cook said, "That is some progress, at least."

Mrs. O'Brien shook her head. "Easy for you to say, Charlotte. You're not one of the struggling parents asked to cover the cost."

The door banged open, and Mrs. Barton rushed in late, all thrilled excitement. "Ladies! Come quick. Such doings! Mr. Craddock and Mr. Cottle have caught a thief! They are outside the lock-up right now!" Her face shone with scandalized glee to be the bearer of such news.

The ladies rushed from their chairs to look for themselves.

Mrs. Barton stretched on tiptoes toward the window latch. "Mercy, open the window, please. I can't reach."

Mercy did so, flinching as it squealed open. Rachel and several others stood craning their necks at the window—Mrs. Barton standing on a chair—while other women crammed into the open doorway of the village hall to watch the nearby drama without interrupting it.

The local butcher, currently serving a term as village constable, stood before the squat stone lock-up, the baker and a wiry youth beside him.

Sir Timothy came striding up Potters Lane, and Rachel's breath caught. With his squared shoulders, set jaw, and determined expression, he looked every inch a magistrate to be respected, even feared.

"Yes, Mr. Cottle? You sent for me?"

"This fellow was caught stealing a loaf of bread."

Sir Timothy looked toward the youth, who looked no more than fourteen or fifteen. "What is your name, son?"

"Jeremy Mullins."

Beside Rachel, Mercy sucked in a breath. "That's Sukey's brother!"

The constable scowled. "A lark, was it, ey, Mullins?"

"No, sir. My pa is injured and can't work, and my little brothers are hungry. I never meant to hurt anyone. Only wanted to help."

Mercy whispered, "Mr. Mullins was kicked by a horse, poor man."

"That don't give you the right to steal, boy," Mr. Craddock snapped.

"I waited 'til the end of the day. Didn't think you'd sell that last loaf."

"Thieving is still thieving."

The youth hung his head.

The baker turned to Sir Timothy. "I demand justice, my lord. This is petty larceny—there's no denying it."

"Petty is right." Sir Timothy sighed and turned to Mullins. "I am afraid Mr. Craddock is correct. Justice must be satisfied. The penalty is six pounds or six weeks' jail with hard labor."

Rachel's stomach twisted. What a harsh sentence for one so young!

The lad's face crumpled and his shoulders slumped. It was clear he hadn't six farthings, let alone six pounds—nearly a year's wages for many poor people.

Sir Timothy extracted his own coin purse. "I shall pay the fine on your behalf, son, if you will accept it."

Around her the women gasped in surprise.

Jeremy's mouth fell ajar. "But, sir, I could never repay you."

"I know."

The baker protested, "That's not fair! If ya spare him, I'll be overrun with thieves!"

Sir Timothy ignored Craddock and kept his gaze on the youth. "Will you accept it anyway?"

Jeremy Mullins stared, thunderstruck. "I will, my lord." His voice trembled. "And bless ya for it."

Rachel stood there, feeling similarly stunned.

"Thank God," Mercy murmured.

Bits of Mr. Paley's last sermon fell on Rachel like rain. *"He appeased God's justice in our place. We can never deserve or repay this gift. We can only accept. . . ."*

Rachel's heart throbbed. O, *God in heaven. Forgive me for being too proud to ask you for help. To accept your merciful grace. A gift I can never earn, "credit," or repay . . .*

The women slowly returned to their chairs, accompanied by whispers and snatches of conversation.

Mrs. Barton shook her head. "Craddock's right. Now every down-on-his-luck chap will be stealing from him."

Mrs. Burlingame sniffed. "He can afford it, greedy guts."

"Goodness, what a gentleman is Sir Timothy," Judith Cook breathed, hands fluttering at the lace at her neck.

Mrs. O'Brien smirked at her. "You're too old for him, love."

"Well, I'm not." Becky Morris fluffed her hair. "What a dashing husband he'd make."

Julia Featherstone waved a dismissive hand. "Like he'd ever notice the likes of us."

"I know." Becky sighed. "Still, a girl can dream, can't she?"

Rachel nodded. *Yes, she could.*

Mercy moved to the front of the room and re-called the meeting to order, other agenda items shelved in the face of this pressing need. "I did not realize the situation had become so bleak. What can we do to help the Mullins family?"

The meeting continued from there, but Rachel could only bow her head and pray—for the Mullins family and for herself. She didn't know what her future held or how she would live, but she felt inexplicable peace descend over her like a warm shawl in winter. She had been too proud to ask for help, but His help, His peace, came anyway.

"Thank you," she whispered.

After the meeting, Mercy and Rachel walked home together. When they neared Ivy Cottage, Mercy was surprised to see Jeremy Mullins loitering outside its gate. Rachel sent her a concerned look, but Mercy greeted him warmly.

"Hello, Jeremy. Hoping to see your sister?"

He exhaled in relief. "Yes, miss. I'm afraid she might have heard and think the worst of me. Or fear I'd been thrown in the lock-up."

"Which you would have been, if not for Sir Timothy's intervention. I hope you have learned your lesson."

"I have, miss. I've never been half so scared in my life."

"Good. Then come in and have some cake with us." Mercy opened the gate and led the way inside.

"I shall go and find Sukey," Rachel offered, starting toward the stairs.

"Thank you, Rachel. I will show Mr. Mullins where to wash his hands."

A short while later the four of them were seated at the dining table, tea, hot chocolate, and cake before them. The cake was not one of Aunt Matilda's better attempts, but Jeremy devoured his piece with relish.

Sukey was stricken to hear the news. "Oh, Jeremy, what were you thinking?"

"I wasn't. At least not clearly. I am sorry, Sukey."

"Mum will break her heart over this."

He hung his head. "I know."

Mercy served him another slice of cake, already planning to send the rest home with him, along with whatever else she could find to spare in the larder. "I am sure if you apologize and promise not to do anything like it ever again, she will forgive you. I know she loves you all very much."

Sukey nodded. "And good thing Pa is on his back or he'd give you a switching. Never mind you're as tall as he is now."

Jeremy grimaced. "I did try to find work first, you know. But few will hire someone my age, and fewer now, when people hear what I did."

Mercy agreed. "I am afraid you are right."

"Why not ask at Brockwell Court?" Rachel suggested. "I would think with it being harvest time, they might need extra hands."

"I asked yesterday, and their farm manager turned me down flat. Said I was too young to do the work, though I am stronger than I look."

Sukey nodded vigorously. "He is, miss. Very strong."

Rachel considered. "Perhaps go again, and ask Sir Timothy himself."

"After tonight? I couldn't ask him to do more for me. And why would he give me a place, when he knows better than most what I done?"

"I don't know if he would or not; I only know that he would be fair."

Jeremy sighed. "Very well. I'll ask. Likely be sent packing, but I'll try."

A short while later, Jeremy left to walk home, laden with a basket of cake, jars of preserves, and a meat pie. Sukey walked him out.

Rachel and Mercy remained at the table, lingering over their tea. They talked over the evening and Sir Timothy's merciful treatment of the young thief, Rachel describing how the scene had affected her and the peace she felt.

Mercy listened with interest, then said, "I am glad to hear it, Rachel. I confess I found myself thinking of Sir Timothy's father. It seemed like something he might have done. I remember hearing the story of how he once spared a woman the workhouse."

Rachel frowned, then said, "I think Sir Timothy is twice the gentleman his father was."

Mercy swirled the dregs in her teacup. "By the way, I am sorry we never got around to your library at tonight's meeting."

Rachel shook her head. "Don't give it another thought. My goodness, if anyone should be apologizing, it's me, for not fully appreciating all you've done for me. I am blessed to be your friend, Mercy Grove."

Mercy smiled. "And I yours."

Rachel rose. "And now I believe I will go and find a new book to read." She winked. "Might as well make the most of my library while I can."

CHAPTER

THIRTY-SEVEN

Lightning flashed and thunder rumbled through the keeper's lodge. Jane groaned. The roof would leak again, and the storm would upset Athena. Jane would have to try to soothe the horse before she harmed herself again or upset every animal in the stable, and likely the ostlers and postboys as well.

Jane pushed back the blankets and rose, pulling on a flannel petticoat, woolen stockings, half boots, and a full-length pelisse. By the time she was dressed and left the lodge, the storm had abated somewhat, though rain fell steadily.

Shawl over her head, she hurried through the archway and across the yard, leaping a puddle as she went. She opened the stable door and slipped inside as silently as she could, not wanting to startle Athena. The stable was surprisingly quiet. When her eyes adjusted, she walked deeper into the building. Horses slept on, or regarded her placidly as she passed. Athena had probably worn herself out, poor creature.

Jane tiptoed around the corner and drew up short. There at the far end, the last stall stood wide open. A hanging lantern illuminated an unexpected scene.

She inhaled sharply.

In the open stall, Athena stood calmly, one leg suspended. Gabriel Locke bent at her shoulder, working away. He had come!

The horse remained peacefully still under his ministrations while he trimmed her hoof. As Jane watched, Athena slowly lowered her head, until her chin lay on Gabriel's curved back. Then she closed her eyes. The mare had fallen asleep, relaxed in Gabriel's care. Fully trusting.

Jane's heart swelled within her, and her throat burned. Perhaps it was time she fully trusted him too.

"Gabriel . . ." she breathed, so quietly she was sure he wouldn't hear. But he looked up, and for a moment held her gaze, his expression measuring. He hesitated, lifting a hand to indicate the work he was in the midst of. She nodded, not wanting to interrupt him until he had taken care of her horse.

As Jane waited, she took in his attractive profile, the dark hair falling over his forehead, and every move of his deft, capable hands. She noticed his broad shoulders and muscular forearms revealed by rolled-up shirtsleeves. She drew in a shaky breath, wishing she were not so poorly dressed. Woolens indeed!

Finally he set down Athena's last leg and opened a jar of salve. "Can you distract her for me while I tend her wounds? Perhaps brush her mane? She liked that, as I recall."

Jane nodded and retrieved her grooming tools. She returned and gingerly entered Athena's stall, murmuring soothing words all the while.

She stroked Athena's soft muzzle and slowly began brushing her mane. The horse stilled again, and her eyes soon became half hooded in pleasure.

"That's the way," he whispered. He applied salve to a wound on the mare's sleek neck. And to a second wound on her leg, near her rump. "Can you hold her tail aside a moment? I don't want to trap any long hairs in this bandage."

"Of course." Jane stepped around, keeping one reassuring hand on Athena's side as she did.

Her hand touched his, and she pulled back. "Sorry."

His eyes held hers. "Don't be."

Jane drew in another breath and tried to focus on her task.

A short while later, they left the exhausted horse to sleep in peace.

"I have not seen her this content since you left. She's missed you and . . . so have I."

Gabriel looked at her in surprise, then a teasing smile quirked his mouth. "Have you a hoof that needs trimming as well?"

"No, my hooves are fine." Jane ducked her head and glanced self-consciously at her half boots, chagrined to see how worn they were. "Though perhaps a visit to a cobbler might be in order."

He stowed their tools and extinguished the lantern. She followed him past the stalls of horses, some sleeping, a few prodding empty feed buckets with their muzzles, or quietly whinnying as they passed.

At the stable door, Jane reached out and touched Gabriel's arm. "Thank you for coming. You're the only one she trusts."

He nodded, his dark brown eyes tracing her cheeks, her eyes, her mouth. When he spoke, his voice rumbled low in his chest. "I would do anything for her. You know that, don't you?"

The intensity of his dark eyes caused Jane's insides to tighten and tingle. Mouth dry, she made do with a nod.

He took a half step closer. "Jane . . ."

A new postboy stepped out of the bunk room, yawning and scratching his belly. "Oh. Sorry, ma'am, sir. Only going out to relieve myself."

Jane said wryly, "Thank you, Fred. For that."

She turned back to Gabriel. "You are welcome to stay, of course. As far as I know, your former room is as you left it. Our new farrier has a family, so he doesn't live here on the property."

"I will stay the night, thank you. I'll want to check on Athena again in the morning."

Would he leave after that? Jane was afraid to ask. To press him. "Well, I had better let you get some sleep. Now that Athena is sleeping peacefully, I have high hopes I shall as well."

She smiled at him but he did not smile back, and she felt the gesture falter. "Well. Good night, Gabriel. Thank you again for coming. Perhaps we might . . . talk more in the morning?"

"Good night, Jane," he said but made no promises.

Jane was wrong. She slept poorly indeed.

In the morning, Jane dressed hurriedly but with care and walked directly out to the stables. She sighed in relief. There was Gabriel, again in Athena's stall. It had not been a compelling dream after all.

"Oh, good. I was afraid you might have already left."

"I would not leave without saying good-bye. Not unless you send me away again."

"I did not!" She protested, then saw he was teasing her. She wished he didn't have to say good-bye at all.

He said, "I have some business in the area. So I thought I would stay for a few days, if you don't mind."

"Of course I don't."

"That way I can keep an eye on Athena."

"I appreciate that. How is she?"

"It will take time for her to heal. But she will be all right."

"Good. I . . . don't suppose I could convince you to take your old job back?" She added a little laugh, hoping he wouldn't hear the vulnerability in her voice.

He chuckled in return—an oddly heartbreaking sound. "No. But thank you for the offer."

"Well . . . thank you again for coming. I hope your uncle can spare you."

"He can. In fact, I am thinking of striking out on my own."

"Are you, indeed? I thought you were out of horse racing for good?"

"I am. But I still want to raise horses. Riding horses, Thoroughbreds, perhaps even carriage horses, if I must. I hope to buy a farm of my own."

"Gracious! You must have won all the money John lost and then some." A little stab of bitterness pricked her at the thought.

He frowned. "I told you, Jane. I stopped betting while I was still ahead. My uncle found out and insisted, thank God. I tried to persuade John to stop, too, but he would not heed me."

"I know. I don't blame you."

His dark brows rose. "You don't?"

"Not anymore." She inhaled deeply. "John was a grown man who made his own decisions, and his own mistakes. I have forgiven him and am ready to leave the past behind."

Good heavens. Jane hoped that didn't seem too forward. She felt her face heat. Would he think she was hinting . . . ? If she was, she had no intention of being so obvious.

He watched her face, his expression difficult to decipher. "I am glad to hear it."

Flustered, Jane turned to the nearby stall. Inside, a familiar chestnut watched them with intelligent eyes. Jane tentatively reached over the rail. "Hello, handsome boy." When he didn't object, she stroked the white blaze on his forehead.

Gabriel said, "He remembers you."

"And I him. I rode him more than once, if you recall, back when you told me he was being boarded here by some *gentleman* away from home."

"I am sorry about that. From here on out, I promise to tell you only the absolute truth."

"Hmm. Are you certain you can keep that promise? I don't know what to think about that gentleman, but I can say unequivocally that his taste in horses is excellent."

He chuckled softly. She glanced over and saw his eyes resting on her intently. Deep and dark.

"Gabriel, I want—"

"Gabriel? Gabriel Locke?" Tuffy called. "Ted, come quick, Mr. Locke is here!"

Tall Ted bounded over, followed by young Joe, beaming at their former leader.

"Gable!" Ted exclaimed, pounding his shoulder. "So good to see you."

The men gathered and buzzed around him like happy bees, and Jane retreated to let them enjoy their reunion.

What she wanted could wait.

Jane walked over to the inn, humming, and found Cadi staring out the window into the stable yard.

"Well, I'll be," the maid murmured. "Mr. Locke is back."

"Mm-hm."

Cadi glanced at her, and her eyes widened. "Good heavens, Mrs. Bell. I don't know that I've ever seen you smile so bright. What—or should I say who—has you smiling like that? I should have known something was afoot when Mr. Locke came all the way to Epsom that day to make sure you were all right."

"Other business brought him to Epsom, Cadi."

"If you say so. And what has brought him back here now, I wonder." The girl's every feature shone with mischief.

"Athena. He's come to tend her wounds. She won't let Tom anywhere near her, as you know."

"Oh sure, and did Athena write to Mr. Locke and ask him to come?"

"Of course not. I did. For Athena's sake."

"Um-hm." Cadi grinned, and Jane couldn't resist a small smile in reply. Bubbles of pleasure tickled her stomach, because something told her Athena was not the only reason Gabriel had returned.

A man came through the door at that moment, and Jane turned, grateful for the interruption. James Drake.

"Good day, James. How are you this fine morning?"

"Hello, Jane. I came to ask you to dinner. . . ." He looked at her more closely, rearing his head back in surprise. "What has you smiling so impishly? You look positively giddy."

"Do I?"

Cadi sent him a meaningful look as she passed. "It isn't a *what*, so much as a *who*."

Cheeky girl. Jane shook her head as Cadi walked away, then turned back to James.

His smile became wistful. "I would have liked to be the man to make you smile like that."

Jane met his gaze a moment, gauging his sincerity. "No, you would not."

"Why do you say that?" He stuck out his lip like a pouty little boy.

"Come, James, don't give me that injured look. I know you like to tease me, and we enjoy each other's company, of course, but I've never believed you had serious intentions toward me."

"I believe the reverse is true." He tilted his head to one side. "I did not think you wanted me to be serious, Jane, where you are concerned. Was I wrong?"

She stilled. "I . . . No, you were right."

"I usually relish being right. But in this instance, I would have rather been wrong."

She tucked her chin. "James, I sincerely doubt your heart has ever been in any danger where I am concerned. Or anyone else for that matter. Tell me honestly—have you ever truly loved someone?"

He lowered his gaze and was quiet for so long she feared she had deeply offended him.

Then he said, "I was in danger of doing so once, a long time ago. But I let her slip through my fingers, out of reach."

Jane's heart pounded dully. "Miss Payne, do you mean?"

He nodded, brows high in surprise.

"Mercy told me. I am sorry, James."

He sighed. "Never mind." He sent her a wry glance. "This is not helping my case with you, is it?"

She chuckled. "No. But I'm glad to know anyway. I did wonder. . . . For all your kind attentions, I always felt you kept your heart at a distance. Now I understand why."

He looked up, considering. "No doubt I have idealized her over time. I have only her memory to relive. She has not aged, her sweet temper not faltered. Perhaps under longer acquaintance, she would not seem as perfect as she does to me now. And she would certainly have become all too aware of my faults. As you have."

She thought of the tension between him and Mercy. But Mr. Drake was her friend too. "James, of course you have faults. We all do. But you are an admirable, likable man. You could still make some woman very happy."

"Are you applying for the position?" His dimpled grin returned.

She shook her head. "There he is again, the James I know and—"

"And what, Jane?"

"And had better send on his way before he serves up more flummery."

He studied her face. "You know, you still haven't told me who had you smiling like that when I arrived."

She glanced at the clock. "Goodness, is that the time?"

He shook his head in mild reproof. "I call that unfair. You make me bare my soul and yet you don't return the favor."

She winked at him. "Exactly."

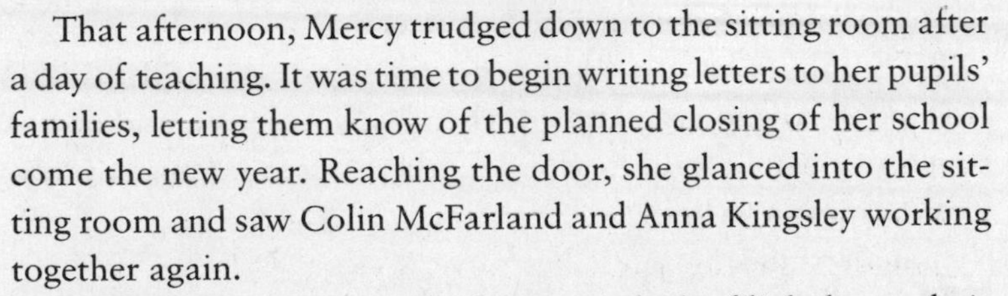

That afternoon, Mercy trudged down to the sitting room after a day of teaching. It was time to begin writing letters to her pupils' families, letting them know of the planned closing of her school come the new year. Reaching the door, she glanced into the sitting room and saw Colin McFarland and Anna Kingsley working together again.

Colin sat bent over a page of figures, a lock of light brown hair falling over his brow.

Thinking herself unobserved, Anna Kingsley studied the young man's profile, admiration shining in her fair eyes.

Colin set down his pencil and slid the paper toward her, expression tense. "I hope that's right."

While his tutor reviewed the numbers, Colin then studied her.

After a few moments, Anna looked up, a bright smile splitting her face. "Exactly right. Well done, Mr. McFarland."

He released a relieved breath. "Saints be praised. And it's Colin, if you please. You make me feel ancient, and . . . we are not so different in age, after all."

Anna met his gaze a moment, then looked down, blushing prettily. "No indeed."

Mercy decided those letters could wait a few minutes more. She left the two young people as they were and went to find a bracing cup of hot tea.

A short while later, Mercy returned and found the sitting room empty. Colin and Anna had left, and with them her excuse to put off her letters. With a sigh, Mercy sat. She propped one elbow on the secretaire desk, and with the other hand picked up a quill and dipped it. She sat there, quill poised, until the ink plopped onto the paper, but not a single word came.

With a sigh, she put the quill back in its holder and held her head in her hands. *Lord, give me strength.*

She heard a knock on the front door, and a few moments later, Mr. Basu ushered in their lawyer.

Mercy rose. "Mr. Coine, I didn't expect you—though perhaps I should have." She gestured toward a chair. "Please be seated."

She reclaimed her chair, and he sat as well.

He began, "I am here in the role of intermediary. Mr. Drake tells me the two of you argued when last you spoke, and he assumes you would wish to avoid another scene that might prove unpleasant to you both."

"I understand."

"He asked me to communicate that he is preparing a room for his . . . for Alice in the Fairmont and asks if it is acceptable that he leave her with you until that room is readied for a child."

"Yes, of course. She is welcome to stay as long as he needs." *Longer, even.* Mercy was thankful for a little more time with the dear girl.

He nodded. "Most kind. By the way, I have just come from explaining Mr. Drake's claim to Mr. Thomas. Talk about unpleasant scenes . . ."

"I am sorry you had to do that, Mr. Coine."

He waved away her concerns. "Perils of the profession."

Mercy said, "I would have almost thought Mr. Thomas would

feel vindicated for his suspicions—for disowning Mary-Alicia and, in turn, Alice."

"I will not attempt to express Mr. Thomas's emotions for him, Miss Grove. But he was sincere in his desire that you should raise the girl, and this has come as a blow to him. As it has to you, I know."

He rose. "Well, I will dispose of the guardianship papers. And will not hear of you paying a farthing."

"Thank you, Mr. Coine. You are the exception to the profession's sometimes poor reputation."

"I do what I can." He smiled kindly. "Again, my apologies for your disappointment."

She nodded and walked him to the door.

For several moments, Mercy stood there, watching him go and wondering how long it took to fit up a room for one small girl. However long it took, it would not be long enough.

CHAPTER THIRTY-EIGHT

Early the next day, Jane stood at the booking desk when Gabriel entered through the side door. She had not seen him since the morning before.

"Good morning, Jane."

"Gabriel. How are you sleeping in your old room?"

"Not well, actually. But it's a beautiful day. We should get out and enjoy it."

She looked up and met his expectant gaze.

"Would you ride with me, Jane?"

He stepped nearer, his tone low, almost intimate. She was probably reading too much into it. It was a simple, innocent request . . . so why did her heart beat hard at his words?

"Do you think Athena is ready?"

"I thought you might ride Sultan, while I ride another horse and keep Athena on a lead. I want to make sure she isn't favoring that leg."

"Good idea. I've been afraid to ride her with her injuries. And I would like to ride Sultan again."

He grinned. "I thought you might."

"But what about you? Old Ruby is still here and no doubt missed you too."

"Oh no. I have a new horse I am becoming acquainted with—bought him yesterday from the Brockwells' farm manager."

"Ah. So that's what you were doing yesterday."

"Yes. Would you like to see him?"

"I would indeed."

Jane summoned Cadi to help her change into her new blue riding habit, and hearing whom Jane would be riding with, the maid eagerly complied.

Gabriel retrieved a top hat and looked handsome in his dark red coat, riding breeches, and tall boots. In fact, he looked every inch the sporting gentleman.

The day was cool but bright. They rode through rolling farmland, scaring up pheasants from the hedgerows as they went, then ventured into Grovely Wood.

As they slowed to a walk on the woodland track, Jane glanced over at Gabriel, admiring the lines of his face and his confident posture on horseback. "You mentioned wanting to buy your own farm. I assume you are looking at land near Pewsey Vale—to be near your uncle?"

"Actually, I am thinking of looking in this area."

Surprise shot through her. "Near Ivy Hill?"

He nodded and studied her face.

Her pulse pounded as apprehension dawned. "Lane's Farm is for sale."

"I know."

"That is very near indeed."

His dark eyes gauged her reaction. "Would that be a problem? We've had our disagreements, you and I, and if you prefer I keep my distance, just say so."

She held his gaze, then looked away. "Those disagreements are in the past."

"Are they?"

She nodded, and lowered her head to avoid a low-hanging branch.

He did the same. "Good."

They rode on a few moments, trotting up a rise.

"So I don't need to keep my distance?" His low voice did strange things to her heart.

She pressed her lips together and gave a shaky little jerk of her head.

Her gesture must not have been convincing, because he asked, "You won't mind having your former farrier so close by?"

Jane's chest tightened. Was he considering moving to the area specifically to be near her? "I . . . don't think so. Though some will think I must have paid you far too much if you can afford to buy your own farm."

"Blame it on inexperience." He winked at her, and she grinned in reply, for they both knew she had paid him very poorly indeed.

He glanced back to see how Athena was faring on her lead. Jane did as well. The mare's gait seemed normal, though her ears went back every time a bird flew nearby. She stayed near Sultan as though she would happily follow him anywhere.

Gabriel looked again at Jane. "At all events, you've learned a lot since then and are managing The Bell well indeed by the look of things. Did I not tell you you would?"

Yes, he had. Before he left, he took her hand in his strong, callused grip and told her he had every confidence in her. His words had echoed through her mind during his absence, when things had become difficult or she'd faced some new decision about the inn.

Now she looked up and held his gaze. "You did. And your confidence meant a great deal—then and now."

"I am glad to hear it. I meant every word."

They emerged from the wood and rode out to Lane's Farm, surveying the land and outbuildings. The farmhouse looked sound, though a little neglected. Nothing a bit of attention and paint couldn't fix.

Jane studied his profile. "What do you think?"

His gaze swept the farmyard once more, then returned to rest on her face. "I like what I see."

They returned the horses to The Bell stables, Sultan and now this second horse of Gabriel's boarding there for the time being. Gabriel applied more salve to Athena's healing wound and changed her bandage. While Jane groomed Athena, he brushed down his new horse, then moved on to Sultan.

Jane finished grooming Athena and gave the mare a final pat. "I'm finished here. May I help you with Sultan?"

"Of course, if you'd like."

She transferred her grooming tools to one hand, opened the neighboring stall, and let herself in. In close proximity to man and horse, the masculine smells of shaving tonic, hay, and leather enveloped her.

Taking a deep breath, she forced herself to concentrate on her task. Together they groomed Sultan, their brushes and hands moving closer, now and again their shoulders touching.

In the adjacent stall, Athena whickered a plea for attention.

Jane smirked. "Someone is jealous." She expected a chuckle from Gabriel, but he was silent beside her.

She looked up at him. His face so near. So unexpectedly . . . tense. The air between them thickened and sparked.

"Jane . . ." he whispered.

His warm breath on her temple made her skin tingle. She lowered her gaze. "Yes, Gabriel?"

She noticed the lapels of his waistcoat were crooked and idly straightened them with her free hand, fingers lingering.

When she looked up, she found his dark eyes riveted to hers. Her heart hammered. He reached out and cupped the side of her face, his intense gaze moving to her mouth. She waited, holding her breath. . . .

A coach horn blared in the stable yard. Jane lurched back.

From the nearby bunk room, ostlers groaned and rustled into action.

"I had better go." Embarrassed and uncertain, Jane hurried from the stall.

She returned to the lodge to change from her habit—and to put some distance between her and Mr. Locke.

Rachel asked Miss Matilda to teach her how to make apple tarts now that the fruit was in ample supply. She agreed and together they braved Mrs. Timmons's ire and took over her kitchen. Following Miss Matty's instructions, Rachel pared and cored apples, boiled them in a little water, added bruised cinnamon, grated sugar, and lemon peel, and left them to simmer while they turned their attention to the pastry. An hour later, the Ivy Cottage kitchen was a floury, cinnamon-scented disaster, but Rachel had made her first gifts of food.

She took one tart to the Mullins family, and the other to Mrs. Haverhill. Rachel suspected her first attempt at baking made Matilda Grove look like a renowned *chef de cuisine*.

The Mullins accepted theirs graciously. Mrs. Haverhill less so. She said, "Thank you, Rachel. But you needn't have done that. You know I don't like accepting charity."

Rachel smiled fondly at the woman. "I know. But when you taste it, you will see it is a very humble offering indeed."

Upon her return to Ivy Cottage, Rachel discovered that invitations had arrived for Miss Bingley's coming-out ball—she, Mercy, and Matilda had each received one.

When Rachel closed the library the next afternoon, she stopped in the schoolroom to ask Anna Kingsley to come to her bedchamber when she could, then continued to her room. There, she spread several evening gowns on her bed, trying to decide which to wear to the ball. She had not had a new dress since their financial calamity, and wondered which of her old gowns would pass for still-in-fashion, yet be appropriate for a woman whose father died five months before. Rachel had earned a little money from her library but could not spend it. With the library likely to close soon, she would have to be prepared to pay back partial subscriptions.

A knock sounded. Rachel expected Anna, but instead Jane's voice called, "Rachel? It's Jane."

Rachel opened the door with a smile. "Jane, come in. What a lovely surprise."

"I hope you don't mind. Miss Matty told me you were up here."

"I don't mind at all. In fact, you can help me choose what to wear to Miss Bingley's ball."

Jane's gaze swept the gowns on the bed, then she picked up the pink gown from out of the trunk before Rachel could close the lid. She held it out and studied it. "I remember this dress. You wore it to your own coming-out ball." Jane studied the pink silk, fitted bodice, feminine neckline, and white lace trim.

"I also remember that Timothy Brockwell could not keep his eyes off you when you wore it."

Rachel stiffened. Did Jane resent that? But when she looked over, she was relieved to see Jane's eyes twinkled.

"And so courtly and formal in his manners that night. As if you were a stranger he'd just met for the first time. An *important* stranger."

Jane held the dress up to Rachel. "I think I knew right away that he was in love with you."

"Did you really?"

"Yes. And it was more than the dress. As sad as your mother's illness was, you grew so much over those difficult years—in beauty and grace and responsibility. You became the lady of Thornvale and a lady in Timothy's eyes. It just took this dress to make him see all the changes in you. And become aware of his feelings toward you."

Jane sighed and laid the dress on the bed with the others. "I should have acknowledged it straightaway. Freed him to court you. But it took me a little while to come to terms with the change. Thankfully, John Bell was there to woo me into doing just that. He looked at me the way Timothy looked at you."

Rachel opened her mouth to apologize, but Jane shook her head. "No. It's all right. I think I've known for a long time that Timothy and I would not be suited as husband and wife. Though dear friends, yes, always. He knows it too. He may have allowed his mother to talk him out of marrying you after the scandal, but he won't let her stall him forever. At least I hope not. I want you both to be happy."

"Oh, Jane. We argued terribly. I told him I was glad to have escaped the noose of marrying a Brockwell. If he ever intended to propose, he won't now!"

Jane looked at her in astonishment. "What? When was this?"

"A few weeks ago. He was so sure I still hoped for a proposal from him after all this time."

"Well, don't you?"

"Yes . . . if I thought he loved me. But he has never said so. Instead he told me his family had reservations about my suitability even before the scandal. I know I should not have let my pride get the better of me, but I grew so angry."

Jane winced. "You know how pragmatic Timothy is. He probably had no idea the effect his words had on you."

"Well, I left him with no doubt of their effect or of my offended feelings."

"But you still love him, don't you?" Jane asked gently.

Rachel exhaled a deep breath. "I do. I cannot help it."

"And Mr. Ashford?"

Rachel shook her head. "I told him I could not accept his offer. I hated to do it, but would it not hurt him worse to marry a woman who loved someone else?"

"You did the right thing. And as far as Timothy is concerned, you know his parents have always held great sway over him. He feels duty bound to marry well, to put his family first."

"I do know. But if I were to be his wife, I would be part of his family. I don't relish the notion of living under Lady Brockwell's disapproving *sway* all of my life. At all events, I shan't have to, because we have parted ways. He was probably relieved. He wished me health and happiness and and went on his way. I believe he may have shifted his attentions to Arabella Awdry."

"Oh, Rachel. I am sorry. Shall I talk to him?" Before Rachel could reply, Jane raised her hand. "No. Forgive me. I have stood between you too often over the years. I won't butt in now. But may I make one suggestion?"

"Of course."

Jane picked up the pink dress again. "Wear this to the Bingleys' ball. Remind him. It would certainly signal your interest."

Rachel shook her head. "I considered that, Jane. But I have decided against it."

"Oh? Then, what will you—"

Anna Kingsley knocked on the door and poked her head inside. "You wanted to see me, Miss Ashford?"

"Yes, Anna. Come in. Have you met Mrs. Bell?"

"How do you do, ma'am."

Jane greeted her politely, then Rachel explained, "Anna here will be celebrating her eighteenth birthday soon, and her parents are taking her to a public ball in Salisbury to mark the occasion."

Jane smiled. "How exciting. We attended a few of those ourselves at your age."

Rachel took the pink dress from Jane. "Anna, I would like you to have this dress."

Anna's lips parted. "Ohhh . . . miss. It is so lovely. But I couldn't."

Rachel noticed Jane's mouth open in surprise as well.

"Of course you can. I want you to have it."

"It's too fine for me. It's too much."

"Please. I insist. If you like it, that is."

"How could I not? It's beautiful."

Rachel held it up to her, much as Jane had held the dress up to Rachel. "I think it will look so well with your coloring. It should be worn by someone as young and lovely as you are, going to her first ball."

She glanced at Jane and saw her friend watching her closely.

"Don't you agree, Jane?"

"I . . . yes. If you are quite certain."

"I am. Why not go and try it on, Anna, and we can see if it needs to be taken in."

The girl's eyes gleamed. "Thank you, miss. I can't wait to show Miss Grove." Taking the dress with her, Anna hurried from the room.

Rachel again felt Jane's gaze on her profile and looked over.

"I know how much that dress meant to you, Rachel. It was kind of you, but . . . I am surprised you could part with it."

"Me too," Rachel admitted. "It was time, I think."

"Then what will you wear to the Bingleys'?"

From the bed, Rachel tentatively lifted an ivory dress with lace trim at the neck and panels of rich gold embroidery.

Jane drew in a breath. "Look at that embroidery! It's beautiful."

Rachel nodded. "I have always thought so. It was my favorite of my mother's." She ran her hand over the lustrous satin. "I thought perhaps Mrs. Shabner might remove the lace, as it has yellowed, and modify the bodice to be more in keeping with current fashion. And perhaps replace the ribbon trim at the waist as well. It is a little frayed."

Jane looked at it more closely. "Yes, I see what you mean." She traced a finger along the embroidered pattern. "This dress is so elegant, Rachel. I think it will suit you well."

"It is more suited to a woman of my years, do you mean?"

"More suited to a woman of your grace and beauty," Jane clarified.

"Are you sure I won't look like a dowd?"

"I'm sure, though Mrs. Shabner won't appreciate not receiving an order for a new dress."

"No, she won't. She will probably grumble and threaten to retire or move to Wishford, as she has done for as long as I've known her."

"Me too. But she knows you are not in a position to spend a large sum on a new dress right now. In Ivy Hill, few are. Present company included."

Half serious, Rachel teased, "Do you promise to wear something old and unflattering, so Timothy is not tempted to look at you instead?"

"There is no danger of that, I assure you. Especially as I have not been invited."

"What? Oh no. I'm sorry."

"Don't be. I don't mind."

Rachel tilted her head and regarded her friend. "You know, I almost believe you. You look rather happy. Has something happened? I know Mr. Drake was paying you a great deal of attention not long ago, but . . ."

Jane shook her head. "Not serious attention."

"I am sorry if he has disappointed you."

"No. He has not injured me. I like James. But there is someone else I like a great deal more." She looked up from beneath her lashes, eyes sparkling.

"Oh, Jane! Who? Do I know him?"

"Not likely! But I shan't say more. Not yet, in case . . . Well, I only mention the possibility so that you don't worry about me where Mr. Drake is concerned, nor hesitate where Timothy is concerned."

"Are you certain?"

"I am."

Rachel walked downstairs with Jane. As they reached the vestibule, Mr. Basu opened the front door for Colin McFarland, then slipped away again.

Colin removed his hat and greeted the ladies. "I am here for another lesson, though I am a few minutes early."

Rachel glanced over her shoulder to the open sitting room door. "I don't think Miss Kingsley is down yet."

Footsteps caused Colin to look toward the stairs behind them. His eyes widened and his lips parted.

Rachel turned to see what had captured his attention. There came Anna Kingsley down the steps in the pink dress. The bodice would need to be taken in a bit, Rachel saw at once, but even so, the girl looked charming in it.

Anna beamed her bright, toothy grin. "What do you think?"

"You look beautiful," Rachel assured her.

"That she does," Colin murmured.

Anna noticed him then, and her smile fell. "Oh! Mr. McFarland, I am so sorry. I quite forgot the time. I'll just go and change."

He slowly shook his head. "Not on my account . . ."

Rachel and Jane shared a secret smile at that and continued to the door.

That evening, Jane was again at the reception desk when Gabriel entered the inn.

He laid his hands on the counter. "I would like a room here in the inn, if you don't mind. At full price, of course."

She blinked in surprise. "Is the stable bed so uncomfortable? You did not complain before."

"I am not complaining now. In fact, I rather missed that small hard bed and hearing Tuffy snore all night through thin walls"—he winked—"but it is not my place to sleep among the horsemen. I am no longer in your employ."

When Jane hesitated, he stepped back. "I don't want to make you uncomfortable, Jane. I can take a room in Wishford, if you prefer."

"And help my competition? Heavens, no."

"Are you certain?"

She opened the registration book and slid it toward him. With a measuring glance at her, he picked up the quill and signed.

She selected a key from the drawer and asked, "Any idea how many nights?"

"Not yet."

"That's all right. I will put you in number four. It's not the biggest room, but it has one of the new feather beds and is most comfortable."

"Thank you."

She stepped around the counter, wondering if she should wait for Colin to return and show Gabriel to his room. But Colin was off polishing boots and would not be back for several minutes.

"This way. Watch your head." She led Gabriel through the

archway and upstairs. She was glad she no longer had to warn guests about the uneven step or loose handrail, or be embarrassed about curling wallpaper, all of which had been repaired. She was, however, still self-conscious as she climbed the stairs ahead of a male guest—especially this particular male. She had not felt so nervous about showing a man to his room since she had shown JD to his months before.

She reached number four and opened the door. "After you."

Inside, she pointed out the basin and towels, then started in on her usual speech about the location of the privy and dining room but stopped midsentence. "How foolish. You already know all this."

"Not at all. I enjoy seeing you perform your role so capably."

"Well, I will ask Alwena to bring hot water. If you need anything else, just let us know."

"I know where to find you."

Jane looked up at him and was disconcerted to find Gabriel's dark gaze boring into hers, just as it had in the stable. Her throat tightened. She reached for the door latch and backed from the room. "I shall leave you to get settled." She gave him a parting smile and said with mock formality, "Enjoy your stay at The Bell, Mr. Locke."

His expression remained serious. "I hope I shall, Mrs. Bell."

Mrs. Burlingame's cart arrived right on time the next morning, and Thora went to open the door. Hetty carried her daughter inside, set her down, and unfastened her little coat.

Betsey's face broke into a smile when she saw Thora. "To-tah," she called, reaching for her.

Thora's heart surged with pleasure. She bent low and stretched out her hands. Betsey toddled over and wrapped her arms around Thora's neck.

Thora scooped her up and straightened, smiling into the little girl's face. "And how are you today, my girl?"

In reply Betsey smeared a wet kiss on her eyebrow.

Thora looked at Hetty. "You have a good day at the inn, Hetty. Talbot and I are planning to have supper with Jane, so we'll bring Betsey a little earlier, if that's all right."

"Of course. Thank you."

Thora turned and set the girl on a rug on the floor, near a pile of wooden blocks she'd brought back from The Bell. She knelt beside her and began helping Betsey build a tower. "See how careful she is!"

When Hetty made no move to leave, Thora looked at her in question. "We'll be all right here. Never fear."

Face tense, Hetty clasped her hands, pulling on her fingers.

"What is it, Hetty? Is anything wrong?"

"No. That is . . . you are not doing anything wrong. You're being incredibly kind, actually. Kinder than we deserve."

"Nonsense. It's my pleasure to watch her."

"I know. But . . . I worry. Worry you'll be disappointed. Patrick is not—He has not . . ."

"He has not what? Asked you to marry him?"

Hetty looked down, flushing. "He has hinted at it. But only because of Betsey, I fear."

"Is she not a good enough reason?"

Again Hetty looked down.

"Forgive me. I am too blunt, I know. I do understand that young women prefer to marry for love. And now that I am married to Walter Talbot, I understand why. But I do think my son is fond of you. More fond than he has ever been of anyone. Will that not lead to love in time?"

"I hope so."

"And do you care for him in return?"

"I do, yes. He knows I do."

"Well then, I don't see the problem. If it's only me you're not fond of, then—"

"No!" Hetty exclaimed, brow furrowed. "That is not true. You used to scare the wits out of me when I worked for you, but now I'm scared for a different reason."

"What reason?" It was on the tip of Thora's tongue to ask the question they'd all been tiptoeing around long enough—if Patrick was Betsey's father or not.

Hetty opened her mouth. "I . . ." She looked away, unable to hold Thora's gaze. "Never mind. I shall sort it. Thank you again."

Suspicion washed over Thora. She steeled herself. "Hetty, if there is something you need to tell Patrick, then tell him and get it over with."

Hetty nodded, fear shimmering in her eyes. "I shall."

Beside her, Betsey gleefully slapped the wooden tower, and all the blocks went crashing to the floor.

CHAPTER THIRTY-NINE

The next day, Jane spent a little time in her flower garden, clearing the dead stalks and fallen leaves that had accumulated over the autumn. Then she went into the keeper's lodge to remove her work gloves, wash her hands, and tidy her hair. As she did so, she noticed the men's glove box on the side table and remembered the errand she'd been planning. She decided to take care of it that very day.

She returned to the inn, found Colin at the desk, and told him she was leaving for a few minutes. He promised to watch over things while she was gone.

Jane walked to the churchyard to bring the gloves to the sexton, Mr. Ainsworth. She had noticed his old, threadbare gloves when he'd moved her flowers, so she had decided to give him a better pair—a pair of John's, in excellent condition. She didn't see the man anywhere about, so she laid the glove box just outside the door to his work shed.

Turning away, Jane paused, surprised to see a man standing before a recent grave—Mrs. Thomas's grave, she believed. He wore a grey frock coat and dark trousers, hat in hand, head bowed. She decided she would quietly retreat and leave him to mourn in peace. But then the man shifted and she glimpsed his profile.

James Drake.

Concerned, she walked toward him. Her half boot scuffed an

uneven paving stone, and he looked up at the sound, expression stricken.

"James? Are you all right? If you prefer to be alone, I'll go. But if there is anything I can do . . ."

"Stay a minute, Jane, if you would."

"Of course." She stood beside him. "I did not realize you were acquainted with Mrs. Thomas."

"I never met her. But still I felt drawn here. To apologize."

"Apologize?"

He nodded. "It was my fault she became estranged from her granddaughter. My fault Mary-Alicia died. She contracted a fever after the birth of her child—our child—and never fully recovered."

Her heart went out to him. "James, you did not know."

"I did search for her. But she'd changed her surname. If I had found her, I *would* have helped her."

"I know you would have."

"I wish I could apologize to Mary-Alicia as well. I went to Bristol to find where she was buried but learned she was given a pauper's burial—and an unmarked grave."

Jane's chest tightened. She knew how that felt. "I am sorry." Jane held out her hand to him. "Come with me."

She took his hand and led him to the west wall. "Mrs. Thomas needed a place to mourn Mary-Alicia as well, and the sexton gave her one."

She showed him the place, the loaf-sized stone lying near the wall. Someone had left a small potted chrysanthemum. Mr. Ainsworth, perhaps?

"I know it isn't the same, but her own grandmother poured out love and tears here, and laid flowers on this spot. You might want to do so as well."

He nodded. "Thank you, Jane."

Jane squeezed his hand, and left him to mourn alone.

When Jane returned to The Bell, she found Patrick standing in the office, hands on the desk, head bowed.

"Patrick? What is it? What's happened?"

"Close the door, Jane."

She did so, concern growing.

"Hetty finally told me the truth—about what happened to her before we met."

"Oh?" Jane held her breath, dread filling her.

"Remember what I told you before? How she made her willingness rather clear at first?"

"Yes."

"But what I didn't mention was that later . . . she cried. I asked her what was wrong, but she brushed it off, so I did too." His jaw tightened. "Now she tells me there was another man, right before she came to The Bell. Hetty got involved with me as a precaution, in case she was already with child—in hopes I would accept responsibility. At least now I know why she cried. She was thinking of him, not me. The man had . . . ill-used her."

"Oh no. Poor Hetty."

She recalled Hetty's determination not to blame Patrick. Her bravado about Patrick's charms, when all along, she'd been hiding a painful secret.

Patrick ran a hand over his face. "She can't be sure . . . but it's likely this other man is Betsey's father."

Jane winced. "As awful as it is, it wasn't her fault. It doesn't have to change things between you."

Patrick looked at her, expression bleak. "Does it not?"

Hetty and Betsey did not come to the farm the next morning. Mrs. Burlingame passed by without passengers and without stopping. Thora instantly began to worry. Was the little girl ill? Or had something else happened?

A short while later, Colin arrived in the inn's gig. He told Thora that Jane would like her to come to The Bell as soon as possible.

"What is it about?" Thora asked.

"I don't know for certain. Something about Mr. Bell, I take it."

Oh no, Thora thought. Now what had Patrick gone and done?

Thora grabbed her shawl, left a scrawled note for Talbot, and followed Colin out to the waiting gig.

The ride had never seemed so long.

When they reached the stable yard, Thora saw Hetty sitting on the side porch, chin in her hands. Jane stood behind her, holding Betsey.

Thora looked from one somber face to the other. "What is it? What's wrong? Colin said something about Patrick?"

Hetty said flatly, "Patrick is gone."

"Gone? Where?"

"I don't know." Hetty shook her head. "He didn't say. He just . . . left."

Thora turned to her daughter-in-law. "Jane?"

"Ted told me he saw him leave on the southbound mail. He carried a valise."

Thora winced. *No, no, no. Not again. Oh, Patrick!* Her heart ached. She had really hoped this time was different.

"Let's look in his room," Jane said. "Unless you don't think we should?"

"It's your property, Jane. I think we are justified, in this instance."

Jane led the way downstairs. Hetty and Thora followed wordlessly behind.

There, Jane handed Betsey to Thora, used the master key to unlock the door, then inched it open.

Thora looked over Jane's shoulder into the small, dank room. No wonder Patrick hadn't wanted to invite Hetty and Betsey to share it. Thora took visual inventory—books on the shelves, clothes on pegs and in the wardrobe, left ajar.

Jane sighed in relief. "He left his things. He must intend to come back."

Thora shook her head. "He left his room like this once before and didn't return for more than a year—sure we would keep his room and belongings waiting for him, if and when he decided to return. It doesn't necessarily mean anything." She ran a hand over the heavy wool greatcoat on its peg. "His favorite frock coat is gone, but he left his winter coat. So perhaps he doesn't mean to stay away long this time."

"Let's hope that's true. But where did he go? And why did he leave without saying anything?"

Hetty's eyes filled with tears. "It's my fault. I told him. Told him everything. And now he's gone."

Thora and Jane exchanged a look. With a pointed glance at Betsey, Thora said, "You told him he might not be . . . someone's father?"

Shamefaced, Hetty nodded. "There was only one other man. I was running away from him when I first came to Ivy Hill. He . . ." Tears swamped her eyes, and she couldn't continue.

"Oh, Hetty," Jane murmured sympathetically.

Thora slipped a finger beneath Hetty's chin. "Now, chin up, my girl. I'd say Patrick might very well be Betsey's father. Just look how beautiful and charming she is, and how she wraps us all around her little finger!"

Jane looked at her in surprise, and Hetty's mouth gaped at Thora's willing suspension of disbelief.

"And Patrick loves you. I know he does." Thora's tone grew husky. "Lord willing, he'll realize that too. But even if he leaves the country again, he'll be back. In the meantime, you and Betsey will always have a place here in Ivy Hill. With Jane, or with me and Talbot."

"Thank you, Thora," Hetty hoarsely whispered, tears filling her eyes anew.

Rachel received a note, hand-delivered to the library by a dark-haired young woman. "From Mrs. Haverhill, miss."

"Thank you." Rachel accepted it, then studied the young woman. "Are you Molly Kurdle, by any chance?"

"I am, miss," she tentatively replied, clearly anticipating a negative reaction.

Instead Rachel beamed at her. "I'm so glad you're back, Molly. And Mrs. Haverhill is as well, no doubt."

The girl smiled shyly in return. "Me too, miss."

The note asked Rachel to meet Mrs. Haverhill at The Bell the following day. No reason was given. Rachel sent the girl an inquiring look, but she shook her head.

"I'm not to say more. But will you come?"

"I'll come."

The next day, shortly before the appointed hour, Rachel walked down Potters Lane. When she reached the High Street, she saw Sir Timothy striding down the Brockwell Court drive.

She raised a hand in greeting. "Hello, Sir Timothy."

His lips parted. "Miss Ashford, I didn't expect to see you here."

He walked in her direction, and she started toward him as well, until they met near the blacksmith's.

"I received a note from Mrs. Haverhill, asking me to meet her at The Bell today."

His eyebrows knitted. "So did I. I wonder what she wants to talk to us about?"

"Perhaps she simply wants to thank you again, though why she included me, I don't know." Rachel hoped the woman had no embarrassing matchmaking scheme in mind.

"Nonsense, she has much to be grateful for where you're concerned." The admiration in his eyes pleased and discomfited her.

"I did very little, but thank you."

He rubbed his chin. "By the way, young Mr. Mullins asked me for work on the estate, when my manager had already turned him down. He told me *you* suggested he come and see me."

"I hope you don't mind. His sister is a pupil at the school. I made no promises, though. I told him only that I knew you would be fair."

Timothy nodded. "He said as much. And he starts next week, helping with the harvest."

"Oh, Timothy! I am so glad. Thank you."

His gaze rested on her face. "I am glad it pleases you. I was happy to help."

Distracted by the warm way he was looking at her, Rachel stepped out into the High Street, not looking where she was going. Sir Timothy's arm shot out and drew her back, just as a chaise raced past. Her hat went flying.

"Oh! Thank you," she panted. Her heart beat hard both from the narrow escape and being pulled against Timothy Brockwell's side.

He looked down at her in concern. "Are you all right?"

"I will be. Once I catch my breath."

Keeping hold of one of her hands, he bent and picked up her hat. "Sorry about that. At least you escaped unscathed. I am not so sure about your hat."

"That's all right."

He dusted it off and placed it back on her head. "There. No harm done. As charming as ever."

His hands lingered on the brim a moment, and sweet tension tightened her chest.

He cleared his throat. "Shall we try that again?"

They looked both ways, and as they crossed the High Street together, he guided her with a protective hand to the small of her back.

Reaching the other side, he opened the inn door for her and they stepped inside. Rachel glanced around the entry hall and into the coffee room but saw no sign of Mrs. Haverhill. They must have arrived before her. A moment later, Rachel saw the carter pass by the front windows, Mrs. Haverhill on the bench beside her and a young woman perched on the back of the cart. Mrs. Burlingame's horse turned and disappeared from view through the inn's carriage archway.

"After you." Sir Timothy held the side door for Rachel, and together they stepped out to meet Mrs. Haverhill in the courtyard.

One of the ostlers helped her alight, and Mrs. Haverhill turned to face them, looking elegant in walking dress and plumed hat, while her young companion wore a simple carriage dress of striped corded muslin that Rachel had seen in Mrs. Shabner's window only the previous week.

Jane stepped out of the inn behind them. "Hello, Rachel, Timothy." She turned to the woman. "Here you are, Mrs. Haverhill, two tickets for the eastbound stage. Colin, help Ted with Mrs. Haverhill's trunk, if you please."

"Yes, ma'am."

"You're leaving?" Sir Timothy's brows rose in surprise.

Mrs. Haverhill met his gaze. "Yes. I asked you here to thank you again and say good-bye. Your subtle hint was timely and taken."

Sir Timothy narrowed his eyes. "I deeded you the cottage, Mrs. Haverhill. How was that hinting you should leave?"

"Well, perhaps not intentionally, but your bequests have given me the impetus and opportunity to spring the trap and fly away. It's time to make my own life somewhere else. Molly is back, God be praised." She put an arm around the young woman beside her. "She goes with me. Almost like a daughter to me, Molly is. The daughter I never had."

Tears brightened her eyes, and in them Rachel saw a reflection of the tender beauty Sir Justin must have seen in her.

"What will you do? Where will you go?"

"We go to Brighton. Many tourists flock there, I understand. Molly and I will carry on the soap-making business we began together. With the funds you've given me, I will set up a little shop and sell perfumed soaps and other things for the visiting ladies to take home with them. We always did mean to go to Brighton, but we never did."

She did not specify whom she meant by "we." She did not need to.

"In the meantime," Mrs. Haverhill added, "I have engaged Mr. Arnold to find a lodger for Bramble Cottage. I may sell in time, but for now I will rent it to someone else."

Sir Timothy nodded his understanding. "I hope you will be happy, Mrs. Haverhill."

She chuckled dryly. "So do I."

The stagecoach arrived. They all stood aside as the horses were changed. Jane disappeared inside to welcome those passengers stopping at The Bell to transfer lines. The ostlers made quick work of the turnout, and the guard signaled a five-minute warning on his horn.

Mrs. Shabner came hurrying into the yard, with a bonnet trimmed to match Molly's new dress—a going-away present. Molly and Mrs. Haverhill exclaimed over the gift and thanked the dressmaker.

Soon Mrs. Haverhill's trunk and valises were loaded onto the stage. The guard opened the door and helped her and her young companion inside. Mrs. Haverhill sat near the window, and for a moment, her gaze held Rachel's. She raised her gloved hand in sober farewell, then faced forward, without looking back.

Mercy stood at the window staring out across the back garden and beyond it to her beloved Ivy Green, where children played on the late autumn afternoon. The children, especially one particular child, lay heavily on her heart.

Knowing she was about to lose Alice, marriage and the possibility of children of her own beckoned like a pain-relieving elixir, just out of reach.

Should she marry Mr. Hollander? She was not attracted to him and doubted he would ever finish a book, but he was not a bad man. In her secret heart, Mercy admitted to herself that if marrying him would allow her to keep her girls school, she would likely accept him.

If Mercy said no to Mr. Hollander, she knew she would be saying yes to life as a spinster aunt in her brother's house and under the thumb of George's soon-to-be wife. Her Aunt Matilda had lived such a life, and she was happy. Or was she?

Mercy went and found her aunt in the quiet reading room and sank into the chair beside hers. "Oh, Aunt Matty, what should I do?"

Matilda set aside her novel and removed her spectacles. "You know, my dear, when I was about your age, I was in a similar situation. My brother was about to marry your mother, and I had to ask myself the same question. Examine my choices, which were few. There was one man I was fond of and would have married, had he asked, but he married someone else. There was one other man who admired me, but I didn't care for him, so I turned him down and stayed here with Earnest and his bride.

"There were times in those early years of the three of us living here together that I regretted my decision. Your mother and I did not always see eye to eye, as you know. But then you and George came along and softened your mamma. And you, especially, were the light of my days. And we are friends even now, thank the Lord.

"Just between us, I was not sorry when your parents decided to quit Ivy Hill for London. Goodness, has it already been ten years ago? No one likes feeling like an unwanted guest in one's own home. These last ten years here—just you and me and our girls—have been some of the happiest of my life, and I am as sorry to see them come to an end as you are. But it needn't be a dire fate. If you are lucky as I was, you will have a special relationship with at least one of your nieces or nephews, and that will make life worthwhile, as it has for me."

"Thank you, Aunt Matty." Thinking through her aunt's words, Mercy concluded, "So . . . you are advising me to remain as I am and hope for the best?"

"Heavens, no. Get out however you can. And take me with you." Matty winked, then added earnestly, "I cannot tell you what to do, my dear. But whatever you decide, I want you to know I love you, and I could not be more proud of you if you were my own daughter."

Mercy pressed her hand, and both blinked back tears.

CHAPTER FORTY

Thora was just stepping outside the next day when Hetty walked through the Angel Farm gate, a parcel in her hands.

"Hello, Hetty."

"You're going out," Hetty observed. "I won't keep you."

"I was on my way to The Bell to see you. Come in." Thora held the door, and Hetty stepped over the threshold but no further.

"Mrs. Bell offered to watch Betsey for me. I've only come to return the things you lent us." She handed over the small bundle. "Here are Patrick's baby things. I laundered them carefully—don't worry."

"I wasn't worried. And you needn't return them."

"Yes, I do. You saved them for Patrick's children. For your grandchildren. It wouldn't be right for us to keep them. I should never have accepted them in the first place. Please forgive me for allowing you to believe . . . to hope."

"Hetty . . ."

"And here is the bracelet you gave Betsey."

Thora glanced at the blue pendant and slowly shook her head. Voice thick, she said, "I've already given her my heart. There's no taking it back now."

Hetty held her gaze a moment, measuring her resolve, then put the bracelet back into her apron pocket. "Thank you, Thora."

Errand completed, Hetty wanted to walk back, but Thora insisted on taking her in their gig. It was a quiet, uncomfortable ride.

Two coaches had arrived at the inn before them, and the yard was busy. Thora saw Hetty's eyes linger on the vehicles.

"Hetty, you are not thinking of leaving, are you?"

"I am."

"But where would you go?"

"I don't know."

Thora handed the reins to an ostler, and the two women climbed out of the gig. Jane came out to greet them, Betsey on her hip.

Thora nodded to her, then continued, "Remember what I said, Hetty. You and Betsey have a place in Ivy Hill for as long as you want it—here at The Bell or with Talbot and me. Right, Jane?"

"Absolutely."

"Thora, that is very kind. And tempting," Hetty said. "But if Patrick left to avoid marriage to me, then I am not simpleton enough to stay here or move in with his mother! I will miss you—something I never thought I'd say and mean it with all my heart, but I will. And so, of course, will Betsey. But she is young, and in time the pain will ease and her heart will heal."

Thora wondered if she was talking about her daughter alone or herself as well.

Jane pressed her hand. "Hetty, please don't leave."

"Leave? Why would Hetty leave?"

They all whipped their heads around. There stood Patrick, wearing his favorite frock coat, a bouquet of hothouse flowers in one hand and valise in the other.

"Patrick!" Hetty breathed.

Thora's heart banged in her chest, and she pressed a hand to the tender spot. *Thank you, God.*

"Where did you go? Ted saw you leave."

"Only for a few days." He set down his valise. "Good heavens, Mamma. Tell me you didn't jump to conclusions and pull Hetty along for the ride! Did you think I'd left for good? What do you take me for?"

"Actually, Thora tried to convince me that you would come back for me," Hetty said. "But I was the one who was afraid to believe her."

"Why? I told you I love you and want you to be my wife." He handed her the bouquet.

Hetty lowered her gaze to the flowers. "But then I told you about . . . Betsey . . . and you left. Without saying a word. And—"

"What about Betsey?" He took the little girl in his arms. "She may not have inherited my suave demeanor or dark hair," he jested, eyes resting fondly on the child. "But she is every bit as attractive and clever and charming—can you deny it?"

Hetty exchanged a look with Thora. "Your mother said something very like that herself."

"Did she indeed? Well, Mamma knew me as a baby, didn't she?" He grinned. "She is most qualified to recognize the similarities."

Hetty bit her lip. "But . . . you never officially asked me to marry you."

"I know. I couldn't. Not until I had something of my own to offer you. Something better than a musty little room in my sister's inn."

"I don't care about that."

"You should. You deserve better."

"You still haven't told us where you went," Jane said, "and why all the secrecy?"

"I left a quick note in the office. Did you not find it?"

"No."

"Probably buried under a pile of bills." He shrugged. "At all events, I first went to Salisbury to talk to the bankers there, since they haven't replaced Blomfield at the bank here in Ivy Hill. Then I looked at a few properties. I didn't say anything because I wanted it to be a surprise, and truthfully, because I feared the bankers might turn me down after the, em, recent misunderstanding with their former partner. But I'm happy and relieved to report they agreed to work with me. I have some money saved and they will loan me the rest."

"Not another loan," Thora moaned.

"Only a very modest one, Mamma."

"A loan for what?"

"I have my eye on a nice lodging house in Salisbury and a smaller one in Wishford. I haven't made a formal offer on either. I want you to see them both, Hetty, and we can decide together. That is . . . if you will accept a simple landlord when you deserve a lord of a manor."

"Of course I will. Oh, Patrick." Hetty's eyes shone, and she rested a hand on his arm.

Thora made a face. "Salisbury is such a big city and quite a long way."

"Not so far. You could visit us on Sundays, Mamma. And I know how much you dislike Wishford."

"But Wishford *is* closer," she pointed out.

"True. The lodging house there is rather small, but it does have a modest apartment for the owners with two extra bedchambers for . . . children. The place needs work, but I think it has potential. There is room for expansion, should we decide to build on, and situated on the river as it is, it could be very successful, in time."

"Sounds promising, Patrick." Thora swallowed hard. "I'm . . . proud of you."

"Thank you, Mamma."

Betsey still in his arms, Patrick gingerly lowered himself to one knee right there in The Bell courtyard. "What do you say, Hetty and Betsey, will you marry me? I know I am not a perfect man, by any measure. But I do love you, both of you, and would be honored to be your husband and your papa."

Hetty dropped to her knees before him and threw her arms around both Patrick and Betsey in a clumsy, dusty, beautiful embrace. "We will."

Even though the future of her library and livelihood were uncertain, Rachel went about her business calmly for the most part. Now and again, a flash of worry would niggle her, but she was learning to pray when that happened. She reminded herself that she had prayed for reconciliation with Jane a few months ago, and now their friendship had been restored. She also thought again of Mercy's many undeserved kindnesses to her. Gratitude filled Rachel anew, and her trust in God grew.

In the meantime, she was determined to make the most of each remaining day in the Ashford Circulating Library, helping patrons and reading voraciously herself. She even attended the next ladies' book discussion, this time about the novel *Emmeline, the Orphan of the Castle* by Charlotte Smith. At this rate, they might soon have to change their name to The Ladies Tea, Knitting, and Book Society.

The day before Miss Bingley's ball, Rachel had tea with Jane. Tucked into a high-backed inglenook in The Bell coffee room, they talked about Patrick's engagement, the situation with the library, and Mrs. Haverhill's surprising departure.

"And Timothy?" Jane asked. "Anything new there?"

Rachel shook her head. "He has not said anything. Nor visited the library lately."

"Perhaps he thinks you and Mr. Ashford are still courting."

"It's possible. Though rumors generally pass quickly along our ole ivy vine. I will say his manner toward me the day Mrs. Haverhill left was quite warm. I confess it gave me hope . . . though I am afraid to hope as well. I don't want to be hurt again."

"I understand, Rachel, but I think you have every reason to hope. You are stronger and prettier than ever, your character sweeter, and you are still young."

"Thank you, Jane."

"Which reminds me . . ." Jane raised a hand, eyes bright. "You are hereby invited to a special dinner next week. We are celebrating."

"Celebrating what?"

"One of us, who is not so young, reaches a significant birthday soon. . . ." Jane coughed for emphasis. "And I can think of no better way to stave off the gloom than a dinner party with friends."

Rachel grinned. "Good idea. With age comes wisdom, apparently."

When Rachel returned to Ivy Cottage, a thick parcel awaited her on the library desk, wrapped in brown paper, sealing wax, and twine. Another donation? Tucked beneath the twine was the printed card of a Bristol bookbinder with her name added in elegant script: *Miss R. Ashford.*

This, then, was a gift. Happy anticipation rippled through her. Was it from Timothy, or was that only wishful thinking? After all, Timothy had recently returned from Bristol. . . .

She slid her nail beneath the seal and peeled back the paper. Inside lay a beautiful leather-and-gilt edition of the novel *Persuasion*, custom bound in one thick volume. The title page carried the attribution: *By the author of "Pride and Prejudice," "Mansfield Park," &c.*

The library already possessed a four-volume set of *Northanger Abbey and Persuasion*, so Rachel felt no qualms about taking the new book up to her room for her own enjoyment. She had adored *Pride and Prejudice* and now looked forward to reading this book by the same author.

Mrs. Timmons called from the passage that dinner was on the table and to hurry along unless she liked cold peas, so the new book would have to wait.

That evening, Rachel changed into her nightclothes and situated herself in bed, bolstered by pillows and a warm shawl around her shoulders. Then she opened the book . . . and drew in a breath. After all her searching for inscriptions in other books, here was one at last:

To Rachel,
You pierce my soul.

Goodness! What did it mean? The handwriting seemed familiar, though it was not signed with a name. Rachel had planned to read only a few chapters, but after discovering that intriguing inscription, she knew she would get precious little sleep that night.

The author began by describing Sir Walter Elliot and his daughters, who decide they must let out their manor house and live more modestly elsewhere. After a few chapters, Rachel began to grow sleepy. *One more page*, she told herself as she began chapter four.

There she read with mounting interest the romantic history of the middle daughter. As a young woman, Anne Elliot had briefly been engaged to Captain Frederick Wentworth. But a trusted family friend argued that because he had little fortune or connections, he was unworthy of her, and Anne had been persuaded to call off the engagement. A decision she came to regret.

"More than seven years were gone since this little history of sorrowful interest had reached its close. . . ."

Rachel could relate. Heedless of the hour, she continued to read, now wide awake.

Captain Wentworth returned from sea a successful man who had apparently shifted his attentions to a younger woman. Meanwhile, a cousin, her father's heir, began pursuing Anne. At seven-and-twenty, she knew she ought to be thankful for any man's interest, but she still loved Captain Wentworth and feared she had lost him forever.

Rachel's bedside candle guttered. She pulled a spare from her drawer, lit it by the flickering stub, and kept reading.

As dawn warmed the sky outside her window, Rachel reached the climactic chapter—Captain Wentworth believing Anne would marry her cousin, and Anne wishing she knew how to prove her constancy.

Finally the captain wrote a letter and, with a look of entreaty, left it where she could not miss it. Staring at that letter, Anne fully believed her future happiness depended on its contents and sat down to read it then and there. . . .

As eager to read the letter as the fictional Anne, Rachel turned the page, and her breath hitched.

What was this? Although clearly a newly bound book, words

had been underscored on the page. Confusion quickly gave way to blossoming hope as she read the underlined phrases:

> I must speak to you by such means as are within my reach. You pierce my soul. I am half agony, half hope. Tell me not that I am too late, that such precious feelings are gone for ever. . . . I have loved none but you. . . .

Rachel pressed a hand to her chest as the words wrapped themselves around her soul and warmed her entire being. She turned the final page and stilled—any remaining doubt fled. There, slipped between the concluding pages, was a small pressed rose with a white bead pinned to its stem.

She picked it up with delicate fingers, tears filling her eyes. It was the flower that had come loose from her hair the night of her coming-out ball, more than eight years ago. Timothy had kept it all this time.

CHAPTER

FORTY-ONE

In the Ivy Cottage sitting room, Rachel held out her arms and turned side to side, showing the Miss Groves her mother's ivory-and-gold gown with the new neckline and trimming.

"Well? Do I look terribly out of fashion? Mrs. Shabner says I do."

Mercy beamed. "No! Rachel, look at you. You are prettier than I have ever seen you. Truly."

"Thank you, Mercy."

"Goodness me. If you don't receive an offer of marriage tonight, I shall be very much surprised." Matilda's eyes twinkled.

"Don't go on so. This is Miss Bingley's coming-out ball. It is her night to be the center of attention, not mine. You don't think I am too showy in this?"

"Not at all. It's not your fault if you outshine every other lady in the room."

Matilda nodded her agreement. "Mercy is right, my dear. You have never been lovelier, inside or out. You have blossomed in spite of it all. Your parents would be so proud of you."

"Thank you, Miss Matty."

Matilda grinned. "And if Sir Timothy doesn't come to his senses now, I've a mind to box his ears."

Rachel smiled, but her stomach tingled with nervous anticipation. She pressed a hand there to calm herself.

"I hope the dress is worth the effort. Mrs. Shabner said having to make over this old thing is the straw that broke the camel's back. She declares she is letting out her shop."

Matilda nodded. "She may just do it this time. But the dress is worth it, I assure you."

Mercy asked tentatively, "Will Mr. Ashford be attending? I happened to overhear Mrs. Ashford after church mention they'd been invited."

"I don't know. I hope he does not stay home on my account. In fact, I will pray Mr. Ashford finds someone new to admire, perhaps even tonight."

They left the schoolgirls in the care of Agnes, Anna, and Mrs. Timmons so the Miss Groves and Rachel could attend the ball together. Mercy tried to beg off, but her aunt argued that she could use some cheering up and should go. In the end, Mercy agreed and determined to enjoy herself as best she could. The evening turned chilly, and they were all thankful that thoughtful Mr. Bingley had offered to send his carriage for them.

As they neared the Bingley home between Wishford and Stapleford, excitement filled Rachel. Lanterns lit the drive and candles glowed in every window of the manor house. When the carriage stopped, liveried footmen appeared to help them alight. Stepping inside, more servants took their capes and mantles. In the great hall, they were welcomed by their hosts, Mr. and Mrs. Bingley. Moving down the line, they congratulated Miss Bingley, and promised Horace Bingley they would have a "capital time."

Mercy soon joined her aunt and the other older women clustered around the punch table, sipping negus or ratafia and talking, while Rachel surreptitiously surveyed the ballroom, looking for Sir Timothy. She saw Justina Brockwell, and her heart lifted, but there was no sign of her brother.

She noticed Mrs. Ashford working her way through the crowd, making sure Nicholas was introduced to as many eligible young ladies as possible. He even danced the first with Miss Bingley herself.

Rachel greeted dour Lord Winspear and several other old friends of her parents, and danced with jovial Mr. Bingley. When he escorted her back to the side of the room, she was surprised to find herself face-to-face with Nicholas Ashford.

He stammered, "Miss Ashford. Good evening. I . . . hope you don't mind. Mother insists I at least try to meet other young ladies."

"She is quite right. I am glad you are here and enjoying yourself. And it was good to see you dancing. You appear to be rather skilled."

He nodded. "I have taken a few lessons from a dancing master. It has done wonders for my confidence."

"Well done."

"I hope you know I am not trying to . . . to make you feel jealous or quickly replaced or anything like that."

"Of course not."

He held her gaze. "I have come to understand that long-held affections are not easily replaced by new ones."

She gave him an apologetic look. "I know I disappointed you, but I hope you meet someone you can love with all your heart. A woman who deserves you."

He managed a lopsided grin. "And who, ideally, returns my affections."

"Yes, wholeheartedly." She pressed his arm. "You deserve every good thing life has to offer, Mr. Ashford."

"As do you, Miss Ashford."

Rachel left him with a smile and walked over to the punch table for a small glass of negus.

She noticed Mrs. Ashford talking to a reserved Lady Brockwell. When Nicholas's mother turned her smile on Lord Winspear, Rachel took a deep breath and approached Lady Brockwell. She reminded herself that the woman had been wronged, whether she knew it or not. And whether Rachel liked it or not, this was the mother of the man she loved.

"Good evening, Lady Brockwell." Rachel curtsied.

"Miss Ashford." The woman's gaze swept over her form, and Rachel held her breath.

"You look lovely, I must say."

"Thank you. You do as well. I . . . wanted to apologize for the unkind way I spoke to you in the library. I know you were worried about your son."

Lady Brockwell inclined her head in acknowledgement. "And I have something to say to you as well."

Rachel steeled herself for a blow.

"Timothy tells me I was wrong to speak to you as I did, and he . . . is right."

Rachel blinked in surprise.

"He also tells me he will brook no more criticism or objections where you are concerned."

"Did he?" *If only he had said that to me.*

"Yes. Old ways die hard, but I am determined not to meddle further in his life—*this* conversation notwithstanding."

She gave Rachel a self-abasing grin. For the first time, Rachel saw a resemblance to Justina, and felt her heart begin to thaw toward the woman.

"Is he . . . not coming tonight?"

"He has not told me his plans. I assumed he would tell you?"

Rachel shook her head.

Something across the ballroom caught the woman's attention. "Well, if you will excuse me, I think I shall remind Justina to save a dance for Sir Cyril in case he comes."

Rachel nodded and watched her cross the room to Justina and whisper in her ear. Apparently, Lady Brockwell's resolve to stop meddling did not extend to her daughter.

Rachel walked over to Mercy and took her aside. "He's not coming." She sighed. "I feel rather foolish now that I raised my hopes. Ah well. I hope you and Matty enjoy yourselves."

"I am sorry, Rachel. Perhaps he was delayed and might yet arrive. I saw you talking to Lady Brockwell. What did she say?"

"She doesn't know his plans."

"Perhaps Justina might." Mercy turned toward Justina and Miss Bingley, who now stood talking and giggling nearby.

"Justina?"

The two close-in-age friends walked over eagerly. "Good evening, Miss Grove. Miss Ashford."

"Hello, girls. Are you enjoying yourselves?"

"We are." Miss Bingley nodded enthusiastically. "Though we wish there were a few more gentlemen in attendance. Ideally single gentlemen possessing good looks and a good fortune."

With a subtle glance at Rachel, Mercy asked Justina, "And will either of your brothers be coming to help our numbers?"

Justina shook her head. "Definitely not Richard. He rarely leaves London. I don't know about Timothy. I thought he would be here, but I haven't seen him."

Rachel looked down to hide her disappointment, and noticed something out of place—a length of ribbon hanging from her waistline.

"Oh no. The new trim is pulling away from the fabric here. Heaven help me if I try to dance a jig in this old thing. It will probably fall to shreds."

Miss Bingley peered closer. "It's not too bad. But yes, better have it seen to before the tear widens. I know! Go up to my room. My lady's maid is up there, and she could easily repair that for you in no time."

"Are you sure?"

"Perfectly. Tell her I sent you. She won't mind—she's a dear. Up the stairs, second door on the right."

"Thank you." Rachel excused herself and went upstairs.

A quarter of an hour later, trim repaired and pleasantries exchanged with Miss Bingley's maid, Rachel made her way back down the stairs. She wondered how long Mercy would want to stay, and if Mr. Bingley would offer to send them home in his carriage, as they had arrived. She hoped they could leave soon.

A gentleman looked up as she descended, and her breath caught. He had come after all.

"Sir Timothy."

How tall and dashing he looked in evening clothes—black tailcoat, brocade waistcoat, light cravat, and breeches.

"Rachel . . . Miss Ashford. There you are. Council business detained me. I was afraid you had left."

"Not yet."

She felt his steady gaze as she descended the remaining stairs, her pulse accelerating with each step nearer to him. Worried she might trip, she gripped the railing with one hand, and with the other held her skirt. Reaching the bottom, she looked up and found him staring at her, lips parted.

Belatedly, he bowed, and she curtsied. "Good evening."

Candlelight from the nearby candelabra reflected in his dark eyes, and perhaps a touch of humor as well. "I feel as though I have lived this moment before. . . ."

She chuckled softly. "Me too, though I am surprised you remember."

His gaze held hers. "Are you really?" He slowly shook his head. "You stunned me then. And you stun me now."

She looked down, self-conscious, and plucked at the skirt. "This dress is old. But I have always liked it."

"You are beautiful in it. But then, you always are."

She looked up again and saw warmth in his eyes brighter than any candle flame. "Thank you. And thank you for the book you gave me."

His gaze flashed to hers. "Did you read it?"

"Every word."

He watched her carefully, expression measuring. "Miss Ashford, are you at liberty to dance with me? Or are you . . . otherwise engaged?"

"I am not engaged. I am free."

"I am surprised but relieved to hear it. I . . ." Noticing the people milling around them, he said, "Will you step into the library with me so we might talk more privately?"

She nodded, heart beating hard.

He gestured for her to precede him across the hall. When they were alone among the many books, he said earnestly, "I deeply regret the way I spoke to you that night in front of Ivy Cottage." He shook his head. "Had I learned nothing in eight years? Again I voiced my parents' concerns, instead of expressing my own feelings for you. My . . . love for you. Discovering my father's hypocrisy has had one benefit. No longer will I be ruled by foolish family pride. I hope you will forgive me."

"I will."

His eyes widened at her quick response, and he stepped closer. How tall he was. How broad his shoulders. How appealing the strong lines of his handsome face.

"When I heard you were moving your father's books out of Ivy Cottage, I thought you were marrying and moving back to Thornvale. I was in torment. From all accounts, young Mr. Ashford is a good man and would make some woman a good husband. But not you, Rachel. I cannot abide the thought that anyone should have that honor except me."

"You are right; he is a good man. But I've told him I cannot marry him."

He nodded, countenance grave. "Rachel, if your feelings are still what they were that night, tell me so plainly. I want to marry you now more than ever."

Rachel felt shy and brave at once. "My feelings are . . . the same as they have always been, truly. I did not mean what I said that night we argued. I have always loved you, Timothy Brockwell. And I always shall."

A smile transformed his serious expression. He held out his hands to her, and she placed her gloved hands in his.

"Were your father alive, I would ask for his blessing."

She grinned wistfully. "You have always had it."

"Now I have only to regret wasting all this time."

Rachel shook her head. "Let's not. Instead, let's make the next eight years the best of our lives."

He held her gaze. "With all my heart."

He stepped closer still, enveloping her in the spicy aroma of his shaving tonic. She relished the warmth of his eyes looking deep into hers, and the awareness that he was going to kiss her at last. He lowered his head with tantalizing slowness, his mouth drawing near. Her lashes fluttered against her cheeks. Her chest tightened in breathless anticipation. Then he touched his lips to hers, softly. Deliciously.

Footsteps approached. Timothy pulled away before she had a proper chance to kiss him back.

Disappointed, Rachel looked over.

Justina stood in the doorway. "Timothy!" she squealed, hurrying into the room. "There you are. You promised me a dance, remember. Oh . . . ! Rachel. Well, never mind. You two must dance instead. I will find another partner. Sir Cyril dances this set with Miss Bingley, but no matter." She grasped Rachel's and Timothy's hands and pulled them back into the ballroom, where they nearly collided with Nicholas.

"Ah, Mr. Ashford, hello."

"Good evening again, Miss Brockwell."

Rachel spoke up, "Mr. Ashford, perhaps you will dance with Miss Brockwell? She is in need of a partner."

"Oh. Yes, with pleasure."

Following after the two younger people, Rachel and Timothy took their place in line together. The music had already started without them, but there were still many steps to dance, and many happy refrains to come.

Sitting in the lodge the night of the ball, Jane heard faint music coming from the courtyard, The Bell's musicians practicing together again to pass the pleasant evening. Jane pulled a shawl around herself, went outside, and sat on her front step to hear them better. Kipper came and rubbed against her skirt, begging her to pet his ears. She obliged him, her foot tapping in time with the melody. Through the archway, she could see the men and their instruments illuminated by lamplight. Tall Ted with bow and fiddle, Colin playing pipe, and Tuffy plucking on his old mandolin. Hetty, she guessed, was probably busy putting Betsey to bed.

Gabriel stepped out of The Bell and, seeing her, walked across the drive. It was strange to see him coming and going like a regular guest, but rather pleasant too.

"Hello, Jane. Beautiful evening."

"It is, yes."

He raised a thumb toward the inn. "Your brother-in-law is in high spirits. Announcing to everyone that he is an engaged man. That is good news, is it not?"

"It is, yes."

He studied her face and his brow furrowed. "What is it? You look sad. Is something wrong?"

"No. All is well."

He did not look convinced. "I was in Wishford earlier. Lots of carriages on the road, heading toward Stapleford. Something going on tonight?"

"The Bingleys are hosting a ball."

One dark brow rose. "You didn't want to go?"

Jane shrugged. "I was not invited."

"I'm sorry."

He sat down beside her on the step and Kipper began butting his arm, looking for affection. "I see you are still spoiling this stable cat." He stroked his fur, then said, "Are you terribly disappointed?"

"No. Nor surprised. It's not the sort of event an innkeeper would be invited to. I used to be in the Bingleys' circle, but that was when I was Miss Fairmont, a gentlewoman."

"You are still the same person, Jane. And have the same worth in God's eyes and to anyone else worth calling a friend."

"Thank you. I knew what I was giving up when I married John. I am just feeling a little sorry for myself. I would have enjoyed spending the evening with my friends."

"They were invited?"

"Oh yes. Rachel and Mercy. And Sir Timothy, of course."

"Of course," he murmured.

"Don't worry. I am all right."

A corner of his mouth lifted. "I was not invited either, if that makes you feel any better. And I hope you count me among your . . . friends."

"Of course I do."

"And our music is no doubt as good." He gestured toward the trio of amateur musicians. "Well . . . not bad," he corrected.

She smiled.

"I suppose they will have fine food at this party? And dancing?"

"I suppose."

He pulled a small parcel from his pocket. "Spiced nutmeats from Wishford. Cadi mentioned you are partial to them."

Little schemer. "Thank you." Jane reached for them, but he set the packet on the top step and stood.

"Later." He extended a hand to her, his dark brown eyes glinting. "Shall we dance, Miss Fairmont?" he asked, using her maiden name in mock formality.

She looked skeptically across the drive. "Here?"

"Why not?"

She listened to the music, realizing it was in three-quarter time. "I don't know that this is the best music for a dance—it's a *waltzer*, I believe."

"A turning waltz, then, unless you deem it inappropriate."

Anticipation tingled through her. "I think it will be all right. There is no one about to scandalize."

She put her bare hand in his and let him pull her to her feet, her shawl falling to the step.

He took a step nearer and slowly pressed his other hand to her back. She felt the warmth of it through her dress.

Drawing a shallow breath, she laid her hand on his upper arm, firm muscle readily evident beneath his coat sleeves.

He tightened his grip on her right hand. She hoped he did not notice how damp it was.

She confessed, "I am dreadfully out of practice."

He looked deeply into her eyes. "Just follow my lead."

She had difficulty holding his gaze in such close proximity and was thankful for the flickering light and shadows that hopefully hid her blush. She focused instead on her hand on his sleeve.

He guided her through the steps. "One, two, three. One, two, three . . . That's it. Now you step forward, now me. . . ." Soon they were turning in graceful circles around the drive.

"You are an excellent dancer, Miss Fairmont."

"Only because I have an excellent partner." She grinned up at him. "What other hidden talents does my former farrier possess?"

He smiled, and the secret promises shimmering there made it difficult to breathe.

Finally the music stopped, and spinning as she was, Jane wobbled on her feet, still dizzy. Gabriel held her a little closer.

"Well done," he murmured, his sweet breath warm on her temple, her ear. His face was near hers. If she looked up, would he kiss her? Her heart pounded at the thought.

She glanced toward the musicians and saw Colin looking their way.

Self-conscious, Jane stepped away. "Th-thank you for the dance, Gabriel."

"My pleasure."

"Now I had better say good night." She retreated into the lodge and shut the door behind her.

CHAPTER FORTY-TWO

On Sunday afternoon, Mercy, Alice, and Phoebe went on a nature walk together. They strolled along Pudding Brook and then down Ebsbury Road, gathering bouquets of colorful autumn leaves: yellow-gold, orange, and russet.

Alice climbed atop the low stone wall bordering one side of the road. Mercy took her free hand to steady the girl as she walked tightrope-fashion atop the wall, her little hand clutching leaves extended for balance.

Mercy remembered doing the same as a child. She smiled approvingly. "You are quite the funambulist, Alice."

Her brow furrowed. "Fyoo what?"

"It's another name for a tightrope walker. It comes from the Latin *funis*, for rope, and *ambulare*—to amble or walk."

Phoebe giggled. "That's a funny word."

Down the road, near Thornvale's gate, a beech tree beckoned, its red-tipped leaves twirling to the ground in a gust of wind. The girls ran ahead to gather some for their leaf collections.

Kelly Featherstone waved to her from near the almshouse, so Mercy paused a few moments to talk to the elderly man. She smiled at something he said, and then looked back to make sure the girls were all right. She felt her smile fall. A man stood talking to the girls.

Mr. Drake.

Her body tensed. What was he saying to Alice? She was torn between wanting to rush over to them and wanting to avoid the man.

Mercy excused herself from Mr. Featherstone and walked with determination down the road, asking God to help guard her tongue—and her heart. Mr. Drake glanced up as she approached, and his own smile fell. Mercy instantly felt the tension between them.

He avoided her gaze and looked at the girls. "Well, good-bye, Miss Phoebe. Alice." He tipped his hat and slanted Mercy a glance. "For now."

In her sensitive state, the simple words sounded ominous.

She glanced over her shoulder as the man strode away, then turned back to the girls. "What did Mr. Drake say to you?" She kept her tone and expression as placid as possible.

Alice watched her face carefully, her green eyes so like his, Mercy noticed.

Phoebe shrugged. "He said he wanted to invite Alice and me to see his hotel and have tea or maybe even iced cream!"

Mercy glanced at Alice. "I see."

Mercy did see. And she realized she could wait no longer to tell Alice of the change to come.

That night Mercy prayed for wisdom and the right words, and the next day she asked Alice to join her in the sitting room.

"Good morning, Alice." Mercy forced a cheerful tone. "I have something to talk to you about. Why don't you sit here, and I will sit next to you."

Alice did so and looked up to her with such trusting eyes.

Mercy took a deep breath. "You know Mr. Drake? Of course you do, you have met him a few times now. He is . . . so kind and he likes you so much that he wants to be your father."

Alice frowned. "My father is dead. He died when I was a baby. Mamma told me."

"I know she did. And now Mr. Drake wants to be a father to you and raise you as his own daughter."

"Why?"

"Because he is your . . . He was a friend of your mother's."

"I thought I was going to live with you. I thought you were going to be my . . . mamma."

Mercy's heart fisted. She bit the inside of her cheek to keep tears at bay. "Nothing would have made me happier. But Mr. Drake was much closer to your mother, so it is his right and privilege to raise you as his little girl."

"Won't I live here anymore?"

Mercy swallowed. "For a little while yet, but Mr. Drake lives in the Fairmont. A beautiful old house—well, hotel, actually. I used to play there myself as a girl. Remember he invited you and Phoebe to visit him? In fact, he is fitting out a bedchamber there, just for you."

Alice's chin quivered. "I want to stay here."

Mercy pressed her lips together. For Alice's sake, she had to squelch her anguish and help the girl believe this was in her best interests. Help herself believe it too.

She took Alice's little hands in hers. "Alice, my dear. There is no reason to be afraid. I realize you don't know Mr. Drake very well yet. Nor do I. But my good friend Jane does. You remember Mrs. Bell, from the inn? I trust her completely, and she assures me Mr. Drake is a kind and generous man who is able and willing to provide for you and care for you. You are a blessed girl, Alice Smith. You have had a mother who loves you, a schoolmistress who loves you, and now a new father who loves you. Let us both try to remember that, all right?"

The little girl nodded, but she did not let go of Mercy's hand.

In The Bell coffee room, Jane sat down to breakfast with her mother-in-law, brother-in-law, and soon-to-be sister-in-law and niece. Thora held Betsey on her lap, deftly feeding the child from her own plate and carrying on a conversation at the same time. Hetty and Patrick, however, could hardly eat for smiling at each other. Jane found herself grinning too. The Bell family was growing, and it felt good to be a part of it.

After she had eaten, Jane excused herself to return to the desk. Thora handed Betsey to Hetty and followed her out, leaving the sweethearts to finish their meal alone.

As the women crossed the entry hall, Gabriel Locke strode through the side door. He wore his dark red coat, leather breeches, and mud-spotted boots. Returning from an early morning ride, Jane surmised, his jaw still shadowed with whiskers.

Thora frowned when Mr. Locke started up the stairs. "Mr. Locke? What are you doing?"

"My room is up here, Mrs. Talbot."

"Your room? Your room is in the stables." She shot Jane a raised-brow look.

"Not any longer, Thora," Jane explained. "You know Mr. Locke has not worked here for some time now."

"I know. But if he is back to help out again, he . . ."

"He is here as a guest, Thora." She waved to Mr. Locke, and he continued to his room.

"A paying guest?" Thora asked her.

"Yes."

"Why?"

"Mr. Locke is considering buying a farm in the area."

"Lane's Farm?"

"Perhaps."

"Then we would be neighbors," Thora said thoughtfully. "Good heavens, Jane. How much did you pay the man before he left?"

Jane chuckled. "Not much at all. He only worked here to help out after John died, remember. He and his uncle raise horses, and now he wants a place of his own."

"On his own, or with you?"

Jane blinked, mouth parted. Thora had come to know her too well.

"On his own . . . for now."

Cadi scurried by, towels in arms, and nearly ran into Thora. "Sorry, ma'am. Excuse me. I am late getting these up to number four, and now Alwena needs me in the dining parlour."

"Number four?" Jane repeated.

Watching her face, Thora quirked one dark brow. "Jane will take them up for you, Cadi. Won't you, Jane?"

"I . . . of course. If Cadi needs help."

"Can't keep a paying guest waiting," Thora quipped, a knowing glint in her eye.

Jane took the laundered towels upstairs and knocked on the door to number four.

"It's open."

Jane nudged wide the door, stepped over the threshold, and stopped.

Gabriel stood at the washstand in his shirtsleeves, braces dangling from his trousers, shaving brush in hand, razor nearby.

He looked over in surprise. "Oh, hello, Jane. I expected Cadi to bring the towels."

"She was busy."

"Forgive my state of undress. I went out riding before the hot water arrived, and . . ."

"Sorry. I will ask Alwena to deliver it earlier."

"I was not complaining—only explaining. I rise earlier than your usual guest, I gather."

She clutched the towels to her chest. "You are certainly not our usual guest."

He turned to look at her. "Does it bother you?"

"No."

"Is my being here causing talk amongst the staff?"

She shook her head. "They seem to like having you here. And Thora is only being Thora."

"I was serious when I said I could remove to the Crown, if you prefer."

"No, don't leave. I am . . . glad you're here."

He walked over, took the towels from her, and tossed them on the bed. "Are you?"

She swallowed. Noticing a smear of cream on his cheek, she raised a hand to wipe it off, but he captured her hand in his and pressed a kiss to the inside of her wrist.

Jane's pulse leapt.

He looped an arm around her waist and pulled her close. Jane sucked in a breath, heart hammering. He framed the side of her face with his free hand, his dark gaze focused on her mouth. He lowered his head, and his lips touched hers. She closed her eyes and leaned in to him, and in response he angled his head the other way, kissing her more firmly, and more deeply.

Jane returned the pressure, kissing him back, ignoring the warning voice in her mind.

He broke away first and rested his forehead against hers. "Jane, we need to talk."

Jane looked at the open door in alarm. What was she doing? This was going too far too fast. She stepped back. "If someone had seen us just now, there would be talk indeed! I had better go. Thora will wonder what I am doing up here."

"Jane . . ."

"We shouldn't make a habit of . . . this, all right? I will see you later. Downstairs."

As she walked away, cold reality washed over her. The road they were on led to marriage and the hope of children. A road she was not ready to travel again.

Rachel went to The Bell to tell Jane her news. She was excited but also a little nervous to do so, wondering how Jane would react. She did not find her at the desk or in the office, but from the window she saw Jane standing in the yard, talking with a coachman.

Rachel stepped out the side door. "There you are."

Jane excused herself and turned to Rachel, brows lifting with interest as she looked at her. Did her expression give her away?

Rachel tightly pressed her lips together, suppressing a smile. She hoped Jane would be pleased.

"What is it?"

Rachel took her hand and led her across the drive to the keeper's lodge. Jane had barely closed the door behind them when Rachel blurted, "Timothy and I are engaged."

"At last!" Jane threw her arms around her and held her close.

"I wanted you to hear from me directly."

Jane released her and looked into her face. "How did it happen? When?"

The two sat down together and Rachel told her everything that had happened at the Bingleys' ball.

"I am so happy for you."

Rachel tilted her head to regard her friend. "Are you?"

"Yes, of course."

She did not look happy. "Jane, what's wrong? Now that it's happened, are you disappointed?"

"No. Heavens, no. I'm sorry, I should not be spoiling your moment with my troubles. I am happy for you and Timothy both, truly."

"Then please tell me what's troubling you, or I shall think the worst."

Jane looked down and sighed deeply. "Very well. . . . Do you recall what you said when you came here before the ball—when your future with Timothy was uncertain? You said you were afraid to hope. That you didn't want to be hurt again."

Rachel nodded. "I remember."

"I understood that, because I am afraid too." Jane glanced toward her bedchamber. "It is only natural to remember pain and want to avoid experiencing it again."

Rachel studied her face in concern. "Jane, what is it? Last time we spoke, you mentioned there was someone you liked a great deal. Has something happened?"

Jane hesitated, nibbling her lip. "I thought I might be ready to love again. Well, romance is one thing, but all the risk and pain that come with it . . . ?" She slowly shook her head.

"What risk are you talking about?"

Jane lowered her voice. "While I was married to John, I . . . miscarried five children."

Rachel's heart plummeted. "Oh, Jane, I am so sorry." She took her hand. "And sorry I wasn't there for you at the time."

Jane glanced up at her. "We were not exactly on good terms then. But, thank God, that has changed."

"Yes. Thank God, indeed."

Jane straightened. "Now, that's enough maudlin talk. Don't forget our celebratory dinner tomorrow night." She squeezed Rachel's hand and smiled bravely. "And now we have another reason to celebrate."

"I would not miss it for the world."

Rachel returned her smile, but her heart remained heavy for her friend.

After leaving The Bell, Rachel walked up the long drive to Brockwell Court. Lady Brockwell had invited Rachel to come to the house to discuss wedding plans. Now that Timothy and Rachel's engagement was official, she seemed determined to make the best of things. Timothy had a meeting that afternoon, so he would not be joining them. He said he was happy to leave talk of shopping, silks, and muslins to them but reserved the right to plan the wedding trip himself.

When Rachel arrived, Lady Brockwell greeted her politely. Her congratulations were cordial, if somewhat reserved. Justina, however, was even more exuberant than usual. She threw her arms around Rachel and kissed her cheek. "Oh, I knew how it would be! Now you and I will truly be sisters. I am so happy!" She embraced her again.

"Yes, yes, Justina. Do let Rachel breathe. Now come and sit down, you two, so we can plan our shopping excursion—you will need a gown, of course, Rachel, as well as clothes for your wedding trip."

Rachel nodded. "Could we ask Mrs. Shabner to make something? She was disappointed I did not order a new gown from her for the Bingleys' ball."

Lady Brockwell wrinkled her nose. "If you would like. Though not your wedding dress itself. We must go to London for that."

Justina beamed. "Oh yes, let's do go to London. I long to go to London. . . ."

Later, when their lists were made and dates settled upon, the ladies took tea together. The atmosphere was far more congenial than during Rachel's last visit.

Afterward, Rachel insisted she would walk home, as the day was still bright and she had so much energy to spare. She felt that she could dance all the way to Ivy Cottage. Even fly!

She restrained herself and walked at a ladylike pace up the High Street. She wanted to call in at Mrs. Shabner's to thank the woman again for making over the dress, and to let her know that it had played at least a small part in her engagement.

But when Rachel reached the dressmaker's shop, she was surprised to find the door locked and a *For Let* sign in the window.

Oh no. Rachel felt disappointed and a little guilty. She was also impressed. After all the years of talking about retiring, Mrs. Shabner had apparently finally done it.

At the end of the street, Rachel saw Mr. Arnold, the property agent, step out of the former bank building, followed by Sir Timothy. She walked toward them, idly wondering what the two had been meeting about.

Mr. Arnold locked the door behind them, then noticed her. "Ah, Miss Ashford!" He waved his hand. "If you require any alteration, you just let me know."

Confusion flared. "Alteration?"

The property manager smiled eagerly as she neared. "You may be leasing this building for your library—is that right?"

Rachel blinked. "I . . . will?"

Sir Timothy corrected him. "Only if it suits Miss Ashford's needs. It is her decision. I was simply investigating possibilities." He turned to her. "I had planned to bring you here later and surprise you."

Of old habit, an objection immediately sprang to mind. She could never accept such an offer! Then she remembered. This was her soon-to-be husband doing the offering.

Noticing her hesitation, Sir Timothy said earnestly, "Your library is an asset to Ivy Hill, and we don't want to lose it over a simple lack of space to house it. I am thinking of the village as a whole."

"The village. Right." Mr. Arnold bit back a smile, a knowing gleam in his eyes.

"I cannot . . . " Rachel stopped herself, then started again. "I cannot thank you enough for searching out a future home for the library."

She looked at both men, but her smile was all for Timothy.

CHAPTER FORTY-THREE

On the night of Jane's little dinner party, Mercy and Rachel walked over to The Bell together, wearing pretty dresses and long pelisses against the evening chill.

When they arrived, Jane met them in the entry hall. "Thank you for coming to celebrate with me, Mercy. And thank you for joining us, Rachel, even though you are too young to empathize." She winked.

"Yes," Mercy agreed. "But Rachel has her own reason to celebrate."

"Very true. And I am delighted for her and Timothy both. And doubly glad we are having this dinner."

Mercy smiled. "Hear, hear."

The three sat down in the coffee room to a meal of green pea soup, spare rib, and New College puddings—a fried dough of breadcrumbs, butter, currants, and nutmeg, which Jane knew Mercy was especially fond of.

Mercy raised her glass of cider. "I wish you joy of your birthday twenty times over, Jane. And to you, Rachel, I wish you joy in your upcoming marriage."

"I do too," Jane said. "With all my heart."

Rachel's eyes sparkled. "Thank you. And you will be glad to know that for my wedding present, Sir Timothy has offered to lease the old bank building so I can relocate my circulating library there. Anna Kingsley will take over the day-to-day management of the place"—she grinned—"as I will be more agreeably occupied."

"That is excellent news." Jane beamed, and glanced at Mercy. "Does this mean you've decided against Mr. Hollander?"

"It means I can make that decision without worrying about the fate of Rachel's library. Though Mr. Kingsley will not enjoy having to remove all those recently installed bookshelves."

"Oh, now he's finished with our stables, he will be glad for the work, won't he?"

"I don't know. I have not seen him in some time."

Jane and Rachel exchanged looks at that, and then the three moved on to talk about other things. They reminisced about old times, studiously avoiding the topic of Mercy's school, and Rachel, Jane, and Timothy's uneasy past. But they could not exclude Timothy from their tales altogether, for he was an old friend to all of them and had featured in so many memories of their younger days—*Twelfth Night* plays, group lessons with the Salisbury dancing master, picnics and parties, and so much more. In fact, Jane began to feel that she might have been remiss in not inviting him to join them.

Over Rachel's shoulder, Jane saw Gabriel Locke stroll through the entry hall, strikingly well dressed in dark evening clothes. Her breath hitched at the sight.

He stopped and talked to Colin, and she had a good view of him framed in the coffee room doorway.

Rachel and Mercy noticed and followed the direction of her gaze.

"Who is that?" Rachel craned her neck.

"Mr. Locke."

"Is he not your former farrier?" Mercy asked. "I recognize him from the coach contest."

"Yes."

Rachel stared, incredulous. "*He* was your farrier?"

"Mm-hm."

"And what is he now?"

Jane's gaze lingered on him. "That is the question."

Mr. Locke glanced over and noticed all three women looking at him.

Jane sent him a sheepish smile.

He walked in and paused before their table. "Good evening, ladies. Was there . . . something you needed, Jane?"

"No. But let me introduce you. Miss Mercy Grove and Miss Rachel Ashford, may I present Mr. Gabriel Locke."

He bowed. "How do you do."

"We are celebrating Jane's birthday," Rachel blurted.

"Is it your birthday, Jane?" He looked at her warmly. "I wish you joy."

"I shall need it. I am afraid I've crossed the thirty-year mark."

"I did that myself a few years ago—and lived to tell the tale."

"Where are you off to?" Jane asked. "I have never seen you so formally attired."

"I have been invited to dine at Brockwell Court, if you can believe it."

"Really?"

He nodded. "I happened to meet Sir Timothy and another gentleman. Another sir. Sir Cecil, or . . ."

"Sir Cyril?"

"That's right. We rode together and they invited me to shoot with them, and dine as well."

"I am surprised," Jane breathed.

"Are you?'

"I only mean . . . you are not well acquainted."

"I have met Sir Timothy a time or two. Most recently when I bought a horse from his stables, though I dealt primarily with his manager."

"That's right."

"And Sir Cyril is a racing enthusiast and was eager to talk about horses. I think Brockwell invited me out of deference to his guest."

"I see." Jane gestured to Rachel. "Miss Ashford has recently become engaged to marry Sir Timothy."

"Has she indeed? That is excellent news. Allow me to offer my hearty congratulations."

"Thank you." Rachel tried but failed to restrain a toothy grin.

"May I congratulate him as well when I see him, or is it a secret?"

"You may."

"Then I will indeed. Enjoy your celebration, ladies."

Jane thanked him. "And enjoy your dinner. Although I'm afraid our simple fare here will pale in comparison after you dine at Brockwell Court."

"The Bell has other charms to recommend it." His smile lingered on Jane's face. "Well, good night."

"Good night."

As he walked away, Rachel whispered, "Is he a guest here, Jane?"

"He is now."

"No insult to Mr. Locke," Mercy began, "but I wonder what Lady Brockwell will say to a farrier coming to dinner."

"He is more than a farrier," Jane replied. "But I agree—not her usual dinner guest." She looked fondly at her old friends. "The world really is changing, and the three of us are proof of that."

For a moment, they joined hands around the table.

Then Rachel said, "Don't worry about Mr. Locke. Lady Brockwell won't have a chance to say much of anything with Cyril Awdry at the table."

They all shared a smile at that, and the last of the puddings.

Gabriel invited Jane to ride again, this time on Athena, while he rode Sultan. He declared she was ready, nearly healed, and needed more exercise. A spirited Thoroughbred was not meant to be kept tethered; she needed freedom to run.

They rode out to old Sarum—or "Stonehenge," as some called it—about nine or ten miles away. A brisk wind made Jane's eyes water and her cheeks tingle with cold. Athena cantered along, her dark mane flying up, her gait strong. Jane had needed this too.

They ascended the raised mound and rode toward the stone

circle within. From a distance the stones had looked large. Up close, they were massive—some more than thrice their height on horseback. The stones shone golden in the late afternoon sunlight. Several stood atop one another like children's blocks, while others lay on their sides as if toppled by a giant toddler.

"I have not ridden out here in years," Jane breathed. "I'd forgotten how magnificent they are."

Gabriel nodded. "It's no wonder there are myths and legends about this place."

His words stirred a memory for Jane. "Sir William Ashford used to tell a story about coming here as a young man hoping to find the words to woo Rachel's mother. He had heard an old legend that if you spent Midsummer's Eve here, you would gain the powers of a great poet. But it rained all night, and he caught a chill and all but lost his voice. He returned to Ivy Hill the next day sopping wet and ill, and proposed to her in a barely decipherable croak. Thankfully, she accepted him anyway."

Gabriel chuckled. "I wouldn't mind a little help finding the right words myself, and the right time to ask you—"

Jane interrupted him. "Those clouds look ominous. We had better head back." She turned Athena's head and urged the mare into a trot.

He rode after her. "Jane, what's wrong? Why are you putting me off?"

She shook her head, not trusting her voice.

"John has been gone more than a year, but if you need more time . . ."

Again she shook her head.

"Is there someone else? Mr. Drake or . . . ?"

"No!"

"Then, what is it?" He quickly surveyed their surroundings. "Come, let's stop awhile. The river is just there. We'll water the horses." They rode a little farther to the bank of the River Till. There he dismounted, tethered his horse near the water, then helped her down. "Now, tell me what's upset you."

She pressed her eyes closed. Throat tight, she managed two words. "Your farm."

"My farm? Why?"

"You want a farm of your own. Of course you do. You want something to pass down to a . . . son or daughter. It's only right you should. Only natural. But I cannot—" Her voice cracked, and she blinked back tears.

"Hey, take it easy. Take your time."

Jane longed to be loved and cherished and held. But how could she destine another man to childlessness? She shook her head.

"Jane . . ."

"John and I were married for seven years, Gabriel."

"I know that."

"We had no children. It was my fault. I cannot carry a child to term."

"John mentioned once that you'd lost a child. Was it more than one?"

She nodded and lifted her hand, five fingers splayed.

"I am sorry."

"You see?"

"Jane, I am very sorry for your losses," he repeated. "But I am not . . . shocked. I knew there was some sort of problem. And I don't think myself such a superior man that I could somehow accomplish what John could not."

"Not John. Me."

"Jane. I have never been married, but I thought God planned it so the two become one—one body. So not *your* fault. You and John could not have children—together. And if we cannot have children together, we will be all right."

"How can you know that?"

"I promised to tell you the truth from now on, remember? So you must believe me. No, I cannot pretend I don't want children. But believe this as well—I don't want to lose you over it. I would rather have you by my side than a dozen children."

"You say that now. But someday you'd regret it. When you're

older and need help. Or want someone to leave the farm to when you die."

"Already planning my old age and even my death, hm? Let's not get ahead of ourselves, Jane."

She shook her head. "Marry someone else. Someone younger who hasn't been married before. Or a widow with lots of children."

"While you sacrifice your own happiness and mine and go through life alone?"

"I may marry again . . . someday. I thought perhaps an older widower, who's already had his children."

Gabriel raised a wry brow. "Who is this widower? I hate him already."

She knew he was trying to cheer her, but her heart remained heavy.

He took her in his arms. "Jane . . . I am three and thirty, and you are the first woman I've ever felt this way about. Do you think I'm going to wait thirty more years in hopes of finding another woman I might love half as much? Even in my gambling days, I would never have taken such a risk."

She managed a grin at that, and he leaned close and pressed a warm kiss to her cheek.

CHAPTER FORTY-FOUR

Mercy sat at her desk in the sitting room, which would not be hers much longer. December was upon them. Mr. Hollander had asked for her decision by Christmas, still a few weeks away, but there was no point in putting it off any longer. She knew what her answer would be, and fairness dictated that she deliver it sooner than later, to give him time to find somewhere else to live. Meanwhile, she was resigned to go on living in Ivy Cottage as her brother's unpaid housekeeper and, most likely, future nurserymaid.

Resolved, she pulled out a piece of stationery, dipped her quill, and began writing. When she finished her few lines, she blotted the letter and sealed it, sealing her fate as well.

Later that afternoon, Mercy was washing down the slate in the schoolroom when Aunt Matilda came to find her, her expression unusually somber.

"Mr. Drake is here to see you," she announced, watching her face in concern.

Mercy's stomach cramped. So soon? She had thought preparing a room for Alice at The Fairmont would take more time.

She nodded bravely to her aunt and then started down the stairs. As she walked, she recalled the awful scene when she'd taken him that letter—his cutting remarks as well as her unjust assumptions and desperate arguments. Indignation and mortification washed over her yet again.

She whispered a simple prayer, "Help me," and stepped into the sitting room.

James Drake turned when she entered. "Thank you for seeing me, Miss Grove."

She stood there, hands clasped, her whole body tensed for another blow. "Mr. Coine has already been here and conveyed your plans."

"I know. That is not why I am here." He cleared his throat. "I have come to apologize. I acted abominably. When I think of how I spoke to you . . . I am utterly ashamed of myself. Never in any other dealings—personal or business—have I behaved so rudely. I would like to try to . . . not justify my actions, but explain."

Too surprised to speak, Mercy nodded and gestured toward a chair.

"I will stand, if you don't mind. But please, do be seated, Miss Grove. You look pale."

Mercy sank into her aunt's favorite armchair, hoping to draw comfort from its familiar embrace.

Mr. Drake's expression struck her as resolved yet turbulent—nostrils flared, jaw tense. He gathered himself, then began. "I realize you have cared for Alice these several months, but I have spent the last nine years regretting how I treated Alice's mother, and that I let her slip from my life.

"When I met her, I was not looking to form attachments; I was looking to buy a hotel, begin my enterprise, my future. But as the days passed with that sweet sunny girl, so refreshingly different from the women I knew . . . I became enchanted. And I believed the feeling was mutual. I knew Mary-Alicia was an innocent, and I should never have pressed my advantage. But the romantic coastal setting, the fine food and wine, the neglectful dowager . . . It was my fault, of course. I didn't stop to think through the consequences. I should have proposed immediately, but I did not. I thought I had more time.

"When I returned from my mother's sickbed and found Mary-Alicia gone, I tried to tell myself her leaving was for the best. I was too young to tie myself down. I had enjoyed a few blissful weeks in the company of a beautiful girl, and she had left without demanding anything of me. I should have been relieved. But I was not. My regret over my cavalier behavior would give me no rest. I had left her vulnerable to consequences unimaginable to a privileged young gentleman but dreaded by unprotected women and their parents the world over."

He grimaced. "I did try to find Mary-Alicia and her employer, but without success. Lady Carlock traveled almost constantly, wherever her fancy took her. I wrote to the Bath address she'd given me, and when the dowager finally returned for the winter and responded, it was only to tell me that Miss Payne had left her employ without explanation. Again, I tried to find Mary-Alicia—I even searched Bristol. But I did not know she had changed her name to Smith. I had little to go on. She'd told me her parents had passed away. She had also mentioned grandparents, but for the life of me, I could not remember where they lived. Eventually, I had to give up the search. But her memory and the memory of my ungentlemanlike behavior were ever with me.

"When I saw the name Ivy Hill on a turnpike survey map, it rang a bell in my mind. Then I remembered: Ivy Hill was the name of the village Mary-Alicia had mentioned, where her grandparents lived. So I came here, to take advantage of the opportunity to establish another hotel, yes, but also to see if I might discover what became of Mary-Alicia. To learn if she fared well, or if not, to somehow help her.

"But here I met no Paynes. And I only recently discovered the Thomases were Mary-Alicia's maternal grandparents. You were there when I learned of Mary-Alicia's fate. . . ." He shook his head, a bitter twist to his lip. "If only I had been able to find her! Oh, the misery of knowing she died destitute and alone in a room over a milliner's shop. A shop I had walked past not once but twice during my search years before.

"Guilt and regret ate at me. I decided I must atone for my part in her death somehow. But there seemed nothing I could do to redeem myself, to right my wrongs."

"None of us has the power to redeem ourselves, Mr. Drake," Mercy said gently. "Only Christ can do that."

He ran an agitated hand over his face. "I know that. Here." He tapped his temple. "But in here?" He slapped his chest. "I had to *do* something. Try to make restitution. But how could I? Mary-Alicia's grandfather wanted nothing to do with me, but I could help her daughter, I decided.

"Then I met Alice, and everything changed. Her age, the story of Mary-Alicia eloping with an officer so soon after our relationship. Never bringing him here to meet her grandparents. The man's career and death suspiciously similar to her father's . . . That's why I searched the records, and went to Portsmouth, and learned what I did."

He glanced up at her. "Even had you not found Mary-Alicia's letter, I knew it in my heart when I looked at Alice. I saw her mother, yes, but I also see myself. I am her father, Miss Grove."

Mercy managed a slight nod. There was no use denying it.

His eyes widened in appeal. "Don't you see? I had been desperate for a way to make restitution. Only to learn I have a daughter—Mary-Alicia's daughter! I am not a particularly religious man, but I do believe in God's involvement with His creation. And never more than when I realized He had given me a second chance to do the right thing—to do my duty. Mary-Alicia deserved to be acknowledged and protected, and I failed her. But I could acknowledge and protect her daughter. Our daughter.

"But then you . . . you got in the way of that. Of what I saw as my rightful, God-given responsibility. I don't say you did so with any ignoble motives. I know you were not trying to take advantage of me, or extort money from me, though I know I accused you of those very things in anger. I was upset, as I have rarely been. But I have heard enough about your reputation and your character to know better than that, once the heat of the moment had passed.

Only then did I stop to consider your feelings. What you stood to lose.

"So again, I must beg your pardon for the things I said and the unjustified manner in which I spoke to you. I hope you will allow that it was a rare lapse from my usual behavior. I am, in general, a kind man. Though clearly not as self-controlled as I thought."

Mercy swallowed. Nothing he had said changed the fact that he would take Alice away and, with her, a large, jagged piece of Mercy's heart. But she could not ignore that he had the decency to admit he'd been wrong, and to apologize.

She forced herself to speak. "Thank you for explaining. For absolving me of selfish motives. Though I cannot claim that for myself, because selfishly I love Alice and don't want to lose her. But I do understand, at least to some extent, as I would do anything to protect her myself, if I could. But as you are her father, then that is your right, not mine, as much as I might wish otherwise. I know I should be glad you feel your responsibility so keenly. It would be even more difficult to give her up to some disinterested parent who would neglect her. But that, I see, you will not do."

"No. Never."

He released a breath and stepped nearer her chair. "Mr. Coine tells me you are willing to take care of Alice here until all is ready for her at the Fairmont."

"Yes."

"I appreciate that. I have to see my father's lawyer about some other matters, which will take me out of town for a week or so. But upon my return, I shall be ready to move Alice to the Fairmont."

Mercy bit the inside of her cheek. "I see."

He shifted. "Miss Grove, I know much of what I have admitted today will not raise your estimation of my character, but even so, I hope you and I might spend more time together. And Alice, of course. I think it would help her to see that you and I are not enemies, but friends. You and Jane are good friends, as she and I are. Is it too much to hope you and I might be as well?"

Torn between astonishment and politeness, Mercy faltered, "I . . . No . . ."

"Good." Mr. Drake drew himself up. "Well, thank you for hearing me out. May I call on you again when I return?"

Feeling light-headed, Mercy nodded and rose.

He stepped forward, hesitated, and then took her long hand in his. "Until then." He pressed her fingers, then released her and swept from the room.

Mercy stood there until the outer door banged shut. Then she dropped heavily into the chair. What had she just agreed to?

The next day, Gabriel knocked on the door to the keeper's lodge. That surprised Jane. He had not been inside since he'd helped her catch a mouse months before.

He held her gaze. "May I come in?"

"Yes. I . . . suppose."

Noticing her hesitation, he said, "We can leave the door open if you prefer, though I had hoped to speak to you privately."

She licked dry lips. "It's all right."

He stepped inside, shut the door, and turned to face her. "I need to make a decision about Lane's Farm. Clearly my plans to buy it make you uncomfortable. . . ."

She lowered her head, but he cupped her cheek and looked into her eyes. "Jane, I love you. I want to spend the rest of my life with you. There is no guarantee any other woman I might marry would be able to have children, and even if there were, I don't want any other woman—I want you. Just as you are. How can I make you believe me? Do I need to retract my offer on the farm? Remain in partnership with my uncle?"

"No."

"I can't go back to being your farrier." He shook his head. "You know what I think about the lot of stage and mail horses—that they are mistreated. I have no interest in being a farrier in a coaching inn ever again. At least I know the horses in my care were better treated because I was here, but long term? It's not how I want to spend my life."

"I understand." Jane crossed her arms. "But I own a coaching inn."

"I know you do. And you have a new farrier who will become more experienced and skilled in time. I am happy to help him—help you—any way I can. But day in and day out? No. I've washed my hands of racing, but I still want to raise and train horses that will be prized and well cared for. It's what I love to do. What I am good at."

"I know it is."

"Jane, I know The Bell is important to you. You've gone through a lot to save it. But do you think you might one day be ready to hand the reins to another? To leave your little lodge and live elsewhere . . . with me?"

Leave her lodge?

Seeing her expression, he went on. "Please do not be offended. But John built this place for the two of you. This was your home together. Not ours. I would rather not begin our married life here. Are there not too many memories here, good and bad?"

She could not disagree. Some good memories of John lingered there amid the sad ones of her miscarriages. Those she was more than ready to leave behind.

Jane spread her hands. "But I can't leave now. We have a whole schedule of improvements and services we'd planned to introduce over the coming months. If Patrick were staying, I think he and Colin could manage the place quite well without me. But Patrick and Hetty are buying a lodging house. Colin has taken on more office work now that his arithmetic has improved, but he is still young and inexperienced, and not . . . family. I would need to hand the reins to someone who had a personal interest in the place."

"You will not consider selling it?"

"This from the man who convinced me not to sell it only a few months ago!"

"I know. But things have changed here at The Bell and in Ivy Hill. Things have improved."

"There are still obstacles. The Fairmont delays have helped us. But eventually we will feel the brunt of that competition and . . ." She turned her face away and squeezed her eyes shut to hold back tears. She knew in her heart that Gabriel was a good man and she should just trust him. But still . . . Deep in her soul, emotions tumbled together, gnawing at her, confusing her. But one thing was suddenly clear: she had to sort out those feelings before she made any life-altering promises.

She was still fighting for composure when he gently turned her back to face him. She opened her eyes and knew he saw the tears.

His own eyes shone with compassion as he took her hand. "I know you're afraid, Jane. But please, don't be."

"Of course I am. I am terrified." She pulled her hand from his. "I'm sorry, Gabriel. I thought I could, but I can't. I can't lose another child and disappoint another man."

CHAPTER FORTY-FIVE

Jane spent a good deal of time praying alone after that, but she now looked forward to church on Sunday. Her soul was hungry for the comfort of Mr. Paley's voice leading them in prayer, and the fellowship of her neighbors and friends.

From her usual place beside Thora and Talbot, Jane noticed Gabriel pause to greet the McFarlands and Tall Ted near the back of the nave. He would have sat among the staff as he used to do, Jane saw, but elderly Mr. Lane entered with his cane, took Gabriel's arm, and gestured him forward to sit with him a few rows farther up. Mr. Lane seemed more frail than when Jane had last seen him. No wonder he planned to give up his farm and go live with his daughter. It made Jane think of her own father. And miss him.

Sitting in the Lane family pew, Gabriel Locke was not far from Jane. She glanced over at him several times during the service.

He sat erect, paying attention, unlike her that morning. If she focused her hearing, she could pick out his low voice among those nearby, repeating the prayers or reciting a psalm. She liked his voice.

She glanced the other way and found her mother-in-law watching her.

Caught.

Thora had no doubt noticed the direction of her gaze and the object of her straying attention.

Jane gave her an apologetic little smile and returned her attention to the service. Tried to, at any rate. She wondered if it bothered Thora that Jane was showing interest in another man. Would she think her disloyal to John's memory? She hoped not. After all, Thora had not remarried for many years after her own husband died.

Beside her, Thora took her hand. Not in warning, Jane didn't think, but rather in companionable affection. Jane leaned her shoulder against Thora's and gently squeezed her fingers.

With one last glance at Gabriel, she asked God to give her courage and direct her steps.

The day before Rachel's wedding, Mercy went up to her room after breakfast and found Alice waiting for her.

"Hello, Alice. I have to help Miss Rachel prepare for her wedding soon, but when I get back, we shall spend the day together, and then I shall help you pack."

"Why do I have to go and live with that man?" Alice asked, and not for the first time.

"You remember," Mercy patiently replied. "Because he is going to be your father now."

Alice frowned. "I want to stay here with you."

Oh, Lord, please help me reassure her!

"Alice, I have loved being your teacher. You will always be precious to me. But it's all right. I am not going anywhere. I will still be right here in Ivy Cottage. And the Fairmont is not so far away. We will probably see each other about the village, and at church, if Mr. Drake attends, and perhaps we could visit each other from time to time. I know I would like that very much. Would you?"

The girl nodded vigorously, and Mercy prayed she had not just made promises she would not be able to keep.

She recalled Mr. Drake's words: *"I hope you and I might spend more time together, Miss Grove. And Alice, of course. I think it would help her to see that you and I are not enemies, but friends."*

Mercy hoped Mr. Drake had been in earnest. It would certainly make the transition easier for Alice. Might it prolong the pain of loss for her? Probably. But for the little girl's sake, she was willing to try.

Miss Rachel Ashford and Sir Timothy Brockwell were married in St. Anne's on a sunny December morning. Rachel wore a pale blush gown with silk embroidery, a matching veiled hat, and for going away, Lady Brockwell had given her a fur-trimmed cape.

Throughout the ceremony, Rachel's stomach tingled with joy. She felt warm and weightless, her heart soaring to realize the day she had dreamed about for so many years had come at last.

After Mr. Paley pronounced them man and wife, prayed over them, and signed their marriage license, she and Timothy exited the church, hand in hand. The smile she had suppressed during the solemn service broke free, and Timothy returned it, warm affection shining in his eyes as he looked at her. Together they passed through a tunnel formed by friends and family bordering the churchyard path, applauding, wishing them well, and tossing seeds of blessings down upon them.

Reaching the gate, Sir Timothy gave Rachel a hand up into the Brockwells' barouche-landau, the top folded back so that everyone could watch the happy couple drive away. The carriage lurched into motion, starting on its way to Brockwell Court for the wedding breakfast. From behind, people called congratulations after them.

Rachel turned on the bench seat to wave to the well-wishers.

Nicholas Ashford stood near the wall, with Miss Bingley on his left and Justina Brockwell on his right. Seeing his smile, the last remnants of guilt blew away like winter's first snowflakes, and her heart felt full.

The churchyard held all the people she loved. Even her parents were there in spirit—their graves and their memories. There was her sister, Ellen. Her friend Mercy, laying aside her worries and sadness for the day to wish her happy. The women of the Ladies

Tea and Knitting Society. Mr. Basu and Mrs. Timmons. Matilda and the girls from the school. Mr. and Mrs. Paley, and so many others. She had even begun to warm to Lady Brockwell.

And there in the middle of them all stood Jane, one hand atop the churchyard gate, watching them go. Across the distance, their gazes caught and held. The moment shimmered, floated in the air, time hanging suspended for one heartbeat. Two.

Rachel was struck by the significance. Unlike all those times when Rachel was young, this time she and Timothy were side by side, riding away together, while Jane was left behind to watch them go. In Jane's face, Rachel saw that the significance was not lost on her either. Was she truly happy for them? Then a smile broke across Jane's dear face, and she waved to them heartily. Rachel waved back, her own smile stretching wide until her cheeks began to ache. Jane *was* happy for them, just as she'd said. Seeing it, Rachel's joy doubled.

Mr. Gabriel Locke came and stood beside Jane in the churchyard, and his presence reassured Rachel. Jane would not be alone for long if Mr. Locke had his way.

Rachel waved until the barouche turned the corner and Jane and the others disappeared from view. Then she faced forward and settled closer to Timothy's side.

He grasped her gloved hand in his and gazed gently down at her.

"All right?" he asked softly.

"Better than all right. Almost perfect."

His brows rose. "Almost?"

She tilted her head and pressed her lips to his, kissing handsome Timothy Brockwell as she had wanted to do for as long as she could remember.

"Now everything is perfect."

He smiled and gave her another long kiss. *Perfect, indeed.*

Jane realized Gabriel had quietly come to stand beside her as Rachel's carriage turned the corner and slipped out of sight.

Neither of them spoke for a moment. They stood together in companionable silence amid the jocularity of those around them.

At length, Gabriel said simply, "I have the deed to Lane's Farm."

Emotions—relief?—coursed through Jane, and she blinked back tears that seemed to spring out of nowhere lately.

Before she could reply, he continued, "I'm not going anywhere, Jane. I love you, no matter what the future brings, and I will wait."

With a gentle squeeze of her hand, he was gone.

The next steps were up to her.

Author's Note

Thank you for returning with me to Ivy Hill. I hope you enjoyed your stay in this fictional village close to my heart, as well as learning more about circulating and subscription libraries in the days before public libraries. If you haven't already done so, I invite you to visit talesfromivyhill.com for more about the series and its setting, including photos, character lists, maps, previews of upcoming books, and more.

Now, just a few notes to share with you. As with my other novels, I have attempted to honor a favorite author or two with fond nods to her work. In this book, you will have noticed references to *Pride and Prejudice* and, of course, *Persuasion* by the wonderfully talented Jane Austen. I hope you enjoyed them.

Speaking of talented, I am grateful for the insightful input of Cari Weber, Michelle Griep, and Anna Paulson. I also want to thank my agent, Wendy Lawton; my editors, Karen Schurrer and Raela Schoenherr; and the entire team at Bethany House Publishers, including Jennifer Parker, who designed the beautiful cover, and Beth Schoenherr, who made the dresses the models are wearing. Gratitude also goes to authors Dani Pettrey, Becky Wade, Karen Witemeyer, Katie Ganshert, Katie Cushman, and Jody Hedlund, who helped me brainstorm book mysteries and romantic situations during our writers' retreats.

Again, I want to acknowledge the real women behind the fictional Ladies Tea and Knitting Society: Beverly, Kristine, Judy, Sherri, Becky, Phyllis, Tiffany, Shari, Kelly, Julia, and Teresa. Were any of your namesakes' shenanigans in this novel inspired by my last visit to your book club? I'll never tell.

Appreciation and fond memories also go to Katie Read of the Pewsey Vale Riding Centre in Wiltshire, England, for sharing the heartwarming story of her horse (a former racehorse) who trusts only one special farrier.

And finally, I want to thank you, dear reader. Thank you for spending time with me in Ivy Hill, and learning to care for its residents as I do. I hope you will come again. I will meet you in the new circulating library, where we'll sit down together over a cup of tea and talk about books and England—two of my favorite topics!

Discussion Questions

1. Were you familiar with subscription or circulating libraries—the forerunners of today's public libraries—or was this new to you?

2. Rachel Ashford struggles to accept charity from others—even from God. Can you relate to this at all? How easy or difficult is it for you to ask for help from others?

3. Both Mercy Grove and Jane Bell yearn for children of their own, but feel they must surrender those dreams. Have you ever surrendered a dream? What did you learn?

4. A few characters in the book experience the sometimes high cost of telling the truth (Mercy handing over Mary-Alicia's letter, Jane revealing her past losses to a suitor, etc.). Have you ever paid a high price for being truthful? What are the risks and rewards of being honest?

5. What did you think about brusque Thora Bell's relationship with Hetty and Betsey? Did anything surprise or touch you?

6. If you were transplanted to Ivy Hill in 1820, what kind of shop or business might you open?

7. Do you belong to any kind of book club or group like the Ladies Tea and Knitting Society? If not, do you think you would like to?

8. What are you looking forward to in Book 3 of the Tales From Ivy Hill series? Do you have any predictions to offer?

Julie Klassen loves all things Jane—*Jane Eyre* and Jane Austen. A graduate of the University of Illinois, Julie worked in publishing for sixteen years and now writes full time. Three of her books, *The Silent Governess*, *The Girl in the Gatehouse*, and *The Maid of Fairbourne Hall*, have won the Christy Award for Historical Romance. *The Secret of Pembrooke Park* was honored with the Minnesota Book Award for genre fiction. Julie has also won the Midwest Book Award and Christian Retailing's BEST Award, and has been a finalist in the Romance Writers of America's RITA Awards and ACFW's Carol Awards. Julie and her husband have two sons and live in a suburb of St. Paul, Minnesota.

For more information, visit www.julieklassen.com and www.talesfromivyhill.com.

Sign Up for Julie's Newsletter!

Keep up to date with Julie's news on book releases and events by signing up for her email list at julieklassen.com.

More Tales From Ivy Hill

The lifeblood of the village of Ivy Hill is its coaching inn, The Bell. When the innkeeper dies suddenly, his genteel wife, Jane, becomes the reluctant owner. With a large loan due, can Jane and her mother-in-law, Thora, find a way to save the inn—and discover fresh hope for their hearts?

The Innkeeper of Ivy Hill
Tales from Ivy Hill #1

More Historical Fiction

The Duke of Riverton has chosen his future wife using logic rather than love. However, his selected bride eludes his suit, while Isabella Breckenridge seems to be everywhere. Will Griffith and Isabella be able to set aside their pride to embrace their very own happily-ever-after?

An Inconvenient Beauty by Kristi Ann Hunter
HAWTHORNE HOUSE
kristiannhunter.com

On the eve of WWI, the mysterious Mr. V hires Rosemary Gresham to determine whether a friend of the king is loyal to Britain or Germany—and she's in for the challenge of a lifetime.

A Name Unknown by Roseanna M. White
SHADOWS OVER ENGLAND #1
roseannawhite.com

When a British plane crashes in WWI German-occupied Brussels, English nurse Evelyn Marche must protect the injured soldier, who has top-secret orders and a target on his back.

High as the Heavens by Kate Breslin
katebreslin.com

When unfortunate circumstances leave Rosalyn penniless in 1880s London, she takes a job backstage at a theater and dreams of a career in the spotlight. Injured soldier Nate Moran is also working behind the scenes, but he can't wait to return to his regiment—until he meets Rosalyn.

The Captain's Daughter by Jennifer Delamere
LONDON BEGINNINGS #1
jenniferdelamere.com

More from Julie Klassen

Visit julieklassen.com for a full list of her books.

After her suitor abruptly sails for Italy, Sophie Dupont's future is in jeopardy. Wesley left her in dire straits, and she has nowhere to turn—until Captain Stephen Overtree comes looking for his wayward brother. He offers her a solution, but can it truly be that simple?

The Painter's Daughter

Abigail Foster is heartsick—the man she loves has fallen for her sister and a bad investment has left her family destitute. When a benefactor offers the Fosters the use of Pembrooke Park, it seems a perfect solution to their troubles. But they soon learn the abandoned manor is shrouded in mystery, and no one seems willing to shed light on the past.

The Secret of Pembrooke Park

With the help of the lovely Miss Midwinter, can London dancing master Alec Valcourt unravel old mysteries and bring new life to the village of Beaworthy—and to one widow's hardened heart?

The Dancing Master

Emma Smallwood and her father have come to the Cornish coast to tutor the youngest sons of a baronet—but all is not as it seems. When mysterious things begin to happen and danger mounts, can she figure out which brother to blame . . . and which to trust with her heart?

The Tutor's Daughter

BETHANYHOUSE